MAY NEVER COME

LYLE WESTBROOK

Copyright © 2022 Lyle Westbrook.

All rights reserved. No part of this book may be reproduced, stored, or transmitted by any means—whether auditory, graphic, mechanical, or electronic—without written permission of both publisher and author, except in the case of brief excerpts used in critical articles and reviews. Unauthorized reproduction of any part of this work is illegal and is punishable by law.

ISBN: 979-8-88640-415-9 (sc)
ISBN: 979-8-88640-416-6 (hc)
ISBN: 979-8-88640-417-3 (e)

Because of the dynamic nature of the Internet, any web addresses or links contained in this book may have changed since publication and may no longer be valid. The views expressed in this work are solely those of the author and do not necessarily reflect the views of the publisher, and the publisher hereby disclaims any responsibility for them.

One Galleria Blvd., Suite 1900, Metairie, LA 70001
1-888-421-2397

IS
Dedicated to:

Larry J. Carter,

John, P. King

Ronald S. Caughorn

Arlie L. Longmire

Stephen F. Thacker

Some say tomorrow is just another day, but will it come and go in its usual way? Or die out before the suns first rays.

The Evil Lords will rule with an iron fist, bringing death and destruction to those who resist.

A New World Order is what they want, to make mankind bow down to a One World Government.

Famine, Pestilence, Starvation, and Disease, are the order of the day. For the wrong he's done, mankind has a terrible price to pay.

From heaven above, the world burns without end. "Oh, Lord, please deliver us from evil," are the cry's of men.

The Earth quakes and lava flows free, as mountains crumble to the sea. But, were we not told this was to be?

"Oh, Lord, will we never learn the lessons of life? The ones taught by Buddha, Mohamed and Jesus Christ."

Black and White, Day and Night, Opposites always fight. One without the other cannot be. No matter who's wrong or right?

With his last breath, I wonder now what the atheist thinks about death.

Will Tomorrow ever come? Has the reign of man really come to an end, or will a new race be born that will learn from history's past.

Before we can understand tomorrow, we must first understand yesterday. Before we can know where we're bound, or what we hope to achieve when we get there. We must first understand who and what we are.

Hello! My name is Duke, the adopted canine son of Nathan L. Masterson, who I call Dad. My mate, Duchess and I, along with our four pups, Duke Junior, Rufus, Molly and, Lucy, have lived with Dad and his human children most all our lives. And I guess as far as humans go, they are some of the best. Unlike others of their race, they look upon us canines as an equal part of their extended family, to be treated as any other member of the family. But then again, if more people had talking dogs, or even cats for that matter, they would no longer see themselves as pet owners, but as parents of adopted canine or feline children.

Now you might think it strange that a dog is telling this story, or that a dog could possibly talk, play chess, write on a computer, or do many of the things humans can. But because of a genetic enhancing drug developed by Dr. Ben Franklin, that he called GEF, we, along with our humans are far more advanced than others of our kind.

But, if you consider that the Holy Bible tells of talking serpents, dragons, demons, and, a whole lot of things that could be interrupted as, what in today's world could be described as UFO's and aliens, this story doesn't seem so far-fetched. Especially when you consider there are over two billion people in the world who believe the Bible is the true word of God.

It all started about a year ago when some pretty odd things happened to our family, which I wrote down in a book named "On the Edge of Tomorrow".

This year, the story continues with just as many strange and unsettling events. So I'm writing this book, which I've dubbed, "Tomorrow May Never Come," to chronicle what many may call Armageddon, the End of Days, or what some believe is predicted in the Bible book of Revelation. However, things are not always what they seem to be, or not even what we think they're going to be. Sometimes they are a lot worse and much different from what has already been written down.

Duke Masterson

Prologue

IN HIGH ORBIT ABOVE THE EARTH

Aboard the Galactic Battle Cruiser Intrepid
Approximately 11,000 BC

The First Fleet of the United Planets of Nirvana came to this star system around the year 300,000 BC, Earth time. They were in search of the Black Lords, the fleeing rebels, who had started the Great War in the Canis star system many light years from Earth. This war brought about the total destruction of four of the systems twelve planets, and the never ending struggle between the forces of Light and Darkness.

The rebels were pursued to this star system where another battle resulted in their capture and imprisonment on what is now known as the planet Mars. For many thousands of years invisible electronic grids, along with robotic drone ships have kept a force field around the planet. However, even though the Black Lords were basically on a prison planet they would not just sit idly by and accept their fate, especially when they had already established several underground bases on this planet, bases that were capable of building many a ship of war. In fact, the Black Lords were confident that some day they would be able to finish the war they'd started so many years before.

After the Black Lords, and the dark demons that followed them, were safely imprisoned on Mars, Admiral Gabriel, commander of the first fleet of Sirius, and most of his commanding officers, decided to colonize the third planet in this system. A beautiful blue planet they would call Earth.

Those who had not lost their family in the Great War and wanted to return home to the Cains system were allowed two of the remaining five battle cruisers for their journey home. However, for those that stayed, a new set of problems would have to be overcome. Earth's atmosphere was much different from their home planets, which meant, they could not live on the surface for long periods without getting sick. To overcome this, on every continent they built many subterranean cities, connecting them with very elaborate tunnel systems. They also engineered the genetic reconstruction of a humanoid species native to the planet. This resulted in a very intelligent species they called human. But even though mankind looked much like those who created him, it would be many thousands of years, before he would understand the true meanings of his creation.

When a rogue meteor hit the Earth in 25,500 BC, resulting in the destruction of the continent of Lemuria and, the death of hundreds of thousands, Admiral Gabriel had ordered a constant orbit of the planet by at least one of the three remaining battle cruisers. With one on patrol through this star system, and one stationed at Moon Base Alpha, he figured the colonies would have plenty of warning if such an event should ever threaten Earth again.

He also ordered the construction of the pyramid shaped ion cannon systems around the surface of the planet. Each of the eight colonies, located far below the surface on the remaining eight continents, would be responsible for their construction. However, because of one problem after another, only ten were fully operational when the next disaster occurred, and not every continent had one. Three were on the continent of what would later become Africa; another on the continent of what would become South America; three on Atlantis; one in the high Himalayan Mountains of Asia and the last two had been constructed by the refugees of Lemuria, who had settled on that spit of land between North and South America.

11,000 BC

Captain Amun sat on the bridge of the battle cruiser Intrepid in high Earth orbit. He had been on duty for about twelve hours now and was about to turn operations over to Commander Montu, the ships First Officer.

"I'm sure glad to see you Commander," the Captain said, "I didn't think this shift was ever going to end."

"I know what you mean Sir; it seems like twelve hours stretch a little longer each time I'm on shift. Is anything exciting going on that I should know about?"

"No, everything seems to be fairly normal. There's the usual shuttle traffic from Earth running supplies to us and Moon Base Alpha." The Captain paused for a moment trying to think if there was anything else. "Oh yes, we did get a garbled message about an hour ago, but couldn't tell who it was from. We checked with the moon base but they couldn't make it out either." As the Captain finished, other bridge personnel were being relieved by the next shift.

Each of the galactic cruisers was mostly triangular in shape, at about 2,500 feet long and 2,000 feet wide. They had a crew of around 1,500 people, 300 canines and 400 android personnel. Each was armed with 200 laser cannons with a range of 1,000 miles, eight ion cannons with a range of 10,000 miles, and twenty Starburst missiles with a range of over 100,000 miles. The Starburst missiles, needless to say, had enough explosive firepower to evaporate small planets or something about the size of Earth's moon. Each cruiser also carried the standard compliment of 150 F-47 star fighters, and each fighter had four laser cannons, two forward and two aft.

"Well, Sir, after another twelve hours it will be our turn to take shore leave. I'm looking forward to spending time on Earth with the wife and kids for a while," Montu commented. "My kids are growing up so fast I can hardly believe my eyes each time I get shore leave."

Each of the three battle cruisers had two full crews which swapped out every three months. The Intrepid, for example, was commanded by Captain Amun for three months, and then Captain Ares and his crew would take over while Amun and his crew took leave below Earth's surface. While on duty, each ship spent a month patrolling the star system, a month at Moon Base Alpha on ready standby, and a month in orbit around Earth.

Just then the communications officer spoke up, "Sir, we're picking up another one of those strange transmissions we got about an hour ago. I think it is Captain Chu Jung aboard the Defiant. He should be about half way back from his deep space patrol to the Martian System."

"Put him on screen, Lieutenant."

At first a fuzzy image of Captain Jung appeared on the main monitor, with the sound intermittent, but soon cleared.

"Cal...Ling...Th...Intrep...id Mars Prison Bas...e has been compromised. A meteor strike knocked out the containment grid. The Black Lords are loose and headed toward Earth with two full battle fleets," Captain Jung informed. "My fighters are slowing them down but we are greatly outnumbered. We should be at your location, in about two hours."

"We'll be ready for the Black Lords, Chu. How far behind you are they?"

"We are picking up at least five hundred ships about a hundred thousand miles to our rear. Most of those are small fighters but there are at least four enemy battle cruisers and about forty smaller battle-frigates. My ship has sustained multiple hits but so far the shields are holding. However, they have damaged our Worm Hole Generator and the best we can manage is warp one."

"Okay, Chu, we'll see you shortly." Captain Amun said, before signing off. Then he turned to his communications officer, "Sound general quarters, lieutenant, battle stations, then contact Moon Base Alpha and all the colonies on Earth. Inform them: SITUATION CRITICAL."

"Sir, the moon base was listening in on our transmission. They have alerted the crew of the Scorpion. Captain Tyr will be here within twenty minutes. The moon base is also powering up their laser and ion cannon generators." Lieutenant Seshat paused for a minute while another transmission came in. "Sir, Admiral Gabriel is hailing us."

"Put him on screen, Lieutenant."

"Admiral," Amun said as Gabriel came into view.

"Amun, since you are the senior Captain, you will have tactical command over this operation. I know I don't have to tell you what you're up against and I know you and you're crew will defend Earth to the last man. I just wanted to let you all know we will be ready here on Earth if the enemy gets by you. Good luck and good hunting."

"Thank you, Sir. Hopefully we will stop them before they get to Earth. If not...Well I know the colonies will finish them." With that, Amun signed off and then ordered his navigation officer to lay in a course that would bring them one hundred thousand miles from the enemy fleet when Captain Jung and the Defiant entered the quadrant. He then turned again to Lieutenant Seshat. "Lieutenant, contact the Scorpion and tell Captain Tyr to take up a position half way between us and the moon. Tell him to initiate a wide pattern code 666-5, at 100,000 miles, on my command." Amun was planning to fire 5 starburst missiles, each, in a wide pattern just as the Defiant entered Earths quadrant. By the time the missiles went off the Defiant would be in a safe area, where all three battle cruisers could then launch fighters to wrap up any enemy ships they might have missed.

"Lord Lucifer," the Denwen's (The Fire Serpent) communications officer said. "Lord Mammon wants you to try outflanking the enemy vessels by going around the back side of sector four and attack Earth from out of the sun. He will send Lord Mahes and his battle group with us."

"That's an excellent idea," Lucifer agreed as he pondered the strategy, "That way the Earth ships will have to split their forces. Tell Lord Mammon we will break off now and meet up with him for the final battle for Earth."

As Lucifer broke away from the pursuit of the Defiant at top speed and started the long roundabout journey to the far side of Earth, he left

Lord Mammon only 110,000 miles from Earths quadrant and less than ten minutes from certain destruction.

When Captain Jung entered Earth's quadrant, he contacted the Intrepid to report his position. At that point the Intrepid and Scorpion both fired five Starburst missiles at the same time. The resulting explosion, ten minutes later, caught Lord Mammon and his ships in a destructive blast that could easily be seen from Earth's surface. The initial blast and resulting shock wave that followed vaporized over 250 enemy ships, including two demon battle cruisers.

When Jung got within a thousand miles of the Intrepid, he informed Amun of the ships that split off from the main enemy force. Amun quickly figured out the strategy of the enemy forces and told Jung to take up a position putting Earth between the Defiant and the Intrepid, to meet the second force head on. Amun then contacted Captain Tyr and ordered him to take out any enemy ships that managed to escape the blast, before joining them in the battle around the planet.

Two hours later the Intrepid and Defiant were in orbit on opposite sides of Earth.

"Sir, our sensors are picking up enemy ships coming out of warp." Commander Montu stated.

"Launch fighter's commander and tell Captain Jung to do the same. Then lock on to their battle cruisers with our ion cannons and open fire."

"Aye, aye, Sir," Montu replied.

Lucifer and Mahes had just barely managed to launch their fighters before receiving heavy fire from the Intrepid and Defiant. They realized at that point Lord Mammon's fleet would not be joining them.

Then the Earth based guns opened up on them with murderous fire. Lucifer ordered the Denwen's fighters to knock out Earths defenses while the rest of the battle group took on the oncoming fighters from Amun's forces. The battle raged for about an hour with each side receiving heavy losses. Then Captain Tyr showed up with the Scorpion, turning the tide in favor of the Forces of Light.

The two enemy battle cruisers were completely destroyed but not before Lucifer and the other Black Lords under his command, abandoned their ships in the escape pods.

After the last shot had been fired, three decks of the Defiant were on fire. She had sustained much damage to her landing and launch bays but she was salvageable. The Intrepid had also received her share of laser blast, but was in much better shape. Captain Amun ordered the Scorpion to accompany the Defiant to Moon Base Alpha for repairs, once the fires were out. What was left of the star-fighters from both ships now landed on the decks of the Intrepid.

"Sir, what are we going to do now?" Commander Montu asked after hearing what had happen on the planet's surface.

The battle on Earth had not gone as well as the one in orbit. The fighters from the Denwen had knocked out the main power reactor core of Atlantis, resulting in a surge that literally blew the continent apart and created a tsunami four hundred feet high. At about the same time one of the enemy battle cruisers came crashing down near a polar icecap, which resulted in an instant meltdown. The results were devastating. Many hundreds of thousands of people and animals died around the world as the flood waters rushed over them. Others managed to find refuge in caves or on the higher mountains, but one thing was for sure, it was going to take thousands of years before mankind would be as advanced as he was at the time of this battle.

"We are going to stand strong Commander, and rebuild. We did it once before and we can do it again." Then a deep sadness came over Amun, he fought to hold back the tears welling up in his eyes as he thought about all the brave men and women that had been lost this day. He also grieved for the loss of families and friends on the surface. They would be sorely missed. At least the tunnels and giant caverns of the underworld colonies had survived and would play an important part in the reconstruction of the surface world and man's struggle to overcome this latest tragedy.

For over five thousand years mankind would roam the surface of the planet in small hunter gatherer bands before once again building great cities on the surface. During that time the Black Lords, who had survived the great battle, would be hunted down, by the Lords of Light, and imprisoned around the planet in the deepest bowels of the Earth.

However, before that happened, they were able to spread their poisonous redbrick of hate and deception, all with the delusions of power and glory, to the far corners of the world. They also formed many secret societies that would turn the hearts and minds of many humans to the dark side. And for their loyalty, the members were given great knowledge in astronomy, architecture, and mathematics.

The Dark Lords were filled with so much hate for the Lords of Light and the human race. They turned into the most diabolical demons which included:

1. Devils or Namaru which once were from the highest house of angels. Lucifer belonged to this group after he turned to the dark side. After his imprisonment in hell he took on the name of Satan.
2. The Defilers or Lammasu were the first of the houses to succumb to hell.
3. The Devourers or Rabisu, from the House of the Wild, which once cared for the animals, sided with the forces of evil and turned against the King of Kings.
4. Fiends or Neberu. Because of them, Lucifer won many early battles in the Great War.
5. The Malefactors or Anunnaki, some believe they tried to enslave mankind, raping human women and started the practice of virgin sacrifice. These are most likely the Nephilim the Torah refers to in Genesis.
6. Scourges or Asharu, were once guardian angels, but more of their number flocked to Lucifer's cause than any other.
7. Slayers or Halaku were once known as angles of death. Their leaders would all be put in cryogenic capsules to ensure they could not escape.

After being deceived by the evil ones for years, some humans turned against the traditional teachings of the Lords of Light. However, there were those who still followed the ways of Hope, Love, and Goodness that the age old Principles of Light, incorporated.

For thousands of years the stories were handed down from one generation to the next, long before they were written down on ancient stone tablets, papyrus scrolls, or the walls of temples. Over centuries of telling and retelling the stories, the Lords of Lights became known as creator Gods, while the Black Lords became a diabolical evil, as they fell further and further from the light.

By the time Christianity came along the seeds of darkness even found their way deep into the very foundations of the Roman church. Many early church leaders were as corrupt and black hearted as any demon in Hell. They manipulated the royal courts of Europe to do their bidding in which war after war was fought in the Holy Land. They also maimed, tortured, and burned thousands of people at the stake during the inquisition, and all this done in the name of a loving, forgiving God who taught just the opposite principals.

Now throughout the world the forces of Light would forever clash with the forces of Darkness. Or should I say, man would slaughter his fellow man over and over again throughout the years, all in the name of whatever god he believed in at the time.

Thirteen thousand Earth years would pass before another great and decisive battle would be fought between the two forces. But, would this battle mean the end of mankind or would he survive, not only the war with the dark demons, but the forces of nature as well.

Chapter One

THE GULF OF OMAN

8 September
Present Day

A lone submarine slid slowly through the waters of the Gulf of Oman, one hundred feet below the keel of a supertanker. By doing this, its commander hoped to mask their passing from anyone who might pick them up on sonar, such as the U.S Navy.

She was an old boat, built by the Russians in 1985, but she had been refitted with the latest equipment available. Her engines had been completely rebuilt and her electronic systems had been replaced with the very best in state-of- the-art technology. However, her crew all knew this was most likely a one way trip.

Before his death in May of 2011, Osama Bin Laden had bought the old sub on the Russian black market, and renamed it, Dhul Fiqar (Prophets Sword). He was then able to secretly buy ten nukes from Pakistan. There were still many within that country's government that was sympathetic to his cause. In fact, over three quarters of Pakistan's population thought of him as an Islamic saint.

The Dhul Fiqar's captain was Malik Abadi, an Iraqi, who had been born in Paris in 1968 where his father was Deputy Ambassador at the Iraqi embassy. This had given him dual citizenship between the two countries. He had been given the very best of educations and after his graduation from university in1994; he spent 12 years as an officer in the French Navy. Most of that time was on nuclear submarines. When the U.S. invaded Iraq in 2003, and killed his parents and his sister's family in 2006, he resigned his commission in the French Navy and joined Osama Bin Laden's fight to rake vengeance on the United States and her allies.

Of course the new U.S. President, Marcus Overton, had now pulled most all of their land forces out of Iraq a few months ago, but maintained a heavy naval presence in the Persian Gulf.

The only good to come out of that war, was it ended the evil reign of Saddam Hussein. However, this did nothing to compensate for all the atrocities committed by the U.S. military on innocent people. Nor did it ever address the punishment of those responsible for the war.

After selling his idea to Bin Laden, Malik had spent the next five years hand picking his crew from all over the Arab world. As they had made their way from a secret base in eastern Siberia where they'd picked up the sub, Malik trained the crew relentlessly before sailing to Karachi, Pakistan, where they picked up their nuclear ordnance of ten, two megaton nuclear missiles. They were now confident and ready to carry out their mission. A mission, if handled right, would make it look like the U.S. had picked a fight with Iran and Iran had responded with nuclear weapons.

It weighed heavy on the minds of the crew as to what they were about to do to the Islamic nations. But, in the end, they figured it was better to die taking a lot of the enemy down with you, than to be dictated over by those who wanted to control the world's oil supply. Even if this meant killing many of your own people for a holy cause, it would be better than living under the oppressive thumb of the world's so called super powers. Besides, except for Iran, these countries were already under the control of the western powers in some form or the other.

From Karachi it was an easy trip across the Gulf of Oman to the Persian Gulf where they would attack the oil fields of Iraq, Iran, Saudi Arabia and Kuwait.

"All stop" Malik ordered as they reached their firing co-ordinates, about twenty miles off the eastern side of Oman near the Strait of

Hormuz. "Bring us up to one hundred feet from the surface, Husam. Then open missile doors one, five, seven and nine and feed the codes into the computer. Our Islamic brothers have gotten rich enough off the Infidels. Now, we will cut off their oil supply and destroy those who dare sell their souls to the western devils."

Even though the boat carried ten missiles and a full complement of torpedoes, Malik was sure four would be more than enough to get the job done. Besides, by the will of Allah, if they managed to pull this off and escape, he had other targets in mind for the United States or Europe.

Huge supertankers were everywhere, some being escorted by gun boats in and out of whatever oil port they were assigned. Tensions in this area of the world were at an all time high since Iran now openly admitted to having nuclear weapons and would use them if any nation tried to invade her as the U.S. had in Iraq. The U.S., along with many European nations, had tried peaceful negotiations until finally getting Iran to promise not to use her weapons offensively. But she insisted that Iran would not be invaded or controlled by the western powers.

"Yes, now is the perfect time to strike a blow that would cripple the world's dependence on oil, and the U.S. would be blamed for it." Malik smiled at the thought.

"Sir, the countdown has begun," Abdul advised.

"Good, as soon as the four missiles are away, dive the boat to 5-5-0 feet and rig for silent running."

"4, 3, 2, 1, Launch," Husam, the second in command said, as he watched the computer screens. "Sir, all four missiles are on their way."

"Abdul, take us down, at 30 degrees down angle and put us on a reverse course from the way we came in," Malik ordered. "Habib, listen carefully for other subs that may be in the area."

The missiles had all reached their designated targets with total devastation. The initial blast and the shock wave that followed evaporated everything within twenty five miles of ground zero. A hundred thousand people died instantly from each explosion and in the coming weeks millions more would die from radiation poisoning. Many warships and supertankers miles from port caught fire and sank.

Burning oil shot out of the pipelines at the ports, filling the sky with black smoke as far as the eye could see. This would continue for months, causing the sun to be blacked out around the world.

And so it was, the beginning of yet another mass extinction had begun. The chaos of another mass extension would once again be loosed on the Earth, which would bring the Four Horsemen of the Apocalypse foretold in Revelation. With wars; famine; disease; economic collapse; nuclear fallout; mega-storms; earthquakes; volcano eruptions; giant tsunamis; and death. The Mayan predictions of doomsday were right on schedule, or, maybe even a little early.

Chapter Two

SHAMBHALA, SOMEWHERE IN THE HIMALAYAS

8 September

We'd been at Shambhala for two weeks and I must say the discipline here was a lot different than any of us were used to. Up an hour before daylight for prayers then a breakfast of cold cereal with yak milk and some fruit or maybe some kind of imitation meat made from tofu and rice cakes. Then off to our different teachers, better known as Masters, to study the meanings of life, the afterlife and, the eternal journey of the soul. This had to do with the inner workings of dharma, karma and, a lot of other stuff, such as reincarnation. This they called enlightenment. But if you ask me, it is real close to cruel and unusual punishment. To be honest though, I guess we have learned a lot about the way the universe works. However, it is a far cry from the adventurous trips we took last Fall, through massive subterranean caverns where we encountered many strange creatures and, wondrous beautiful cities. But, we'd promised Gabriel we would come here to learn how to let go of our inner self, which would help us in the battle against the Black Lords. And a promise is a promise.

It all started last October when Dad, Nathan Masterson, got an e-mail from his old buddy, Steve Franklin. Because Dad has a Ph.D. in archaeology, Steve and his father Ben, wanted him to help check out a very interesting cave system not far from Ben's house on the coast of British Columbia. What we found was a vast underworld filled with talking Sasquatch called Guardians, little demons with a mouth full of sharp teeth, and flying, fire-breathing dragons. And, it seemed in every chamber we passed through, we found something new and unbelievable.

After many days on a boat, passing from one subterranean chamber to another, through an elaborate connecting tunnel system, the Guardians took us to a crystal city called Avalon in the middle of a giant subterranean lake, called the "Sea of Endwebu". That's where we met Gabriel, an android replica of the commander of the First Fleet of the United Planets of Nirvana.

You can forget what you've been told about aliens. They do exist here on Earth. However, the ones we met were not little gray beings with big heads and large black eyes, which most abductees describe. In fact, they looked much like the human race, except most have slightly elongated heads, with azure blue eyes, and blonde hair. Or at least these were the type of alien beings we encountered. But, from what I understand, the First Fleet was made up of many different races from what used to be the twelve planets of the Canis star system. So I guess the aliens look more like the different races of humans here on Earth.

They claimed to have come to the Earth, in the distant past, from the planet Sirius and the eight remaining planets of the Canis star system. Gabriel told us they were in pursuit of a rebel fleet that caused the total destruction of four planets in that system during a Great War. When they were found here in this system, another battle ensued resulting in the imprisonment of many Black Lords and dark demons on the planet Mars. It was then Admiral Gabriel and the First Fleet, decided to stay and colonize the Earth.

He also informed us that it was these alien races of the First Fleet, which started mankind by genetically altering the DNA of a little known bipedal primate with their own DNA. This was done to form a race of beings, much like themselves, that could live on the surface of Earth without succumbing to the atmospheric difference between this planet and theirs.

It took years of gene splicing and artificially-inseminating females of both species before the creature they called "human" was born. Admiral Gabriel and the original settlers of the planet then came up with a system of periodically going into "suspended stasis" every thousand years to keep from deteriorating in Earth's atmosphere. However, a thousand years on Earth was like a single day to them, because of the size of their home planet and its rotation around its sun. While in "suspended stasis", an android clone, an exact look-a-like, right down to skin texture, would fill in for that colonial leader until it was once again time for him, or her, to resume their duties again as colony leaders. Of course, in most cases, even in suspended stasis, an individual was kept informed as to what was happening in his or her domain. This was done by way of a mental download between android and the being in suspended stasis. I said in most cases, because there were a few places where there was no android to fill in for the ruling Lord. Such was the case in the Andean underworld, where our exploration team ended up last year.

Anyway, getting back to last year's adventures, after we returned home in northwestern Montana, we battled an evil organization called the Black Dragons. They were a bunch of evil drug-lords and tomb-robbers from Colombia, who were led by Beltran Velasco. He was trying to steal a medallion from our local veterinarian Dr. Patricia Smith, which he believed to be the key to great treasures in a long lost mountain pyramid complex in Guatemala.

The FBI and CIA also got involved in the case after this guy's goons attacked our island with U.S. helicopters. We found out later that Velasco was part of an ancient secret society that was trying to take over the world.

We put an end to Velasco and the Black Dragons after Dad and Steve put together an exploration team and went down to the sacred mountain in Guatemala. There we found another underworld tunnel system to South America, where we encountered an array of many Ice Age animals, dragons, demons, many underworld tribes, huge cities, and, a space craft the creator race had left there thousands of years ago.

Our team consisted of Dad, Dr. Pat Smith, her father Dr. John "Dusty" Smith, archaeologist, Mr. Yang, Ben Franklin's cook, and me in M-I-1. In M-I-2 was, Steve Franklin, his wife Jane, our electronics and communications expert Ron Clayhorn, FBI agent Fred Holtz, and my brother Max. In M-I-3 there was our Security Chief, Arlie Longhire, Jay Perry cryptographer and PhD of Religious Studies, Larry Carver, historian, Steve's son Dr. Sean Franklin M.D, and my other brother Lobo.

An M-I unit is a 48 foot Masterson Industries-Tactical Motor Home. Or, a state-of-the-art motor home with some very advanced electronics and weaponry. Dad's brother Lamar provided them for our trip. Lamar is the head of Masterson Industries, a chemical and munitions factory in Georgia, which he inherited from his father, Leroy, upon his death, about twenty one years ago.

In Guatemala, we found The Mountain of the Gods, as we called it, with two pyramids that shot killer laser beams and was full of ancient knowledge and mystery. This is where we took out the bad guys. However, on the way down there we came across some pretty interesting sights, such as the pyramids at Tula and Teotihuacan in central Mexico, the 100 foot waterfall we went over in the southern part of that country, and then there was the lake in northern Guatemala that 40 foot crocodiles called home. It was all very exciting and we learned a lot about what is truly a whole different history of the origins of mankind and the many mysteries this planet has yet to reveal.

To get to Shambhala, Gabriel had sent a star-shuttle, piloted by a couple of androids named Robbie and Robo. It was these two androids that had brought us back to Ben's house last year from Avalon. They had already picked up Larry, Jay, and Ron from East Tennessee before getting to our house in Montana, where we got on board.

From there, we flew to the British Columbia coast and picked up Steve, his wife Jane, my brother Max, and Mr. Yang, from Ben Franklin's home. The flight over the Pacific had only taken a little over two hour before the Chinese coastline came into view. Then the Himalayas, with their high, jagged peaks, and snow caps, came into view. A few minutes later as the ship slowed for landing. Robbie and Robo brought us down on a mountain plateau, over twenty thousand feet high. And, we didn't have to wait long before a greeting committee exited from a concealed doorway in a nearby vertical rock wall of the mountain.

Pat brought the rest of our group in the supply ship from the Andean underworld, which included her father Dusty, Arlie, Fred, Sean, his new wife Kinna, and their canines Lobo and Howl. They arrived just five minutes after we did, so we all went down to Shambhala together.

After we were all together, the greeting party led us to what looked like a very modern subway train inside the mountain. As we got on board one of the greeters told us to fasten our seatbelts and to enjoy the ride. However, he didn't tell us just how fast we would be traveling. I've heard of modern bullet trains that can go a couple hundred miles-per-hour in Japan and Europe but we were traveling at over 350 mph. The super-fast train took us through much the same type of tunnels and chambers we'd seen last year in the Andean underworld. Each chamber was just a little different from the next, with its own brand of flora and fauna. It almost reminded one of a giant zoo, except the animals in each chamber were from different time periods, dating back thousands of years. And, it seemed the few villages we passed were also inhabited by humans from the different geological periods, as well.

When we arrived at the city of Shambhala, we were greeted by King Chogyal, Headmaster Jangbu, and the other Masters, with much warmth and enthusiasm. After the usual handshakes and introductions, we were shown to our rooms on the northeastern side of the city near the city's Enlightenment Center.

The city spread out over a few square miles, just like many other major university towns, with all the different pavilions, modern classrooms, libraries, and laboratories. Here the students are taught all the sciences and arts as other schools around the world, but to a much higher degree. After all, these beings have the technology to cross the vast distances of space. Here too, students are taught how to become one with the universe, as well as the true beginnings of mankind.

Our quarters were very elegant. We were very surprised to find that our rooms were as good as, or better than, those of a five diamond resort. Much like the rooms we had at Avalon at the crystal palace in the Canadian underworld. Our group was assigned to the seventh floor of a pagoda styled building where we had magnificent views of the city. Our humans were divided up into six rooms. We canines however, were at the far north end where our five rooms had been built with dogs in mind. Everything was at a paws reach. Our beds were big overstuffed pillows that made you feel like you were sleeping on a cloud. We also had a TV, a computer, and a telephone, all adapted for canine use. However, the only channels you could get on the TV were of past lessons of the great Masters, or the meditation chant, to help one find a higher level of consciousness. The bathroom, for us canines, was much like the one we used at home, with the bigger, floor level bowl toilet and pushbutton flush. The shower was equipped with a sensor soap dispenser, automatic showers with brushes, and a pushbutton blow dryer. All you had to do was get into the small pool and press a button. You were then automatically soaped up, brushed, rinsed, blown dry, and brushed again, all in a little over five minutes.

Since we've been here at Shambhala, we found out that it was one of the original nine colonies of the Lords of Light, and was many thousands of years old. Even though it has the illusion of being on the surface world, it's actually far below the highest mountains on Earth. There is what looks like a real sun that rises and sets each day and a moon that comes up each night. There is even a regular amount of rain fall each week. Dad figured it worked much like a buildings sprinkler system in case of a fire, but on a much larger scale.

The city itself is about twelve miles long by ten miles wide. But, the chamber the city is in was enormous, about 50 miles across with its ceiling at almost a mile high. On the outskirts of the city there are many vegetable gardens and fruit orchards with elaborate irrigation systems that stretch as far as the eye can see.

Around three thousand people live here on a permanent basis, with only a few hundred students who come here each year from all over the world to learn from the Shambhala Masters. There are beautiful temples, pyramids, and many stone and wood houses that reach several stories high. Then there are the fabulous flower gardens, magnificent waterfalls and beautifully forested parks with golden walking paths. All kinds of wildlife including many species of birds, yaks, dogs, bears, snow leopards, and even a tiger or two that seem to roam freely throughout this chamber without fear or apprehension from the human inhabitance. Fish of all kinds are also abundant in the many streams, rivers, and lakes in this truly magical place.

We also found out the residents of Shambhala, like the other subterranean colonies around the world, have extremely long lifetimes since there is no disease or sickness of any kind here. Even the ordinary humans, that live here, may live for more than a thousand years.

Like Gabriel at Avalon, King Chogyal, is the political leader here. He was one of the original battle cruiser captains of the First Fleet, second only in command, to Admiral Gabriel, but unlike Gabriel, Chogyal and most of the Masters, and Elders here at Shambhala, are from the planet Nirvana. They look much like most oriental people do, with black hair and oval-shaped eyes. However, you can tell the human population from the alien beings, because the aliens all have beautiful dark blue eyes. They are also taller than most humans, and have a strange glow, or aura about them.

King Chogyal and the twelve Masters all wear long flowing robes of different colors. Of course, here everyone wears a robe. Even the students have to wear them. Ours were of different colors depending on what class or level of understanding you were in. It was kind of like Karate school where you start out with a white belt as a beginner, and end up with a black belt as an expert. However, in the case of the Masters, it was to indicate what specialty they taught.

"Hurry up, Duke," Duchess barked. "We're going to be late for Master Cimba's meditation class and you know how he feels about that."

Master Cimba was a little Pekingese who was in charge of teaching all us canines the workings of the universe and the meaning of enlightenment. He started each morning with an hour of meditation before moving on to an hour's stroll through one of the many parks, where he pointed out the animal and plant life and explained about chi, life force energy, and how we were all connected to The One. The humans learned much the same things in their classes.

The things we experienced in last year's travels put many of us far ahead of others in our party who had not been able to go with us to the subterranean chambers. Dad, Pat, Steve, and the rest of last year's exploration team were taught by Headmaster Jangbu, who was in charge of all the Dharma Masters and their classes. He was second in command only to King Chogyal, here at Shambhala.

Each morning I helped Duchess with the pups and Arista's little dog Skipper, making sure they all got to class on time. Then my brothers, Lobo, Max, and I would join Dad and the others in their advanced class.

David's daughter Arista and her stepmother Angela, along with Dawn and Kinna, studied under Master Amrita, one of only three female masters. Jane's father Dusty and the former FBI agent Fred Holtz attended Master Woo's class. I think the only reason Fred and Dusty attended a different class than Dad, Pat and the other members of the exploration team, was because they had not been given the GEF inoculations until last year.

Of course, Pat had not gotten her first shot until last year as well, but Pat is of a purer bloodline to the creator race than anyone else, and her abilities are far more advanced. We found that out when she brought a small animal back to life, returned King Drac's youth and healed one of our dragon friends from the injuries he had suffered from a giant serpent.

It's too bad our dragon friends were not able to come; I was looking forward to seeing them again. But there were just no accommodations here for dragons. The closest would have been many miles away to the south where the Asian dragons lived in a huge chamber of their own. Of course, you know how dragons are about their territory. No, the more I think about it, I can understand why it just wouldn't work out.

"Okay, dear, let's go," I answered, as we ran out the door to where the pups, Skipper, my brothers, and Howl were patiently waiting.

"It's about time, Papa," Molly grumbled as we all headed down the path to Cimba's class.

"Papa, can Rufus and I go with you and our uncles to Grandpa Nathan's class today?" Junior asked. "We're tired of the same old routine day after day."

"Believe me, Son, if you think Master Cimba is boring you, don't want to come with us. All they do in Dad's class is sit around talking about the inner self, dharma, the universe, and past lives."

"I like Master Cimba," Lucy spoke up. "He's quite informative," she paused before continuing, eyeing her two brothers. "I won't mention any names, but if certain somebody's would pay attention to what they were told, they might just learn something."

Chapter Three

NEW YORK CITY

8 September

Marcus Overton was the first African American to ever take the presidential oath of office. He'd been elected, in a landslide victory because of the changes he had promised to bring to a divided nation. Overton was tall, about 6'2," with short black hair and an athletic build. He had promised to get our troops out of Iraq, change the tax laws to include the very rich, find better energy sources lowering our dependence on fossil fuels, raise the level of the educational system, and provide a healthcare system to cover all Americans.

Ten minutes after the detonation of the nuclear missiles in the Middle East, President Marcus Overton was informed. He was in the middle of a speech on universal peace at the U.N. Building in New York City. By the time the secret service agent rushed up to the podium and whispered the news in his ear, the representatives of the other world governments were also being told as their nations were preparing for an all out nuclear war.

There was a sudden uproar as the general assembly received the news in their headsets. The Russian Ambassador pounded his fist on the table where he sat, as he accused the President of hypocrisy, talking peace while all the while threatening war with Iran.

The Iranian Ambassador suddenly yelled, "Death to America," as he got up and shook his fist at the President.

Then the whole assembly erupted in a yelling match.

"I can assure you we did not launch those missiles!" the President fired back. "We have been trying to peacefully negotiate with Iran ever since my predecessor left office in January of 2009." Marcus wiped the sweat from his brow. "We had worked out an agreement and were just about to sign a nonaggression treaty with them on the fifteenth of this month. This doesn't make any sense. Why on Earth would we jeopardize the world's major oil supply and bring the wrath of the super powers down on ourselves? Not to mention the loss of our own naval vessels in the area."

"To bring the rest of the world under U.S. control," the Chinese ambassador accused. "Everyone knows you've been stockpiling your oil reserves for many years now and have had the technology to get a hundred miles to every gallon of gas since the seventies, so if ever there was a sudden oil shortage it would not affect the U.S. like it would the rest of the world."

"Let's not jump to any conclusions," Marcus pleaded. "Give me a chance to get to the bottom of this matter. I promise to keep the U.N. and the world informed of our findings." With that, the President walked from the podium as Secret Service agents quickly escorted him to the underground garage and into a waiting limousine.

Once out of the building they found the streets of New York City a maze of traffic, as the five car escort made its way to JFK and the safety of Air Force One. As soon as they had left the building, Marcus had his aide, Tom Vitt, place a call to the CIA director, Miles Standish, the Joint Chiefs, FBI director Stan Miller, and the new Vice President Katherine West. He told them to gather as much information on this incident as possible and meet him at the White House situation room in an hour.

"Sir," Vitt said, just after they boarded Air Force One. "Miles Standish is on line one."

Marcus took the call in his secure office as he buckled his seat-belt for takeoff. "Miles, what have you got for me? How many ships did we lose?"

"Sir we've lost most all the surface vessels of the Sixth Fleet. They were either sank from the shock waves or rendered dead in the water from the EMP. In either case, the high amount of radiation will kill any initial blast survivors within a very short time. However, there is a chance the two subs assigned to that fleet could have survived if they were submerged at the time of the blast, but as of yet there's been no word." Miles paused before continuing with more bad news that was just coming up on his computer. "Sir, we just found out, Iran is now charging Israel with this atrocity and they are prepping their nuclear missiles for a retaliatory strike."

"My, God, Miles, if we don't stop this before it goes any further this could mean the end of the world as we know it. Do we have an overall casualty count yet?"

"Not yet, Sir, we can only estimate at this point, but it doesn't look good. Our experts have decided the missiles must have been at least two megatons each, which vaporized the major oil fields and everything within a twenty five mile radius on detonation. Then with the prevailing winds the radioactive black smoke will kill millions within a few days. Our people say within a month, everyone from the eastern edge of the Mediterranean Sea to the foot hills of the Himalayas, and from the southern border of Russia to the Indian Ocean, could be dead or dying, especially if Iran retaliates with nukes."

"Do we know who did this, Miles?"

"Not yet, Sir, NORAD said the missiles were fired from, or just off shore of Oman. They had a relatively short flight path so it's hard to pinpoint the exact spot of launch. The most probable scenario is that they were launched from a rogue submarine, which would narrow the possibilities considerably, as to who fired them."

"Okay Miles, we're taking off now, stay on it and I'll see you at the White House when we get to Washington."

"Tom," Marcus said "get the president of Iran on the phone as soon as we get air born."

A million things ran through Marcus's mind as the plane ran down the runway. Ever since he had taken office, it had been one crisis after another. Last year a plot had been uncovered to assassinate him. The then Vice President and CIA Director, it seemed, belonged to an evil, secret organization that was trying to take over the world, and he was standing in their way. Before it was all over, it was also discovered that over a third of the government was involved in this organization. Needless to say, all of these people were fired, impeached, or imprisoned. Except for the former V.P. and CIA chief, they were believed to have gone down in a plane crash somewhere over the Atlantic.

"If it hadn't been for that Masterson incident, I probably wouldn't be here now," Marcus thought to himself, shaking his head in disbelief.

"Mr. President," Vitt said, bringing Marcus back to the here and now. "The President of Iran died in the explosion that took out that countries main oil depot. It seems he was doing an inspection of that facility when it happened. Iran is now in the hands of its military."

Chapter Four

HIMALAYAN UNDERWORLD

8 September

Today started much like every other day had since we've been here at Shambhala. After we accompanied Duchess and the pups to Master Cimba for morning meditations, my brothers and I headed over to Dad's class with Master Jangbu. However, when we got there we saw something that was absolutely amazing. The whole class, who normally sat on small pillows in the lotus position, was levitating at least two feet off the ground. Each was in a deep meditative state, with their hands together in a pyramid shape, and held out slightly from their bodies.

"Whoa Duke, I think we must have missed a few lessons," Lobo woofed softly, as we took our places next to our humans.

After Max sat down between Steve and Jane, he too, tried to assume the same position, but found it impossible. "I guess we dogs are just not made to levitate," he whimpered with disappointment.

"I'm not sure that's true, Max," I told him, as I sat down next to Dad. "We just don't understand how it's done yet."

After getting as comfortable as I could on my pillow, then taking many deep breaths trying hard to relax, I was finally able to let go of the physical world around me. Soon, I found myself connected with Dad's mind, sort of piggybacking on his thoughts as it were. Now, I understood what plane of existence he was on. It was like flying. We could go anywhere in the world we wanted, and even travel through time and space.

We remained in this state of mind for about thirty minutes before coming back to present. It happened rather suddenly when a strange vibration went through us. I guess you could say it was something like an electric shock to our systems. Not even Master Jangbu knew what had happened, but we all knew something was very wrong in the world when we fell back to our pillows with a thud.

A half hour later, everyone was gathered in the Great Hall, where King Chogyal told us there had been a huge rift torn in the Earth's magnetosphere. Everyone listened with horror as he delivered the news. And if the hole was not repaired quickly, the Earth would suffer another mass extinction. He also said that everyone in the subterranean chambers around the world should be safe, but those on the surface would be in grave danger. The King could not say for sure what caused the great rift. However, he did tell us there was an unusually high level of nuclear radiation in the atmosphere, in and around the Mid-East.

The Great Hall was more like the throne room of a great palace. The walls, of which, were curved in an oval-shape, about 80 x 100 feet, with large oval windows evenly spaced around the room. There were also long white marble columns every ten feet around the structure, reaching up to the fifteen foot high balcony that semi-circled on two sides of the room. The domed ceiling went another twelve feet beyond to a very ornate skylight. The floor looked to be made of a royal blue marble, with pure gold poured in around the edges. Large, ornate statues of gods and demons alike, which control man's emotions and desires, rested under the balcony's overhang. On the north end of the room there was a small raised platform of about four feet high, twenty feet long, and ten feet wide. Here, thirteen huge, overstuffed pillows of different colors were placed for the King and the twelve Masters to sit on. On the wall above the platform, was a giant monitor screen, currently showing Gabriel and all the other subterranean leaders, or their android equivalent.

Everyone knew what "nuclear radiation" meant. World War III had, probably just begun, and the future of mankind was doubtful at best. When we heard the news, everyone felt a great sadness that seemed to engulf their entire being. "Is there something we can do to reverse this tragedy before it destroys the world?" asked a Japanese woman from Master Amrita class.

"I'm afraid all we can do, is pray for the poor souls that were lost this day, and for the many more that will be lost in the weeks to come." Master Jangbu told us with sad eyes.

"We are now able to monitor the situation in the troubled area," the King informed us from his golden pillow. At that point, the screen behind the throne changed to show the area in question. "Someone has detonated at least four nuclear bombs, in four different countries. I'm afraid the devastation to the world's largest oil fields is total."

Dad raised his hand with a question. "Sire, if what you say is true, and I have no reason not to believe it is, the whole world will soon be fighting over whatever oil is left, even if it means the total destruction of the Earth. So my question is, what can we do to stop this from escalating?"

Just then an aide ran in and whispered something to the King. With this, the students were becoming a little uneasy. Some of the Shambhala Masters tried to calm them by walking among their students answering questions the best they could, but how do you explain to someone that the world they once knew, is now gone, and would never be again.

"To answer your question Nathan," the King finally responded, as his aide hurried away. "I'm afraid it's already too late. I've just been told, the country of Iran has now launched nuclear missiles at the country of Israel, and Israel responded with their own missiles. Needless to say those two countries no longer exist. Other countries around the world, are also readying their nuclear arsenals. If any more are set off, it will only be a matter of hours before the radiation levels, worldwide, will be so high mankind will not be able to survive on the surface again for at least two hundred years, if ever. A giant hole has already been torn in the magnetosphere layer of the upper atmosphere, letting in enough solar radiation to kill everyone in and around the Mid-East, many times over."

"The best we can hope for at this point, students is that the other countries of the world stand down, and the rift in the Mid-East heals itself," Master Jangbu spoke up from where he sat beside the King. "But if that were to happen, many millions, possibly billions would still die before the hole could be closed."

This time, Pat raised her hand. "Could we close the rift with our ship?"

Master Jangbu whispered something to the King before he answered her question. "My dear, your supply ship could not possibly handle the task at hand. What you would need is a Galactic Battle Cruiser."

Then Gabriel spoke up from the screen behind the King. "I think a battle cruiser can be obtained, Chogyal. But what worries me is, we can get the nations of the world to stand down long enough to close the rift."

"Sir, if you can get me and my team into a battle cruiser, we will do our best to restore the hole," Dad volunteered.

"I have no doubt about that, Nathan," Gabriel said. "But how do we convince the leaders of the world not to escalate this situation?"

Then our electronics engineer, Ron Clayhorn, raised his hand. "Sir, if you can tap into the worlds communication and military satellites, we might be able to electronically disarm their land based ICBM. However, they would still be able to launch nuclear missiles from their ships at sea, or drop nuclear bombs from long-range aircraft."

Dad, Steve, Ron, Arlie, Larry and Jay grew up together in Knoxville, Tennessee. They were all over sixty now, but only looked to be in their thirties, because of the inoculations they received as teenagers with Ben Franklin's GEF serum.

"Yes, that just might work." Gabriel said, as he pondered the possibility. "If we shut down their first response launch capabilities, we might just be able to convince the nations of the world to pull together and save people, instead of destroying the world and everything in it. There might even be a possibility that we can shut down their other nuclear options as well." Gabriel paused for a moment, and then looked to Pat. "Queen Patamaya, we're going to need to place, at least some of the thousands of displaced people from around the world, in the underworld colonies. Have you completed the necessary upgrades to your realm?"

"We're about 90 percent done with restoring the great cities, and 75 percent finished restoring the road system. However, in some of the chambers, where the cliff dwellings have been abandoned for thousands of years, we still have a lot of work to do."

"Sir, we're making headway, but were having trouble getting the different tribes to except King Gukumatz and the Zipacna, as equals," Dusty spoke up. "In fact, most tribes still think of them as devils, and want to slaughter them for all the wrong they have done."

"I can understand how they feel," Gabriel said. But Gukumatz and the Zipacna were not in control of their actions, they were just puppets of one of the Black Lords." Gabriel thought for a moment. "You will have to get a handle on this situation fast, or face the possibility of an all out civil war."

"We understand that, and are working on the problem, but I believe it's going to take some time before the healing begins," Steve's son, Sean spoke up.

The debate over what to do about the crisis went on for another hour before we decided on a course of action. It was King Chogyal who finally suggested that Queen Patamaya return to her realm, with Dusty, Sean, Kinna, Arlie, Fred, Dawn, Arista, and her dog Skipper. Of course, Duchess, the pups, Lobo, and Howl would also go with Pat. They needed to prepare the Andean Underworld for the refugees, which would soon come pouring through.

The rest of our team would be accompanying King Chogyal and his daughter Dohna to Moon Base Alpha where we were to take the Galactic Battle Cruiser, Intrepid, to close the rift.

Chapter Five

THE WASHINGTON D.C. BUNKERS

8 September

By the time President Overton got to the situation room in the new bunkers below the White House, most everyone he'd asked for was there. The Joint-Chiefs, Vice President Katherine West, Secretary of State Mavis Henley, FBI Director Stan Miller, CIA Director Miles Standish, along with Tony Barker the Secret Service Chief, and a few other cabinet members.

Just before the meeting started the President was told the Secretary of Defense, Hugh Hageman, had died of a heart attack shortly after hearing news of the bombings. Unlike most everyone else in this room, Hugh had been a long time friend of Marcus, dating back to their college days. His counsel would be sorely missed, especially now.

After telling the others about Hugh, the President called for a moment of silence before he started the meeting.

"Ladies and gentleman as you already know, Iran and Israel are gone, as well as most of the Middle-East, and the other superpowers are getting ready to start World War 111 over the remaining oil deposits around the planet," The President said, as he took his chair at the end of the large oval conference table. "Does anyone have any suggestions, which does NOT include launching our nuclear missiles?"

Just then the large screen on the far side of the room came to life. "Mr. President, it's good to see you again. We thought you might be in the situation room by now," Dad began, and then proceeded to let him know what we'd come up with. However, he left out the fact we were at Shambhala and we were going to the moon to retrieve a galactic battle cruiser. But, Dad did explain how the world's nuclear ICBM arsenal had been disarmed and their military communication satellites would be disrupted if they tried to launch nuclear weapons from ships or aircraft. He also told them about the rift in the magnetosphere which, if not closed and soon, would flood the Earth with solar radiation. And finally, how they needed to get as many people as possible underground until radiation levels return to more normal levels.

"Who the hell is this guy and how did he tap into our tactical communications screen?" General Wells, Chairman of the Joint Chiefs, yelled. The General was a man in his mid fifties who had spent all of his adult life in the army. He had short, fiery red hair and emerald green eyes that danced around the room looking for an answer.

"Calm down Dan," the President told him. "This is Nathan Masterson. He helped us out of a very tight situation last year, if you recall." Then the President asked, "Mr. Masterson, can you assure us the other superpowers won't attack us."

"Sir, all I can tell you is that the same message I just gave you, was also given to the other nuclear powers of the world at the same time. As far as I know, everyone has agreed to stand down until they find out for sure who started this mess. However, like I said before, the solar radiation coming from the rift is going to literally raise the temperature around the world to critical levels. In other words, if we can't fix this sucker, the surface of the world will be uninhabitable for a very long time. Even if we can seal the rift, the amount of black, contaminated, smoke coming off the oil fields may cause a blackout of the sun. Sir, I think you can imagine what that might lead to; a nuclear winter, possibly another Ice Age after a total melt down of the poles, or any number of disastrous possibilities."

"Mr. President, I say we have an ideal opportunity here to get rid of our enemies," General Wells interrupted. "This guy has no idea what he's talking about. If I remember right he's an Archaeologist for god sakes, not a nuclear physicist."

"Oh, but he does General," advised the little lady seated at the far end of the table. Dr. June Vanderbilt, the NRC secretary, had no idea why she was sitting in on this meeting, until now. "We have been studying these possibilities for many years and came to the same conclusion this man has. But what I want to know is how they plan to seal the rift."

At this point Miles Standish spoke up, "You can take it from me, Mr. Masterson here, knows some pretty interesting people, who shall we say, belong only to the highest circles of science and technology."

Last year Miles had worked on a case with Assistant Director John Brown from the FBI. They uncovered the plot to kill the President and helped put an end to many of the corrupt politicians in the government. But, they also found out that many of the modern science theories of the origins of man were completely wrong.

"And, I can assure you, as far as science goes, these people are the best-of-the-best in their field," Miles continued.

"Mr. President," Dad spoke up, "if the U.S. and the other powers of the world can work on the problems of: A. Figuring out who detonated those bombs, and B. Getting as many people as you can underground. Hopefully, we'll be able to handle the rift."

"We will work on both problems and if there is anything we can do to help seal the magnetosphere, let us know," said the President.

After Dad broke the connection, General Wells was still upset about him being able to tap into a top secret facility at ease, his face turning beet red as he continued to berate Dad. "And did you see those robes he had on? Has he turned into a Buddhist monk, or what? No, I don't think we should put our faith in somebody who is obviously out for his own fame and fortune to save the world."

"General, if you had ever seen Masteson's file, you would know the man is truly an American hero," Miles told him in a serious tone. "And his father LeRoy Masterson also served his country well, and had the highest respect of many of the most important people in Washington.

So before you question his motives, I would suggest you do your homework." At this point Miles leaned forward in his chair and looked the general in the eye. "Just the mere fact that he can tap into this room ought to tell you something about the friends he has."

"People, let's get back to the problems at hand," the President interrupted, seeing the anger rising on the Generals face. Then he turned to Wells and the other Chiefs. "Do we know who set these bombs off and where they got them?"

"Mr. President, we think they were set off by a rogue faction following Osama bin Laden. They are probably pissed off because we killed the SOB." Admiral Randolph Parks offered. "We believe they somehow got their hands on an old Russian nuclear-sub and refitted it with the latest state-of-the-art equipment. Our intelligence reports said such a sub left Siberia about six months ago, but at the time we had no reason to suspect anything unusual." Then the Admiral reached into his briefcase, pulled out a folder and handed it to an aide, who projected the two pictures from within on the screen. "We took these satellite photos of a Russian sub in Karachi Pakistan a week ago. This is where we think they may have obtained their nuclear-ordinance"

Parks was a stocky built, bulldog of a man. He stood 5'11" and weighed around 185 pounds. His ice-blue eyes were said to have frozen people where they stood whenever he got upset. But for the most part, his gentle features and high intelligence gave most people a false sense of ease. Something like how a cobra's gentle swaying almost hypnotizes its prey before it strikes.

"I didn't know Osama bin Laden had a Navy," The Vice President spoke up for the first time, from where she sat to the Presidents right. "Have we been able to locate this sub and destroy it?"

"No Ma'am," the Admiral told her. "When the bombs went off, all our communications in the area went dead. As far as we know, we've lost the entire Sixth Fleet. However, there is a chance at least one of our two subs, connected to that fleet, survived."

"Admiral, if there is a rouge sub, or subs, out there, how long before we can stop it?" The President asked with concern. "I would hate to think these terrorist could sit off our shores and target our cities."

"Sir, we are doing all we can to find this bastard," Parks confirmed. "We have every ship and plane at sea on high alert. If this sub is still alive, it's only a matter of time before we find it and kill it."

"I hope your people are working with the other navies of the world," the FBI Director, Stan Mille spoke up. "Even though this looks to be an older Russian sub, could it be mistaken for one still being used by their Navy? And if by chance you should sink the wrong one…..well, I think you can see the possible repercussions of such a mistake."

Stan didn't much care for the Admiral or any of the Joint Chief's for that matter. They had always agreed with the former Vice President and CIA Director, who most everyone had come to despise. Stan was still not sure the Joint Chief's were not part of the same group, but there was no hard evidence to tie them together.

"We have contacted the Russian's to confirm the boat in question, but under the circumstances they haven't been very cooperative, claiming we would use such information to attack their sub-fleet," Parks told them.

"Randy, you will make the finding of that sub your top priority," Marcus ordered as he pointed at the screen. Then he turned to the Secretary of State, Mavis Henley. "Mavis, contact the other superpowers and advice them, of our suspicions about this sub, and who we think are behind the attack on the oil fields. Tell them, whatever help they can give us in hunting this guy down will be greatly appreciated."

"I'm already on it Mr. President," Mavis said, as she started typing out orders to her staff, on her laptop.

"Now," Overton continued, "how many people can we get into those new underground facilities around the country, and how fast can we get them there?"

Like the underground White House bunker, which interconnected with other underground Washington facilities, through a complex tunnel system, nine other super-secret subterranean facilities, capable of housing 2,500 people each, for twenty five years, had been under construction for the last nine years. Those who will inhabit these facilities would include scientist, technicians, medical personnel, military personnel, and the country's most prominent civilian aristocracy.

The bunkers had been started just after the previous President took office, and were now just about complete. Except for the Washington facilities, each one had been built into a remote mountain of at least 3,500 feet high, with four in the Appalachian states, four in the Rocky Mountain States, and one in the Brooks Range of northern Alaska. They were built with at least ten levels, going down at an angle so no one level would be directly above another. Each level was approximately 80 to 100 feet from floor to ceiling and 1,200 feet wide by 1,500 feet long. Each level was designated for a particular purpose, such as living quarters, science labs, livestock, water supply, and security. On some levels there were even parks with many trees and small lakes or large water fountains. Then, each one had a state-of-the-art-hospital, a level for growing food, and of course, a level for storage: food, vehicles, weapons, and so on. And, they also had a full sized landing-strip built directly into the mountain that was big enough to land the biggest civilian and military aircraft. At over three hundred billion dollars apiece, many in the finance department thought they were a waste of time and money. However, there was a lot of unnecessary spending in the last administration, the biggest, being the Wars on Iraq and Afghanistan.

Then the President turned to General William Farmer, the head of the Air force. He was a tall man over six feet with sandy hair and dark brown eyes. "Bill, can we count on you to provide transportation?"

"Yes, Mr. President, but who do we fly and where do we fly them to?"

"A list will be made available shortly General," The Homeland Security Chief, Jefferson Davis said, with a slow southern drawl. Jeff came from Vicksburg, Mississippi where his father had taken part in so many Civil War reenactment battles it was only natural for Jeff to be named after the President of the Confederacy.

"We've changed the list a bit to include a few names the former President conveniently left out," Jeff informed.

"Jeff, it will be up to you and Debora to contact those people and get them to the debarkation points within the next twenty four hours," Overton told him.

"Sir, we've already started calling, but what do we do if some of them cannot be found, or for some reason cannot go?" Debora Downs, the head of FEMA inquired. "Do we try to find replacements for that person, or just leave the spot unfilled?"

"If you can find someone with the same qualifications, give them priority over a less qualified person," Katherine West answered. "However, if your down to the last minute and have not filled a spot, fill it with anyone you can."

"Okay, people, if no one has anything else," Marcus paused to see if there were any questions. "Then, I think we should get cracking, there are many lives depending on us this day. Let's not let them down." With that he got up and exited the room with, Tom Vitt and Secret Service Chief, Tony Barker close behind.

Chapter Six

GULF OF OMAN 4:30 PM
8 September

After ten hours on a southerly course, at a speed of 10 knots, and a depth of 550 feet, Malik ordered the Dhul Fiqar to periscope depth. The sea was filled with ships of all sizes, trying to escape the devastation. Many of these ships would never see port again; their crews were already dead or dying from not only the massive amounts of radiation in the air, but from the poisonous gasses given off by the never ending fog of black smoke. The very sky seemed to literally be on fire, even at over 280 miles away from where the nearest missile went off. A strange lightning filled the smoke as it crept across the heavens like the harbinger of death. Malik swallowed hard; he had only meant to destroy the oil fields, but if what he was seeing was spreading like he thought it was…..he realized they may have just ended all life on earth. As he turned the scope in the direction from which they had just came, his stomach turned over in a fit of extreme nausea. He wanted to puke, and was barely able to control the urge for now.

"What's wrong?" Husam asked when he saw the color drain from Malik's face.

Malik didn't answer; he just stood there staring in disbelief at the carnage on the surface. Then, Malik finally stepped away from the periscope and let Husam see for himself what they had started.

"May Allah be praised," Husam said with awe. "They are paying now, for all their deceit and treachery."

"Husam, do you see that strange lightning that seems to crackle and spark like the end of a lit fuse?" Malik asked. "If that's what I think it is, we may have torn a rift in the world's magnetosphere wide enough to let in solar radiation from outer space. That would mean, within six month there would be nothing left alive on the surface of the entire Earth."

Husam thought for a moment before he realized the implications of what Malik had told him. "But, that would mean..."

Malik just nodded, then ordered the boat back down to 5-5-0 feet, and to resume course. They would stay on this course until they cleared the Arabian Peninsula, then head south to the island of Madagascar, off the east coast of Africa.

"Sir, what the hell happened?" Lieutenant Paula Jones, asked Captain Josh Worthington of the USS Tennessee.

The Tennessee had just gotten to the Persian Gulf on the fifth of September. She was the very latest in U.S. nuclear attack-subs. The new Virginia-class sub was close to 400 feet long, with a crew of 137, making it one of the biggest in America's sub-fleet. It carried the Tomahawk cruise missile, which extended her strike range without having to use nukes. From her vantage point at periscope depth, just off the coast of the U.A.E, she could keep track of the comings and goings of most every ship passing, through the Straits of Hormuz.

When the missiles were fired, the Tennessee and the Dhul Fiqar were separated only by that spit of land that juts out from the Arabian Peninsula to form the Strait, half, belonging to the UAE and half belonging to Oman. The instruments on the Tennessee had told the crew the directions the missiles had come from, so they knew it had to be another submarine.

"I think someone just started World War III," Worthington answered.

"But why would…and what…?" Jones stuttered, for a moment with panic, her thoughts going back to her family in Baltimore, Maryland.

Lieutenant Jones stood about 5'8" with raven hair and dark blue, almond shaped eyes. Her face was real easy on the eyes and her slim, firm body was kept in shape with a rigorous exercise program. Paula, at thirty-three, was as level headed as anyone in the Navy. She had come from a long line of Navy people, dating back to John Paul Jones, the famous Revolutionary War Hero. But, for a moment there, she almost panicked as the thought of a nuclear war mushroomed in her mind.

Captain Worthington had dark brown hair, gentle brown eyes and was tall for a submariner, at six feet. At forty, he had finally received his captain's eagles and a command of his own, after many years of crawling up the ranks. Even so, he had reached this point a lot sooner than many of his classmates from the Naval Academy.

After sending numerous messages and getting no reply, the Captain decided to get the hell out of Dodge. With the surface looking like a scene out of "Dante's Inferno," it didn't take a brain surgeon to realize there was nothing left in this part of the world except the dead and dying.

"Sir, our instruments are showing extreme water and air temperature," Lt. Jones reported, after a seaman brought it to her attention.

"Dive the boat to 5-0-0 feet, and check the gauges again," Worthington ordered. When the boat leveled at 500 feet, very near the bottom, the water temp was closer to normal, but even at that depth the temperature was still rising. Josh ordered the Tennessee to full speed, and headed for the Gulf of Oman. As soon as they passed through the Strait of Hormuz they followed the coastline of Oman until they were finally able to turn south.

Two hours later, Jones asked. "What, do we do now? I mean if World War III has really taken place there is no one left.

"Lieutenant, until we know for sure what has happened, we must continue on as a ship of the U.S, Navy," Josh told her. "It may just be a limited nuclear strike of the Middle East. But regardless of how long it takes, we must hunt down the bastards responsible for this mess and kill them." Josh thought for a few minutes trying to figure out what he would do if he were the one behind the attack.

"Sir, we have a distant sonar contact at five miles astern," Seaman Bob Bixby reported.

"They're behind us," Chief Petty Officer, Clive Cloverdale stated.

"Sir," the radio officer, Ensign Ben Brooks spoke up. "It's the Chattanooga."

The Chattanooga was a Sea Wolf class attack sub, and was the second sub assigned to the Sixth Fleet. She had just started her patrol route near the borders of Kuwait and Iraq when the bombs went off. And now like the Tennessee, the Chattanooga, was hunting for the enemy.

Chapter Seven

HIMALAYAN UNDERWORLD

8 September

After Dad disconnected from his brief conference with the president, preparations were made for the rest of our family and friends to be taken to the Andean underworld where we would, hopefully, join them after resealing the rift. Gabriel agreed to send a ship to collect the families of Larry, Ron, and Jay along with Ben Franklin's daughters, Phyllis and Mary in Knoxville, Tennessee. Then it would pick up Dad's brother Lamar and family, in Georgia, and his sister Caroline and husband Ron on the Caribbean island of Crab Claw Cay, before heading to the Andean underworld.

On her way home Pat would pick up Ben Franklin, and his extended family, in British Columbia, and then swing down to Montana for Pedro, Chiquita, their new baby Nathanya, and their little Jack Russell terrier, Hombre, who lives with us on Masterson Isle. While there, she would also collect the sheriff of Flat Head County, Peggy Stone Carter, and her new husband Joe, along with a few close friends, including Ken Amberson and his wife Linda.

It had only taken an hour to get our things together and catch the bullet train back to the surface, as our emotions seemed to be going in every direction at once. I guess it was a good thing to have learned what the Masters taught us about controlling them, because under the circumstances, it was easy to see how one could become panicked.

When we reached the surface, another ship was waiting next to Pat's. It was also a supply ship; the only one King Chogyal had left. They were oval or disc-shaped, about 100 feet across and approximately 30 feet thick from top to bottom. These craft had four decks, two for cargo, one for the crew, and of course the bridge, which appeared as a small domed rise above the fuselage.

A grayish-red haze covered the sun as it began to sink in the west and even here, the air was filled with the smell of burning oil. We quickly exchanged our goodbyes with hugs, handshakes and kisses, or licks on the nose from Duchess and the pups, in my case.

King Chogyal had put Master Jangbu in charge while he, his daughter Dohna, 20 of his best men and another 50 androids, as well as our team, started off for Moon Base Alpha. The robotic staff in charge of the base had already begun the initial startup procedure on the Battle Cruiser, Intrepid. These old ships had sat idle for many years at the moon base and needed a few hours startup time before space travel was possible.

Dad had asked the Kings permission to pilot the supply ship, and was given his blessing at the controls. As we lifted off, Pat and the rest of the Andean crew appeared on the main screen. "We just wanted to let you all know that our hopes and prayers go with you."

"Ours go with you as well. We'll see you guy's soon in Akakor," Dad told them as he engaged the engines and we went from a hover to almost 2,000 mph in about ten seconds.

"If we are lucky, by the time we get there the Intrepid will be all ready to go," Chogyal said, once we finally got underway.

"Sir, do we have enough people to actually run a ship as big as a battle cruiser?" Larry asked.

"I must admit, it will probably be a bit awkward at first, but I think we'll be able to manage once everyone learns their stations, and however long it takes us to get the old girl up to speed," Chogyal replied. "You have to understand, these ships have not seen action for about 13,000 Earth years."

"If I remember the stories correctly," Jay spoke up, "they were heavily damaged in the last battle with the Black Lords."

"Yes, it was a terrible time that almost destroyed mankind, and in some ways, is similar to what the planet is facing now," Princess Dohna spoke up.

She was a tall for a woman, about six feet, with jet black hair and hazel eyes. I couldn't help thinking she was truly an angel, as I stared at the softness of her face. We learned later she, like Chogyal and Gabriel was well over 300,000 Earth years old. However, to look at her you would think she was in her early thirties. But, even if you considered that one day on Nirvana, was like a thousand years here on Earth, that would still make her over three hundred years old. But, Dad thought it had to be from the period of time they spend in suspended-stasis. This process was supposed to rejuvenate, heal, and restore the body to a perfect being each time it was used. Now that's what I call holding your age well.

"Yes, our battle cruisers were all damaged to different degrees," Dohna continued, "but Commander Clakrin and his android staff at the moon base have had plenty of time to make them like new again. In fact, I believe Gabriel had mentioned something about taking them out for deep space trials soon. Maybe if we can close this rift in the Earth's magnetosphere, he'll allow us to take her out for a spin around the galaxy."

"That would be great," Max woofed, "just think of it Duke, we could be the first dogs to see the Milky Way up close and personal."

"No, you wouldn't be the first, but certainly the first in a long time," the King corrected. "When we first came here we brought many canines with us. They were a very important part of our extended families, and crew, much like you are, Max, to Steve and Jane, or like Duke is to Nathan and his family."

The old supply ship handled well, for a craft that had not been used in thousands of years. The trip to the moon only took a little over four hours. But then we were able to speed her up a little after we entered space. However, it was not until we went around to the dark side that we found the huge base at the bottom of an enormous crater.

Moon Base Alpha was an extremely large facility. A very large domed structure over five miles in diameter, dominated the center. Eight smaller domed structures, each about 2,000 feet in diameter, spread out in a circular pattern around it. Long tunnels of about three hundred feet connected the smaller domes with the larger one. Connected to three of these smaller structures with laser tethers and a long docking collar at one end, were three huge battle cruisers.

Off in the distance, we spotted pyramid like structures as we slowed and came in for a landing on Intrepid's E-deck landing bays. Suddenly, we all had a feeling of being here before, but knew that was impossible, so we shrugged it off and marked it up to nerves.

Robbie and Robo were there to greet us. Gabriel had sent them along with a few others to help expedite this operation. The base Commander, Rudrin Clakrin, was also there to welcome us and provide whatever we needed. After the handshakes and introductions, we proceeded to the bridge by way of three large elevators, where we found a crew of androids going over the last detailed check list before takeoff.

"Everything seems to be in order, Rudrin," Chogyal acknowledged, after taking a quick scan of the instruments and monitors around the oval-shaped bridge. "It looks like your personnel have done an excellent job of restoring this old gal to her original glory."

"Wow, this is incredible," Jay said, in awe of all the high technology as we entered the circular room.

Dohna then took us over to a set of controls where she pressed a button, and a huge screen came to life. In fact, this screen was at least six feet wide and curved around half the bridge. It allowed us to see not only the moon base and the surrounding area, but, with a few more button presses, far out into space.

Larry again noticed the many pyramid structures that circled the base at about five thousand yards and asked what they were for.

"They are the laser and Ion cannons that defend the base," Dohna responded.

"Oh yeah, I remember now, like the ones we saw last year in Guatemala and Akakor."

"Exactly," Dad told him. "But Dohna, there is something I don't understand. How, is it this base was never discovered by all the moon missions of the 1980's?"

Dohna just gave Dad a look, with those big almond eyes, as if to say, "Oh, but it was."

It was then Commander Clakrin said goodbye and headed for the elevators, and Chogyal headed over to where we were standing. The King then took each of us around the bridge assigning each one a special station. Dad, who seemed to understand the systems like he'd done this all his life, helped Princess Dohna, show the rest how the instruments worked. Dad was put in charge of piloting the ship for now, while David, Angela, and Yang ended up with tactical, in charge of the weapons systems, Ron sat at the communications station, while Larry and Jay were assigned to navigation stations. Steve and Jane would stand by in case someone needed medical attention. Dohna along with Max and I, would continue to circle the bridge helping out wherever we were needed, and of course the King would be in command of operations.

Robbie and Robo were in charge of the hundred or so android personnel we had on board. Commander Clakrin had loaned us about fifty of his androids for this mission. They would make sure everything on the ship functioned the way it should, such as, engines, weapons, and basically everything that fell under the heading of Engineering.

Chapter Eight

ANDEAN UNDERWORLD

9 September

Pat made good time crossing the Pacific, but ended up making a few more stops than originally planned. After collecting Ben Franklin, Ming, Mayling, and Gertrude (my mom) on the B.C. coast, they stopped in Seattle to pick up Dad's daughter Lynn and her extended family. And finally a quick stop at Masterson Island in Montana to pick up Pedro and his family. Another ship had already collected the extended family members of our team on the east coast and would meet them at Akakor.

Less than four hours later, both ships landed in the false volcano on the Island of the Sun, in the middle of Lake Titicaca.

"It's good to see you again, my Queen," Prince Draco greeted, as he and the First Dragon Squadron bowed their long necks low.

"And you as well, Draco," Patamaya responded as the rest of the crew and passengers exited the two ships. "How is the High Council doing with the preparations?"

"Everything should be in order, my Queen. After tonight's festivities honoring your return, the long empty houses of many underworld cities have been renovated, and made ready for the influx of humans from the surface. We have also found empty housing around Lake Akakor that once belonged to the Zipacna that are no longer with us."

"How are the remaining Zipacna, or should I say Olmec, accepting this new development?"

"It was King Gukumatz idea and his people accepted it with open arms, but I think it may be his aim to show the council and the different tribes, that they are no longer the evil demons they once were."

"Well I hope it works. The last thing we need is a civil war down here."

While Draco made his report to the Queen, Arlie, Sean, and Fred went over and talked with the rest of the squadron. They had a special bond with these particular dragons. Last year, when the squadron was first formed by Dad to defeat the evil demons that held the city of Akakor. Pat rode Draco, Dad rode Ragnon, Arlie rode Dagon, Fred rode Fagon, and Sean rode Zargon. At that time there were two rookie dragons in the squadron without riders, Ragtar and Hagnar, but since then, they have acquired chieftain's sons for riders. Tomka, the son of Bolontiku stood up proud as he held Ragtar's reigns, as did Agab's son Naumy with Hagnar's. Both dragons and riders looked smart in their shiny new uniforms, and since it was now the squadron's job to keep the peace in the underworld, everyone had been given a military rank.

Tomka and Naumy had graduated, at the head of their class from the new academy in the Chamber of Akahim. There, both human and dragon, not only learned how to become efficient squadron members by becoming, one with the other, but learned to speak every underworld language, plus a few from the surface world. They also learned math, history, reading, and writing, as well as the use of just about every weapon made in both worlds.

I guess you could say, some of the lives of our original team, had changed dramatically since last year when they decided to stay in the underworld with Pat. Arlie Longhire, an ex-special ops operative for the CIA, and Fred Holtz, the ex-FBI man, were now the two main instructors at the academy and were proud of their achievements. To date they had graduated over 21 dragon and rider teams that would form up three full squadrons. But, now that they had established the academy, the training period would now go for a full year instead of six months.

Sean, Lobo, and Zargon had been assigned to Councilman Agab's people, in the Chamber of the Tree of Life. Since Sean was a medical doctor, their original assignment was not only to provide protection, but medical care for the people in the surrounding chambers as well. And they became part of Agab's family when Sean and Agab's daughter, Kinna, got married and my brother, Lobo, married Kinna's wolf, Howl.

Pat's father, Dusty, had been assigned the duty of Goodwill Ambassador to all the tribes of the underworld. This kept him very busy, traveling throughout the many chambers from Guatemala to the tip of Chile and everywhere in between. Tomka, and Ragtar, along with Naumy and Hagnar accompanied him as his assistants, when they were not on squadron duty. However, except for times like today, to welcome the Queen home, or some other ceremony, the original squadron seldom got together as a single unit anymore. I think maybe it was because Pat was always busy with the affairs of state, and the fact that Dad was not here to take command.

After everyone had departed the ship, they were transported to Akakor in our M-I units, or Masterson Industry 480 Tactical Motor homes.

Queen Patamaya, along with Arlie, Fred, and Sean flew with the squadron to Akakor, while Dusty led the others in M-I-1. When the queen flew in over the huge city island the cheers of the people could be heard throughout the massive chamber.

Akakor, the capital city of the Andean underworld, was at the center of a huge island, which was thought at first to resemble a huge octopus, with its arms outstretched in all directions. However, after looking at it more carefully, we discovered it was constructed to mimic an unknown galaxy. Perhaps the one the ancients came from.

The city itself measured about three by five miles, with a large pyramid in the central plaza. A beautiful temple to Viracocha was on the east end of the plaza. Here, the people were taught the true stories of mans creation, and the original construction of the subterranean colonies. The United Underworld Library and Educational Center was on the south side. Here too, the histories continued in three dimensional holograms, right up until last year when we liberated Akakor. An identical building sat on the north side, but it was the new headquarters for the Andean Underworld Government, much like the congressional building in Washington, D.C. And, on the west side of the plaza, was the Grand Palace where the Queen lived with her entourage.

Yes, the city was now a sight to behold, because, almost every square inch of the central plaza was covered with pure gold and studded with precious gems, including the buildings and roadway. The beautiful homes of the Akakor citizens lined the outer edges of the city, down the length of what looked like eight outstretched octopus arms.

Pat and the other chieftains had really done a great job of restoring the city to its original glory. I mean, if you could have seen it last year, you would think they had torn everything down and rebuilt a whole new city. Last year the whole plaza, along with the steps of the pyramid, ran red with blood from the cannibalistic demons which lived here. The Zipacna flew through the different chambers, on their camulatz, raiding the many underworld tribes and taking sacrificial victims. The camulatz were a basilisk like creatures, a cross between a bird and a snake, with long venomous fangs, and a sixteen foot wingspan.

During last year's battle, it was here in the Royal Palace, that Queen Patamaya killed the evil Namaru class devil that had controlled King Gukumatz and the Zipacna people for so long. It was strange though, because after the demon had been destroyed, King Gukumatz and his people had no recollection of the evil that had possessed them, or the atrocities they had committed over the years. Since then the Zipacna have been known as the Olmec, because they resemble the people of the great stone heads found in southern Mexico.

As the squadron landed atop the steps of the palace, King Drac, Agab, Bolontiku, King Gukumatz, and all the other members of the High Council were there to meet them.

"How was your trip, my Queen?" Bolontiku asked, as he bowed low.

"It was going well, until some crazy's decided to blow up the world," she responded.

The chieftains looked at each other as if not quite sure what she meant by that.

"We need to get things ready now to receive a whole lot of new people in a hurry." Pat told them. "Our ships have just left to pick up as many people and supplies as they can before the surface becomes uninhabitable."

As the understanding of the enormity of this event sank in, King Drac spoke up. "We received your communication about the bombs in the Middle-East, my Queen, but we had no idea they would affect the rest of the world in such a way."

"Well, it was a lot worse than we originally thought. I mean it was bad enough when the first set of nuclear missiles went off, but when the second set also exploded in the region, it caused a tear in the magnetosphere layer of the upper atmosphere, allowing radioactive solar rays to pour in, making a bad situation a whole lot worse."

"Will Nathan, Steve, and the rest of the team be returning to us soon?" Agab asked with concern.

"They went to see if they could somehow seal the rift in the magnetosphere, but...." Pat turned away, as tears started to well up in her eyes from worry. Ever since Dad had saved Pat from the tomb robbing drug lords last year, she had fallen very deeply in love with him. And, Dad felt much the same way about her, but because he had been through two failed marriages already, Dad was a little gun-shy when it came to matters of the heart. He was scared to death of failing again.

Agab stepped over, taking her hand in his and looking deep into her blue eyes, just as the M-I units came to a stop at the bottom of the palace steps. "They will be safe, my Queen," he whispered, before they all turned and welcomed the new arrivals.

Chapter Nine

TACTICAL SITUATION BUNKER
Washington, D.C

The President and his staff had reconvened in the situation room just after breakfast the next day. He had addressed the nation on national TV at 7: 00 pm the night before, advising the people not only to stay indoors, but to get as deep underground as possible. Needless to say the subway tunnels of the major cities quickly became very crowded, as did the underground parking lots of the biggest buildings. Many people just moved down into the basements of their homes. But, what they didn't know was that most all these people would be dead or dying within a week from solar radiation or starvation. And within a month, maybe two, even more would die from diseases contributed to few sanitary facilities with clean water.

"Dr. Vanderbilt could you give us a breakdown on what is actually happening and what we can expect to happen in the next few days," the President asked.

"Well, what basically happened was, when the first bombs went off it weakened the magnetosphere, which are those weird looking figure-eight lines you see crisscrossing the planet." June used a small laser pointer to show the lines on the main viewing screen. "As you can see, the sun is constantly bombarding us with solar radiation. It is the magnetosphere barrier, or the electromagnetic field, that keeps most of these particles from hitting the Earth. But, even when this barrier is functioning properly some of these radiation particles find their way to the surface, which some feel is the biggest cause of skin cancer. When this occurs from time to time in the Polar Regions, we call this phenomenon, the Aurora Borealis, otherwise known as The Northern Lights, or Aurora Australis, known as the Southern lights, in the southern hemisphere."

"Yes, but what are we faced with now," General Wells spoke up, trying to speed up the narrative.

"When the second set of bombs went off, they tore a large hole in this section of the barrier." Again, June pointed at the screen. "What we can expect to happen now, is massive amounts of subatomic particles hitting the planet without any kind of protection. In other words, within the next few days it's going to get hot, real hot. So hot as to make the Sahara Desert in summer, feel like an iceberg off the Greenland coast in winter. And not just in the Mid-East region, but it will soon encompass the whole world, unless of course, Dr. Masterson can somehow close the magnetosphere barrier. Then all we have to worry about is the possibility of a polar meltdown, or possibly another Ice Age. Then, there are the mega-storms, earthquakes and volcanic eruptions created by any one of the fore mentioned scenarios. None of which are going to leave the planet anything like mankind has seen in the past twelve to thirteen thousand years."

"It would seem the human race is screwed regardless of whether we fix the rift in the magnetosphere or not," Debra Downs, the F.E.M.A director, spoke up.

"Yes, well the difference is how long it would take for the Earth to recover. If the rift is not fixed man may never walk the surface again. However, if it is fixed, we may be able to go topside again within five to twenty years, depending on worldwide radiation levels," June replied.

"I think we get the picture June," the President commented, shaking his head at the possibilities facing mankind. Then he turned to General Wells. "Dan, can you tell us how the evacuation of our most important citizenry to the subterranean facilities is going?"

"Mr. President, we have filled, at least seven of nine to full capacity, but the one in Alaska and the one in New England are at present, a little over half. We should have most everyone on the lists, safely underground by this time tomorrow." Wells paused a second to check some paper work. "There's a few here however, that have either died, are out of the country, or just can't be found."

"If they have not been found within twenty four hours, fill their position the best you can," the President advised, then turned to Admiral Parks. "Randy have you got anything for us this morning?"

"Mr. President, we received a garbled message from what we think is the Tennessee, but there was so much interference from the radiation it was hard to be sure. As you know the Tennessee was one of the two subs assigned to the sixth fleet. And, if we are reading the message correctly, we also believe the Chattanooga is still alive. We think they are presently on the trail of the rogue sub, but hopefully we'll know more when they've moved out of the affected area."

"Is there a possibility this rogue sub is still armed with nuclear missiles Admiral?" The Vice President asked.

"Yes Ma'am, we have to assume they still have nuclear missiles on board and are most likely to use them on U.S. targets if they get half a chance. However, with the advanced technology aboard both the Tennessee and the Chattanooga, we should be able to take her out before she has a chance to fire her missiles, possibly even before she knows we're there."

"Admiral, have you calculated the possibility of what this rogue sub will try to do next?" Miles Standish asked.

"We have a few scenarios drawn up, but when you're dealing with terrorist, it's hard to tell what they'll do for sure." The Admiral pointed toward the screen, as an aide brought up a world map. "At present, we believe they are headed for Madagascar to get out of the hot zone. From there they could continue south and swing around the coast of South Africa into the Atlantic Ocean. It is at this point they would have at least three options. They can head northwest to the Caribbean, continue west around the tip of South America, into the Pacific Ocean, then north to attack Americas' west coast, or they can continue south to Antarctica and try to hide out for a while before picking another target."

"It seems to me they have a forth option as well Admiral," Stan Miller said. "They could head east from Madagascar and take the long way around to the Pacific via the Indian Ocean."

"What counter measures have you set up Randy?" The President asked.

"Sir, we are setting up a line of subs across the Atlantic at this point," the Admiral pointed with one of those laser pointers to a line of subs slowly making their way south. "The French and English have also agreed to help us hunt this guy down. Australia, India, and even New Zeeland, have agreed to spread four of their subs throughout the Indian Ocean. Hopefully we will box him in, somewhere around the southern tip of Africa."

"Mavis, has our relations improved any with the other world powers?" The President asked the Secretary of State.

"A little, but even those that consider this attack was not directly related to the U.S., thinks this country is responsible in a round-about-way, because of our unjust invasion of Iraq back in 2003. They feel we over reacted instead of letting the U.N. handle the situation or accepting the fact our Intel was wrong about the W.M.D's." Mavis paused and took a sip of water. "Even though we took out a so-called evil dictator in Saddam Hussein, we caused the death of tens of thousands of innocent civilians who were just defending their homeland. And for most in the Arab world, vengeance on America and her allies will last forever."

"Well, it looks like they've killed a whole lot of their own people with this attack," General Wells spoke up.

"According to Pakistani intelligence reports we received through unofficial channels, the attackers were out for revenge, not only for the U.S., but the Arab countries that sold their oil to the U.S. and her allies," Miles offered. "However, I don't think they had any idea things would turn out the way they have."

"Are you saying you don't think they wanted to blow up the world?" General Wells asked, becoming a little irritated with Standish.

"I'm saying, I don't think they had any idea of the damage, or repercussions, they would cause when they attacked the oil fields with nukes," Miles replied. "I think they thought they were acting as Allah's punishers." Miles paused for a second before continuing. "Besides, I doubt these fanatics know anything about nuclear-fusion or the consequences there of."

"Regardless of what they intended," Admiral Parks spoke up, "the main thing at this point is to make damn well sure they can't use the missiles they have left."

Everyone nodded their head in agreement. "Okay," the President finally said, "If no one has anything else, we will meet back here in the morning at the same time, unless of course there is a new development."

With that said, the only ones to leave the room were the Joint Chiefs. The rest just sat there, stunned, as the realization of what the world was now facing began to sink in.

"May God be with us, because mankind is going to need all the help we can get," Katherine West prayed.

Chapter Ten

THE BATTLE CRUISER INTREPID IN LOW EARTH ORBIT

9 September

D ad brought us into a low Earth orbit over the affected site. The area was invisible to the naked eye, until Princess Dohna pressed a button on her console, which brought a photo-optic filter down over the main screen. At that point, the massive tear in the magnetosphere became very clear. It was now a thousand miles wide and almost stretched around the world, as did the radioactive black smoke still coming from the oil depots in the Persian Gulf. It reminded one of the Bible passage, where God tells Noah he would not destroy the Earth with water ever again and sends a rainbow. Then adds it will be fire next time. Well, I think we were now seeing the fire and it wasn't pretty.

"Raise shields," Chogyal ordered.

"My God!" Jane exclaimed. "How are we going to fix that?"

"We are going to try to pull the tear together with a magnetic tractor-beam," Chogyal told her.

"Something similar to zipping up your pants, I'll bet," Larry speculated.

"Well, I hope it's that easy, but sometimes this procedure can be a little problematic," the Princess informed us. "The last time we tried it, there seemed to be no end to the complications before we finally got it fixed."

"How many times has this happened?" David inquired.

"It has happened many times during Earths history," King Chogyal replied. "Oh, every time a large meteor comes through the upper atmosphere or when a super volcano goes off or massive earthquake hits."

"Or when the Black Lords attacked," Dohna interjected, just as she ordered Yang to lock onto the rift with the tractor-beam.

"The affects can be devastating to the surface, causing long lasting mass-extinctions." The King continued. "Sometimes it takes thousands of years before the animals, or humans, can once again emerge from the underworld caverns."

Just then, Ron informed us that Admiral Gabriel would be hailing us from the bridge of the Defiant shortly. He was presently in route to the moon base to take command of the battle cruiser, which he would use to pick up survivors from the surface and place them in the moons biosphere.

"Admiral Gabriel," Dad said. "I thought he was still in stasis."

"He was, until this morning," Chogyal informed. "In fact, it is time for him and a few others, to once again, be revived and assume command of their realms. That's the way it's been since we arrived here on this planet. But you already know that, Nathan."

"I guess, I just wasn't thinking it was time yet," Dad replied.

"I didn't know the moon base had a life support system for humans," Steve said, as he looked over at Chogyal, changing the subject.

"Oh yes, it can hold over 5,000 people, in the base's underground biosphere. The subsurface of the moon is much like many of the subterranean chambers on Earth, with beautiful parks, and gardens. In fact it is very similar to Shambhala," Chogyal described. "And another 3,000 can be put into the suspended stasis chambers indefinitely."

"Oh, look it's working," Angela said, as she looked up from her station, between David and Yang, and marveled at the technology of this craft.

Everyone stared for a long minute as the rift slowly came together at one end. But at this rate it was going to take at least a day, maybe even two, to get the hole completely closed again, that is of course, if the rift didn't open on the opposite end faster than we were closing.

"It's too bad we can't do something about the radioactive fallout caused by the bombs," I woofed.

"That should dissipate into the upper atmosphere in a few years, but most of it will most likely fall back to Earth with the rain and snow," Dohna explained. "And of course, it's possible the black smoke could block out the sun long enough to cause another Ice Age."

"Sir," Ron spoke up. "We have an incoming transmission from Admiral Gabriel. He is now on board the Defiant and headed for Earth."

"Put him on the screen, Mr. Clayhorn," the King said.

"Chogyal, are you making any headway with the rift?" The Admiral asked, as his image materialized on the main screen.

"Yes, Sir, after the crew figured out the instruments, it didn't take long before we were able to start closing. However, it is a lot wider than we first thought and will take a bit longer to close," Chogyal informed.

"I understand. We sure don't want a repeat of the problems we encountered last time," Gabriel answered. "But, we do have to speed things up as much as possible, because our long-range sensors have picked up an asteroid, about 10x7 miles, on an Earth bound trajectory."

"Where is the asteroid now, sir?" Dohna asked.

"It just passed Mars and is traveling far faster than what we've seen in the past. Odin is sending Captain Tyr and his crew, who have also just come out of stasis, to the moon base as we speak. They will take the Scorpion and assess the situation while you finish closing the rift. Then you will join them and together either change its course or blow it up. In the mean time I'll send down all my supply ships to gather up as many people off the surface as we can carry."

"Sir," Dad spoke. "Are the subterranean chambers filled to capacity yet?"

"Major Masterson, it sure is good to see you again. Yes, we will have them filled worldwide within the next seven hours," the Admiral answered.

It was a little hard for us to differentiate between Admiral Gabriel and his clone that filled in for him when he was in stasis. They looked exactly the same; tall, slim, with blonde hair and dark-blue eyes. I guess the only difference was that the Admiral wore a uniform and the clone always wore long flowing white robes with a thin golden belt around his waist. Last year when we discovered the subterranean caverns in Canada, and sailed through the interconnecting tunnels to the island called Avalon, Gabriel's android clone showed us a hologram of Admiral Gabriel, who informed us of how they had, came to this world, fought the Black Lords, and then colonized the planet. But we never met the real Admiral in person. So, what did he mean about seeing Dad again?

"Sir," I don't think we've ever……" Dad started.

"Oh, I can understand your confusion, Major," the Admiral cut him off in mid sentence, "but believe me, I have known you and your team for a very long, long time. We'll have to get together soon and talk about it when I visit Akakor, when Viracocha comes out of stasis. But, for now, let's close that rift and stop that rock before this planet is no longer inhabitable."

"Aye, aye Sir," Dad responded in a military manner, not really knowing why.

Then, after a brief acknowledgment of the rest of us, including Max and I, the Admiral signed off. Afterwards, King Chogyal stepped over to Dad's station and whispered. "I know you don't remember, but you and the rest of your team, including the ones that are with Queen Patamaya at Akakor, and a few others, were once part of the Admiral's original crew, on this ship. Of course, after we decided to colonize the Earth, the Admiral turned over the ship to a rotating command. At that time, you and your companions became part of Captain Amun's crew.

"But, how can that be?" Dad asked, a little skeptical. "Those things happened thousands of years before we were even born."

"Nathan, you and the others, are not here by accident or by some random chance of fate," Chogyal informed. "I guess what it amounts to is that you have come home."

As I listen to their conversation, from where I sat at Dad's left in a seat just made for canines, I became more and more confused.

"Look at those massive storms headed across the Atlantic," Jane announced suddenly, bringing us back to matters more urgent.

"The ones at the poles, I think, are even bigger," Steve observed, pointing to the screen as everyone looked up from their station.

"All those poor people," Jay said. "I hope the Admiral can….." He was going to say save them, but then realized that only a very few, out of so many, could be saved by the Admiral. The rest had little hope of survival on the surface.

As we looked on, a sense of deep sadness came over us all, for those innocent people that were doomed to die this day, from the stupidity of mans greed, hate, and vengeance.

Chapter Eleven

JUST NORTH OF MADAGASCAR
10 September

"Abdul, bring us up to periscope depth," Malik ordered, returning to the bridge after getting a six hour nap.

"While you were resting, I thought about what we have done," Husam told Malik, in a whispered voice so no one else could hear. "Is there any way we can fix the hole in the magnetosphere? Or are we all doomed to die from this mistake in our judgment?"

Malik thought for a few minutes while waiting for the sub to reach periscope depth. "In time, the rift may close by itself, depending on how big it is. But from what we saw yesterday….." Malik just shook his head. "If it is still there, or has gotten bigger, all life on the surface of the planet will be…."

"What is it Malik?" Husam asked when he looked up again to see Malik's face.

Malik smiled. "Husam I think the rift is closing, we no longer have that lit-fuse lightning. But, it is a little early to tell for sure. Pray to Allah, we see no more of this phenomenon."

Just then, the sonar operator, Habib, reported. "Sir, I'm picking up an unusual return and…, well ah, maybe you can know what it is."

Malik took the earphones and listened. He looked at the screen which showed the return at eight miles off the port stern, "Husam we have company." Malik paused as he continued to listen. "All stop, rig for silent running, pass the word, don't even dare to make the slightest sound," he whispered, then wrote on a piece of paper. "It's the new American propulsion system for their Virginia class subs."

"Sir, we have sonar contact," Bixby reported. "Or at least had contact for a few seconds at about eight miles off our starboard bow."

"If it was the rogue, he may be headed down the west side of the island like Paula speculated."

"All ahead full," Captain Worthington ordered. "Lt. Jones, plot a firing solution. Chief Cloverdale, rig for silent running and ready tubes one and two. Talk to me Bixby."

"There's nothing sir, it's as if he just vanished."

"No, he's just playing dead," Josh guessed. Then after he thought for a second he ordered, "Mr. Brooks contact the Chattanooga and let Captain Northfield know what we have."

"How do we know this subs not a friendly?" Lt. Jones asked. "I mean every navy in the world is probably looking for the rogue by now."

"Oh, we're not shooting until we're sure, Lieutenant, but until then we have to assume he's the enemy."

"Sir," Brooks spoke up. "Captain Northfield is now two miles to our stern and is turning east to cover that side of Madagascar. He suggests we go down the west side and catch the rogue between us on the south end."

"That's a good idea," Josh agreed. "Bixby, what kind of return was it?"

"Sir, it sounded just like one of those older model Russian attack subs. You know like the Kursk, of the Oscar II class."

"Yeah, I know the ones you mean. But I heard the Russians did away with most of them after the Kursk sank," Josh thought as he pulled at his chin."

"Sir, tubes one and two are ready," Chief Cloverdale reported.

"What's our position, Lieutenant Jones?"

"Sir, we are now 5.5 miles from the last sonar contact."
"All ahead slow, Chief."

"Malik, what do we do?" Husam whispered, with the sweat rolling down his face.

"Wait," Malik mouthed the word, while holding a finger to his closed lips.

Then the sonar operator, Habib, handed Malik a note that read. "Two subs, one at five miles to our stern, the other heading off to port at 6.5 miles. Both have their outer doors open and are ready to shoot."

Just then the radioman, Ali, handed Malik a note that said: "They are hailing us, sir."

"Put it on speaker, Ali," Malik ordered.

"This is Captain Worthington of USS Tennessee, to the commander of the unknown submarine five miles off the northeast coast of Madagascar. Please identify yourself or risk being sunk."

Malik thought for a moment before he responded. He knew they could neither out run nor fight, their way out of this situation. So he decided to try a ruse. "Oui, Captain Worthington this is Captain Perrier Lafitte of the French submarine Charles De Gaulle," Malik responded, faking a heavy French accent. "We have been put on high alert, to help you Americans hunt down a possible rogue sub operated by Al Qaeda terrorist. But I find that a little hard to believe, don't you?"

"Yes, it does seem a little strange," Worthington conceded. But, we did track the missiles as they were launched, and a submarine is the only scenario that makes any sense."

"Where would they have gotten a submarine, and a crew to operate it, Captain?" Malik retorted. "I don't know of too many Arab countries with submarines in their Navies, except for, maybe, Iran. Iran would also have the nuclear ordnance for such an attack." Malik paused. "Or, do you think it possible, the missiles may have come from a surface ship, perhaps from an oil tanker with a converted hold?"

"Well Captain, I guess that is a plausible possibility," Josh conceded. "But Al Qaeda could have also gotten the sub from the Russian Black Market, and I suppose the missiles too. But, I'm guessing the missiles came from Pakistan."

"Oui, Captain, but where would they have gotten a seasoned submarine crew?" Malik asked. "You know as well as I do, it takes years of training to actually sail a modern submarine, especially, in a manner that you suggest." Malik paused. "I'm sorry, Captain Worthington, but we'll have to debate the possibilities of this dilemma at a later date. We are late for our next check point and will have to be on our way."

"Well, it's been nice chatting with you Captain Lafitte. Good luck and good hunting to you, sir. And be careful of that rogue bastard, any idiot stupid enough to use nukes on the oil depots, is crazy as they come."

"Oh, I will Captain," Malik said, as he signaled his helmsman, Abdul, to go to full speed ahead. "Maybe we can get together after this is all over, and have a drink some day, if there is still a world left after this mess."

"I'll look forward to it Captain," Josh said as he signed off.

While Josh and the alias, Captain Lafitte were having their little chat, both the Tennessee and Chattanooga alike sent inquires of this Capt. and boat to the Atlantic Naval Command. The returned message confirmed the fact there was indeed a French captain and submarine of those names on patrol in the Indian Ocean off the east coast of Africa.

Malik had known this, because he had served on that boat when he was in the French navy assigned to the UN. However, the Charles De Gaulle had put into Port Elizabeth, South Africa the day before for a problem to their starboard bow plane. Even though the problem was a minor one, it would require a part that had to be specially made, which would take at least two more days to repair. And by the time this information was finally received by the American boats, the Dhul Fiqar seemed to have once again disappeared.

"Where's that boat, Bixby?" Josh asked, mad at himself for being taken in by such a ploy.

"I'm not sure sir," Bixby responded. "I tracked it off to the southeast for about an hour until it just disappeared."

Josh shook his head, "They should definitely be in range of our sonar."

"Brooks radio the Chattanooga and see if they have a sonar contact," Worthington ordered. "Chief, take us up to periscope depth; let's see what the surface looks like."

"Aye Sir," Cloverdale responded, then repeated the order to the helmsman.

As Josh looked through the periscope, he could see that the sky had changed dramatically from the scene over the Persian Gulf. There was no longer the black smoke or the many death ships as far as the eye could see. Even the fire in the sky and the strange lightning seemed to be diminishing. However, to the north, the sea was now churning into one hell of a storm, with 80 mph winds and 40 foot seas. Josh had seen many storms in his day, but this monster had to be the biggest he'd ever encountered.

For a long moment he watched as the white caps rose up and spilled over and over again, getting a little bigger each time. It was almost hypnotizing, and for a few seconds he found himself on the distant beach where his family spent their summer vacations. In his vision, Josh was only ten, his dad had yelled at him to get back from where he played near the surf, building a sand castle, oblivious to his dad's concerns. He would have drowned that year when the huge wave came out of nowhere and dragged him out to sea, but a surfer pulled him off the bottom and brought his limp body back to shore where they were able to revive him.

"Sir, the Chattanooga reports negative contact on the rogue boat," Brooks, suddenly reported bringing Josh back to reality.

As the periscope went down Josh said, "Chief, dive the boat to 8-0-0 feet, speed 28 knots, and come to a heading of the last known position of the rogue."

Chapter Twelve

ANDEAN UNDERWORLD

10 September

In just a little over twenty four hours the two supply ships had brought nearly 10,000 new souls to the Andean Underworld. The M-I units were kept busy shuttling the newcomers from the landing pad to the city of Akakor. At the United Andean Underworld Government Building, they were greeted, registered, and given a full physical check up. Here too, they would also be given Ben Franklin's G.E.F. drug, so they would not only stay healthy, but be able to communicate with all the different tribes, including the dragons, and canines. Then, over the next two days they were shown the real story of man's creation and development, at the Educational Center.

Once, everyone was registered and had taken the newly adopted Oath of the Andean Underworld, they were assigned a chamber and transported there via the newly restored ancient gondola system, which traveled along at a mere 30mph near the ceiling of each chamber. Because of the slower speed it allowed the occupants an opportunity to see the true wonders of this amazing world. Once they reached their assigned chamber, they were shown to their living quarters, and depending on their education and training, assigned jobs.

"My Queen, and members of the High Council," Bolontiku, the former Chieftain of Akanis, began as he opened the morning meeting.

"With our habitable human chambers nearly at full capacity, our food supplies are beginning to run low."

"This situation came up so fast it has not allowed us the proper growing time for our most important crops of beans, corn, wheat, rice, and potatoes," Agab, the former Shaman and Chieftain of the Chamber of the Tree of Life, spoke up.

"At this rate we only have enough food reserves for another month," King Gukumatz, former King of Akakor, added.

"I will have the supply ships bring in enough food to get us by for a few more months but, we need to figure out how the ancients fed so many people the last time a disaster struck the Earth," Queen Patamaya told them. "I'll check the old records and let the council know my findings in a day or so."

"Your Majesty," King Drac spoke, "food is not our only problem." Many of the new-comers still think we dragons are evil beasts, and call us "the spawn of the devil." In some chambers they have even shot at the squadrons that are there to protect them."

"You would think after three days of indoctrination at the Educational Center they would know better. But, I'll have Dusty and his escorts weed out those that can't except the dragon kind and put a stop to it. It may be that we'll have to expel them from the underworld altogether if they don't comply with our ways," the Queen responded. "And, let me make this clear, if anybody shoots at you, you have every right to defend yourself."

Dusty raised his hand to speak. He had sat in on this meeting so he could ask the council for help with his duties. With the influx of so many people he could no longer patrol all the chambers with just three men and two dragons. "King Drac is right. I've heard many newcomers say demeaning remarks toward the dragons. In fact, there were a few times when we just left a chamber rather than put up with such nonsense. I feel if the council doesn't act on this problem soon there will be violent hostilities breaking out all over the underworld."

"I vote we arrest these people and have them brought back here for trial," Agab spoke up.

"At this point I think that would only aggravate the situation," Dusty replied. Because, we honor the right of free speech, arresting these people would only be detrimental to the future of the underworld. However, I do believe we should give them fair warning, that that kind of behavior will not be tolerated. And if it persists, those responsible will be exiled from the underworld. Or sent to a chamber of exile until they could fit into the underworld society"

"All in favor of Dusty's proposal say Aye," Patamaya called for a vote on the matter, before the others had time to think about it. Everyone raised their hands in agreement, so the motion passed. The Queen then asks her secretary to send a memo advising the chamber Chieftains. She also promised to look into the matter of assigning more people to help Dusty.

The next morning, while Pat was busy at the government building with matters of state, Dawn, Arista, Duchess, and the pups were beginning to settle into the very nice rooms at the palace. They overlooked the beautiful blue lake that stretched beyond the palace grounds. The top two floors of the palace had been assigned to the family and friends of our original exploration team, who became known as the White Knights of Avalon.

While some suites overlooked the lake, others had views of the beautiful courtyard and the golden plaza beyond. The palace was huge, taking up the whole west end of the city. It was over five hundred feet long, one hundred feet wide and fifteen floors high. The upper seven floors were made up of forty eight suites each. Most of these were set aside for the royal court and visiting Chieftains.

The lower three floors of the palace had large banquet and ballrooms, with blue-marble floors, giant golden columns spaced evenly around domed ceilings. This building could easily rival any grand palace in the world.

The surrounding grounds of the palace offered beautiful, manicured courtyards, with many flower gardens. Huge fountains with colored lights, dotted the landscape every hundred feet or so, spraying water high into the air. As one walked around the grounds on the golden tiled pathways a person could easily loose one's self in the beauty of it all. Here the troubles and tensions of the day seemed to quickly fade away.

"Aunt Dawn, can we go outside and explore the city?" Junior inquired, as he and Rufus looked out the window at the wide lake beyond the palace grounds.

"Well, if you'll give me a few minutes we'll all go for a walk," Dawn replied. "I want to check out the library again, but I guess we can take a look at some of the other buildings as well." She paused for a moment as a thought came to her. "Maybe, some of the others would like to go as well, so why don't you guys check with the rest of the family and friends before we leave. While you're gone I'll call and see if it's alright for us to take a tour and if we need an escort or not."

"We can do that," Molly barked as she and the other pups headed for the door.

"However, be real careful when you ask Pedro and Chiquita, that you don't wake the baby."

"We will," Lucy woofed as she and Skipper headed out with Arista.

About thirty minutes later a group assembled in Dawn's suite. Other than her, Arista, Duchess and the pups, were Anthony and his family, Lynn and her family, and Joe and Peggy Carter.

"We tried Grandma Gertrude and Mr. Ben's room," Molly reported, "but they were not home."

"Oh, that's right," Dawn remembered, "they went to visit Sean, Kinna, your Uncle Lobo and Aunt Howl, this morning at some place called the Chamber of the Tree of Life."

As they came down the steps to the foyer, Naumy (Agab's eldest son) and Tomka (Bolontiku's son) were just entering the giant double doors of the palaces east side. They were clad in the dress uniform of second lieutenants of the United Underworld Dragon Squadron.

"Ah, there you are Miss Masterson," Naumy said, as he came over and took Dawn's hand. "My name is Naumy and this is Tomka, we met you last May on your Aunt's island, at the wedding ceremonies."

"Oh yes, I remember you guys," Joe spoke up. "You had just entered the academy and were about to start flight training when you got back."

"Yes we graduated last month. With honors I might add," Naumy injected.

"The Queens aide said you wanted to take a tour of the city, and sent us to show you folks the sights," Tomka spoke up.

"But, where are your dragons?" Molly asked wagging her tail. "Are you going to fly us over the city?

"No, that's not allowed except in an emergency or some kind of celebration," Naumy informed. Besides, Hagnar and Ragtar are on leave at Dragon Isle for the next few days, to visit relatives."

"So, if you'll follow us, we will get this tour underway," Tomka said. "And, if anyone has any questions, please don't hesitate to ask."

"We might as well start out with the new Library and Educational Center and work our way around the plaza," Tomka said, as they descended the palace steps.

As they entered the Educational Center, the group encountered another group who had just finished the last of a series of five holographic imaging rooms where they watched the true history of mans origins.

All newcomers had to pass through here after they were done over at administrations in the government building. Here, they learned all about the creator race, the war with the Black Lords, their imprisonment on Mars, the colonization of Earth, and the creation of the underworld. They also learned about a mass destruction that destroyed the continent of Lemuria and about the escape of the Black Lords about 15,000 Earth years later. Then, there was the second battle in this solar system with the Black Lords, which caused the destruction of Atlantis. Then, in yet another room, they learned how Nathan Masterson and a team of brave explorers came down here a year ago, with Queen Patamaya and freed the cities of the Andean underworld from an evil demon. But, there were some that could not, or would not, accept this story.

"I don't care what they say, there is no such thing as aliens that created the human race," an outspoken priest, in his forties told his group of four other priests and five nuns.

"Sir," the guide said. "I know it's hard for you to accept, but I can assure you everything you've seen today is true."

"Who do you think you're trying to fool, my son?" another priest, who looked to be in his fifties, asked.

Naumy thought he could be of some assistance, to the young guide, and went over to help. After introducing himself he asked the priest, who seemed to be the leader of the group, "May I ask where you folks are from and how you came to the underworld?"

"We were in a small parish just outside Albuquerque, New Mexico when we were abducted by...." Suddenly the group realized what Naumy was trying to do, and knew they had been wrong about an alien race, because the UFO that brought them here was not exactly manmade.

"I'm sorry for my rash statement earlier," the priest apologized. "But it's just so hard for us to accept after years at seminary, learning the teachings of the Bible. Our faith teaches that aliens and UFO's don't exist. Then to find out they not only exist, but are responsible for the creation of man. Well, you can see how confusing that could be."

"Sir, your religion, along with so many others around the world, is not necessarily wrong. However, you will now have to learn a whole new way of interpreting the text of your Bible," Naumy said with a smile.

The group just nodded with understanding as Naumy returned to where the others waited.

"Young man, you showed a lot of tact in the way you handled that priest," Joe Carter told him. "Remind me to put in a good word to your commanding officer for you."

Two hours later, after they had finished touring the city, they met back at the palace for lunch in the main dining room. Queen Patamaya and the underworld Chieftains were also there, but they sat at a special made table to accommodate the enormous size of the dragons. The table sat much higher up on one end, which allowed humans to sit at the same level as the dragons. It was more like ten long tables connected in a rectangular- shape with a huge section missing from the middle. This allowed the food to be raised and served from a section of the kitchen below by a hidden elevator mechanism in the missing center section. All the other tables were served in the usual way.

As everyone dined on soup, salad, and terror-bird sandwiches, in such a beautiful setting, where the giant western windows allowed one to see the courtyard and lake beyond, it was hard to think about all the destruction happening on the surface.

Who would have thought the lives of so many could have changed so dramatically in just the span of one year.

Chapter Thirteen

ON BOARD THE INTREPID IN LOW EARTH ORBIT

11 September

"I think we are just about done here," Chogyal said, as the ship finished off the last few miles of rift closure. "Thanks to this fine crew and their expertise, we have accomplished in a matter of hours what might have otherwise taken a week."

"Sire," Princess Dohna spoke up. "Maybe we could let the androids relieve the crew while we take lunch in the mess-hall and deal with that other matter."

"Oh, yes, my dear, I think that is a good suggestion. Call the replacement android crew to the bridge. Then we'll retire to the mess-hall for a bite to eat."

While we waited a few moments for the replacement crew, King Chogyal and Princess Dohna sat at their stations staring out at Space, the Earth and other celestial objects as if they were in some kind of meditative trance.

I looked up at Dad, from where I sat near his station, with a look that asked, what's up with those guys.

Dad just shook his head, as if he didn't know. Then he asked, "Sire, what heading should we take?"

Chogyal then turned to Larry, who was filling in as navigator, "Put us on an intercept course with the Scorpion, Mr. Carver. We'll see if we can help Captain Tyr with that meteor."

"Aye, aye Sir," Larry responded in a military manner without really knowing why.

As the co-ordinance was then laid into the ships computer, our android relief showed up and we all headed down to the mess-hall. On the way there we had to pass the medical bay, which gave Dad, Steve, Jane, and even Max and I the strangest feeling we'd been there before. This strange Déjà vu then spread quickly to the rest of our team.

Suddenly, images of Maggie's face came across Dad's mind making him feel weak and disoriented as other images started pouring in. Maggie was Dad's second wife and David and Dawn's mother. It was if we were all seeing the same thing at the same time, all being part of the same dream. We found ourselves inside the sickbay, which was suddenly full. Many people were being treated for what looked to be severe burns caused by laser blasts. It was like the whole ship was on fire. Then the ship would rock now and then, like we had been hit with a missile, or possibly a cannon blast.

As we made our way around the operating bays, looking into each one and seeing doctors and nurses running every-which-way, Dad stopped dead in his tracks. A cold sweat began to run down his face, as we watched what was happening. In this room we saw Steve, Jane, Sean, and Maggie standing over a bed, frantically trying to save a patient in a flight suit. His face and most of his body was black from burns and much of his hair was gone on one side. No matter what they did, it was to no avail, and as he died, he held Maggie's hand, telling her he loved her.

On the far side of the same room, a dog lay in a smaller bed, where someone who looked like Pat worked, with Dawn and an older man, to save his life. But that was not to be either. And as they put the sheet over their heads we realized who they were.

Just then in this crazy dream, if that's what you want to call it, Joe, Arlie, and Fred, followed by Max, Lobo, and my sisters pup, Spike, also in flight suits, walked straight through us as they came to find out how the two on the beds were. Then Joe, David, Angela, Dawn, Jay, Peggy, Ron, and Larry also crowded into the operating bay, right through our real bodies. When Steve, or at least the Steve who stood by the bed, looked up and just shook his head, a sense of great sadness filled the room.

"They saved our lives," Joe said, as tears came to his eyes.

"And, they saved this ship and all aboard her," someone by the name of Commander Montu said as he made his report to the Captain.

"Major Masterson," King Chogyal called sharply, bringing us all back to reality. "Is there something wrong?"

"No, Sir, I, ah, just felt a little disoriented for a moment," Dad responded. "But I seem to be alright now."

"Talking about disoriented, did you guy's see what I just saw?" Jay spoke up. "It was like being here at a different point in time. The whole sickbay was packed with patients being treated for burns. I'm telling you, I've never seen anything like it."

"Yes, I think whatever we experienced, it affected us all the same way," Jane said, as the color returned to her face.

"Maybe we should get something to eat," Steve suggested. "It may be that we've been under too much stress over the last couple days."

We then made our way down the corridor to the elevator. This would take us one deck down to the officer's mess. On the way, it occurred to Dad that there was another shorter way to our destination. We could have just taken the elevators from the bridge to the mess hall. Then he knew we'd been routed this way by the King and Dohna, on purpose. They knew we would experience what we had.

By the time we entered the officer's mess everyone had fully recovered from the Déjà vu affect of the sickbay. The large oval room manned by android personnel was what one would think a ship of this size should be. In fact, the dining room could have passed for a fancy 5-star restaurant. Many red overstuffed booths circled the walls with swing out tables for easy access to different size tables. Many green plants also dotted the huge dining area. Here we found a few humans having lunch at three rounded tables in the center of the room, but other than that, the dining hall was empty. But then, we only had a skeleton crew on board at this time.

Chogyal and Dohna led us to a very large table at the back of the room, which would accommodate our number. Here, we were seated in overstuffed chairs, but as soon as we all sat down, things changed again to a different time. It must have been earlier that same day we saw in the sickbay, because there was no fire, no injured personnel, and Dad and I sat with Joe, Peggy, Maggie, Steve, Jane, Max and Arlie around this same table. Suddenly the whole room was full of people, coming and going, eating and talking quietly amongst themselves. Two tables over, a much younger version of Steve's dad, Ben Franklin, sat with Nathan's dad, Leroy Masterson. They both wore the uniform of fleet captains, except, Ben's had the insignias of Chief Medical Officer, and Leroy's indicated he was the Chief Squadron Commander for this ship.

"I don't understand," Max said, as he looked over at me confused. "I thought a Major out ranked a Captain, but it looks like those guy's clearly out rank Nathan."

So I had to quickly explain the difference between the Naval and Marine ranking systems. But I'm not real sure he understood the difference, even after I broke it down for him. Sometimes it can be real hard to understand humans and the way they do things when you're a dog, even if you're smart like Max and I.

We saw a pair of waitresses, in this other time period, which looked exactly like, Mr. Yang's wife and daughter, Ming and Mayling; they were taking orders from the table next to ours. A young second lieutenant, who looked like Dad's son Anthony, told them to tell Yang how good his stew was. Others at that table resembled Dad's daughters Lynn and Dawn and his other son David and wife Angela. They were sitting with Sean, and Lobo. Then, as we looked around the room, it dawned on us that all our family and friends were represented. Some wore squadron uniforms, while others wore those of the medical staff, and then there were those of technicians, specialist, and general ships officers of all different ranks.

It was just about then the klaxon sounded, signaling everyone to general quarters-battle stations. Shortly afterwards Captain Amun came over the intercom telling everyone about the escape of the Black Lords from the penal colony on Mars. He said they were heading for Earth and it was up to us to defend the planet to the last man if need be. Then he ordered all fighter squadrons to launch-bays, and wished us luck.

The hair on my back began to stand on end, as we saw everyone get up and leave at once. At that point three androids started serving our lunch, and again we were brought back to the here and now.

"Sire," Dad said. "I think you know what my friends and I have been experiencing. Would you mind telling us why and what this is all about?"

"As I tried to tell you on the bridge earlier, your journey has brought you and those closest to you, full circle," the King replied. "This has little to do with what's happening on Earth at present, it's just our way of letting you know who you really are."

"But, Sire, we saw our bodies, or at least distant relatives that looked like us, in stasis at Avalon last year, when we visited Gabriel," Steve spoke up.

"That's right," Max barked, "we were in those capsule coffins with the glass tops."

At this point, Yang spoke up. "I believe Gabriel told us they were our great ancestors."

Chogyal and Dohna just nodded in understanding, and held a hand up, as if to say, give us a chance to explain. "Yes, and in a way they are your great ancestors," Dohna agreed. "But what Gabriel didn't tell you, because he felt you were not ready at the time, was the bodies you saw were actually clones made at the time of your original death."

"What do you mean, "original death"?" Dad asked.

"All of you were first born on Sirius, long before the Great War with the Black Lords," Chogyal began, as the rest of us began to eat our lunch, but listen with all ears. "In a lot of ways, life in the Canis Star System was much like it is here on Earth, except more highly advanced. And until the Black Lords turned to the dark side there was little or no death."

"You all joined the fleet at about the same time," Dohna smiled broadly, remembering the time as if it was yesterday. "It was about five years before the rebellion, and after your graduation at the academy you all were assigned to the first fleet and this ship."

"Admiral Gabriel took a special interest in you, Nathan, after your commanding officer was killed in a fierce battle over my planet of Nirvana." Chogyal said. "It was you who took charge and led the rest of your squadron into the murderous fire of the Rebel forces, and won the battle. You were made squadron commander after that and led your star-fighters to many victories."

Dohna continued the story. "Then, after we had the Black Lords imprisoned on Mars, you and Maggie were married. For many years you lived happily in the house you built on the mountain just above Avalon. The Admiral always said we would not have won so many victories if it hadn't been for you and those who followed you. In fact, all of you became like sons and daughters to him."

"And when you and Duke died that day defending the ship and the people you loved so much, the Admiral, King Adonai and the Great Creator, El Shaddai, figured out a way that you could all be reborn, and for that matter all of mankind", Chogyal informed. "Reincarnation," Jane guessed, understanding now how and why the process started.

Dohna nodded in agreement before continuing where her father left off. "In fact, you all have died and been reborn thousands of times over the years, living many lifetimes on your long journey back to who you once were."

I looked up at Dad, "Now you know why you have all those weird dreams."

"However, until this life, when you were given Ben Franklins G.E.F. serum, which slightly changed your DNA, we were unable to bring you home, so-to-speak," Dohna continued. "Then, last year, Gabriel decided to give you a booster shot to speed things along. He made that decision to help you with the obstacles you would face in the Andean Underworld. And with another mass extinction possibly drawing nigh, he thought the booster would help all of you better cope with circumstances."

"That reminds me," Chogyal spoke up, as he raised his glass of wine for a toast. "I would like to congratulate each one of you on a job well done. If it had not been for you the Andean Underworld would still be under the control of a Namaru class demon, and many more lives would have been lost."

As everyone finished off the last of their lunch, Dohna suggested. "We should be at the rendezvous site in about fifteen hours. So, why don't we all try to get some well needed rest before our arrival?"

"I could sure use some sleep," Angela spoke up as she looked in David's direction, with a smile.

"I should contact the president to let him know the rift has been sealed," Dad said as we got up from the table.

Chapter Fourteen

WHITE HOUSE BUNKER
11 September

As everyone took their seats around the big oval table in the Tactical Situation Room, the big viewing screen on the south wall came to life. "Mr. President," Dad said, as they all came into view. "We have been successful in closing the rift for now. But I'm afraid there was nothing we could do about the damage it caused or that of the bombs."

"Does this mean the people of the world can once again live on the surface?" The president asked.

"Sir, all this means is the rift has been sealed for now. All the ultraviolet radiation that was coming through that portal has been stopped, or at least reduced to normal levels. However, on the surface, the region that was once called the Middle-East has been totally wiped out, and everything within a thousand mile swath around the middle of the Earth, from the eastern Mediterranean, is dead or dying. There are millions of dead fish washed up along coastlines of countries within those parameters. And you probably already know about the many storms throughout the Atlantic and Caribbean that have wind speeds of over 280 mph. Some have gone as far north as Greenland. In the Midwestern U.S., on top of all the flooding, you have literally hundreds of tornados sweeping across the land from Denver to the Atlantic and from the Gulf of Mexico to Canada, while most all of the western states are on fire. It is like this over most of the world. Even now giant looking hurricanes are forming over and around the North Pole. Sir, it looks as if those nukes have triggered a lot more than first anticipated."

"And how do you know all this," General Wells asked.

"Well sir, I'm in a position to know. You might say I have a bird's eye view of everything."

"The only way you could know that, is if you were on the international space station," General Farmer spoke up.

"Is that where you're at, Mr. Masterson, on the space station?" the Vice President asked.

"Not exactly, but something like that, Ma'am. Let's just say my whereabouts should not be your main concern. Besides, my location is on a need to know basis only."

"Mr. Masterson, I'm the president of the most powerful country in the world and there is no one who needs to know more than I do."

"Sir, don't let that lie go to your head. For I can assure you, it has been the downfall of many powerful Kings, Emperors and Conquerors throughout history," Dad replied, in no uncertain terms. "In fact, it's that kind of thinking that's put us where we are now, in a fight to save mankind from extinction."

"Young man, are you saying this mess is the fault of the United States," The VP asked. "Ma'am, I'm not blaming any one country. I'm just saying governments around the world vie for more and more power every day, instead of addressing the needs of their people. Hell, the only time that happens is when it benefits some crooked politician on Election Day. But, this power struggle has now reached critical-mass and is threatening to tear the world apart, so let's try to fix this problem before we start throwing accusations."

"I apologize, Mr. Masterson," President Overton said, as he realized the truth in Dad's words. "Is there anything we can do at this point to help stop the storms or put out the fires that are ravaging our country?"

"Sir, all you can do now is hope and pray we can stop this asteroid," Dad switched the main screen to the deep-space probe the scorpion launched just after she left the moon.

"It is about ten miles long by seven miles wide and is approximately 200,000 miles this side of Mars. We have done the math on this one and if it is not stopped, it will hit the Earth in exactly twelve days, eight hours, and twenty minutes."

Everyone in the situation room was stunned as they stared in disbelief at the giant rock. No one said anything for a long while, as fear set into each of their minds. It was like they'd been handed a death sentence.

Then General Farmer spoke up. "We have the SDI (Space Defense Initiative) to knock it out before it hits the Earth." The General was referring to the system put up in Earth's orbit during the Cold War to deter a nuclear exchange between the U.S and the Soviet Union. The SDI, installed during the Reagan administration, were laser satellites, to be used to knock out any incoming ICBM's.

Dad switched the screen back to the situation room. "Well, General I hope you don't have to rely on such archaic technology, but I guess if we fail in our efforts to knock this thing out, or to divert its course, then it won't matter what you throw at it. I'll let you know in a couple of days how we did. Until then, may God bless and keep you all safe." With that Dad ended the transmission.

The room was quiet for a few minutes while everyone tried to digest what they'd just seen. Then June Vanderbilt said, "Well, at least they closed the rift," trying to initiate something positive. "This means, if they can stop that rock, the Earth may be back to normal in just a few decades."

The President looked at each person in turn around the room. The Joint Chiefs had nothing to say for a change. Finally, Vice President West spoke, "Was it my imagination… because I got the impression he was traveling to the asteroid, and was going to try to destroy it in deep space."

"It seemed that way to me as well, Katherine," Overton said after a moment of thought. "General Farmer, is there any way this could be possible?"

The General looked up from his laptop computer and said, "Sir, the only way that could be remotely possible is that he is on an alien space craft traveling at near the speed of light. And we all know there is no such thing, so I don't know where he is or how he knows what he does."

"How sure are you, General, that there is no such thing as aliens and their craft on Earth?" Miles Standish asked, as he smiled slightly from across the table.

Knowing full well there were alien craft on Earth, General Farmer and the other Joint Chief's began to show signs of being caught in one of the biggest lies ever told to the American people. "If there were aliens on Earth Sir, I can assure you we would know about it," the General responded as sweat formed on his upper lip and forehead.

Just then, Tony Barker leaned over and whispered something in the President's ear.

"Oh yes, let him in," the President responded.

When the door opened, General Mark Baker, the Commandant of the Marine Corp and the unofficial fourth member of the Joint Chief's, walked in with his aide, Major Sarah Wheaton. Baker was in his early forties, slim with military cut brown hair, and brown eyes. As he took his seat next to Admiral Parks he apologized for being late.

"I understand, Mark," Overton said, "But right now we're trying to get to the bottom of something." Overton turned back to the other chief's, "General Wells, do you and Admiral Parks agree with General Farmer, or not?" The President asked.

Wells looked at Parks and nodded, "Yes Sir, we have no knowledge of aliens or their craft on Earth."

"What about you, General Baker?" The Vice President asked. "Do you have any knowledge of an alien race on Earth?"

Mark thought for a moment and took a sip of water while trying to figure out how to phrase his next words. He pulled at his chin as he looked around the room at the others. "Like the other Chief's have stated, I could say there's no such thing, however, they, along with Mr. Standish and Mr. Miller here, know better. Even before Roswell, the military, the CIA and even the FBI knew for sure they existed. But because these races are far more advanced than humans, we tend to down play their existence to the world, and encourage the science world to do the same. So, yes they exist and they have been here a lot longer than mankind has. Hell! There are some that think these ET's may even be our creators." With that, General Baker sat back in his chair and watched the reactions of the others. The other Chief's gave him cold angry stares that would melt lead.

"Before you got here, General, we were in contact with Mr. Nathan Masterson who said he was on his way to stop an asteroid from hitting Earth in about twelve days," Mavis Henley stated. "We were having a little trouble figuring out how he was going to do this, since he was not forthcoming with his exact whereabouts. The only thing General Farmer could think of was that he had to be on an alien craft."

"Did you say Nathan Masterson?" Mark said, with surprise. "It's been a long time since I heard that name. "My Uncle, retired Brigadier General Joe Carter, used to talk about a Nathan Masterson all the time. If I remember the story right, Uncle Joe was Masterson's wingman during the Vietnam War. He said Nathan was one hell of a fighter pilot, an ace many times over, and should have gotten the Medal of Honor on their last mission. But, I think Uncle Joe said he was shot down over enemy territory and was believed to be dead."

"He was shot down alright," Miles Standish spoke up. "But then, six months later, Masterson walks into the U.S. Embassy in Bangkok Thailand."

"That can't be the Masterson we just talked to, General. He looked to be no more than thirty five at the most, which would make him too young for the Vietnam era," the VP said.

"Well, Ma'am, Uncle Joe always said Nathan looked like he was barely old enough to have graduated high school, let alone being a major in the Marine Corps."

The discussions went on for another hour before the meeting was adjourned. But, in the end they concluded Dad and his team of explorers had made contact with an alien race at some point, while bringing down the evil empire of Beltran Velasco in Guatemala last year.

Chapter Fifteen

INDIAN OCEAN, SOUTH OF MADAGASCAR

11 September

While running patrol routes, off the southern coast of South Africa for the UN during Malik's service in the French navy, he learned all about the deep narrow canyons that lined the bottom of the Indian Ocean. They ran from the south end of the island of Madagascar to the southern tip of South Africa. However, while these trenches offered perfect cover, they were at a depth of 2,000 feet or more in places and when your crush depth is 2,800 feet, you have to be very careful. And, they could not get more than 16 knots while using the new Whisper Drive Propulsion system, or WDP for short. This system allowed them to travel, even though at a slower speed, without being heard by another sub, or at least not heard so as anyone would think it was another submarine.

"Sir, how long do you think the Americans will continue to look for us before they move on?" Husam questioned.

"They won't give up easily, my friend. We were extremely lucky they accepted our story without challenge. But I'm sure by now they know about our little ruse and won't make the same mistake twice," Malik replied, as he leaned back in his chair at the captains station. "No, I think it would be wise, of us, to stay hidden here in these narrow gorges for a while longer."

"Sir," Abdul interrupted, "we are coming up on our next turn."

Malik had learned every turn many times over, while serving on the Charles De Gaulle, but the Dhul Fiqar was over 20 feet longer and 10 feet wider. Malik's eyes were now glued to the outside monitor as he calculated the distance and allowed for the larger dimensions. "Turn in three, two, one, now, Abdul, hard right rudder." A terrible scratching sound was heard on the port side. The boat had barely hit the rock wall on the port side of the trench. Rocks fell onto the hull, making a clanging echo throughout the boat. This caused a pressure pipe to spray water one deck below the bridge, but was quickly brought under control by the crash team. Malik's eyes didn't leave the screen, as a hard turn to port was now coming up fast. "Hard left rudder, Abdul, and slow us down to five knots," he ordered, with a sigh of relief after they had made the turn. After that Malik ordered an all stop.

"That was close, Malik," Husam told him.

"I think we need to slow down and rethink our position. The trenches ahead are even narrower than these and we may not be able to maneuver them with this big boat," Malik replied, as he tried to remember what lay in front of them. Then he took another look at the charts to make sure of their bearings. "We have come more than a hundred miles since our encounter with the Americans, Husam. If we raise the boat 500 feet, out of this hole and continue on at 16 knots using the WDP, we may be able to slip by them without detection."

The Tennessee and Chattanooga had crisscrossed the area, on both sides of the island, many times over, for the last several hours, without success. Their long range sensors also showed no traces of the rogue sub. Capt. Worthington and Lt. Jones studied the deep sea charts once again hoping to find something they'd missed.

"Do you think they could have gone into these trenches?" Paula asked, as she pointed to the large cracks in the seafloor.

"I considered that," Josh said, shaking his head, "but, it would be awfully tight down there for a boat of that size. They would have to know every twist and turn down to the last foot, possibly the last inch in some places."

"But where else could they have gone so fast as to be able to avoid our sonar?"

"You've, got a point. It would have been almost impossible," Josh replied. "Chief, prepare a probe and program it for depth of 2,000 feet at 30 knots," Josh ordered.

"Aye Sir," Chief Cloverdale replied sharply. Then after a few moments, "Probe ready to launch, Sir."

"Launch probe," Josh ordered.

The probe was eight feet long and eighteen inches in diameter. It could be manipulated by a joystick, like a videogame, and it sent back sound, as well as visual images. It was good for about a hundred miles before the fuel ran out, but, it could also be retrieved, refueled, and reused.

As Chief Cloverdale manipulated the joystick, his screen showed the parameters of the canyon walls. From where the probe entered, it was another 800 feet to the bottom, and 120 feet wide from wall to wall. After thirty minutes, and about 17 miles, the canyon walls narrowed down to about 80 feet wide. From there they went back and forth, narrowing down then widening out, turning one way then the other, for many miles, but still no rogue. Then after an hour the sound of falling rock on a metal hull was picked up on the sonar. Bixby immediately put it on speakers, "Sir, I think we have contact."

"Have you got a visual, Chief?" Josh asked.

"No Sir, but the sound is coming from about five miles ahead, give or take a mile or two."

"Mr. Brooks, notify the Chattanooga, of our position and let them know that we have possible contact at five miles. Lt. Jones, flood tubes one and two, and open outer doors. Let's kill this son-of-a-bitch, and go home, before he gets away again." Josh thought for a second, and then ordered the Tennessee to a depth of 1,500 feet.

"Sir, we're ready to fire," Lt. Jones reported.

"What have you got for me, Bixby?"

"Nothing, Sir, I thought I had something for a second but it….faded too fast to make out what it was."

"What about you, Chief, is there anything on the probe?"

"We're coming up on the rockslide now, Sir, but whatever caused it is long gone. Do you think the slide could have sunk them, Sir?"

"Not a chance," Josh replied.

As soon as the Dhul Fiqar came out of the canyon, Malik ordered an almost due west course, and increased speed to 16 knots. He also had the boat brought up to a depth of 1,000 feet; from here the bottom would come up fast as they headed toward the South African coast. But Malik was not planning on putting into port, he just wanted to, hopefully, avoid the Americans by making an illogical maneuver and throw them off his trail.

"Sir," Habib spoke up, in not much more than a whisper. "We have an American sub at 6,000 yards to our starboard stern, and closing fast. But I don't think they have picked us up on sonar yet, or at least they haven't turned in our direction." Habib waited a few moments, listening very intently to the American sub continue on a zigzag pattern in a southerly direction.

"Load stern tubes as quietly and quickly as possible," Malik ordered. "At least if they do attack us we'll be ready for them."

Chapter Sixteen

DEEP SPACE

Onboard the Battle Cruiser Intrepid
12 September

As we made our way to our quarters for some well deserved sleep, images of the distant past came and went across our minds. For some odd reason we all knew exactly where we were supposed to go without having to be shown the way. Mine and Dad's quarters were on D-deck, just opposite the briefing room for the pilots, and one deck above the launch bays. On the door were the names of everyone who shared these quarters, ours read: Major Nathan Masterson, Captain Duke Masterson, Captain Joe Carter and Lieutenant Spike Carter.

As we entered the room we again seemed to be instantly transported back to another time, a time of great sorrow. Joe sat on his bunk, weeping, with his canine Spike who looked a lot like one of my sister's pups, and was presumably his RIO (Radar Intercept Officer), as I was at that time to Dad. Then a knock on the door jarred us back to the present.

A male android stood at our door wearing a white jacket and black pants. He then introduced himself as Gofor, and said he'd been assigned by commanders Robbie and Robo as our personal valet. "Is there anything I can do for you Major Masterson or Captain Duke?

"Well, for one, you can make these awful visions stop," Dad replied, a little irritated at having to relive the past every time we entered another doorway.

"I'm sorry Sir, but I have no control over your vision. However, if you require something such as food, clean uniforms from the laundry, or that sort of thing, just let me know by pressing my call button on your console."

"Thank you, Gofor, but all we need right now is a hot shower and a few hours sack time," I barked.

Our room was laid out with four bunks, two twin-size beds for the humans and two rounded overstuffed pillow beds for us canines. Dad's and Joe's bunk had three large drawers underneath, while mine and Spike's had only one. A small light with a dimmer-switch was inset into the wall above each bunk allowing one the comfort of reading in bed, or working on an alien version of a highly advanced computer system.

Along the port wall were four very comfortable chairs around an oval table about four feet in diameter. There were two heads, or bathrooms, one for us canines and one for the humans. As you entered the large doorway the humans were to port and canines to starboard. In the wall between the two was the laundry chute.

All in all, they were not bad quarters, the beds were very comfortable, everything was at easy access, and, oh yes, there was the large wraparound screen, which took up the better part of one wall and continually showed where you were in space. It was neat to lie in bed and see all the distant stars and planets zip by as we flew through space at incredible speeds.

As I checked the drawer under my bunk, I found three sets of uniforms, a casual, a dress, and a flight suit, which resembled the survival suits, Uncle Lamar, gave us last year before we headed south through Mexico on our exploration exploits. Dad found socks, underwear, and pajamas in his drawers. He found his uniforms, hung up, in a closet located next to the door to the head.

After we showered and put on fresh clothing, we sacked out for a few hours. However, our sleep was plagued with dreams of the ancient past.

When princess Dohna called on the intercom seven hours later telling us to report to the bridge, we still felt drained from the lack of good restful sleep. But, duty calls and all that stuff, so we put on a fresh khaki uniform of the Fleet Marines, complete with name bars and rank insignias, and reported to the bridge, as ordered. It felt good to get out of those robes we'd had on since we left Earth. Of course, we sent them down the laundry chute almost immediately.

The Intrepid was now alongside the Scorpion. As the elevator door opened, Dohna motioned us over to take seats with her and Chogyal at the command center. The King was engaged in conversation with a figure on the main viewing screen.

"Chogyal," Captain Tyr said, "It sure is good to see you again, you old space wolf. How long has it been, a thousand or two thousand Earth years?"

"It was when we all got together for the last Fleet Dance at Avalon, three thousand years ago."

"Oh yes, I remember now. That was when Odin and Zeus had a little too much to drink and got into that little tiff about who was the better looking, Freya or Aphrodite. Then Thor and Apollo had to quickly break things up before they got out of hand."

Chogyal laughed at the thought. "I think that's why we haven't had a dance since."

"Yeah, I kind of miss those dances. We had so much fun and it gave us an opportunity to visit with everyone and catch up on old times," Tyr remembered the comradeship, as a sense of longing came over him.

"I'll see if I can't talk Admiral Gabriel into having one at Akakor when Viracocha comes out of stasis, next year," Dohna commented. "But for now, Captain Tyr, what can you tell us about this rock we're after."

"It has a solid iron core unlike any I've ever seen before." Tyr switched the screen to show the asteroid, and then broke down what the scan reports showed. "In fact if I didn't know better; I'd say it had been purposely created."

"By whom and for what purpose?" Chogyal asked.

"Well, we're pretty sure it originated at or near a low Martian orbit; about two days ago," Commander Freyr spoke up. "Even though, we have seen no indication of demon activity on the surface. But, they could have manipulated our long range sensors to continuously show nothing unusual." Commander Freyr was second in command of the Scorpion, and twin brother to Freya. Of course, the present crew of the Scorpion originally came from the planet Valhalla in the Canis Star System, but now resided in the subterranean colony of Asgard in Northern Europe, ruled over by Odin.

"I'm sure they still have their underground bases and have most likely rebuilt a sizeable fleet over the years," Dohna commented. "That's where they assembled their battle cruisers just before they attacked us last time."

"Do you think this rock could be some kind of bomb to destroy Earth?" Dad spoke up for the first time.

"That is a possibility," Commander Freyr said. "So let's destroy it before it gets to Earth and then attack the demon colonies still on Mars."

Those from the planet Valhalla always were a little too eager for battle. Chogyal thought to himself. "First, let's make sure what this thing is made of, and second, let's make sure it was the work of the demons and not some random combination of events," Chogyal suggested. "To begin with, I think we should take core samples to make sure what type of iron we're dealing with and how much magnetite it has in it."

"You're right, of course," Captain Tyr agreed. "If we try to blow that thing up and it's full of magnetite, we could blow ourselves up with it. But if we let it get to close to Earth, and they use nuclear missiles, that would not be good either."

"I agree, Tyr," the King said. "So I suggest we lock on to it with a magnetic tractor-beam and pull it off course, while a probe takes the samples. My navigation team is already figuring a course to head this monster into deep space."

Jay and Larry looked at each other confused and then realized Chogyal was giving them a direct order. "We have the co-ordinance, Sir," Larry said after a two minute delay.

"We need to tow or push the asteroid thirty degrees to starboard; to this point, Sire." With that, Jay showed the area on another section of the screen, as an arrow pointed to the location. "At that point the asteroid should miss the Earth by 80,000 miles. It would then be spun around in her gravity-field and slingshot out on a course for deep space." A mini-graphic showed the desired effect in yet another insert on the screen.

"That's awfully close," Dad said. "What happens if the Earth's gravity field pulls the rock in, instead of slinging it back out into space?"

"Yes, I see your point," Larry said considering the possibly. "But, if it is further out, the asteroid will eventually hit another planet, or in time make its way back to Earth. Either way, if the figures are not exact, the potential for another disaster are extremely high." Just then Tyr came back on the screen. His navigations officer confirmed Jay and Larry's calculations. With that, Chogyal ordered Mr. Yang to launch a probe into the asteroid. The Scorpion launched a second one a few seconds later.

In only a few moments we had the results back, 50% Iron magnetite, 30%, iridium and the other 20% was made up of many different metal and chemical elements.

"Just as I feared," Chogyal observed. "That rock has about the same metallic makeup as the one that came down over the Tunguska region of Siberia a little over 102 Earth years ago. Except this one is a lot bigger."

"I must have been in stasis," Tyr said. "But from what I was told, when updated on world events, the thing exploded in the upper atmosphere."

"That's right," Dad spoke up. "If I remember my history right, there was a blast equivalent to twenty five modern nuclear bombs, some thirty seven years before mankind had such weapons. In fact, human scientists are still trying to figure out for sure exactly what it was."

"That was a small one compared to this monster," Dohna said. "This one is over four times bigger and I think......" she paused for a second then asked Jay and Larry to run the projected course of the asteroid. "Where exactly would it hit Earth if we don't stop it?"

A few seconds later Jay came up with the location. "It would hit the Earth around what we call the Bermuda Triangle."

"Just as I thought," Dohna continued. "In that area, on the sea floor, there is one of the highest deposits of methane-hydrate on Earth; if this rock ignites it, there would a fireball that would consume the Earth in a matter of a few days. In fact, it would leave the Earth in much the same condition as Mars is now."

"Would that not indicate the Black Lords?" Tyr asked.

"Not necessarily," Chogyal said. "Remember the one that hit the Gulf of Mexico sixty five million years ago. The one some believe wiped out the dinosaurs. We had not arrived in this quadrant yet, the Black Lords had nothing to do with that one."

"May I make a suggestion," Dad spoke up.

"Of course you can, Major Masterson," Dohna said. "We welcome your input and that of your team as well.

"Why don't we push this rock out of harm's way, and then investigate the demon colonies on Mars?"

"That's an excellent suggestion Major," Chogyal spoke up. "It will take the effort of both our ships to move this rock to its new course, and then we can make sure the demon legions are where they are supposed to be." At that, he then turned to Mr. Yang and ordered a tractor beam be engaged. The Scorpion did the same on the other side of the huge rock. But, from the start the size and speed of the asteroid was going to prove a challenge, even with two ships.

Chapter Seventeen

ANDEAN UNDERWORLD CITY OF AKAHIM

12 September

Today, Queen Patamaya and the underworlds High Council traveled to the city of Akahim, the home of the United Dragon Squadron Academy. Soon many hundreds of residents from all over the underworld would come here for the Pairing Ceremonies. This is where the new cadets at the UDSA would be paired together with their squadron partners. Then, both dragon and human would remain as a team throughout their length of time in the service.

Tomorrow, Queen Patamaya and a few other Chieftains would give a short speech to inspire the new cadets. There would also be exhibitions, by First Squadron, to show just how efficient a dragon squadron can be against an enemy. I guess you could compare this show to the exhibitions put on by the Navy's "Blue Angels" across America.

It was here at Akahim last year we received a great deal of knowledge about the evil demon that controlled the city of Akakor. And, it is also here that the Andean underworld historical records are kept.

Located two chambers north of Akakor, this chamber like many others, is the home of a vast number of Ice Age animals. The Mammoth, Mastodon, Giant Ground Sloth, Toxodon and many other giant species share a large grassy plane that stretched out for miles in all directions east of the river. Here also were predators, such as Dire Wolfs, Saber Tooth Cats, and giant Short Faced Bears.

Here, as in Shambhala all the chambers, now that the computers had been fixed, were regular day/night cycles, with what looked like a real sun, during the day, and moon and stars at night. The ancients must have understood the importance of making it as much like the surface world as possible, because without it, there would be no plant life. Even human and animal life would not survive very long down here without the regular yearly cycles. But now, each chamber once again experienced all four seasons, as they had when they were first built by the ancients. This was all controlled by a timer on the main computers. It was set to slightly raise or lower the temperature as day turned into night and as the weeks and months passed into years. For example, in winter the temperature was on average 25 degrees cooler than in summer when it stayed mostly in the mid 70's.

Rain fall was also quite common now that everything was up and running properly. This was done with an elaborate aqueduct system built into the ceiling. When it filled to a certain level from rain water filtering down from the surface, it automatically tripped a sprinkling system that filled the chamber with a rain storm, complete with a generated wind from huge fans in the ventilation ducts.

Pat couldn't help but marvel at the differences from when we were here a year ago. At that time the underworld computers had been down or only operating at fifty percent for at least a thousand years. I mean, very little was operating as it should down here. Most all the chambers were dark and desolate with many scary creatures around every turn, but now they were bright and full of life like they were meant to be.

In this chamber, the city of Akahim was just to the west of the main river, and because of the way the mountains came together it was unseen until you were directly in front of it. The outer wall was over forty feet high and fifteen feet thick. It curved across the front of a giant fissure, connecting two huge granite mountains. The inner wall was only slightly smaller in height and connected to the outer wall by two, 200 foot runways, each 50 feet wide, and equally spaced along their 500 yard length. Beyond that, the great city was built on the cliffs of the two mountains that rose over 1,500 feet above the river below. For over 2,000 years, the many rock and timber housing structures, all painted bone white, had sat unoccupied. However, many of the bigger ones had now been turned into barracks, mess halls, and classrooms for human and dragon alike.

At the very top was a spectacular palace, with a golden dome-shaped roof. This structure's lower two floors were now being used as an office building for all military and police matters throughout the Andean underworld. Only a few of its many suites, which made up the upper floors, were being used by teachers, flight instructors, and administration officers as well as their families, as housing. It was here Queen Patamaya, and the High Council, would be staying during the festivities.

One level below the palace was a beautiful temple where the bodies of Viracocha, Xolotl (twin brother of Quetzalcoatl) and others of their kind still lay in stasis. When we passed through here, a year ago, we were met by the holographic images of Xolotl and four others who told us all about the evil Zipacna at Akakor and how to defeat them.

The Queen and High Council were here at the temple a day early, to ask the image of Viracocha about the problems they were facing with the influx of so many people to the underworld.

As they walked, two by two up the winding pathway, with Patamaya and King Drac leading the way, Colonel Longhire, and Lt. Colonel Holtz, the academy's commandant and deputy commandant, came down to meet them in their white formal dress uniform. I have to admit, with the golden buttons on the jackets and a red and gold stripe down the outside legs of the trousers, these smart new uniforms made Arlie and Fred look very official.

"Your Majesty's, and honored members of the Andean High Council," Arlie said as he and Fred bowed slightly. "If you will follow us we'll show you to the Hall of Records, in the great temple."

"Lead on, Colonel's," Patamaya said in a very formal manner, as she smiled slightly and winked at the two men when she was sure the other council members couldn't see. Arlie and Fred had become very close friends over the last year and she didn't want them to think she took herself too seriously.

Fifteen minutes later everyone stood in a large oval-shaped room with polished marble floors, and large columns, as was the style of most of these structures. And here too, there was a central alter platform, much like those we'd seen in temples all over the underworld colonies. On the floor was a circle about twelve feet in diameter surrounded by equally spaced golden tiles. On these, one council person stood per tile.

Pat stepped onto the platform, inserted her medallion into the proper niche, and started to manipulate the proper symbols on the ancient alien computer. Soon, a holographic image appeared in the center of the circle. It was the image of Viracocha himself. He was a tall, bearded, white man, with blonde (almost white) hair, sapphire blue eyes and a slightly elongated head. He, like Gabriel and most all those from the planet Sirius, looked very similar in appearance, but they had very different individual personalities and characteristics.

"How can I be of help to you, my daughter?" the image asked.

"Oh, Great Father, the next destruction is upon us, but the new world has not yet begun," Pat started. "The underworld is filling fast with many people from the surface, and we call upon your great wisdom to advise us as to how to feed them. We would also like your knowledge as to the discipline to handle so many displaced people."

Viracocha spoke as if he knew most, but not all, of what had happen since he had been in stasis. "If the end has started, something has happened to upset the balance," he said. "Yes, the fourth destruction is nigh, but there should still be enough time to prepare, unless man himself has triggered the inevitable. If that is the case, it will be very hard to feed so many people without being properly prepared. You must turn every uninhabited chamber you can into farmland and then check the records computer for a procedure called Rapid Plant Acceleration. With so many humans from different tribes, there will be many racial, or tribal, disputes. However, what you have done so far with this problem is good, but you need to reinforce the unification idea until everyone understands, there can be no room for their petty prejudices in the underworld colonies." With that, Viracocha looked around at the other council members.

"King Drac, I'm sure glad to see you again, you don't look a day older than the last time I saw you, in fact you look a lot younger. I hope my great, great granddaughter has met with your approval."

Drac let out a puff of smoke and bowed slightly, before he replied. "Yes, she has restored me to a much younger age. I can even keep up with Draco now."

"How is the Prince," Viracocha inquired.

"He's doing excellent now that he is in charge of the dragon half of the UDSA."

"Oh, yes, I heard about that. It was formed by Nathan Masterson last year to defeat the Zipacna. It does my heart good to know, both human and dragons are working together for a common cause." With that Viracocha turned to Agab. "Agab, old friend, how are you and your people coping with the newcomers."

"Sire, the Chamber of the Tree of Life is now filled to capacity. I am seldom there anymore because of my duties on the Andean High Council, but I hear everyone does their part to insure the common good of all. My oldest son, Naumy has joined the United Dragon Squadron, while my second son, Ekno has taken over my duties in our chamber. I'm also happy to report that my daughter Kinna and her new husband Sean Franklin, from the surface world, are now expecting a child."

"It sounds like you have everything under control, Agab. How is your wife Akna, dealing with the new accommodations in Akakor?"

"It was a little hard at first for her to adapt to big city life, but now that she has made a lot of knew friends things, are going much better."

Viracocha acknowledged each council member in turn, always asking the state of his or her chambers. In all, there were 72 subterranean chambers this council was responsible for. They stretched from the mountains of Guatemala to the tip of South America. Sometime only two abreast, but mostly three across, at between 50 and 75 miles in diameter, connected by a series of tunnels that were on average five to seven miles long. Each of the 12 council members had the responsibility of six chambers, with Queen Patamaya ruling over all of them. That is of course, until Viracocha, once again comes out of stasis. Then he will take over the Queen's duties. This was one of only three colonies that did not have an android replacement for their leader when in stasis.

"I think you are all handling the situation the best you can under the circumstances," Viracocha finally said. "It sounds like you have your share of difficulties, but as long as you all stand together everything will work out for the best. But, always remember you hold the future of planet Earth in the palm of your hands. If you close your hand too hard, you may squeeze the life out of it, and if you don't close it hard enough, everything will get out of hand, and you will lose control."

"Thank you, Sire, for hearing us here today, we will see you again when you come out of stasis," Pat said, as they all bowed slightly to show respect.

"I will look forward to that day, my daughter." With that Viracocha's image dissolved.

Chapter Eighteen

WHITE HOUSE BUNKER

13 September

The President and members of the cabinet watched the monitors as they revealed what was happening on the surface. The already terrible storms were continuing to grow in intensity. They now ranged from pole to pole, and except for just a few isolated areas, covered the entire planet.

In the Pacific, the "Ring of Fire," had come alive, as volcano after volcano began to erupt, Alaska, Japan, Hawaii, New Zealand, the mountains of South America, and Mexico, along with the Sierras and Cascades of the American west. Even the ones that had been dormant for hundreds of years began to show signs of activity. The smoke and gases from those mountains blotted out the sun for the last five days, and the experts felt certain this would most likely trigger another Ice Age if it continued.

"Many earthquakes, above a magnitude 8.5 were also felt around the world." June Vanderbilt pointed out as she aimed her laser dot at the screen. "They leveled whole cities in just a matter of minutes, caused rivers to change course, and created great fissures to open up across the globe. In America, the Mississippi River has now become a giant lake, twenty five miles across and stretches from Lake Superior to the Gulf of Mexico. In the western states, everything west of the Sierras and

Cascade mountain ranges is now a group of small islands, as tsunami after tsunami has hit the Pacific coastline from Mexico to Canada. Much the same thing is true on the other side of the country as well, with land east of the Appalachian range and Deep South." June paused for a moment and took a drink of water before continuing. "The areas in and around the Mid-East, including the Mediterranean regions of southern Europe and North Africa, is still inundated with so much radiation all that was picked up was static when satellites were turned in that direction. This was also true for a thousand mile swath around the middle of the Earth, which glowed red from the radioactive fallout."

After watching the screen for over thirty minutes the President finally asked her to turn it off. "I've seen enough," he said as he shook his head in disbelief. "I guess there's no doubt now as to whether Masterson was right or not about conditions on the surface. So tell me, what we can do about it." No one spoke a word, because there was absolutely nothing that could be done. "Debora," Overton said, to the FEMA Secretary. "What are we doing for our civilians on the surface?"

"Sir, we have done all we can do," she responded, irritated at the hopelessness of the situation. "After we filled the new underground bunkers around the country, there was not much we could do for those left on the surface. The only thing we can do now is plan a rebuilding strategy for the day we are able to return topside."

The president seemed to be devastated by the news. "That's unacceptable," he said, angry at himself for not being able to do something to help.

"Sir, we did make contact with that rouge sub," Admiral Parks spoke up, trying to inject something positive and get onto a different subject. "It was off the coast of South Africa two days ago but, they escaped before we could eliminate them."

The President now had a different look about him. It was the look of anger, an anger that bordered on rage. He then looked in the direction of the Joint Chiefs, and in a voice that sounded almost demonic, he said, "Admiral, I don't want to hear how the son-of-a-bitch got away. I just want to hear that the people responsible for the end of the world are dead." With that he adjourned the morning meeting.

Chapter Nineteen

OFF THE COAST OF SOUTH AFRICA

14 September

With the Island of Madagascar far behind them now, the storm that raged above the Dhul Fiqar was nothing like Malik had ever seen. The water churned to a depth of over 500 feet. Even at 700 feet it was hard to stay on course. Malik finally had to order the boat to a 1,000 feet before full control could be regained.

"Do you have the Americans on sonar, Habib?" Malik asked, hoping they had lost them in the turbulent waters off South Africa.

"I see two faint returns on sonar, the closest at nearly five miles to our starboard stern and the other at over eight miles to the port stern. But, with the WDP engaged I don't think they are able to pick us up," Habib replied as he studied his screen. "They continue on a zigzag course, trying to get lucky with their scans."

Malik stepped over to the charting computer to locate their exact position, once more. He had already checked and rechecked it five times in the last hour. He knew they could not out run the Americans at only 16 knots. But, if they engaged the main drive the enemy would close within firing range in a matter of a few minutes.

They were now headed south- south-west at fifty miles east of Durban, South Africa.

"Habib let me know the next time they go to starboard." The only thing Malik could do now was something the Americans would not expect.

Then, fifteen minutes later his chance came. "They are turning now, sir," Habib reported.

"Abdul, come to a heading of 2-2-0 degrees," Malik ordered. This new heading would take them on a southwesterly course, to Antarctica if they stayed on it long enough. However, with the world Navies chasing you, where else could you hide a boat of this size if not among the massive ice floes? After thirty minutes he asked, "Are the Americans still following, Habib?"

"No sir, in fact we have now put over ten miles between us, and the distance is growing fast," Habib reported.

"We will now see if this, Captain Worthington, is as smart as he thinks he is," Malik commented to himself in a whispered voice.

"This guy is shrewd!" Josh said, as he shook his head. "Where in the hell could he have gone?"

"Do you think he put into port, somewhere along the South African coast?" Paula asked.

"I doubt he would chance surfacing anywhere near civilization with most every Naval ship in the world out to kill him. Besides, with that storm raging topside, I doubt he would even be able to maneuver in such seas," Josh replied. "No. My guess is that he has either got some kind of knew propulsion system that is so quiet we are unable to pick him up, or we are following the wrong course. Hell, I don't know Paula; maybe both possibilities are true."

"But where else could he go?" Jones asked, as she stepped up to the charting computer. "Unless they turned south and headed for Antarctica." Then she laughed at the thought.

Josh thought for a moment about what Paul said. "Lt. Jones, that's exactly what they've done," he said excitedly as if a light bulb had just come on. "That's the only explanation that makes any sense. "Mr.

Brooks, send a message to Atlantic Naval Command and ask if the Russians have developed an extra quiet propulsion system for their subs. After that, advice the Chattanooga that I suspect our quarry has headed to Antarctica and we need to break out the cold weather gear."

"Aye, Sir," Brooks replied.

Josh stepped over beside Paula, at the charting computer to get an exact bearing and chart the new course. "With the fifth fleet coming south in the Atlantic, he will have nowhere to go except west through Cape Horn off the southern tip of South America or south to Antarctica," Paula said, as she pointed at the possibilities on the screen.

After Josh did the calculations, he ordered the new course, depth, and speed, "Chief Cloverdale, plot our course at 2-2-0 degrees, at a depth of 1-0-0-0 feet, at 30 knots."

"Aye, aye, Sir," Cloverdale said, then repeated to the helmsman what he had been told.

"Mr. Brooks, tell A.N.C. we are headed for Antarctica in pursuit of rogue," Josh ordered as the boat turned to the new course.

An hour later Brooks received a message from A.N.C., "Sir," he said, as he handed the teletype to Josh.

Josh read the message, then handed it to Paula who was standing across from him at the charting computer.

It read: THERE ARE RUMORS OF A POSSIBLE NEW PROPULSION SYSTEM DEVELOPED BY THE RUSSIAN'S. IT IS SAID TO BE EXTREMELY QUIET AND MAY SOUND MUCH LIKE THAT OF WHALE SONG. BUT, WE HAVE NO HARD EVIDENCE OF ITS EXISTANCE.

GOOD HUNTING AT THE SOUTH POLE, TENNESSEE. MAY GOD GO WITH YOU, THE CHATANOOGA AND ALL MANKIND?

"Bixby," Josh said, after he handed the message to Paula. "Have you picked up any whales in the last few hours?"

"Sir, we've been getting whale sounds for the past two days. They're very common in these waters," Bixby replied.

"Have any of these soundings headed off to the south?" Paula asked.

"Yes, Ma'am, but, many species of whales pass through these waters on their Antarctic hunting migrations all the time," Bixby replied, a little curious as to why they wanted to know about whales all of a sudden.

As soon as the Americans were no longer picked up on their sonar screen, Malik ordered the boat to full speed ahead. They had now put twelve miles between them and the Americans and he felt they now had a fighting chance to out run or avoid their pursuers. However, in the back of his mind he knew that no matter how long they were able to escape the other boats; he and his men would not survive, for they had caused the death of at least a third of the world's population and would be punished accordingly, if not by man, by Allah himself.

"Malik," Husam said, as he came on duty and saw Malik deep in thought near the charting computer. "What is wrong, my friend? Have the American's found us again? I woke up when I felt the main engines start up."

Malik smiled, "No Husam, we are running free without our shadows, for the first time in three days. I've put us on a course of 2-2-0 degrees, which will take us to Antarctica." Malik drew a line across the computer screen with his finger to show Husam their course. "Our only chance is to hide in the ice until our pursuers are no longer a threat."

"I understand," Husam said, as Malik turned the bridge over to him so he could get some much needed sleep.

Chapter Twenty

DEEP SPACE

Galactic Battle Cruiser Intrepid
15 September

We, along with the Scorpion, had tried to push and pull this asteroid off its present trajectory, for two days now, but the rock was just too big. Even with both ships at full power; we were not able to move it more than a few hundred yards off course. At that rate, it might miss the Earth at this range, but it would be awfully close.

"I don't like it," Chogyal said, after we were all seated in the conference room just off the bridge.

"Do you think we should try to vaporize it with Starburst missiles?" Dohna inquired. "Or would that cause too many fragments to rain down on Earth?"

"I've thought about that," the King replied. "I think, given the composition of this Asteroid, most all of it would be vaporized if we hit it with a Starburst. However, if that's what we decide to do, we need to do it soon, so there won't be the possibility of fallout over Earth."

"How many Starburst missiles do we have and how many do you think it will take to destroy this thing?" Dad asked.

"Oh, we have about fifteen, but it shouldn't take more than one, two at most," Chogyal answered.

"How far away do we have to be when we fire this missile?" Larry asked.

"I think the maximum range is a hundred thousand miles," Dohna replied. "But given the speed this rock is traveling, we could back off at least twice that far, or more."

"Well," David spoke up, from where he and Angela sat at the other end of the large oval table. "We're not doing much good pushing and pulling on this thing, it's just too big. So I vote we go to plan B."

A little under two hours later, both ships were 300,000 miles from the Asteroid. All the data had been entered into the targeting computers and the countdown was down to 4, 3, 2, 1, "Fire the missile, Mr. Yang," Chogyal ordered. At that point, both ships fired one missile each at two different angles. Fifteen minutes later an explosion almost as bright as the sun lit up the alpha quadrant of space between Mars and Earth.

"You were right, Sir," Angela spoke up. "Long range scanners are showing very little or no debris from the explosion."

"Sire, the Scorpion is hailing us," Ron informed.

"Chogyal, do you think we should go check the demon colonies on Mars?" Captain Tyr asked, after he appeared on screen. "We need to make sure they haven't escaped again, and are once again scheming to attack Earth."

"Okay, Tyr, I guess since were out this far we might as well make sure the demons are behaving themselves," Chogyal replied, a little annoyed at Tyr's persistence about going to Mars.

Just then Max walked over to where I was seated next to Dad. "It sounds like we're going to Mars, Duke. Do you think we'll be the first dogs to set paws on the red planet?"

"I don't know Max. The demons may have evil canines or we may not even land on the planet. With our probes and penetrating scanners, all we may need to do is pass over it a few times."

Dad laughed slightly as he overheard our conversation. "I think Max wants to be first at something on this trip," he said just above a whisper.

"Well, I just want to feel like I've accomplished something. You know, something I can tell my grandpups about when I'm old."

"You're not even mated yet," I said. "Let alone have any pups."

"Well, that's another thing I have to do before I get old."

Then Dad said as he remembered some of our exploits of last year, "How many dogs do you know that have explored ancient ruins, fought demons in the underworld, and been to outer space. Not to mention fighting with a full grown jaguar, and living to tell about it."

Max thought for a moment. "Well, since you put it that way, I guess I have done a lot that is meaningful and worthwhile."

"We couldn't have done it without you Max," Dad told him, which boosted his ego out of sight as he trotted back to his spot next to Steve and Jane.

"We're having a few problems with our WHG (Worm Hole Generator)," Chogyal informed Tyr. "So we won't be able to reach light speed until Robbie and Robo are able to fix it. "However, if you want to go on ahead we should be able to join you in about twenty to twenty-four hours."

"Okay, Chogyal, have a good trip and we'll see you when you get there." With that, Tyr ended the transmission and in a blink of an eye, the Scorpion shot out of sight.

Everyone was thinking that if the trip to Mars was going to take at least a day, maybe more, under impulse drive, it would give us time to get to know the ship a little better. Since Dad was an old fighter pilot, I could sense he was itching to check out the fighters down on E-deck. In fact, this is something he'd wanted to do ever since we came on board.

So while Steve, Jane, and Max checked out the sickbay with Jay, Larry, and Dohna, Dad and I checked out the launch-bays with the King. Everyone else retired to their quarter for some more R&R.

When the elevator doors opened, we once again found ourselves in a time long past. We stood for awhile just outside the elevator as E-deck personnel rushed around readying the old F-47 star-fighters for takeoff. The fighter crews exited eight elevators hurrying to their ships which were now ready for launch. There was Joe Carter, Arlie Longhire, and Fred Holtz, just to name a few of our present day friends who were also part of this ancient squadron.

Everything seemed so surreal, as Dad and I climbed into the lead ship. Then the engines fired, and at full throttle, the ship launched down the bay at an incredible speed. Only then did we return to present time and realize we had just watched the last launch before our first death.

"Are you alright Nathan?" Chogyal asked, as he put his hand on Dad's shoulder.

"I don't think I'll ever get used to these visions," Dad replied, as the color started to return to his face and sweat beaded up on his brow.

"You should learn to embrace them, for they are you and you are them. By accepting your past you can control your future," Chogyal said philosophically.

"Sir, what happened out there?" I asked. "How did Dad and I get…?" Something caught in my throat and I was unable to finish the sentence.

"I don't know for sure, Duke," the King replied. "Captain Amun was in command at the time. The ships logs didn't go into that much detail, except to say that you both died heroically, saving your ship and all who flew aboard her."

Steve and his group were also having their share of déjà vu in the sickbay, as they saw themselves tending to the sick and wounded. When the episode was over, Max pointed out the glass covered rejuvenation-capsules, that were now in almost every unit of the med-bay but were nowhere to be seen in the visions of the past.

"That's because the rejuvenation-capsules were not developed until many years after that battle took place," Dohna informed them. "In fact, it was because we lost so many during that battle that we developed the med-bay rejuvenation-capsule to restore the vital functions of the body. It will usually bring a person back to life within forty minutes, taking up to two hours after a death."

"Last year at the Mountain of the Gods in Guatemala, Dusty, Queen Patamaya's father, died from a rare form of cancer," Steve spoke up. "But, when he was hit with a strange blue light from the alter area, he came around shortly afterwards."

"Yes, that was the Light of Life," Dohna explained. "They were built into the pyramids around the world, but were just too big to install on our ships. However, the med-bay rejuvenation-capsule uses a very similar technology."

"I thought the pyramids were laser cannons used for defense," Jay spoke up.

"Yes, that's correct. But they can also be used to heal the body," Dohna informed us. "Of course, modern archaeologists think pyramids were used as tombs by the ancients because most contain what they interpret as a sarcophagus or burial capsule, even though almost no bodies were ever found. But then, your modern human scientists have a tendency to misinterpret a lot of things."

Jane raised her hand with a question. "Dohna, you said earlier the M-B-R-C usually brought a person back to life. Have there been times when it didn't work?"

"Yes, but they are rare. Only one or two out of a thousand have not been able to be revived with one of these units."

"We saw Pat bring an animal back to life by just touching it, last year," Max said. Then, there was the dragon, Hagnar, who almost died when a giant serpent literally squeezed the life out of him. He was revived when Pat touched him with her healing hands."

"There are very few among us over the years that have been given the power over life and death. But yes, they do exist, and Queen Patamaya is one of them. If you will remember, Jesus was another," Dohna explained, as they walked toward the elevators.

Later, after meeting Steve's group in the mess hall, we all sat in silence while picking over our lunch. Even Max had trouble eating, and that's very unusual. Most of us were in deep thought of what we'd learned over the past two hours. It was about then the klaxon sounded. "Now hear this. Now hear this," the robotic voice announced. "The Scorpion is under attack from the Demon colonies of Mars."

Chapter Twenty One

ANDEAN UNDERWORLD
Pairing Ceremony at Akahim
15 September

Everyone was excited this morning as they began to take their seats for the Pairing Ceremonies. Both dragons and humans alike had come from all over the realm to witness the new class take their partners and the exhibitions put on by First Squadron. Of course, all the exotic foods the people had brought for the evening feast, would round out the days actives.

These festivities were the idea of Queen Patamaya and the other council Chieftains, to bring the people of the underworld closer together. If all went well, this type of exhibition would be held for the graduation ceremonies in June. Hopefully by then however, it would be the graduating class putting on the aerial-acrobatics.

This would also be a chance for everyone to make new friends and exchange stories. Old time residence that had been down here for hundreds of generations would now be able to mix and mingle with the newcomers from the surface world.

Just east of the road and separated by 200 yards of grasslands, the twin outcroppings of huge boulders, towering in layers to a height of 150 feet and stretching for about 120 yards, would serve as seating for most everyone. However, because of their huge size, the dragon clans did seem to dominate the boulders to the north while humans and canines took up seats on the opposite outcropping to the south.

The same was true for their barracks and mess halls at the academy. The human cadets occupied the southern side of the two granite mountains while the dragon cadets would be on the northern side. They would come together for classes on one of the many wide bridges connecting the two.

The many colorful flags and banners of the academy, and all the underworld kingdoms, flew from numerous poles around the city of Akahim. As everyone took their seats, the Queen led six members of the High Council down the south runway of the inner wall, in a slow procession. Behind her were the 14 human cadets that would be paired with a dragon today. On the north runway, King Drac and Prince Draco led the rest of the council, followed by the 14 dragon cadets. All the cadets were dressed in their new academy uniforms and felt a little anxious as the ceremonies began.

When the two groups reached the center section of the outer wall, Queen Patamaya stepped up on the temporary podium to address the gathering.

"I would like to welcome you all here today for the first annual Pairing Ceremonies of the United Dragon Academy," Patamaya, dressed in a long flowing blue gown, announced as the crowd cheered. The dragon guests, let loose many fireballs, followed by wing flapping and foot stomping. "I know many of you are new to the underworld and are still trying to adapt to this environment, and I'm sorry about the events on the surface that have brought you here. The stupidity of mankind has never ceased to amaze me. However, if we work together as one, we can rebuild all that we've lost with a much stronger union in your new home here in the Andean underworld." Pat paused as the guests again let go with many cheers, barks and, fireballs.

"I am happy to announce, this year we have four female cadets and I will be watching their progress with interest over the next school year. As you all know, I am part of the First Dragon Squadron, so I encourage you girls out there to enlist in this great school. But for now, I'm going to give the podium over to councilmen Bolontiku, King Drac, and Agab, so they can start the parings while I get ready for the exhibitions." With that the Queen walked off the stage, mounted Draco, and flew to the staging area on the palace grounds.

As the three took the podium, another round of cheering, fireballs, and foot stomping resounded from the crowd. Bolontiku took the mike and explained how the ceremony would proceed. "King Drac will call the name of a dragon cadet, and then Agab will announce a human rider. The two will then step forward, address each other with a short statement about themselves, such as name, age, and from what chamber they're from. This will be followed by an oath to the other, to always defend and protect each other, as well as the laws of the United Andean Underworld with their very lives, if need be. Then, the human will mount his or her dragon, fly down and land in the gap between the two boulder outcroppings where they will wait in a neat, single row, until all 28 cadets have been paired. This will be followed by a flyby by all the cadets. Afterward, they will land again in the same area to wait for the First Squadrons exhibitions to end, at which time I and other Chieftains will end the ceremonies with the academy theme song."

Pat had just gotten her new shinny flight suit buttoned up and joined the rest of First Squadron, when Bolontiku made an announcement about Dad. "As you all know, the true leader of the First Squadron, Nathan Masterson cannot be with us today because he was called to other duties in deep space. However, his dragon companion, Ragnon, will lead First Squadron out."

That was their cue to take off. Pat climbed up on Draco's back once again like she'd been born there, and then looked back at the others. Arlie and Dagon, Fred and Fagon, Sean and Zargon, Tomka and Ragtar, and Naumy and Hagnar were all mounted and ready to go. Ragnon took the lead in a V-formation as they took off from the high palace grounds and dropped down quickly, clearing the heads of the councilmen on the outer wall by only a few feet. They first flew over the dragon guests and then circled around after a couple miles and flew over the human guests. A mammoth was heard in the distance, trumpeting their passing, as the crowd erupted again in cheers and fireballs. Then, after the first flyby, Ragnon dropped out and stood with the cadets, while Pat and Draco took the lead, in a missing man formation, and put the squadron through some pretty fancy maneuvers. They did rollovers and giant loops, some just a few feet off the ground. They then skyrocketed toward the ceiling, over 3,000 feet above, and dove straight down, pulling up only seconds before impacting the grassy turf.

The OO'S and AHH'S of the crowd went on for some time before First Squadron ended their aerial-exhibition with a fireworks display and the academy theme song.

After First Squadron finally landed, the guests came down from their seats on the boulders to congratulate the new cadets. Pat and the First Squadron also answered questions of those thinking about joining the academy. Many pictures were taken as they talked for over an hour before finally heading off toward the many food tables that had been set up for the night's festivities.

Up at the palace, the festivities had to be held outside on the beautifully manicured grounds, because the grand ballroom was not big enough to accommodate more than a few dragons at any one time. Besides, having it outside meant everyone could enjoy the music, dancing, and fireworks that resounded over the city and throughout the chamber.

After dinner, Queen Patamaya and Arlie started the dancing. The music was provided by the many musicians that had recently come to the underworld from the surface, and it wasn't long before everyone was waltzing around the palace courtyard. It was lucky for the humans and canines that the dragons dance was a beautiful aerial-display. Otherwise, they would have to have a separate section to themselves.

When her dance with Arlie was through, Pat walked through the guests, shaking hands like a politician running for re-election. "Gen. Carter, it's so good to see you again," Pat said as she extended her hand. "What have you done with your new bride, Peggy?"

"I think she went to the restroom for a moment," Joe replied.

"General, what did you think of our little show today?" Arlie asked.

"I was shocked and amazed at the maneuverability of your squadron. But then, I'm still trying to get used to dragons, let alone flying ones. But then, it took me the longest time to get used to talking dogs."

"Well, if you would have told me a year ago such creatures existed, I would have sized you up for a straitjacket," Sean said, as he and Kinna stepped over with Lobo and Howl to join in the conversation.

At that point, Peggy returned and hugged Pat. "Who would have guessed that our local veterinarian was the Queen of an underworld kingdom?"

"Believe me, Peg, not that I'm complaining mind you, but I would be very content to still be the Kalispell Vet."

Fred walked up at that point and shook everyone's hand. "General, can I interest you in a job?"

"What kind of job?" Joe responded his attention piqued.

"Well, with Nathan gone, we could use a good flight instructor."

"But, I've never flown on a dragon before and wouldn't know where to begin."

"A year ago, we didn't know anything either. But, because of our situation, Nathan started flight school. And in a matter of a day's training, we all became dragon riders right out there." Fred pointed at the expanse beyond the city walls.

"I didn't," Dusty said, as he walked up and shook Joe's hand along with the others.

"Hi Dusty," Peggy said, as she give him a hug.

"Hey, can anybody learn to be a dragon rider?" Anthony asked, as he and Matt walked over with Lynn, Karen, and the rest of Dad's family, to give Pat a hug.

"Hi, guys," Pat told them, as each came up for a hug or a scratch behind the ears as she did with Duchess, the pups and Skipper. "I'm sorry I haven't been able to visit with you, like I'd wanted to, but being Queen of the underworld keeps you very busy."

"That's okay, we know you're busy, but we just wanted you to know we still love you," Arista told her.

"Well, I love you guys as well, and I'll see if maybe we can get together soon for a trip to the chamber of the Tree of Life in the M-I units."

"We'd like that very much, Miss Pat," the pups woofed in unison.

Chapter Twenty Two

WHITE HOUSE BUNKER

15 September

President Overton had been in a bad mood ever since he realized he could do little or nothing to help the people left on the surface.

He had canceled the last two morning meetings in the situation room and spent most of his time pacing the floor of his plush quarters. His wife Marissa, a mocha skinned beauty with an athletic figure, long raven hair and beautiful blue eyes, tried to calm and comfort him, to no avail.

"No, Marissa, this situation is my fault. Even though he didn't tell me anything about a rogue submarine blowing up the Mid-East, I should have listened to what Masterson had to say last spring when he tried to explain about a coming apocalypse. But it just sounded so fantastic at the time. To be honest, I thought the man had lost his mind." Marcus stepped over to the bed and sat down next to his wife who was stretched out reading some of the material we had brought back from the underworld. Marcus had decided to show her the file to get a second opinion. An opinion he had come to rely heavily upon over the years.

"These pictures are incredible," Marissa said, as she looked at the huge cities, underground seas, and enormous creatures, including the flying dragons of the Andean underworld. "My god, Marcus, do you know what this means? If what I'm reading and seeing in these pictures are true, it means the human race was started by an alien culture from another galaxy."

"Yes, yes, I know," Marcus rolled his eyes at the thought. "That's crazy, is it not? Almost laughable, would you not agree? I mean, he sounds like one of those nuts that claim to have been abducted. And yet, there was something about it that seemed to ring true, especially what he says about an apocalypse supposedly due on December, 21, 2012. But, I think it has come a little early. Don't you?"

"Well, the 2012 date is based on the Mayan calendar. And from what I understand, the Maya predicted the end of the world on that date over seven hundred years ago. But, what I'm talking about is who built these underworld cities?" Marissa held up the pictures of Akahim and Akakor. "They look old, very old, and some of these structures are built into the cliff face, like in this picture of Akahim."

"Yeah, so," Marcus said, not understanding what she was getting at.

"Don't you understand? This could truly be the answer of mans origins on Earth. For many years now, science has had a very hard time explaining how mankind came from the caves of the Stone Age and started building structures such as Stonehenge and the Pyramids with such mathematical accuracy shortly thereafter." Marissa continued to look at the file with awe. "Look at this, Marcus," she said, after finding a picture of the Hall of Records room in the lower recesses of the Mountain of the Gods, in Guatemala. "That looks like it could possibly be an ancient computer, but look at the holographic image of the man on the center alter."

"Or, it could be a Hollywood studio for all we know," Marcus said skeptically, as he scanned the photo. "The bottom line is that we don't know if any of this is true, or how we can use it to help those poor souls caught on the surface."

"In the book of Revelation does it not say something about the death and destruction, the Four Horsemen of the Apocalypse would bring," Marissa said, as she got to her feet in search of her mother's Bible.

"It says a lot of things in Revelation about the destruction in the end days," Marcus replied, after thinking for a moment. "In fact, the whole book is about the rise of the Antichrist. Then of course, there's that part about the upheavals of the Earth, wars and rumors of wars, pestilence, and the death of one third of the population of the planet. But these things have always happened throughout mans history."

"Yes, your right, they have occurred over and over again," Marissa said, as she shut another empty drawer without success. "But the question is, has so many of these events ever occurred at the same time before, like they are now?"

"Well, now, that I don't know, but I'm sure they probably have," Marcus told her, as she finally gave up the search and returned to the bed. Then he asked, "Where's your mother's Bible?"

"I'm pretty sure it's in one of those boxes we hurriedly put in storage before coming down here," Marissa answered, pursing her lips, still trying to remember where it was. "But anyway, my point is that we have all the signs of the end times happening as we speak. And, if that is the case, there is nothing at this point anyone can do for the people on the surface. It's not your fault some maniac decided to trigger the apocalypse."

Marcus thoughts returned to the book of Revelation for a moment. "Well, who do you think the Antichrist is, and what about the battle of Armageddon?"

Marissa thought for a moment. "I'm not sure, but if you look back, over the years, you can almost see a pattern developing to undermine the world's economy, topple certain governments, and create anarchy around the planet. If you can figure out who's behind it, I think you'll have the Antichrist."

"Do you think it could be an organization, instead of an individual?"

"Do you know of any organization that doesn't have a leader or a board of directors?" Marissa answered, as a thought came to her. "Or maybe in this case, seven directors, as the beast with seven heads and ten horns, that's referred to in the book of Revelation. But even at that, the seven would most likely have a chairman or supreme head of the organization."

"When we captured Raul Velasco last year, he referred to the Illuminati as a group of very powerful individuals around the world, trying to bring about the New World Order. I just wonder if this is the seven headed beast mentioned in the Bible," Marcus said, as he tossed the idea around in his head. "Of course, I've heard of the New World Order, but I never thought of it as a diabolical entity before. I thought it was a good thing, meant to bring about world unity."

Marissa flipped her laptop open and typed in, Illuminati. "Look here, Marcus," she said, as website after website came up. She then clicked on the first one and began to read, how it was supposedly founded in Ingolstadt, Bavaria by Adam Weishaupt on May 1, 1776. She continued to read how Weishaupt, a Jesuit-taught atheist and freethinker, had started the secret society to combat the power of the church so science could flourish.

As she scanned the many websites over the next hour, she found how the Illuminati, believed by some to have merged with the Freemasons to form a secret society within a secret society and how they had progressed to the present day with an agenda to now overthrow and replace all the world's governments with the NWO.

"Listen to this," Marissa said, as she read from a website that came up under the title of "The New World Order, the Zep-Tepi also known by various other names such as, the First Time of Osiris, a new Order of the Ages, Novus Ordo Seclorum or the New World Order. These are different organizations with the same purpose, some dating back before the flood to the corrupt "Golden Age of Incarnate Demons," in ancient Egypt. Their agenda, in modern times, is to create an evil one world government with the multinational authority over, world banking, oil production, world trade, and military operations, just to name a few. This is what Weishaupt tried to establish into the fundamental principles of the Illuminati."

"Sounds to me like Weishaupt just wanted to obtain the power the church already had, and transfer it into a secret underground society with a world domination agenda." Marcus commented after listening to what Marissa read.

"Are you saying the Catholic Church is an evil entity, Marcus?" Marissa asked, as she thought about the possibilities.

"Well, in my opinion the Catholic Church is just as corrupt as the Illuminati. If you will remember, at one time the Roman Church, more or less ruled Europe. At that time it was one of the most evil entities the world has ever known. Don't you remember the Inquisition and all the other atrocities carried out by the church? Hundreds of thousands of innocent people were killed in the name of Jesus, a man who taught Peace, Love, and Forgiveness. And to hold this power for as long as they did, they convinced the European nations the Pope was Gods emissary on Earth." Marcus paused. "I guess what I'm trying to say is, that the Roman Empire never really died. They just disguised themselves as Europe's soul saviors. By doing so, they were in control of Europe's economy, education, science, and religious beliefs. If I remember my history correctly, it was Emperor Constantine who adopted Christianity into the Empire as the state religion. However, he didn't actually become a Christian, himself, until he was on his deathbed years later. But what's all this got to do with Masterson and his report about these underground aliens?"

"There are many references to the Lords of Light battling the Black Lords in this file," Marissa told him. "After the last battle, about 13,000 years ago, many of the Black Lords walked the Earth influencing the minds of men until most all were finally rounded up and imprisoned in the bowels of hell by the Lords of Light."

"Doesn't it say something in the Bible about a war in Heaven?" Marcus asked.

"Exactly," Marissa told him. "I think the Illuminati, or whatever they called it in the long ancient past, was started by the human followers of the Black Lords, not only to undermine the Lords of Lights, but to enslave the minds of men."

"Does that mean everything we were taught in school about our county's founding's, or in church about our religious beliefs, were just a bunch of lies or half truths designed to bring about the New World Order?" Marcus asked, as the possibility crossed his mind.

"I don't think so, but we do have to figure out how to bring down this evil atheistic system before it takes over the world."

"Do you still believe in God? I mean if mankind was created by an alien race, does that not say the Bible and most of our religious text is untrue?" Marcus asked, unsure of what to believe at this point.

"I believe the Bible is true and God is very real," Marissa told him. "However, I feel it is encrypted with many hidden meanings. For example, you don't really believe Eve talked to a serpent, do you? Or that Cain married an unmentioned sister, which would have meant Seth would have had to also marry a sister. Especially, since Adam and Eve only had three sons according Genesis. Because, if they had of mated with their unmentioned sisters the genetic DNA would have broken down within just a few generations, and mankind would have been reduced to blithering idiots. What I'm saying is; there has to be more to the story than what we've been told."

Marcus thought for a moment then said, "I think some of the problem is that the Bible has been written and rewritten so many times, that much of the original meanings have been lost over time."

"And before it was ever written down, the stories were told and retold through oral-traditions, for who knows how many generations," Marissa stated, as she pondered the possibilities.

They both sat quietly, thinking of these many, different possibilities and how they could have changed the world they knew and loved.

Chapter Twenty Three

THE SOUTHERN ATLANTIC
16 September

The last two days of this cat and mouse game, of speed up, slow down, and zigzag course changes, had proved most interesting. It seemed, every time the Tennessee or Chattanooga got a sonar return on the Dhul Fiqar, they lost it within seconds.

At least for now the surface storms had subsided, which allowed them to go to periscope depth and have a look around. Since the Tennessee and Chattanooga left the southern tip of Africa, they had slowly made their way west-south-west toward the Weddle Sea. Which is located just south of the Orkney Islands and between the Antarctic Peninsula and the Ronne Ice Shelf. Now dodging icebergs at a depth of almost a thousand feet, the two subs silently pursued their prey toward the southern continent.

"Sir, we're picking up a distress signal, approximately ten miles off our port bow," Ensign Brooks reported.

"Who's sending it?" Josh asked.

"It's a 400 hundred foot, Argentine cruise ship, called the Southern Cross #5," Brooks replied. "They specialize in Antarctica cruises. It seems they got stuck in the ice when they tried to retreat from a storm with hurricane force winds and thirty foot seas. They've been stuck for the last two days and are becoming desperate for help."

"Why, can she not pull out now?" Paula asked, a little skeptical of the situation. "I mean, those type ships are built with icebreaker bows and very powerful engines."

"Their Captain said an engine had been damaged during the storm so they didn't have enough power to pull free before the ice froze over," Brooks replied.

"Sir, we have a whale contact about four miles north of the cruise ship," Bixby suddenly reported.

"Very good, Bixby," Josh said. "Chief Cloverdale, sound general quarters and ready tubes one and two. Lt. Jones, plot a firing solution for that whale sound. I think we have found our rogue."

"Sir, I have two torpedoes in the water headed straight for us at 6,000 yards, and closing fast," Bixby reported again.

"Ready countermeasures," Josh ordered. "Chief, on my mark, fire countermeasures and dive the boat to 1-5-0-0 feet, at a thirty degree down angle to port. Talk to me, Bixby."

"The torpedoes are now 4,000 yards out, Sir; 2,900, 2,800, 2,700, 2,600, 2,500." Every twenty seconds Bixby called out another reading.

"Flood tubes one and two and open outer doors," Josh ordered.

"1,300."

"Fire countermeasures at 800 hundred yards and take us down fast." Josh looked at his watch and timed the seconds before the torpedoes reached the countermeasures and exploded.

The explosions rocked the boat violently, rupturing many pressure pipes that sprayed water everywhere. Suddenly Bixby reported two more torpedoes, but this time it was the Chattanooga firing. She had been monitoring the situation from 5,000 yards off the Tennessee's starboard side, at a depth of 700 feet.

"Bixby, where's that whale?" Josh asked. Now at full speed, Josh was counting on closing the range before firing.

"Sir, he is now 5,000 yards to the west of the cruise ship and about 4,000 yards from our position."

"He's going to use the cruise ship as cover," Paula said. "Not if I can help it," Josh said. "What's his depth, Bixby?"

"1,200 feet Sir, It looks like he may be trying to dive under the ice shelf, and escape."

"Chief, bring us up 300 feet," Josh ordered. "Bixby, what's our distance?"

"About 3,500 yards, Sir."

"Fire tubes one and two."

"One away, two away," Cloverdale reported.

Just then two explosions had erupted 1,000 yards west of the cruise ship. The Chattanooga's torpedoes had missed their target by only 200 feet, as they slammed into the massive ice sheet. They did, however, break up the ice enough to free the cruise ship from its icy grip.

Three minutes after the Tennessee's torpedoes went off, the ice sheet broke up even more, but by then, Bixby had lost track of the rogue.

"Do you think we hit him?" Paula asked.

"No, I think he fired his countermeasures and dove under the ice just before impact," He told her. "And that's, where we have to go now if we're going to get him, but first, Brooks, see if the cruise ship still needs assistance," Josh ordered.

"Sir, they are now underway and are headed for the Tierra del Fuego region of Argentina," Brooks responded, after a short exchange with the captain of the Southern Cross #5.

"That was close," Husam said, as he looked at Malik with sheer terror in his eyes, after the last two torpedoes went off just above them in the ice shelf.

"Come now, Husam, you knew this was a suicide mission when you signed on," Malik reminded him.

"Yes, but.....I now want to live," Husam replied with an unsteady voice, the color drained from his face. He then, came close to Malik and whispered so the rest of the crew wouldn't hear. "If I could take it all back, undo what we've done, I would do it in a minute. May, Allah forgive us for the wrong we have done our brothers and sisters." It was now plain to see, Husam had thought about what they had done, and was overwhelmed with guilt.

Malik knew how Husam felt, he too would like nothing more than to undo the past eight days. But now he had to find a way to not only live with himself but try to live in a world unlike he had ever known. He tried telling himself it was the will of Allah, but now he wasn't even sure he stilled believed in God. Only by staying alive could he hope to help in some small way; to re-sow the seeds of life and atone for the great wrong he and his crew had done.

Malik now believed it had all been a lie. A lie told over and over again for thousands of years. A lie told to inspire mortal men to kill each other. This was done in the name of a religion that promised immortality, by a loving God. But what was really crazy was that, Christian, Jew, and Muslim all believed in the same God. They just called him by a different name. This meant the lie would continue, the lie, which was really spun by governments, terrorist, and religious radicals, and had nothing to do with a true God.

Malik put his hand on his friends shoulder, "I understand how you feel, Husam, but we need to pull ourselves together and find a way through the ice."

Husam wrapped his arms around his midsection. "I think I need to lie down for awhile. My stomach is unsteady."

As Husam left the bridge, Malik ordered the boat to 1,800 feet and a course of due south. He also ordered the speed to all ahead slow. At this depth, and speed they could pass safely under the ice without fear of collision, and the course would bring them right up to the continental shelf. From there, Malik was unsure what direction he would take, but he would have a couple of hours to go over the charts and decide which way to go.

Just then Habib spoke up. "Sir, we have sonar contact at two miles to our stern."

"Damn those American's!" Malik exclaimed, as he momentarily lost his composure. "What's their speed and depth?"

"They have matched our speed, depth and course, Sir."

Malik sighed a bit of relief, because he knew all the Americans could do under this ice shelf was to shadow his boat. "May Allah deliver us out of the hands of the infidels," he silently prayed to himself out of habit as he turned on the outside lights and monitors. He saw the thick white ice shelf above them, which turned the water a beautiful aqua blue. "So peaceful", he thought, as the boat slid through the water toward the continent.

Below the screen, on the readout, Malik noticed a change in water density, along with a rise in temperature. It was rapidly becoming fresher with a lot less salt content. But, the fresher water only extended 80 feet to either side of the boat. It was much like they were headed up a river of fresh water. This phenomenon piqued Malik's interest. "It has to be coming from the continent," he thought.

"Sir," Habib spoke up again. "We have another sonar contact, this time it's about five miles directly in front of us. But, it's nothing like I've ever heard before."

For a moment, this new information left Malik without a clue as to what it could be. It couldn't be the Americans. "Not even they have a boat fast enough to get in front of us that quick," he said. "Is it a metallic contact, Habib?"

"Yes and no," Habib said shaking his head, unsure.

Malik stepped over to Habib's station and looked at the screen. The blip was there, and then it wasn't, it fading in and out like a false image, but yet it was slowly moving toward them. He then listened to Habib's headphones. The object was giving off a faint low level buzzing sound, much like a mosquito that gets too close to ones ear in the middle of the night.

Malik looked at the range readout; it was now at 6,500 yards. A different readout, told him the object was oval in shape, about 125 feet long by 115 feet wide. He stepped back to the outside monitor but was unable to spot the object. Then suddenly, the boat lost all power. They were now dead in the water, completely in the dark, and in danger of sinking.

Chapter Twenty Four

HIGH MARS ORBIT

17 September

When we reached the Scorpion, she was fine, with no sign of battle damage except for a couple laser blasts to her starboard side. It had taken us less than an hour to get here after we received her distress call. It seems when the call came in, Robbie and Robo had just finished fixing the wormhole generator, so the last twelve million miles went by in a snap.

It was shortly before we entered the wormhole that Dad and I joined Chogyal, Dohna, Steve, Jane, and Max, at the central command center. The king then explained how we all would soon be promoted in rank and how we needed to get the feel of command.

"Sire, there's something I don't fully understand," I said, as we sat down. "When the Black Lords were imprisoned on Mars after the first decisive battle in this star system, how is it they were able to keep their starships?"

"Well, that very question bothered Admiral Gabriel and his senior officers for the longest time after the second battle over Earth many years later. It seems the Black Lords and their dark demons had built many undetected subterranean factories on Mars when they first came to this system. Their leaders knew we would be coming after them and wanted to be able to replace or repair their ships," Chogyal explained.

"And with the many ores available to them on Mars, they had plenty of options when it came to building material and could turn out a fully loaded battle-cruiser in less than ten Earth years," Dohna added.

"We should have sent a cruiser to destroy those facilities after the second battle, but we had lost so many in that battle we almost abandoned the Earth colonization project altogether," Chogyal continued. "And by the time we had decided to rebuild, we figured with most of the Black Lords now imprisoned on Earth, the dark demons left on Mars would be of little threat."

It was about then we came out of the wormhole and slowed to impulse power.

"What happen, Tyr?" Chogyal asked, as we entered orbit and made contact with the other ship.

"I'm not sure at this point, to tell you the truth," Captain Tyr responded, as he materialized on the bridges forward screen. "We had just come out of the wormhole and slowed to impulse, when we were hit with two laser blasts. Our instruments showed a single demon fighter firing at our starboard engines. He made only one pass before our laser cannons were able to lock on and destroy him. But what's so baffling is that the planet's surface defenses didn't open up, or that there were no more fighters. It makes no sense for just one small fighter to attack a Galactic Battle Cruiser."

"Yes, I can see your dilemma," Chogyal said, as he stroked his chin in thought.

"Have you launched fighters or a recon ship to the surface?" Dohna asked.

"Not yet," Tyr responded. "I was just about ready to launch a pair of fighters to investigate the surface, but I don't want to put troops down there and not be able to retrieve them."

"It does sound like a trap," Dad said. "I suggest we pull back to extreme high orbit, while we send a probe down to the surface."

Suddenly, Mr. Yang spoke up a little excited. "Sir, we are getting multiple contacts all around us. They are ships much like this one."

"Mr. Clayhorn, try hailing them," Chogyal ordered.

"Sir, they are already hailing us," Ron informed.

"Put them on screen," Dohna ordered.

The main screen then split, showing Captain Tyr on one side, and the figure of a Sirius Fleet Admiral they had known since their days at the Academy. Everyone immediately rose to attention and saluted as they greeted the newcomer. Admirals Gabriel, Uriel, Raphael, and even Prince Lucifer, (before he changed over to the dark side), were best of friends, with this Admiral at the Galactic Star Academy on Sirius and had all graduated together. Captains Amun, Adams, Odin, Thor, Tyr, Chogyal, Zeus, Viracocha, and Poseidon, to name a few, had all graduated the very next year.

"Captain Chogyal, is that you?" The figure asked, while returning their salute. "And Tyr, you old son of a star hound, you guys haven't changed a bit in all these hundreds of years." Of course, he was talking about years on Sirius, because a year on Sirius is equal to a thousand years on Earth.

"It's sure is good to see you again, Admiral Michael," Chogyal replied. "But, what brings the second fleet to the Beta Quadrant?"

"King Adonai sent me here to upgrade the First Fleet," Michael said.

"I'm sorry, Sir, but, I don't understand," Chogyal stated with a puzzled look on his face.

"Well, do you remember those members of the First Fleet? The ones Gabriel allowed to return home after the Black Lords were imprisoned on the planet you call Mars?"

"I remember that," Tyr spoke up. "They wanted to either return to their families, or had decided they wanted no part of the colonization of planet Earth."

"The Admiral let them take two of our Battle Cruisers, if I recall correctly," Dohna said.

"Yes well, after they got home and told their families about this planet called Earth, the word began to spread like wildfire. The people soon began to petition the King relentlessly to open this quadrant to interstellar travel. Even when Prince Immanuel returned home about two years ago and told King Adonai how strong the demon influence was on Earth. He had explained to his father in great detail of the brutality, hate, idolatry and debauchery of the human race. However, our people still wanted to come here and see for themselves."

"Well, Sir, this is not exactly a good time to open Earth up as a tourist destination," Dohna told him. She then proceeded to explain the recent events Earth had experienced and how we were trying to reverse, stop or at least slowdown any escalations to those events.

The Admiral listened with interest to all she had to say before smiling and offering his help. "Well, I haven't come all this way not to see my old friend Gabriel. Besides, I have brought him a present from the King. Four new Galactic Battle Cruisers to replace those he lost and the ones a quarter of his command returned home in. But, you'll have to staff them with a crew, my officers and men are going back to Sirius with me when we leave. However, we will stay long enough to make sure your crews have been trained properly and Earth is once again stable. Oh, and before I forget, you do know Prince Immanuel is planning to return to Earth soon, or at least that's the latest rumor at the Grand Palace on Sirius."

"Sir, not to change the subject, but we had been attacked, by a single fighter, just before you showed up," Captain Tyr, interjected. "We thought it was a demon ship from the surface of Mars, but we're really not sure at this point where it came from."

"Admiral, we were just about ready to launch a probe to survey the planet for any recent activity," Chogyal informed.

"I see. Well, would you like some help or can you handle it by yourself?" Michael asked.

"I think we can handle it, Sir, but if you'd like to stick around for a few hours while we wrap this up, we can all returned to Earth together," Chogyal offered. "If not, we'll see you when we get back."

It was about then, that all hell broke loose. A blast from ion-cannon on the surface barely missed the Scorpion. Then, a swarm of demon fighters came out of the sun with cannons blasting. Our klaxon sounded the call to battle stations and our shields were automatically raised.

A strange feeling came over Dad and me and when Chogyal looked over at us with that knowing look and nodded, we started for the launch bay where Robbie and Robo met us with our flight-suits, then showed us to our fighter. It was a brand new F-48 Star Fighter. This puppy was a little bigger and much faster than the old F-47's, and it also packed a lot more punch.

As we climbed into the cockpit, we noticed there were no windows. Instead, there was the internal wraparound monitor like on the bigger ships. We found two seats, one behind the other like most Earth based fighters have. Dad took the forward seat, which automatically contoured to his body, as did the rear to mine. On Dad's console were weapons, steering, speed, and vector systems. I was in control of, shields, navigation, inertia dampeners, communications, cloaking, and the main viewing screen, along with a few other things, but I was unsure at this point what they were for. Dad sat back and said to himself, "My complements to Commander Clakrin and the moon base crew, this baby is sweet."

While we were getting ready to launch, the Intrepid and Scorpion took up new positions 25,000 miles further out in space. The new position would give us enough room to maneuver and take us out of their surface ion-cannon range. In space those cannons would have a range of 10,000 miles, but because they were land based and subject to the pull of the planets gravity, even though less than on Earth, the range was cut in half.

The Scorpion launched 100 of their new fighters first, but Dad and I soon attacked with 25 from the Intrepid. Ours were manned, mostly with android pilots, because of our limited human personnel, while the Scorpion had a full complement of 150 fighters and the crews to man them.

When we got to the battle, the demonic fighters outnumbered the Scorpions three to one. So we went for the end run, attacking the enemy on their port flank. They were so involved with the Scorpion's fighters that we were able to take down over fifty before they knew we were there. We were then able to split the enemy forces in half and proceeded to knock them down one by one. After twenty five minutes of very intense fighting, we had them on the run.

Admiral Michael had also pulled the second fleet back out of harm's way, but not before launching his own fighters to attack the surface. Since they were still using the old F-47, which looked similar to the enemy ships, it was a good thing they were not part of our battle.

When the battle was over, we had only lost two fighters. The Scorpion had lost four, and Admiral Michael had lost three. But, in the end, the demons had lost most of their surface cannons and most of their fighter force, or so we thought.

As we landed on the stern end of E-deck, the thought occurred to Dad and me at the same time, "Those that we now call demons were once very much a productive part of the Canis star system. Even Lucifer was a prince at the Grand Palace and was good friends with many of our high ranking officers. However, we now fight each other to the death. It made no more sense than Christian killing Muslim or Muslim killing Jew in this day and time." I thought how strange it was the way history continually repeats itself over time and space. We pondered, for a moment, how much further our two cultures would have advanced over the years if we had not spent so much time trying to destroy one another.

Chapter Twenty Five

WHITE HOUSE BUNKER
17 September

Two more days had passed without a morning meeting. In fact, the President was thinking of canceling them altogether unless something important happened. Even though Marcus knew down deep it wasn't his fault, he blamed himself for not being able to do more for the people stranded on the surface. He now had a two day old growth of beard, and for every day that went by he slipped deeper into a dark depression as he tried to think of some way to help them.

Admiral Parks had received the news about the near miss at Antarctica, but since the rogue was not sunk, he thought it best to delay telling Overton until there was a confirmed kill. He certainly didn't want to anger the President needlessly with near misses.

The sun had not been seen for at least five days in the northern hemisphere, and it was now snowing heavily from the North Pole to southern Georgia. Even in the southern hemisphere where it would normally be spring, the weather was getting colder. However, even under these conditions, movement had been detected on the surface, which indicated there were still some people and animals that had managed to survive under the harsh conditions. But most had died and thousands of bodies were lying everywhere; in the streets, in cars, in housing basements, in subways, and in underground parking lots.

Some had starved to death or succumbed to the elements, and still others died from marauding, mutant, cannibalistic mobs. Those few, lucky enough to have survived, would most likely die within the next few weeks. Unless, they could find an old civil defense shelter or one of those backyard bunkers built back in the fifties and early sixties still full of food and supplies, they didn't stand a chance.

The President ordered Gen. Wells and Gen. Farmer, to put out food, blankets, and medical supplies, for the poor souls in areas where the most movement had been recorded.

Even though no one mentioned it, everyone believed it was just a matter of time before all life on the surface would either end or mutate into something the world had never seen before. Overton had ordered his medical scientists at all the underground facilities around the country to study the new diseases being born on the surface and try to come up with vaccines to treat them with. If they couldn't find a cure, the air-borne pathogens from the decaying bodies would probably kill more people than the Black Plague during the middle-ages. And then of course, there was always the chance these new viruses would eventually find their way into the underground bunkers.

"I wonder if that's not what happened after all the other mass extinctions," Marcus said. He and Marissa had been swimming in the 72' x 48' pool, located on the third sublevel of the underground White House facility. They were now having drinks in one of the eight spacious hot tubs spaced evenly around the pool. Marissa had talked him into coming down here in hopes it would improve his mood.

This was much more than a 200' x 125' oval shaped room with a swimming pool. It also contained a tropical garden with many flowers and small trees. There were also around twenty five round tables where the staff could have lunch while listening to restful music. Even the 100 foot domed ceiling, with its big white clouds floating lazily across a simulated azure sky made a person feel relaxed. The whole east wall was made to look like a tropical beach with the ocean in the distance. Yes, here one could easily forget they were in an underground bunker contemplating man's future on planet Earth.

"I mean, when the dinosaurs were wiped out, they were replaced over time with the giant mammals, and so on and so forth. Maybe it's just man's turn to go extinct?" With that he shrugged his shoulders and took a sip of his rum and coke.

"Or maybe it's just another segment in the age old battle of good and evil," Marissa told him, a little disgusted with his attitude. She had never seen him so emotionally down before. It was as if he was giving up. "Look, we have to stay focused here. I know things look bad, but we're going to get through this one way or the other and rebuild a whole new world, a world full of love, compassion, and forgiveness, a world where all mankind will be treated equally without hate, suspicion, and deceit."

"Now you sound like you're suddenly an advocate of the New World Order," Marcus said, throwing up his hands like he didn't understand. "I thought you said that was a bad thing?"

"The New World Order the Black Lords are trying to bring about, is a bad thing because it takes away mankind's freedom to choose. They want to dictate what you can or can't believe in, and treat you in a subservient manner with no voice or say in anything. In their society, I doubt if you would have ever stood a chance of becoming President."

"Why do you say that?"

"Mainly because, you're a well-educated black-man who deeply cares about his fellow man. Like the way you beat yourself up for being unable to help those poor souls on the surface." Marissa paused and took a sip from her Mai-tai. "You also care about the rights and freedoms of mankind, to right the wrongs, and to have a say in man's future. In the New World Society of the Black Lords, people like you and me would probably still be picking cotton in the Deep South. In fact, most of mankind, red, yellow, black, and white alike, would not be much more than slaves to their overlord masters. Just picture in your mind Nazi Germany in the late 30's and early 40's, then multiply that times ten. It would be much like it was during the rule of the Roman Empire." Again she paused for a sip from her drink, and then smiled as a thought came to her. "Hell! Someone like you would have probably ended up nailed to a cross back in those days."

"Like I said the other day, the Roman Empire never died they just took the form of the Catholic Church."

"Yes, I think you might be right. I think it says something in Revelation that in the End Days there will be two beasts. One is the Antichrist that comes from the sea. The other is a religious leader called the False Prophet. I think this could very well be the Pope in Rome."

Just then, Tony Barker, the Secret Service chief, stepped over and informed the President, there were two men to see him in the duplicate of the oval office.

"Who are they Tony?" Overton asked.

"Sir, one is CIA Director Standish and the other is from the NSA."

"The NSA," Marissa repeated with surprise.

"Okay Tony, give me a minute to get dried off," Overton said, as he stood and grabbed a towel. Then, after putting on a terrycloth robe, he told Barker to have them brought to the pool. He had decided to talk with them here, with Marissa present, to get her opinion on what they had to say.

Chapter Twenty Six

ANDEAN UNDERWORLD

17 September

True to her word, Pat had set aside the next week for her friends from Kalispell. She had planned a trip to the chamber of the Tree of Life with Dawn, Arista, Skipper, Duchess, and the pups. They would be accompanied by Lynn, Anthony, and their families, along with Pedro and Chiquita, their new baby Nathanya and their Jack Russell Terrier, Hombre.

M-I-2 and 3, had been set aside for this trip because Dusty would have M-I-1, in a chamber far to the south where a dispute had broken out between the people of Amaru Meru and a group of unruly newcomers. According to the initial report, some recent newcomers from the surface were trying to separate themselves from the local population by rebelling against local authority. So Dusty and his team were being sent to see if they could defuse the situation before it got out of hand. When Dusty had asked Joe and Peggy Carter if they would like to tag along, Joe jumped at the idea, but Peggy decided to go with Pat and the others, going north, because of the female companionship.

The Masterson Industries 480 tactical motor home was equipped with the very latest in computer software and very capable of taking care of their occupants in just about any situation. They were armed with two 50.cal. machine guns located fore and aft, just under the head and tail lights. A 20mm cannon was mounted in the nose, with two 30.cal. machine guns located on either side of the vehicle, mounted on hidden, retractable arms. They were also armed with two sets of rocket launchers, which came up from the roof when in tactical mode and could fire up to eight Excalibur rockets each. These special M-I rockets had surface to air or surface to surface capability. These units could also be used as a boat by switching everything over to aquatic-mode after driving into any large body of water. At that point, the wheels recede into a secret compartment and two rear-propellers drop down from under the taillights. And at the rear, midpoint of the unit, a rudder drops down from a hidden compartment. In this mode the M-I 480 can get up to 25 to 35 knots in water and almost 90 mph over the road. Other than that, these units were very comfortable, 48 foot motor homes with plush interiors.

The two M-I units were ready and waiting at the palace gates by 7:00 am as everyone climbed onboard. Pat would drive M-I-2, leading the way through the different chambers. Ridding with her, were Dawn, Arista, Skipper, Duchess, the pups, and Peggy Carter.

After giving Anthony and Matt a quick lesson on the operation of one of these units, including weapons systems, everyone else climbed into M-I-3, with Matt Dawson, (Lynn's husband,) at the helm and Anthony, (Dad's oldest human son), in the copilot's seat.

The route would be a little different from the one we took south last year. This time they would be traveling through the western most chambers in order to avoid the Chamber of the Great Swamp. It was in that chamber last year, that Hagnar was almost killed by a giant snake, and if it hadn't been for Pat's miraculous healing powers, he would have been a goner for sure.

Of course, the chambers roads and bridges have had a complete overhaul since then, which would probably make it safe enough to travel through. However, Pat felt there was no reason to take unnecessary chances when you didn't have to. Besides, it would only add one days travel to their journey.

"I can't wait to see Grandma Gertrude," Molly stated. "How long will it take to get there, Ms. Pat?"

"Oh, maybe a couple of days," Pat replied.

"It's not fair that she lives so far away," Lucy spoke up.

"She's always lived far away," Junior reminded.

"I hope we see some of those giant elephant animals we saw off in the distance at the mating ceremonies," Rufus commented.

"Those are mammoths," Arista told him.

"Or mastodons," Skipper added.

"Well, the pups are excited," Pat said smiling, as she looked over at Peggy, who occupied the copilot's seat.

"Well, I think everyone's excited," Peggy responded. "We're all happy to get away for a few days and see a lot more of this amazing subterranean world. I heard the stories of your exploits last year, but I had no idea it was so vast, or filled with so much wildlife. In fact, until I came down here and saw it for myself, I found Nathan's stories of this place a little hard to believe."

"That's much the way I felt when I first saw it," Pat said, as they started onto the bridge to the western tunnel of Akakor. When they emerged from the seven mile tunnel, the landscape turned into wide grasslands that sloped gently downward to the west. But the true beauty of this chamber was not revealed until you were at the central intersection, where they turned north. Everyone, in each unit, had their noses glued to the windows. Off to the east were high mountains, like in the chamber of Akahim. And far off to the west was what looked to be a great ocean.

"Wow!" Willard exclaimed, as he saw a giant bird being chased by a couple of saber toothed cats about a 150 yards off the road to the east. "Dad, did you see that?" He asked.

"See what, son?" Matt asked, looking off in the direction of the huge ocean, and keeping an eye on M-I-2 at the same time.

"There," Anthony said, as he caught movement out the corner of his right eye. "Good Lord, look at that, Matt." At that point the huge, flightless bird, known as a Phorusrhicidae, or terror bird, kicked one of the Smilodons, or saber toothed tigers, so hard it landed only feet from M-I-2.

Pat brought her unit to a screeching stop and waited for the chase to continue on the other side of the road. "That's odd," she said to Peggy. "Those two species are from two vastly different time periods. The Phorusrhicidae is from the Cenozoic, about 62 to 2 million years ago and the Smilodons are from the Pleistocene era about 1.8 million to 10,000 years ago."

"This would be a paleontologist dream world." Peggy said in awe over the barking in the back.

"Cats," Molly barked. "I hate cats."

"Look at those huge teeth," Rufus said.

"I bet they could bite the head off that bird without any problem," Junior commented, as he ran from one window to another.

"You guys just settle down and behave," Duchess told the pups. "You're too old to act like little puppies."

"But, Mama, we're just trying to see what's happening," Lucy told her.

"Arista, why don't you bring Skipper," (her four year old miniature Dachshund), "and come sit with me?" Dawn said, after noticing how afraid the eleven year old was.

"Aunt Dawn, I was just comforting Skipper, because he was so scared," Arista said, not wanting anyone to know that she was the one that was afraid.

Matt brought M-I-3 to a stop just in time to avoid crashing into the back of the other unit. "If this is a sign of things to come, it's going to be one hell of a trip."

"I wonder how many more surprises we'll have before we get back to Akakor," Lynn said to Karen and Chiquita, as she looked out the window just above the table.

Pedro sat feeding Nathanya on the sofa, giving Chiquita a much needed break, while his little Jack Russell terrier, Hombre, kept the other three children company at the large port window. "Maybe we should have stayed back at Akakor," he said, a little concerned about the situation. His English was much improved from when Dad invited him and Chiquita to come live with us at Masterson Island last year. Now, with all the lessons they'd taken over the internet, it was hard to believe he and Chiquita had been uneducated migrant workers from Guatemala, hunted by tomb robbers and drug lords. And, since they had come to live with us at Masterson Island, they'd been granted full citizenship for his help in bringing down the Valasco's last year.

"Nonsense," Anthony told him, from the copilot's seat. "I don't think there's anything in the underworld this puppy can't handle," referring to the M-I unit. "I mean, just look at this tactical display," he back waved a hand at the computer in front of him. "Hell, we could take on an army if need be."

"But that doesn't mean I would purposely take my daughter to where a battle is being fought, senor," Pedro responded, now trying to burp Nathanya.

"I think we'll do just fine," Lynn spoke up. "Dad and his team saw a lot worse things down here that we'll encounter on this trip, and they came through just fine."

Karen looked over at Lynn, "As your Dad might say, sit back and enjoy the adventure."

Just then, Pat started forward again. "Well, I guess the excitements over," Matt said, as he too drove forward.

"Yuk," Paige said, as they passed where the two big cats had finally brought down the ten foot Terror Bird.

"Double Yuk" Megan said, as she ran over to where her mother sat at the table with a sour look on her face and tears welling in her eyes. "Mama, there's blood and feathers all over the….."

"I'm sorry you had to see that, sweetheart," Karen told her, as she hugged her close. "But that is what happens in the wild animal kingdom. Sometimes it's kill or be killed."

Chapter Twenty Seven

SOMEWHERE UNDER ANTARCTICA

18 September

The Dhul Fiqar and the Tennessee had both been knocked out by some kind of powerful EMP, (electromagnetic pulse), which left them disabled for over five hours. The Chattanooga had only been four miles behind the Tennessee, but when they suddenly lost contact, Captain Northfield knew something was very wrong. After searching for nearly a whole day in a wide zigzag pattern, he took his boat back out to open water and sent a message to ANC and waited for orders.

"Sir, it's been almost twenty four hours since the Tennessee disappeared," Lieutenant Robert Dixon, the boats XO, said in frustration. "And we don't have a clue as to what happen to her. Shouldn't we….."

"No, Mr. Dixon, we should not give up, not until we know for sure what happened to the Tennessee and the rogue," Northfield interrupted.

William Northfield had been in the navy most of his life and had never experienced anything like this. He was now in his late forties, stood five foot eleven, with balding salt and pepper hair. And because he'd been passed over for promotion a month ago, he had decided to retire as soon as his boat returned home. He had an exemplary service record and was tired of being passed over by younger officers. Hell, there were admirals in the navy younger than he was, so he felt it was time to go somewhere he was more appreciated.

"Sir, I was just going to say, the only way we're going to find her is to go back to that weird underwater river where she disappeared," Dixon advised.

"Yes, I thought about that, Bob, but it may mean we will disappear as well. However, as of right now, that seems to be our only option," Northfield conceded, coming up with blank for an alternative plan. "We'll wait here for two hours. If we have not heard back from ANC we'll head back to where she disappeared," he finally said.

The strange craft Malik had seen just before they lost power had locked a tractor beam on to the Dhul Fiqar and drug it back to a vast subterranean chamber under the continent of Antarctica. The same fate had also befallen the Tennessee. Limited power had been restored to both boats and the crews ordered out. They would now be taken before the King of this realm under heavy guard. They were not shackled or bound in any way, but it was clear from the start that those who got out of line would be dealt with severely.

The guards were all lined up on the dock as the two crews exited their boats. They didn't seem that different from any other military in the world. They were dressed in navy-blue jumpsuits, and carried a weapon that could, depending on the setting, blow a twelve inch hole through eight inches of solid steel, or just stun a man or beast to a debilitating state. Josh and Paula would later relate these weapons as looking like something Gandalf, from R. R. Tolkien's Lord of the Rings, would carry. They were basically made up of some sort of crystal attached to a long staff. Last year, on at least two occasions, we'd seen these weapons used in battle, so they must be the weapon of choice for most cultures of the creator race. But, come to think about it, in the different mythologies around the world, the supreme deities such as, Odin, Zeus, Poseidon, and Viracocha to just name a few, were able to throw down lightning-bolts, or in Poseidon case shoot lightning from his trident, whenever the need arose.

"Where do you think we are?" Husam asked Malik. "And where do you think they're taking us?

"I don't know, Husam, but I think our fight is over," Malik replied, as they exited the boat and saw the most beautiful city he had ever seen spread out over many hilltops, off to the left of the huge docking facilities.

The city was located in an enormous chamber that was many miles wide and at least 5,000 feet to the ceiling. It seemed to be on an island, or islands, surrounded by many circular canals. On the largest central island, there were four huge white pyramids located at the top of the highest of the surrounding hills. They seemed to represent the boundaries of this beautiful city, because there was nothing but high mountains, great forests, and large rivers with stunning waterfalls, off in the distance.

The city itself was made up of many ancient Greek and Egyptian style buildings, with colossal size statues, temples, and a grand palace. On one hill was what looked like a great temple with a sculpture of a man riding in a huge chariot pulled by great winged horses. The gold trimmed central plaza was filled with people dressed in white robes, who stared at the prisoners as they were marched to the grand palace and lined up on either side in front of the steps. There, at the top of the palace steps, the King, his wife, two of their ten sons and the palace guards, met the crews of the two subs.

"I'm King Poseidon," the figure at the top of the twenty foot high stairway said, in a loud booming voice that seemed to resonate throughout the city. He was a tall man that looked to be in his early fifties, with a muscular build. He had shoulder length white hair and beard, with dark blue eyes which seemed to penetrate all the way to one's soul. He was dressed in long, flowing, blue and white robes with a thin gold crown around his head and in his right hand he held a gold-colored trident. "I would like to welcome you to Atlantia, the second kingdom of Atlantis. This is my wife, Cleito and two of my sons, Atlas and Gadeirus." They were all dressed in similar but slightly different robes.

"Am I dreaming?" Paula asked Josh. "Or have we really found the lost continent of Atlantis?"

"I'm not sure. I think they may have found us," Josh replied. "But whichever the case, I don't think we're going home anytime soon." Josh then stepped forward. "Sire, we mean you and your people no harm. We were in pursuit of these...."

"Yes, we know who you are and why you're here," the King said with a heavy sigh. "You were trying to kill these people," he pointed at Malik and his crew, "for the wrong they have done to mankind when they set off the bombs." The King paused for a second as he inspected this officer closely. "They truly deserve to die for such an atrocity. But then, if all men were killed for the wrongs they've done, the human population of Earth would be nonexistent. Tell me Captain, how you would have felt if a foreign country invaded yours, killing your family and those most dear to you? Would you not want revenge? Or would you just turn the other cheek, as it says in your religious texts? Or maybe, you are one of the many that can only see the wrongs of others, and not what you or those you represent have done."

"Sire, we represent the U.S. Navy," Paula spoke up proudly, "and have to obey the orders handed down from our government."

"So what you are saying is that you follow blindly, and do whatever your government tells you, no matter if it's right or wrong," Cleito responded.

"The only ones you have to fear, or be concerned with, are the Black Lords and dark demons. Their influence stretches far and wide into every country and culture on Earth," Atlas commented as he walked slowly with two imperial guards in front of Malik and his men. "In fact, they thrive on your petty wars, deceiving you into thinking that killing your fellow humans is something your God wants you to do."

"The Black Lords," Malik said, a little confused.

"Yes, the Black Lords and those that follow them, are the ones that pit human kind against one another to the point of bloody wars, slavery, human sacrifice, and every kind of human oppression that you can imagine," Atlas explained.

Then Poseidon spoke up. "We will explain more later for now you will join us for lunch." He then turned with his wife and sons and led the way to the banquet hall of the great palace.

The great hall was built much like many of the others we'd seen in palaces throughout the underworld, with its blue marble floors and evenly spaced white columns holding up a domed ceiling, complete with a skylight. This one also had a balcony that extended out twelve feet that encircled the room.

After everyone was seated at the twelve very large oval-shaped tables, a variety of foods was brought out and placed before them. There was stuffed peacock, hare marinated in orange sauce, as well as clams, squid, fish, and lobster dishes to choose from. There were also many fruits, vegetables, soups and breads to pique ones taste buds.

On a raised platform on the north end of the room, Josh and Paula, along with Malik and Husam, sat at the even bigger royal table with Poseidon, Cleito, and their sons, Atlas and Gadeirus. The palace guards also stood at attention around the room, with their staff weapons ready in case these newcomers posed any kind of threat.

"Sire, is this truly Atlantis?" Paula asked, before trying the stuffed peacock. "I thought Atlantis was destroyed in a great cataclysm and sank beneath the waves, over 13,000 years ago."

"It was destroyed in a great battle with the Black Lords," Gadeirus explained. "However, Atlas and I had just brought this kingdom on line when the attack came. So when a series of laser blasts hit Atlantis's main ion reactor core, causing the mid-Atlantic continent to blow up, we moved most of the survivors to this continent, and renamed it Atlantia after our home planet. But you'll see what I'm talking about after lunch when you are shown through the historical archives at the Temple of Enlightenment."

"Sire, how long will we be staying here with you at Atlantia?" Malik asked, as he tried the soup.

"For as long as you like," Poseidon responded. "Many humans have already been brought here to survive what will most likely become, because of you, the next mass extinction on the surface world."

"It sounds like you were expecting these people to attack the Mid-East oil fields with nuclear weapons and destroy the world," Josh said, as he pointed at Malik and Husam with great loathing.

"If it had not been them, it would have been someone or something else," Cleito offered. "I guess what you don't understand yet, is that the next mass destruction is inevitable. Regardless of who or what starts it. However, we thought there would be a little more time for us to prepare."

"Mother, I still think our projected date will still prove to be accurate," Atlas suggested. "These bombs were just a mere distraction of what is to come."

"I agree with Atlas," Gadeirus spoke up. "I only hope the Admiral can come up with some solutions before it gets here. Because, if the underworld lords are not ready....well you know what happened last time."

"Yes I remember all too well, it turned my hair white overnight," Poseidon said. "That reminds me, I have a computer conference with Gabriel, Chogyal, Odin, and Queen Patamaya, coming up soon. I'll go over the problems with them at that time, and get their thoughts on our new guests."

The two sub-crews just looked at each other in confusion, not believing their ears. But then, it was hard for any of them to accept that they were in an underworld kingdom far below the continent of Antarctica. To them, it was as if they had sailed into another dimension with a different reality.

After their delicious meal, Atlas and Gadeirus led the two crews to the Temple of Enlightenment. There, they were shown the holographic history of the ancient ones coming to Earth, the battle with the Dark Lords over 300,000 years ago, and the colonization of planet Earth. They also learned how the creator-race used their own DNA to create mankind, which they called the Children of Light. They were then told of the sinking of the continent of Lemuria from a huge asteroid strike, and the terrible Ice-Age that followed. After that, there was the total devastation from the second battle with the Black Lords fifteen thousand years later, and then yet another Ice-Age.

"Are you telling us our religious beliefs are unfounded or that our God does not exist," Husam asked, not believing the things he had seen, and upset at what these people were telling them.

"Look around you and tell me what you see," Gadeirus said. "Do you think we arrived yesterday? You probably have heard stories of what is considered cultural mythologies about the different gods and goddesses from around the world. Why do you think those cultures came to believe the way they did? They, like you, had to have some kind of foundation for their belief system."

"We're just showing you what was and what could be again," Atlas told him in a soothing voice. "If you look at the history of your belief system and those of the rest of the world, you will find many similarities. It is an age old story, told and retold in many different ways, by hundreds of cultures around the world."

"The story has changed over the years as oral traditions often do, but the main theme of the Torah, the Christian Bible, and the Koran live on," Gadeirus explained. The theme of all three religions is and always has been one of love, peace, and forgiveness and that these lessons should live in the hearts and minds of all mankind forever."

"I'm afraid it will take a while before we truly understand just what you are trying to tell us," Paula commented. "It is hard to just let go of something you have been taught all your life."

"We are not trying to change your beliefs," Atlas told her shaking his head. "We are just trying to put them into a proper perspective. Look how many times you're Bible has been written or rewritten to be adaptable to the interpretations of the many Christian sects. Or how many, of what was considered the Apocrypha text, or the so called lost Gospels, and Gnostic gospels were conveniently left out. And if you look closely at the early text of the Bible one can find many verses that make little or no sense."

"Such as, Eve talking to a serpent, and Cain, taking a wife when his parents only had three sons and this, at a time when they were supposedly the only people on Earth," Gadeirus explained. "Then Cain goes down into the land of Nod and suddenly there are all kinds of people. Then you have all the angels, dragons, demons, and what many in the modern world believe are descriptions of UFO's."

"I guess when you put it that way, what you have told us seems plausible," Josh said, as he considered the possibilities. "I've never thought of it like that before."

"It's not your religion that is at fault, it's the way you interpret the text you have, and those that deceive you into believing a false doctrine," Atlas informed.

Chapter Twenty Eight

DEEP SPACE

Between Mars and Earth
20 September

We were now on our way home again and for the first time since we'd taken on this project, we were able to get some well-deserved R & R. Before we left Mars, we'd checked out the many demon colonies scattered over the planet, such as the one in the Cydonia region where the famous Face on Mars was discovered by the first Viking Orbiter in 1976, and found no recent activity. Except for the recent firing of their ion cannons, that had opened up on our ships during our brief skirmish. There was no indication of a possible fleet that could attack Earth.

Admiral Michael had left for Earth with the Second Fleet, a few hours before we had.

He had chosen to travel at warp speed to save time and see if there was anything the Second Fleet could do to help Admiral Gabriel with collateral damage on the planet. However, it's kind of hard to clean up the mess twelve nuclear bombs and a tear in the magnetosphere can cause. About all you can do is try to save as many people as possible.

Chogyal and Captain Tyr decided to return on just impulse power to make sure we hadn't missed anything that would cause us more trouble down the line.

"I'll bet Gabriel will be glad to see Michael," I told Dad as we climbed into our bunks. "He'll also be glad to get those new Battle Cruisers. Do you think the Admiral will put you in command of one of the new ships?"

"I don't know Duke, I'm not sure I want to command my own ship yet. However, it is something to think about." Then Dad looked up at Maggie's picture, as he must have so many times in the long distant past, before falling into a deep sleep.

About six hours later we both woke with a start. Dad jumped from his bunk and called the bridge. Dohna had the con. "We have to go back," Dad told her. "The demon bases are not on the planet, they are on Phobos, Mars's largest moon. That's why we missed them with our scans."

"Are you sure?" Dohna questioned. "Phobos is so small there couldn't be much of a base, and Deimos, Mars's second moon, is even smaller yet."

"Well, I'm not positive, but if I wanted to hide a strike force from prying eyes I would put it in the last place anyone would suspect of being an operational base."

"Why don't you and Duke come to the bridge while I run this idea by father?"

"We're on our way," Dad told her, then added. "Maybe you should also contact the Scorpion and run it by Captain Tyr as well."

By the time we got to the bridge, the ship was headed back to Mars. The wormhole generators had been engaged so we were now traveling at warp speed. This meant we would be back in high Mars orbit, in less than an hour.

"What made you think of the moons as possible strike force bases?" Chogyal asked, as we entered the bridge, off the elevator.

"Sire, it was those new fighters we have. I was so impressed with them, I was dreaming about how and where they were made, at Moon Base Alpha ...Well, then it hit me, where else would you hide a strike base."

We came out of warp 15,000 miles from the planet and quickly established orbit. With the Scorpion on the opposite side of the planet, at about the same distance, we could keep an eye on the two small moons without worry of being jumped by surprise.

Phobos was the larger of the two at about 27x21x19km, with a deep crater on one end. Phobos was also the closest to the planet and orbited it every 7.3 hours. Deimos was much smaller at 15x12x11km but much further out. Its orbit took about 30.3 hours. They were not like other moons in this system, but more like asteroids caught in Mar's gravity field about two billion years ago.

Within twenty minutes after we established orbit, Dad and I were all suited up and ready to go. Robbie and Robo would fly the second fighter and act as our wing man. The Scorpion would also launch two fighters to check out Deimos while we had a look see at Phobos.

We were cloaked and invisible to their sensors, so Dad brought us in slow and easy, careful not to trigger their alarms. And, after looking the moon over very carefully without our sensors picking up anything unusual, we were about to return to the Intrepid when a large doorway opened up in that huge crater we had spotted on one end. Three medium sized ships soon exited. At about the same time the Scorpions patrol reported six dozen demon fighters exited the smaller moon, Deimos, and formed up with the larger ships before going to light-speed in the direction of Earth.

A half hour later we sat with King Chogyal, Dohna, and the rest of our crew in the conference room just off the bridge of the Intrepid. Captain Tyr, Commander Freyr, and the Scorpions top officers also sat in, via communication screen.

"The ships that left Phobos were much larger than a supply ship but nowhere near as big as a battle cruiser," Dad said, as he pointed to the pictures we took with our fighters cameras.

"They look something like the old corsairs used in the Great War," Dohna said. "They could do more damage than three squadrons of fighters, and were just about as fast. They carried a crew of about three hundred, and could get much closer to a target, with almost as much firepower as a battle cruiser. However, we quit using them because of design flaws in the core reactors."

"If I remember correctly," Chogyal spoke up. "There were not enough safety features built into the reactor, such as dampening fields and automatic shutdown before critical mass. This meant the ship would just explode without warning, when certain temperatures were reached."

"You're right about that," Tyr agreed. "I lost a good friend to one of those explosions at the battle of Draco. And it was shortly after that the Admiralty decided unanimously to quit using those ships."

"Well, it would seem the demons have redesigned and probably gotten the bugs out of their ships," Chogyal said as he brought an image of an old corsair up to compare it to the ships we'd seen leaving Phobos. "They seem to be about the same in length and width, but it looks like a much improved version of the hypersonic engines, increasing both impulse and warp capability."

"This new design looks like it has more armament," Dohna pointed out. "They still have the two ion cannon pods, fore and aft, but look how many laser cannons they've added, at least five on each end and three on each side."

"What are those objects amidships?" Dad asked. "The old design doesn't seem to have any."

"Yes, I saw that," Chogyal said. "But I'm not sure what they are, maybe Robbie and Robo can give us some idea." He then called the two androids to the conference room.

Five minutes later the pair explained the strange object was most likely the safety features for the new more powerful engines, and the object directly behind the first was probably a more powerful shield generator with cloaking capability.

"If these ships are headed for Earth, we could be in for a hell of a fight," Commander Freyr commented.

"Yes, I've sent an alert warning to Admirals Gabriel and Michael as soon as the demon ships went to light speed," Dohna told them. "But the question now is, what do we do about these two moon bases?"

"Well, you know the standing order, handed down by King Adonai himself, that we cannot attack unless we are under attack," Tyr said with disgust. "He might as well have tied our hands behind our backs as far as these demons are concerned."

"I'm not sure why he restricted us so, but I think it has something to do with Lucifer," Chogyal said shaking his head sadly. "The King keeps hoping he will give up his evil ways and return to the fold. But then, that's no different than any other father. I think we would all feel that way if it were our child."

"Doesn't the earlier attack on us, give us cause to counter-attack their moon bases?" I asked.

"I think so," Dohna agreed.

Then Max spoke up. "I wonder if the ships we saw leave the moons are the only ones that have left. I mean others could have left before we arrived, could they not?"

The others thought for a moment as Max's words sank in. "You know, Max is right, we don't know how many demonic ships have already left here for sure, or just where they're going" Jane told them.

"I think we'd better get home, just as fast as we can," Dad suggested, as a sudden sense of urgency came over the crew.

"I agree," Tyr said. "We can always come back and take out the moons at another time."

Chapter Twenty Nine

WHITE HOUSE BUNKER

21 September

The President called a meeting, in the situation room, at 9:00 a.m. to discuss a new development. In attendance, along with usual cabinet members, was a forty three year old NSA agent. He was tall, about six feet, and athletically built, with dark brown hair and eyes.

"Mr. Standish, I'll let you make the introductions and explain the reason for this meeting," Marcus said, as he gave a slight backhand wave to Miles, giving him the floor.

"Mr. President, Madam Vice President, and members of the cabinet," Miles acknowledged, from his chair midway around the large oval-shaped conference table. "This is Raymond Mendez from the NSA. He has something to tell us about some interesting transmissions his agency has picked up lately."

At first, Ray was a little taken aback as he looked around the table. He was not used to speaking to so many high-level people at the same time, but figured now was not the time to be squeamish. "As you all know, last year we brought down Beltran Velasco, one of the most infamous tomb robbers and drug lords the world has seen in recent years. And by doing so we uncovered a diabolical secret society trying to take over the world, under the guise of the New World Order. We also found out many of the members of that organization were high level people in our government, which included Representatives, Senators, and many of our top military officers. Even the then, Vice President and the CIA Director were believed to belong to this group."

"What's your point," General Wells spoke up. "They were found out and dealt with accordingly. I mean that is old news, so why do we continue to go over it?"

"Let's give the man a chance, Dan," the President said, giving the General a stern look.

"The point, General, is that we didn't even scratch the surface, this organization stretches worldwide. And now, since the bombs went off in the Mid-East, the same type of coded transmissions we picked up last year, have increased tenfold."

"Just where are these transmissions coming from?" Homeland Security Chief, Jeff Davis asked.

"They usually originate somewhere in the Swiss Alps. For reasons unknown, we've been unable to pinpoint the exact location. Within minutes after receiving said transmissions there is usually a response from, Brussels, Beijing, Washington, Moscow, and London. Before the bombs went off, there were also many responses from Rome and countries in the southern hemisphere. But, I guess the radioactive fallout in the red zone has disrupted those signals."

"What kinds of information are in these transmissions?" The Vice President asked.

"They are sent in the form of coded email," Ray said, as he looked at the faces around the room. "The codes are changed every time a new email is sent, but we got lucky recently and broke the last one. Here is the last coded message sent yesterday around noon our time." Ray, then put the message up on the viewing screen.

It read: TO ALL MEMBERS: EVERYTHING IS STILL ON SCHEDULE. OUR BROTHERS HAVE LEFT THEIR RED HOME TO OPEN THE PIT. GIVE THEM ALL THE HELP YOU CAN.

"And exactly what is that supposed to mean?" General Farmer spoke up.

"Sounds like some kind of religious rhetoric to me, Bill," the Vice President commented.

"Well, what we think it means is the proponents of the New World Order are going to play their trump card, so to speak, and start the battle of Armageddon with help from an unknown source," Miles told them.

"We have reason to believe the people who sent this message are the Illuminati of old. However, they may go by the name of Bilderberg's today, and may or may-not be connected to the modern day Freemasons. It is believed the two groups merged about two hundred years ago and have slowly been shaping the governments of the world into a single, One World Government, better known as the New World Order," Ray continued. "But there's no solid proof the two groups are truly connected in any way. However, there are some that believe the United States was an Illuminati experiment from the very beginning, and there is a lot of circumstantial evidence to that possibility."

"But I thought the Illuminati was an atheist organization," Mavis Henley spoke up.

"Well, Madam Secretary, it's a little complicated to understand exactly where they stand religiously," Miles explained. "It was thought by some that the Illuminati was started by those who wanted to bring down the Roman Catholic Church in the seventeen hundreds, or at least cripple their power, so they would have more freedom in science exploration. When they were exposed, and many killed, most of the freethinkers of that day, and for many generations to follow went into hiding or joined other secret societies such as the Freemasons. Needless to say, the scientific community and the church have been at odds ever since. Even to this day many scientists reject the idea of a God, or anything to do with religion altogether."

"I thought you said they wanted to bring down world governments?" Marcus questioned.

"Well, I think their agenda today is more like uniting the world governments under an all-controlling single government," Ray corrected. "In the beginning they wanted to take down the European Monarchies because they were, more or less, controlled by the Church of Rome. However, when they allegedly merged with the Masons, who some believe had already merged with the Knights Templar a few centuries before. The agendas of all three have now evolved into what it is today, a secret society, within a secret society, within a secret society. And the only ones that truly know what's going on are those few at its central core."

"And there is no mistaking their agenda now," Standish interjected. "It is to enslave the world under one all powerful government, controlling Economics, Science, Trade, Labor, and the Militaries of the world."

"That's a crock of crap," FBI Director, Stan Miller firmly stated, after staying quite as long as he could. "I have been a member of the Masons for many years and have never heard of such a preposterous proposal. To even suggest the Masons are a diabolical organization is totally against everything they stand for."

"I agree," Tom Vitt joined in. I too am a long time member and all of these allegations go totally contrary to the Masonic code, which is to build a better world for all mankind."

"I'm also a member, Mr. President," Tony Barker said.

"That makes four of us," Jeff Davis broke into the conversation with his slow southern drawl. "And they're right, Mr. President, this makes very little sense. I mean just look back at how many of our Presidents have been Masons. Many of our founding fathers were also Masons and their principles were the very foundation this country was built on. Yes, I will agree that over the years our country has made many mistakes, giving into the same moral wrongs man has been guilty of since he first walked upright. Things such as greed, hate, and lust for money and power, but I believe we'll, under the provisions of our constitution, be self-correcting and emerge as the greatest nation on Earth."

"Well, I can tell you right now there are a few flaws in our constitution, or at least in the Declaration of Independence," Marcus rebutted. "It says that: "ALL men are created equal and endowed by their Creator with certain unalienable Rights, to Life, Liberty, and the Pursuit of Happiness. And yet, there were those among the signers of that document that were slave owners. And, being a distant descendent of slaves in this country, I could never figure out how they could justify such an atrocity in what was supposed to be the beginnings of a free nation. Even when the slaves were freed during the Civil War, most black people in this country were still treated like second class humans, on both sides of the Mason/Dixon line." Marcus paused. "Nor, could I understand how the native tribes could be taken off their lands and put on reservations, be forced to abandon their cultural beliefs, and accept the way of the white man, all this after damn near being exterminated by the U.S. government. NO! Ladies and gentlemen, this country, stole their lands, and broke every treaty it ever made with the American Indian." Marcus paused. "I guess what I'm saying, is that the truly great words written into our Declaration of Independence and the Constitution, only applied to rich, white people. And this is what many of the Masonic forefathers were actually trying to establish, and not freedom for ALL men."

No one said a word for a long moment, as they thought about what the President said.

"Sir, you're probably right," Stan Miller, finally spoke up after carefully considering the President's words. "And yet, today we have a great grandson of slaves, as President. As Jeff said earlier, the constitution should be self-correcting if we follow its principles." Stan paused a second. "However, we may never know for sure who's behind the End of Days scenario. All this talk of the Masons, Illuminati, or even the Bilderberg group has all come up in recent years to mislead us from the real evil that is now upon the planet. I mean, we can speculate all we want, but without any real proof, all we have is conjecture. What we need to do now, is determine for sure where this evil comes from, and put an end to it. Even if it means fighting the final battle of Armageddon, wherever that may be, now that the Middle East has been blown to hell."

Marcus commented. "Hell, for all we know at this point, the final battle site could be anywhere, or engulf the entire planet. I know if I were the devil, I would want to change the battle plan to one no one knew about." Then, realizing they were gaining little ground he decided to end the meeting. "We'll meet back here in three days unless someone has some real answers before then that we can act upon. Mr. Mendez, thank you for your input, we will be looking forward to hearing more from you in the near future." With that Marcus rose and left the room.

Chapter Thirty

ANDEAN UNDERWORLD

22 September

Dusty and his team had gone south after leaving Akakor to the great city of Akanis, where High Councilman Bolontiku had once been the head chieftain. This was one of the three largest cities in the Andean underworld, along with Akakor and Akahim. It was located in a very large picturesque chamber with high mountains, large rivers, and many forests, supporting a wide assortment of wildlife. But the city itself was designed more like the city of Shambhala than its sister cities and supports a population of around 8,000.

It had taken three days to get there and of course they had to stay another day visiting with city leaders and noting all the complaints the locals wanted Queen Patamaya and the high council to address. Then of course, they were wined and dined with all the pomp and circumstance of foreign dignitaries, so it took longer than expected before being on their way again.

When they finally did get underway again, it took another two days and four chambers to get to Amaru Meru, better known as the Gateway of the Gods. This city was only half the size as Akanis but very impressive, none the less, with its white pyramid, and Temple of Viracocha. It was here a giant golden disc existed, which some believed could actually transport worthy souls to their home planets. However, even though a huge golden disc did exist in the Temple of Viracocha, the knowledge of how to activate it had long been forgotten. It was also here that one of the biggest confrontations between locals and newcomers existed.

M-I-1 had been met at the city gates by the local squadron commander, Captain Bitol and his dragon, Captain Paragon, who escorted them to the regional Government Building. Dusty and the rest of his crew had been here a few times before, so they were acquainted with the captain and his squadron as well as the city elders. So after the introductions to Joe, the captains explained the situation, as they all walked down the hundred foot runway of the large office complex. Naumy and Tomka, along with their dragons Hagnar and Ragtar, stayed with M-I-1.

"My men and dragons have undergone insults, slurs, and humiliations of all kinds since these newcomers have arrived. We have repeatedly tried to calm the situation by reassuring them they are welcome here, but I've never seen such bigoted, opinionated, overbearing beings in my life." Bitol said, shaking his head.

"Just last week one of my patrols was shot at in a residential area in the north quadrant of the city," Paragon informed. "I know it must be hard on them, being uprooted from their homes on the surface and brought down here where the customs, religions, and environments are completely foreign to them. But if they keep this up we will have to expel them from the underworld altogether."

"I agree," Dusty said. "And I will bring it up to the Queen and High Council. The newcomers must be made to know that that kind of behavior will not be tolerated anywhere in the underworld."

Once they reached the doors of the Palace they were met by five city elders who escorted them to the nearest large conference room.

"Dusty, its sure good to see you again," Ajbit, the chief elder greeted, as he took Dusty's hand in his and bowed slightly. He was a short, mocha skinned man, about 5'4" with black hair and deep blue eyes, who had to constantly look up at Dusty's six foot frame. He and the other elders were clad in traditional colored robes according to the department they represented. Ajbit's was gold in color.

After Joe was introduced, Ajbit also tried to explain what they were up against as they took their seats. "Most of the newcomers have become a welcomed addition to our city. They adapted very quickly to our ways and now take an active part in our cultural ceremonies. However, there are a few that are always causing trouble."

"How many newcomers did Amaru Meru receive?" Dusty asked.

"We got about five hundred," Elder Tabai spoke up. Tabai wore a green robe and was in charge of the agriculture, flora, and fauna of this chamber. "However, there's about fifty or sixty poor souls that seem to think they can come down here and push us around, giving orders, demanding this or that."

"We have tried everything we know to get along with them, but for some reason they think they are so much better than we are," Elder Chibirias interjected. Chibirias wore a white robe. She was one of two female elders, and in charge of education.

"This sounds like the same problems that have plagued the surface world for hundreds of years," Joe spoke up. "A group moves to a new location and soon tries to take over or conquer the local inhabitants. That's how most of Europe colonized the rest of the world, and the very concept that has led the surface world to where it is today."

"But what do we do about these people?" Ixtab, the other female elder, asked. She was the Public Relations elder and wore a blue robe. "If we kill them, we are no better than they are. And if we do nothing, we risk others believing their venom and thus escalating the situation."

"Well, we've had many such incidences all over the underworld. The Queen and High Council have come to the conclusion that we may have to expel the trouble makers from the underworld," Dusty explained. "Have you isolated or arrested those responsible?"

"Yes," Nacon answered. He had on a red robe, and was in charge of civil defense, fire and police. "After they started shooting at our dragon squadrons, we had no choice. We put them in one of the smaller isolated chamber to the southwest where a tribe lived until they were wiped out by the Zipacna a few years ago." Nacon then called the chamber up on a four sided viewing screen that came up from the middle of the table. "As you can see, it has about a hundred dwellings cut into each cliff-face of the four mountains with plenty of cultivatable land. And there is also enough deer, rabbits, wild boar, turkeys and fish to provide them with meat, and a sizable lake with three rivers, that will give them plenty of fresh water. The northern connecting chamber has a very primitive swamp with many dangerous creatures, such as great serpents, huge crocodiles, and large vampire bats, just to name a few."

"Yeah, we came through one of those chambers last year before we liberated Akakor. Damn near lost Hagnar to a giant snake," Dusty commented. "I would hate to imagine what their fate would be if they strayed into that one. However, the chamber that you put them in resembles the chamber of the Tree of Life, with its cliff side dwellings, fast rivers, small game and fertile soil."

"What about using one of these?" Joe asked pointing to the chambers to the east and south of the penal chamber.

Nacon then called them up on a split screen image. "This is the one to the south," he explained. "As you can see, that desert is over eighty miles across, with poisonous serpents, scorpions, small rodents, and little water. I guess they might be able to cross it, but it would be risky. Then the one to the east is mostly a huge forest, with plenty of wildlife, such as mammoth, mastodons, saber tooth cats, large bears and dire wolfs. Of course, there are the smaller mammals here as well, deer, rabbits, and wild boar. But I guess the most interesting thing about this chamber is the family of man-ape that dwells here, about fifty or so in all, as I recall."

Joe wasn't sure he believed that one, but with all that he'd seen already in the underworld he wasn't about to totally discard the possibility. "How many people did you take to this penal chamber?" He asked trying to get back on track.

"Ten of the worst offending families, forty eight people altogether, including children" Elder Ajbit answered, as he looked at the list in front of him. "We told them if they changed their ways we would consider bringing them back to Amaru Meru, but this would depend on their attitude and the judgment of the high council."

"We left them with plenty of supplies, enough to last about six months, including their guns and ammunition, plus plenty of vegetable seeds, and carpentry tools" Elder Chibirias explained.

"Well under the circumstances, I don't know what else you could have done short of killing them," Dusty said. "I will let the Queen and High Council know that I approve of your course of action, and will suggest to them that others who do not respect the laws of the underworld, be dealt with in a similar manner."

"It's only been two weeks since the surface world was disrupted," Joe commented. "It may take a while for those people to adjust to a completely new environment, along with the truth about human development and religious ideas. I know Peggy and I are still trying to make sense of it all."

Dusty, Joe, and the crew decided to spend the night in Amaru Meru that night at the palace, before heading back to Akakor the next morning. The small palace, what we would consider an average sized modern Hotel, was just not big enough to accommodate dragons yet, so Ragtar and Hagnar were able to find quarters at the brand new police facilities just down the street. Here they able to visit with their dragons friends from Second Squadron. However, the crew was able to dine together in the grand ball room, and then took a tour of the city, led by Captains Bitol and Paragon.

Before going to bed that night Dusty emailed his report to the Queen and the High Council, telling them all that had happened. The next morning he found new instructions on M-I-1's computer: TRAVEL TO SAID CHAMBER AND CHECK OUT FACILITIES. MAKE SURE THE FAMILIES THERE ARE IN GOOD HEALTH AND WILL BE ABLE TO ADAPT TO THEIR NEW ENVIRONMENT. PLEASE KEEP US ADVISED.

Chapter Thirty One

ANDEAN UNDERWORLD

Chamber of the Tree of Life
22 September

It was in this chamber last year that we met Agab and his family. We learned their tribe had inhabited this cavern for almost 13,000 years. They came to the underworld shortly after the last battle with the Black Lords to escape the carnage on the surface where a tribe they called the serpent-people had either killed or made slaves of many of their people. Agab's people stood, on average, between 5' 2" and 5' 5", with mocha-colored skin, black hair, and dark brown eyes.

We also found out why this chamber is named for the Tree of Life. Located on the far side of the big river there's a massive tree that gives off a golden glow. It was easily the biggest tree I'd ever seen. Agab told us last year, the tree was the reason his forefathers had settled here in the first place so many years ago, because its fruit totally restored one's body to perfect health. However, we didn't find this out for ourselves until a few days later in a chamber far to the south.

Since, Agab had taken the office of High Councilman for this chamber in Akakor and his oldest son Naumy had joined the First Dragon Squadron, his second son Ekno had assumed the duties of local chieftain and shaman here. Of course Kinna, Agab's daughter, had married Sean who was stationed in this chamber, with his dragon, Zargon, and canine Lobo, as the local healer and protectors of this chamber.

Pat and the others arrived on the afternoon of the 19th, and found the cliff dwellings right where she remembered they were. In this chamber the family dwellings are built into the cliff-face of a high mountain. When they got to the dwellings everyone stared in amazement at the site before them, as they stood on the edge of a cornfield. A small river of about 25 feet across and 10 feet deep ran past the full length of the mountain. On the other side of the river about 200 feet above the cavern floor were about 105 dwellings. They were designed in a pyramid-shape with seven levels; 21 dwellings were on the bottom tier and nine at the top. On each level, a terrace or balcony ran the full length of the tier outside the dwellings. Each tier was about ten feet high with oval-shaped doors and windows for each dwelling.

To get to this strange looking structure, one had to cross the river on a stone bridge on the far west side where huge boulders came down to meet the water. Then after maneuvering through the large rocks you walked the 600 foot length of a crescent-shaped beach below the cliff-face. At that point, you had to circle around more giant boulders that hid a secret rock pathway, which led up through a low narrow passageway to the first terrace.

Pat led the way since she had been here before and thought she knew all the secrets of this place, but before the day was over she would find out how little she did know.

"I forgot how much of a climb that was," Pat said as she reached the landing, with the others close behind.

Here Ekno, his wife Kim, along with Ben Franklin, Grandma Gertrude, Ming, Mayling, Kinna, Howl, and a few of the local tribal councilmen met the Queen and her party. Here too, were Ben's daughters, Phyllis and Mary, and their families, including my sisters Gracie and Missy, and Missy's pup Spike. Everyone was all dressed-up in formal attire and bowed when Pat first stepped onto the terrace.

"It's good to see you again, my Queen," Ekno stated as Pat approached. "We hope you enjoy your visit to the chamber of the Tree of Life."

"It is good to see you again, Ekno and the good people of this chamber," Pat said. "But please, we are here on vacation and wish to be treated as friends and or relatives, not royal dignitaries."

It was then everyone relaxed a bit and hugged, kissed, licked noses, and shook hands or paws as the case may be. The pups of course started in telling Grandma Gertrude, Aunt Howl, and the other dogs about all the strange animals they'd seen getting here, while Pat introduced everyone to Ekno, his wife Kim, and the rest of the locals.

"Yes, we had a lot of excitement on the way here," Dawn told Ben and the others, as she gave them each a big hug. "There were terror-birds and saber-toothed cats in one chamber, and in another a huge heard of mammoth made us wait for over an hour while they crossed the road."

"Yeah, I thought that lead bull was going to charge us when that calf touched M-I-2 with his little trunk," Willard told them.

"It's a good thing his mama came when she did or we might not have gotten here at all," Arista commented.

At this point Ekno and Kim led everyone inside through a circular doorway at the center of the balcony. And after a few minutes of following a series of interconnecting stone stairways and pathways through a massive inner cave system, they came to a very large room near the top of the pyramid. It was at least forty feet long and thirty-five wide, with large murals telling the history of Agab's people on the walls. A large table had been sat up in the center of the room with all kinds of delicious food. There was roasted venison, baked rabbit, and poached trout, with corn on the cob, yams, green beans, at least two kinds of freshly baked bread, and of course four big bowls of freshly cut fruit from the sacred tree.

"This is our new tribal assembly room," Ekno explained. "I hope you will be pleased with our humble efforts to honor our Queen with this banquet."

"OH, it's wonderful! Thank you all for this delightful surprise, thank you so very much. And, yes I'm deeply honored by your hospitality."

After everyone sat down at three other big tables on the opposite side of the room, with a plate of food and a glass of fruit punch, Pat said, "I don't recall this structure having so many different tunnels. When we were here last year it seems to me we had little trouble finding Agab and Akna's quarters."

"Well, because of the influx of all the newcomers, we've had to expand our internal storage units, as well as activity centers," Kim explained. "In all four dwelling complexes we've had to make extensive excavations, updating old apartments, putting in new food storage chambers, and replacing old plumbing and electrical systems. We even put in an ultramodern laboratory for our new Councilman Ben Franklin." Kim pointed at Ben across the room where he was being filled in about Dad and his team saving the world from space.

"Kinna, where is Sean, Lobo, and Zargon?" Peggy inquired.

"Oh, they were called away to deliver a baby in the chamber to the southeast," Kinna responded, glad to finally be part of the conversation. "Poor woman, she's had a very hard pregnancy. Sean said the last time he checked her, he thought the baby may be breech." At that Kinna shuddered. "I just hope I don't ever go through something like that."

"Oh, you're fine," Howl woofed, as she looked up from her plate of venison steak.

"Kim, did you say there were four dwelling complexes?" Pat asked. "I thought this was the only one in this chamber."

"Oh no, there is one on the north wall, the south wall and the far eastern wall near the tunnel road, and each one is about the size of this one," Kim answered. Because, this one is centrally located, it was where our ancient Chieftains chose to live."

"Well, I guess I got confused, because this is the only one we visited on our way through last year."

"Yes, father told us how Mr. Nathan was in a hurry to get home and was only able to stay a couple nights, before moving on," Ekno said. "But, everything worked out for the best, because you, Mr. Nathan and the rest of the team, were able to destroy the evil demon in Akakor and unite the underworld tribes."

"If it were not for your efforts, we would still be fighting the flying serpent warriors," Kim added. "So thank you, my Queen, for all you have done for us."

Over the next three days Pat and the others had a chance to visit with Ben and his family. Duchess and the pups sure did enjoy their visit with Grandma Gertrude, Howl, and Uncle Lobo when Sean got back. They made fast friends with Gracie, Missy, and Spike. Even Pedro, Chiquita, and Hombre made many new friends and were asked, by the high council to become permanent residences of this chamber. And after thinking it over for a couple of days, they accepted the offer.

The group was also shown the rest of the chamber. The three other dwelling complexes and on a trip to gather fruit at the Tree of Life, they saw the face of the great Lord Punch carved into one of the western mountains, much like the Presidents of Mount Rushmore.

"He is the protector of the Tree," Kim whispered to Peggy.

"Look at his blue eyes," Lynn spoke up. "They must be made of the biggest sapphires in the world."

During their stay Pat stayed in touch with the rest of the realm, as well as the whole of the underworld around the planet, via computer. With a special adapter she was able to see and hear, as well as be seen and heard, by those she was in contact with. It had disturbed her a little when Poseidon explained to Gabriel and the other leaders at the monthly conference, about the two sub crews he'd taken in.

"It is my feeling that extra precaution should be taken with these people. Just look to the surface to see what they are capable of," Pat told them. "These are men of war and can kill without feeling any compassion for the people they slaughter."

"I agree," Thor spoke up. "If they get loose in the underworld they could influence the newcomers with their petty bickering and cause all kinds of havoc."

In the end it was agreed by all that the crews should be returned to the sea unharmed. But first, they would be allowed to stay a few weeks while they were taught the true story of man's origins. Then after much thought, Gabriel relented in the end, and decided to let Poseidon make the final call as to their fate. He said the creator race should lead by example. And since we have lost so many of our children to the dark-side over the years, maybe it was time we forgave them for their rejection so many years ago and try once again to teach them the true meaning of the Principles of Light.

Chapter Thirty Two

THE UNDERWORLD OF ANTARCTICA

25 September

To see if these people could change their way of thinking from a military mindset, of war, death, and destruction, to a gentler, caring, attitude toward all life, the two sub crews had been taken to different chambers by a fast rail system much like the one at Shambhala. The two sub crews would also be allowed the freedom to explore everything within the boundaries. In each chamber there were communities where newcomers had recently been introduced to the customs and beliefs of the longtime local inhabitance. They too were having a little trouble adjusting, but it was only because their surface world had been torn apart and the worry of loved ones left behind.

The crew of the Tennessee was taken to one of the larger chambers located near the center of the continent. This chamber was over seventy miles across. Here the grass filled rolling hills gave way to clusters of evergreen trees, forming little forests here and there. There were also many animals of all kinds,' animals, from the mighty mammoth to the small packrat. Near the center of the chamber, four major rivers, with aqua-colored water flowed over three hundred foot waterfalls into a huge lake, twelve miles long by three wide, with an average depth of over 200 feet.

A wall encircled metropolis of about 3,000 people, spread out on the lakes north shore. It looked like most medium-sized cities of the underworld, combining ancient simplicity with modern technology. Of course, the buildings of the main square had the usual pyramid, a few monuments, an educational center, and a government building, which was used for just about every kind of social gathering there was. But, in this chamber there was no grand palace or elaborate temple complex, like so many other cities of the underworld. Even the individual family dwellings looked like medieval huts with thatched roofs and mud walls for their exterior facades. However, on the inside they would rival, if not surpass, the most modern state-of-the-art three bedroom house of the twenty first century. At the cities west gate, the crew was met by the thirteen member local high council.

"Captain Worthington, Lieutenant Jones, I would like to welcome you, and your crew, to South Point," Azaes greeted, as he extended his hand. "We call it that because this chamber is the southernmost point of the world, or should I say the underworld." As he shook their hands, Azaes, the twin brother of Diaprepes, the youngest pair of Poseidon's five sets of twins, introduced the rest of his council. Then Josh introduced his crew.

When a mammoth trumpeted somewhere far off in the distance, Paula said, as she shook Azaes hand. "I would never have guessed there were elephants at the South Pole in a subterranean chamber."

"There are no elephants here," Azaes corrected, shaking his head for a second before grasping what she was talking about. "Oh, you must mean the Mammoth herd that moved in a few years back. Yes, they do quite well in this chamber, as I hope you and your crew will. Most of our recent newcomers are adjusting much better than expected, under the circumstances."

"How many newcomers do you have here?" Ensign Brooks asked, as he shook hands.

"We were blessed with five hundred new souls, as was every other chamber on the continent of Atlantia," A councilwoman named Cay told him. "Of course, we had to add many new homes to our little city, but I think things have worked out for the better so far."

"Speaking of new homes," Azaes said. "I guess you folks would like to see where you will be staying. It's a brand new building, much like what you would call a hotel on the surface. It has over eighty rooms and all the amenities including: queen size beds, HD-TV's in each room, swimming pool, and a spa.

"Wait a minute. Where did you get TV's?" Josh inquired.

Azaes smiled, "Captain, we have monitored man's progress since their very beginnings. When we're not in stasis, sometimes we even walk among the people of the surface world. However, your technology is still archaic compared to ours, so I think you will find the TV's in the underworld are far more advanced than any you've ever seen before."

"If you and your crew will follow me I will show you to your quarters, Captain," Cay said pointing the way into the city. "We will give you a few days to get settled in before assigning you to your new duties here at South Point. So feel free to go where you like or ask what you will. I'm sure you'll find the people here very happy to help you in any way. However, if you desire to go outside the confines of the city wall, you will need an escort. There are some big predatory animals in this chamber that would be glad to have you for dinner, but come to think about it, most of you wouldn't make much more than a snack."

The crew of the Dhul Fiqar was taken to a similar chamber to the east of South Point, where Azaes's twin brother, Diaprepes, was in charge. Here they were also met by the local council and made welcome. And, except for a few members of the crew who remained skeptical of their new host, Malik and his men thanked Allah for this chance to make amends.

The crew was taken to their new quarters after the introductions, and shown the city they would, at least for now, call home. Here again, the building was much like a fancy hotel with eighty beautiful rooms, and by putting two to three to a room, the whole crew was placed on the fourth floor. They were told, like the crew of the Tennessee, of their complete freedom within the city walls and warned of the dangers beyond.

"I'm not sure I trust these people," Husam said to Malik, after they were alone in their new room.

"Why is that?"

"After what we did, how many people would just take us in and set us up in such nice quarters without wanting something from us?"

"Husam, have you not been paying attention?" Malik asked. "These people are actually beings from another star system. They're so far ahead of mans knowledge and technology it is like the difference between Neanderthal and modern man. Don't you understand they, and others like them, are the real parents of mankind?"

"Do you really believe that?" Husam said, while staring at his friend in total disbelief. "Do you just disregard all you've been taught about Allah, Mohamed, and the Koran?"

"No, I still believe in the Koran, but I now understand what the text really means, or should I say, I understand it better now than I ever did before. The Christian and Jew are not our enemies, nor are any other religious group," Malik told him while studying something outside the large oval-shaped window.

Husam stepped over to the window to see what had captivated Malik's attention.

"Tell me, Husam, what you see just east of the central plaza."

"I see a big pyramid," Husam replied, shrugging his shoulders, not understanding the meaning. "It looks similar to the ones at Giza, in Egypt. So what?"

"Well, I guess we know now who really built these magnificent monuments."

A long moment went by before Husam responded. "OH, now I understand what you're saying. These beings really are from……." Husam didn't finish the thought as the full impact of Malik's meaning finally hit him.

"Come on, Husam, let's get the rest of the crew and go sightseeing," Malik prodded as he headed for the door.

The Chattanooga once again zigzagged its way under the ice-shelf, five hundred feet off the bottom where the fresh water river flowed from the continent.

"Sir, we are five miles from the continental shelf and still no sign of the Tennessee or the rogue," Lt. Dixon said, as he too looked at the GPS display monitors. "We have been over this same stretch of ocean about a hundred times in the last week, and still nothing."

"Sonar, is there anything, anything at all?" Bill Northfield asked for the tenth time in the last hour.

"No Sir," Trevor Horton replied. He had been on duty for over twelve hours now and was getting very tired of listening to whales, seals, and penguins.

"Sir," the communications officer, Ensign Sam Parker spoke up. "We are receiving a call from the Portland. They are entering the Weddell Sea and are requesting our status and the status of the Tennessee."

"That's Frank Foster's boat," Bill said. "Advise the Portland as to our present situation, Mister Parker." Then Bill turned to Bob Dixon. "I hope he brought plenty of help, because this doesn't make any sense. There is no way those two subs could have totally disappeared without us knowing about it."

"I know what you mean, Sir. If they had killed each other we would have heard the explosions, or at least found some debris. If they just lost power and sank, we would have picked them up with one of our probes that have searched every inch of the bottom for a hundred square miles, over the last week."

Bill thought for a minute, and then said, as he sat down at the command station. "There's a saying by Sir Arthur Conan Doyle, written into one of his Sherlock Holmes novels, but I can't remember the quote exactly. It goes something like this, "When you have considered all the possibilities and still come up empty, whatever is left, no matter how absurd, has to be the answer." So let's try something new, Chief, head us straight for the continent at ten knots, and let's see if we can find the source of this mysterious river of fresh water."

"Sir, we are picking up a strange anomaly about two miles in front of us, and it's headed straight for us at twenty knots," Horton reported, after fifteen minutes on the new course.

"Chief Kelly, go to general quarters, battle stations," Bill said, just before everything went dead.

But instead of being taken into the underworld like the others, a message appeared on the communication computer, which read: "DO NOT FEAR FOR THE OTHER BOATS OR THEIR CREWS. THEY ARE SAFE AND WELL TAKEN CARE OF. PLEASE GO FROM THESE WATERS AND NEVER RETURN, OR FACE THE CONSEQUENCESES." With that, the boat returned to normal without the slightest hint that anything had happen.

"Who or what in hell, are we dealing with here?" Bill asked with frustration in his voice, at the inability to do anything about the mysterious power loss. But as he thought about it Bill, realized the answer. He now knew they would be literally powerless to find the Tennessee, as the full implications materialized in his mind. "Mr. Parker, contact the Portland and let her know we need to rendezvous before we go any further with this operation. Chief Kelly, put us on an intercept course with the Portland in the Weddell Sea."

"What do you think happened?" Lt. Dixon asked, as he sat down next to Captain Northfield.

"I don't know, Bob, but whoever sent that message obviously has far greater technology than anything our boats have. They can shut us down at will and there's nothing we can do about it. Let's just hope they were telling the truth about Josh Worthington and his crew."

"What if we tried another probe?"

"I have a bad feeling they would not only shut it down, but come after us and the Portland as well." Bill paused for a second as the boat turned to the new course. "Mr. Parker, as soon as we clear the ice-shelf send a message to ANC and advise them of our situation.

An hour later the Chattanooga broke the surface of the water one hundred feet from the Portland and a thousand feet from the ice-shelf. It was 3:00 a.m., with the temperature at thirty below zero, with little wind and no clouds. Captain Northfield and Lieutenant Dixon stepped out onto the small lookout platform atop the Chattanooga's sail, donned in heavy parkas. Captain Frank Foster and his XO Lt. Paul Wilson did the same on the Portland.

"We have a big problem here, Frank," Bill said, as the two boats came within voice range. "We are dealing with what has been deemed unspeakable by the Naval Department."

"Yes, we received a similar message about the same time you did, Bill," Frank informed. "I think all we can do now is wait for orders from the ANC, and pray the captors of the Tennessee are not hostiles."

"Josh Worthington is a good friend, and I'd hate like hell to lose him, but there's nothing we can do against such technology."

Just then, Bob Dixon looked skyward and saw what he thought was a meteor shower. But, after many explosions and what looked like tracers streaking the night sky. "My God!" He suddenly exclaimed pointing at the heavens, as he realized what was happening. "There's a huge battle going on in space."

At that point, Dad and I flew over the two boats in pursuit of a demon fighter.

Chapter Thirty Three

IN ORBIT OVER ANTARCTICA
25 September

After we figured out a full scale invasion of Earth was underway, the Scorpion and Intrepid returned home to find the Defiant and the Second Fleet already engaged in a huge battle around the entire planet. Max had been right. What we saw before we left Mars orbit was just the last of the demon invasion fleet. It turned out they had amassed a huge fleet with updated weaponry over the last 13,000 years, and would have been more than a match for the three galactic battle cruisers of the first fleet. The demons had at least four battle cruisers, two hundred corsairs and fifty F-47 class star-fighters to defend each of the larger ships.

As soon as we came out of hyperspace, Admiral Gabriel sent us to defend the southern hemisphere, while the Scorpion defended the northern pole. It was obvious the demons had no idea the Second Fleet had arrived from the Canis System. But even with the extra fleet, the battle had gone back and forth many times before the Lords of Light could declare victory.

I think the tide of battle finally changed in our favor with our return, because afterwards, the demon ships started to fall like rain. However, the real threat now was the possibility the demons had landed troops, or worse yet, found their way to the underworld and freed the Black Lords.

Of course, the job now was cleaning up the few demon ships still threatening the Polar Regions. We had already taken out a battle cruiser and were now trying to finish off the last of the corsairs and their fighter escort. Dad had sent ten fighters to attack each corsair while our other five fighters divided the smaller demon ships. With their attention diverted by our fighters, the Intrepid was able to destroy a battle cruiser with her ion cannons. But, she did sustain some battle damage when her shields started to fail late in the fight. Even with our new advanced fighters, the new armament of the demon ships made it harder to take them out than we first thought.

"We have two demons on our tail, Dad," I said as we came low over the ice shelf.

"I see them, Duke, but we have to take care of this one first." Dad replied, as four laser blasts just missed our port engine. That's when we spotted the two American subs, just sitting on the surface almost surrounded by ice. Dad fired the forward cannons at that point, and we watched the demon craft explode. Then he fired the aft cannons and sent another spiraling into the ice. Before our last pursuer could react, Dad hit the thrusters and went vertical in a giant arch that put us directly behind the third demon ship. With a single blast from our forward cannons, it too spiraled into the sea about a thousand yards from the subs.

I quickly sent the subs a message on the A.N.C frequency. "Don't worry, boys, the skies are safe now with Masterson and Masterson on the job."

"Who are you and what are you doing on this channel?" Came, the reply from Captain Foster on the sail of the Portland.

At that point Dad found them on the radio, as he brought our F-48 low and hovered 100 feet above and between the two boats. "Are you boys lost or do you need help with a mechanical problem?"

"This is Captain Frank Foster of the USS Portland. I repeat, Sir, who are you and what country do you represent?" Frank said a little more forceful.

"This is Major Nathan Masterson of the First Fleets Galactic Marines, and I guess you could say I'm representing all the nations of Earth at present, Captain, even though I'm a U.S. citizen. If you'd like I can arrange for a meeting so we can talk face to face."

"I'll give you my reply in five minutes," Frank answered, a little uneasy.

Lt. Wilson had the look of worry on his face. "Sir, you're not seriously considering a meeting with this guy, are you? It has all the earmarks of a trap."

"What do you think, Bill?" Frank asked. "Shall we meet with this pilot and find out what's really going on? I mean, if this guy wanted to sink us, we'd probably stand a better chance in a canoe going over Niagara Falls."

Bill thought for a moment and then agreed. "Yeah, I think you're probably right, Frank, if his intention were hostile we'd be on the bottom right about now. Besides, he may be able to tell us what happened to the Tennessee."

"Okay Major, Captain Northfield and I will meet with you," Frank replied, after five minutes had passed.

"If each of you will stand alone on the sails of your boats, I'll arrange for a pickup in two minutes," Dad told them before heading for the Intrepid at high speed.

As we landed on E-deck the two naval officers were being beamed aboard to B-decks med-bay where they were met by Dohna, Jane, Steve and Max.

"Hello Captains, I am Princess Dohna of Shambhala and I would like to welcome you to the Galactic Battle Cruiser Intrepid, of the First Fleet of the Canis star system." Dohna greeted. "This is Captain's, Steve and Jane Franklin, of our Galactic Marines; they are our Chief Medical Officers.

"If you don't mind gentlemen we would like to make sure you have not suffered any ill effects from being transported aboard," Jane said, after shaking hands.

The two men looked around at the all-white walls of the med-bay, at the very human looking persons standing in front of them, and even the normal looking dog wearing a khaki uniform with lieutenant's bars. "If you'll just step over to the screen and remove your parkas," Steve said, indicating to the 6x4 foot monitor. "We'll get you squared away in no time."

"Forgive us for staring, but we were led to believe aliens were little gray beings with big eyes," Bill Northfield said, after finally finding his tongue.

"Yes, well, those beings do exist but, before you return to your boats gentlemen, you'll learn not only who we are, but exactly who and what you are," Dohna said with a smile. "And I'm guessing it's going to surprise the hell out of you."

When each man had been scanned for any abnormalities and checked out okay, they were taken to the bridge to meet King Chogyal. But, he and the rest of the bridge staff were in the process of landing the last two fighter squadrons. However, he promised to meet with them in the conference room before they left. It was there, Dad and I found the two sub captains waiting patiently with Steve, Jane, Max, and Dohna. They were fascinated with the ship and were asking questions faster than the three humans could reply. So they were very surprised when Max supplied some of the answers.

"Hello gentlemen, I'm Major Nathan Masterson and this is my RIO, Captain Duke Masterson," Dad said as he extended his hand. "We would have been here sooner, but I thought it best to clean up a little first."

"So you're the one we talked to out on the ice," Frank Foster said, as he pumped Dad's hand.

"That was some aerobatic display you put on out there, Major," Bill Northfield commented as he too took Dad's hand. "Your fellow officers here have explained a little about the Black Lords, but there's a lot we don't understand."

Dad looked over at Dohna, "Have they not seen the hologram on the beginning yet?"

"We were just about to show them when you came in."

Just then a beep sounded, before Chogyal's voice came over the intercom. "Dohna, could you bring Major Masterson and Captain Duke, to the bridge for debriefing? And Mr. Franklin you and Jane are needed in sickbay, ASAP."

"Aye Sir, we'll be right there," Dohna replied, then looked at Dad with worry on her face.

"Gentlemen, if you'll excuse us for a few minutes while we take care of a few things, I'm sure this hologram will explain a lot of our situation," Dad told them as he entered the program into the computer.

Five minutes later, we were sitting with Chogyal and Dohna at the command center of the bridge, and Chogyal informed us this would be piped throughout the ship. We didn't know it at the time but, it was also being telecast throughout the underworld kingdoms, around the world, as well as to all nations on Earth.

The main screen was divided into a pyramid. At the top was, Admiral Gabriel, and Admiral Michael, who were in a huge conference room at Moon Base Alpha, with a few Vice Admirals and Captains from both fleets. All the underworld leaders were spread out on the lower levels of the pyramid.

Dad and Pat made eye contact almost immediately, before Gabriel began to speak. "I would like to commend the officers and men of the combined forces of the First and Second Galactic Fleets of the Canis Star System," the Admiral stated with pride. "On this day we were able to, once again, fight off the demon forces and uphold the principles of the Great Creator El Shaddai and King Adonai. But, even though we won a battle, the war continues, and will go on until we can once and for all, free the Earth of Hate, Fear, and Deception, and replace these things with Love, Hope, and Freedom for all that dwells upon it."

The Admiral paused a long minute before continuing. "At this point, Captain Adams will read the names of those who gave their lives today. They will be deeply missed, may their courageous spirits be reborn to us soon."

After Captain Adams read the eighty seven names, of those who died in the battle, sadness gripped the hearts of both fleets. A few moments of silence followed, as a prayer was offered by a Commander in the Second Fleet. Then Admiral Gabriel read the names of the officers and men who would be given special commendations and a raise of rank for valor. These also included the names of the White Knights of Avalon and the dragons of the First Dragon Squadron for their liberation of Akakor last year.

I thought it a little odd when he failed to mention Dad and I, not that I thought we needed a promotion or even a special mention. However, I soon found out why.

"There are two more names I would like to mention, that have needed mentioning for a long, long time now. They have, over many lifetimes, shown their loyalty to the Lords of Light, their courage in battle, and their ability to lead with honor. They are two of the finest officers in the First Fleet, and it makes me proud that from this time on, you can address Major Nathan Masterson as Major General and his canine, Captain Duke Masterson as Colonel of the First Fleets Galactic Marines. And, I am also happy to announce they will soon take command of one of the new Galactic Battle Cruisers Admiral Michael has brought us from the home system."

At that point the bridge crew of the Intrepid erupted with shouts of praise with everyone coming over to congratulate Dad and I. Dad looked over at Chogyal and Dohna after everyone returned to their stations. "Did you two have something to do with this?"

"Nathan, the Admiral and I agree you two are ready now for your own command. You and your team have proven yourselves time and time again over thousands of years, and should have been promoted long before now," Chogyal said, with pride. "With this defeat, the Black Lords and the many legions of demons that follow them are going to be even more determined in their quest to rule the Earth. So we need all the seasoned battle commanders we can get."

"Well, thank you for your praise, Sire, but do you really think we should have been promoted over the ranks between our old ones and our new ones?" I asked.

"Believe me, Duke, you both very much deserve the ranks you now have," Dohna spoke up before the King could answer. "Besides father and I were not the only ones that put your names in for promotion. The list goes on and on from your fellow officers, both on the Intrepid and the Andean underworld, including Queen Patamaya, King Drac and the dragon kind, all the way up to Admiral Gabriel himself."

We sat there a moment thinking over our new positions, when Steve, Jane, and Max returned from the sickbay. "How's Captain Hon," Chogyal inquired. He was one of the few human pilots Chogyal brought with us from Shambhala. His fighter had been hit many times over, but somehow he managed to get it back to the ship.

"He'll be just fine now that we got him into the restoration capsule," Steve said, as he led Jane and Max over to congratulate Dad and I.

"Did the two sub Captains return to their boats?" Max asked, after the hugs and handshakes were shared, reminding us of our guests.

"I'm sorry gentlemen for the delay, but it turned out to be more of an honors ceremony than a debriefing," Dad said, as we returned to the conference room.

The two men were looking out, what they thought were windows, at the continent of Antarctica far below the ship. "Yes, we heard," Bill Northfield said, as they returned to their seats.

"And we saw the hologram," Frank Foster spoke up first. "But Sir, I don't mind telling you, we find this a little overwhelming. Would you have us believe that mankind came from an alien race and that our religious teachings have all been wrong."

Dad looked at each man and shook his head, as he considered how to explain. Why was it so difficult to accept? But, then I reminded him, telepathically, of how skeptical he was when we first learned of the creator race.

"Gentleman, I understand how you feel. I felt the same way when a few friends and I first discovered these beings, or should I say when they awoke an old knowledge buried deep in my subconscious."

"Not to change the subject, but can you tell us what happen to the crew of the Tennessee," Bill Northfield asked, after filling in the sketchy details of what had happen up to their disappearance.

"We can do better than that," Dohna said with a soft smile, as she pressed a set of buttons on the console in front of her.

"Mister Clayhorn, would you arrange for a link with the crew of the Tennessee on Atlantia and patch it through to this conference room?"

"I'll see to it right away, Captain," Ron replied, remembering Dohna had also gotten a promotion in rank.

While Ron arranged for the link, we continued to explain how Steve had found the caves in British Columbia last year, which triggered the chain of events that has now brought us here.

After about twenty minutes Ron beeped in. "Captain, I have that link you wanted."

"Thank you, Ron," Dohna said, as a screen came up in the middle of the conference table.

On the screen, Josh and Paula suddenly appeared sitting by a swimming pool, enjoying the facilities of their new environment. "Bill, is that you and what's Captain Foster doing there?" Josh asked, surprised to see the two officers.

"We...A... What...Happen...To you and your crew," Northfield said, a little dumbfounded at what he saw.

"Oh you guys are NOT going to believe what happened to us and the rogue," Josh said shaking his head. "We were under the ice shelf in pursuit of the rogue, when all our power suddenly went dead. After a few minutes we all lost consciousness. When we awoke, it's as if we had entered another time and place. There was a beautiful city with a huge pyramid, a King who claimed to be Poseidon, and an underworld kingdom that I found impossible to believe at first."

"It's like being in a dream," Paula offered. "All the myths and legend that science has completely rejected as fact are actually very real."

"They showed us a holograph that explains all of this, but even then it took about a week before the reality began to sink in," Josh told them, as he looked a little closer as to the room the two officers were in. He could see the window-monitor behind them, which clearly revealed the Earth far below their position. "Where are you guys? You're not on any submarine I've ever seen. You look like you're on the space station."

Bill and Frank looked at each other with a question mark. How, can we explain this without sounding completely crazy, they thought. Frank Foster finally found his tongue. "Would you believe we were abducted by aliens and are in a high Earth orbit?"

"After what we've seen in the last week, we are ready to believe just about anything," Paula told them.

"Hey, did you guys see that battle in space?" Josh asked. "We were able to watch it on the big screen TV in our rooms. They tell us it was real, but...."

"Yeah, we saw it up close and personal," Bill told him. "Three of those demon ships were shot down within a few hundred yards from where we were."

They talked for another ten minutes before Ron lost the communication link.

Chapter Thirty Four

WHITE HOUSE BUNKER
25 September

When the battle above the planet first began, Admiral Gabriel thought it best to make sure the children of Earth knew who their real enemy was. So he tapped into every communication satellite around the world and instantly became the only face on every TV on Earth. He figured if there was anything that would truly unite mankind under one cause, it would be the threat of a global invasion from space. He also knew if it failed, the human experiment may soon come to an abrupt end.

In the White House bunker, at 7:15pm, the screens of every monitor suddenly came alive with the raging battle in space. At first everyone thought it was a rerun of an old "Star Wars" movie, until Gabriel appeared and explained that what they were seeing was very real. He also explained how the dark demons of Mars had escaped and were now threatening to free their Black Lord masters, imprisoned in the fiery abyss. "My children, I tell you now, this is the time to put aside your petty differences and embrace your fellow humans as brothers, no matter his religion, skin color, or ethnic background, because if you don't, and you continue on your present course, you will be in danger of becoming extinct."

"Are you the Admiral Gabriel, Nathan Masterson, told us about?" Overton asked from his chair in the replica of the Oval Office, where he sat with the Joint Chiefs.

"I am, and believe me when I tell you, Nathan's, words were very true. The only enemies that should concern you are the Black Lords, the demons legions that follow them, and the misguided humans under their control. They are the ones that tempt and influence mankind into doing wrong to his fellow man."

"Oh, you mean as in blowing up half the world like the Islamic terrorist did in the Middle East a few weeks ago," General Wells said sarcastically.

"Or the unjust invasion of Iraq and the slaughter of thousands of innocent people in 2003," Gabriel retorted. "For every wrong you do, a greater wrong will be done unto you. This has gone back and forth for centuries, and is now at a point where the future of mankind is at stake."

"Is there anything we can do to help win this battle?" Marcus asked.

"This battle is beyond your archaic weaponry, but it can be fought in many ways, up here with galactic warships, or down there in the hearts and minds of all the peoples of Earth. The only thing you can do is change your ways. Instead of trying to destroy or rule over your fellow man, always trying to impose your will with an iron hand. You should truly adopt the Principles of Light, and disregard anything that goes against those teachings. If we lose this battle up here, the only thing that's going to save you down there, is not giving in to the Black Lords. You have to believe from the deepest part of you, that the teachings of Buddha, Jesus, and Mohammad are true and let their principles guide your lives."

With that there was a strange silence as the leaders of the world digested Gabriel's words. As they watched the battle go back and forth in space, they now knew beyond a doubt, the true meaning of all the holy books of the world's great religions. They now knew those books had been warning mankind for thousands of years of the impending danger that was now knocking at Earths door. And for the first time, they were terrified, not only of the Black Lords and the dark demons, but of their own stupidity. Gone, was the pompous arrogance that most people in power had, as they realized how little power they actually had.

Then, one by one, each leader swore their allegiance to the Lords of Light and promised to incorporate the principles thereof into their nation's charters. They also promised to put aside their petty differences and work together for the common good of all mankind.

Later that night Gabriel, Michael, and the other high officers of both fleets, had finished giving out commendations, the President met with his cabinet in the situation room. After everyone was seated, General Wells confirmed the transmission from Gabriel was real and in fact the battle in space did indeed take place. He also confirmed the existence of crashed space craft around the world.

"Mr. President, I have two sub commanders near Antarctica claiming they were taken aboard one of those Galactic Battle Cruisers," Admiral Parks informed, shaking his head in disbelief. "They said they met Major Masterson, or should I say General Masterson now, and some other officers. All this happened after they watched Masterson shoot down three demon star-fighters just above their position in the Weddell Sea. They also reported talking to Captain Josh Worthington of the USS Tennessee and his executive officer, Lt. Paula Jones, who disappeared a week ago while on the trail of the rogue. However, Worthington and the rest of his crew were not on the battle cruiser, they were in some subterranean kingdom far below the surface of the Earth, if you can believe that."

"Yes, well Masterson gave me some material, earlier this year, which might explain the whereabouts of Captain Worthington, his crew, and even these alien races doing battle above Earth," the President informed. "But at that time, I thought it was all a bunch of bull crap and failed to see the humor in this sick joke. Of course now, I wish I had listened to what he had to say."

"Mr. President, do you still have that material?" General Farmer asked. "If you do, we might be able to bring these alien bastards down."

"Why would you want to bring down the Lords of Lights, Bill?" Katherine West asked.

"Because they pose a threat to our way of life," Dan Wells spoke up, before Farmer could utter a response.

Now, the President was beginning to understand just what Raul Velasco had told them about the conspiracy to bring about the New World Order. As he looked around the room, he wondered how many more of his cabinet was on the side of the Black Lords.

"General Wells, if the Lords of Lights were hostile to humans, or stood in the way of our development in any way, I can assure you, sir, we wouldn't be here. We're talking about a race that has protected, nurtured, and given mankind the fundamental knowledge to survive against all odds. And, if it were not for them, the human race would now be under the threat of being totally eradicated from the face of the Earth," Marcus said, making it clear where he stood on the matter. "With a show of hands, how many others in this room feel the way Dan and Bill do about the Lords of Light?" The only response came from Admiral Parks, but a few others had the look of uncertainty on their faces.

Even though as president, he had approved of each member of his cabinet, how was he supposed to know who belong to a diabolical organization, trying to take over the world, and who doesn't??

Now, Marcus was unsure who he could trust, or if he was truly the Commander and Chief over the military. Was it really possible that a shadow government actually existed, and was the real power behind the government? Was it all a bunch of smoke and mirrors designed to fool the people into thinking they actually had some say in our government? If these things were true, it would mean the President of the United States was nothing more than a puppet on a string, dancing to an unseen puppeteers tune. And if this was the case, it would explain why nothing, or very little, ever gets done to benefit the people, no matter who, or what party was in office.

"Ladies and gentlemen, we have learned a lot here today," Marcus finally said, with a thoughtful, mellow voice. "We now know we are not alone in the universe, and what most of us were taught as the origins of mankind, will now be subject to a different interpretation. An interpretation I feel that has been there all along, but we were too blind, stubborn, and arrogant to see the truth. We have much to discuss and think about, but because of the lateness of the hour, I think we should call a recess until tomorrow morning. So if no one has anything else, I will see you all here at 11 a.m."

Fifteen minutes later Marcus returned to his quarters to find Marissa still trying to piece together the material Dad had given them. She had watched the battle in space earlier that evening on TV and now knew for sure this was no joke, or hoax.

"Have you found anything new?" Marcus asked, before kissing her gently on the lips and then going to fix himself a drink at the bar. "Even after watching the battle, I still have trouble accepting these beings as Gods."

"That's because they are not Gods and don't claim to be," Marissa answered.

"I thought these beings created the human race," Marcus said, a little confused.

"That's true, but just because you have children doesn't make you a God." Then Marissa quickly thumbed back through the material looking for a page she'd seen earlier. "Here it is," she finally said. "When Masterson, Franklin, and Yang, the cook, first met Gabriel at the crystal palace in the Canadian underworld, Yang asked him if he was God. Gabriel told him, "No, that would be the Great Creator of all, El Shaddai."

"You know, this sounds a lot like the Bible," Marcus said, after a thought occurred to him. "Wasn't Gabriel and Michael archangels? I think Gabriel was the messenger of God, while Michael was his warrior angel."

"You might be right about that, but if you were one of the original authors of the Bible, trying to put down on paper for the first time, the many, long told oral traditions spanning thousands of years and hundreds of cultures, what exactly would you say? How would you explain these beings from another star system with powers beyond belief?"

"I see what you mean," Marcus said, finding a place to sit down next to his wife on the sofa, being careful not to move the papers she had scattered all about. "I guess I would try to tell the story using the only words I knew to describe the events, which would mean exaggerating them with plenty of supernatural and religious overtones." Then Marcus's expression turned dark, as he took a sip of his Scotch and remembered what he'd learned in the situation room.

"What's wrong, Marcus?" Marissa asked, noticing the change in his mood.

He thought for a long moment before answering. "I think I now know what that NSA agent was trying to tell us the other day." Just then the phone rang. "Mr. President, could I have a quick word with you?" Miles Standish asked.

"Sure Miles, Marissa and I will meet you in the Oval Office in five minutes."

Five minutes later, Marcus and Marissa met with Miles Standish, General Mark Baker, and Director of the FBI Stan Miller, in the Oval Office of the White House bunker. General Barker had expressed his concerns about the Presidents safety. Of course he didn't know for sure, he had no hard evidence, but he felt there might be a governmental coup being hatched by the Joint Chiefs and a few others of the cabinet.

"Why do you think the Joint Chiefs would try to take control of the government, Mark?" The president asked.

"Well Sir, there are many reasons," Baker responded sadly. "The idea, of course, didn't start with the Joint Chiefs, but with those very powerful people, shall we say, behind the scenes of our government that feel they have a score to settle. In fact, the military was trying to stay neutral through all this, until you showed your support for the alien race earlier this evening."

"You see, when you ordered the arrest of so many governmental officials and prosecuted those officials to the letter of the law last January, it pissed off some very powerful people," Miles stated. "The silent, nameless people with big money, who have been running this country for many decades, out of view of the general public. For example, every president after Eisenhower has been kept in the dark about the aliens, UFO's and the true story behind Roswell, no matter how bad they wanted to know. But that's only a small example of their power, as JFK found out in Nov. 1963." Miles paused before continuing, "However, most within the government are on your side. Even some of those that don't necessarily agree with your policies, would give their very lives, if need be, to defend you."

"So what do you think I should do about this situation?" Marcus asked, "I mean, none of you have any hard evidence verifying your suspicions."

"Well, there are the inner department emails that in a roundabout way hint of a takeover, Sir," Stan Miller commented.

"Sir, I do know the Joint Chiefs were real upset after today's meeting and are planning to go after these aliens regardless of your approval," Mark informed. "I think Admiral Parks is going to order our subs at Antarctica home for debriefing."

"Have they destroyed the rogue yet?" Marcus asked.

"I don't think so. In fact, I think the rogue has disappeared altogether. It was probably captured by the aliens that captured the Tennessee. Captain Northfield reported it was in some kind of giant underground complex where the aliens have lived for thousands of years."

"How do we stop a military-coup by the Joint Chiefs?" Marissa asked.

"By pulling the teeth of the tiger," Stan suggested.

Chapter Thirty Five

ANDEAN UNDERWORLD
26 September

Dusty and his team had decided to make camp by the large river, in the chamber just east of the one where Ajbit had exiled the rebels of Amaru Meru. While here, they would designate this chamber with an ID number, as they had done throughout the underworld. They gave this chamber the number designation of 48-5390. The first number (48) stood for its location within the 72 chambers of the Andean underworld complex. The next number, (5) represented the size of the chamber, which were rated between 1-9, so this one was about average in length and width, about fifty miles across. The next number, (3) on a scale of 1-6, represented the type of chamber it was, desert, swamp, forest, jungle, mountains, or many lakes or rivers. This one had at least three out of the six, with forest, mountains, and rivers. The next number represented the flora and fauna, again on a scale of 1-9, with nine being very high with each. And the last number represented human population, which was on a scale of 0-9. Of course, they were not sure yet if perhaps a small tribe didn't live here, but there was no sign of any human population in this chamber so far.

Here, the forest was so dense very little light filtered down to the chamber floor. This created an almost primeval atmosphere once you got fifty yards off the road, where many varieties of trees grew in abundance.

Under the night sky, Dusty's team sat talking about the great battle in space around a nice campfire. Even here, in this remote subterranean chamber where the stars were nothing more than small pinpoints of light built into the ceiling, they'd picked up the battle and Gabriel's address on M-I-1's computer monitors.

"So, with Nathan being promoted to a Major General I guess you'll be leaving us soon," Dusty said to Joe.

"Why do you say that?"

"I think what Dusty is saying, Joe," Tomka spoke up, before Dusty had a chance to respond. "If General Masterson is given a new galactic battle cruiser he'll most likely want you to come with him."

"Wow, now that would be the life, flying through the galaxy at light speed, exploring other planets and protecting Earth from the forces of evil," Naumy said, as he threw another log on the fire.

"Now don't you be talking like that, or getting any fancy ideas about leaving without me," Hagnar spoke up from where he lay, a short distance away.

"Oh, you know I wouldn't go anywhere without you Hagnar, but its okay to dream a little every once in a while." Naumy paused a moment. "It's just that I've never even been out of the underworld and would like to see a little bit of the surface world and maybe even the stars beyond, before I die."

"Well, I've seen the surface world and it's not a good place to be right now. And, I don't know if I want to even consider taking a commission on a battle cruiser," Joe finally said, after taking a long minute to think about it. "For now, I'm just happy to be alive, have a wife that loves me, and to know the new friends I've made here in the underworld."

"Yes, I understand all that, but don't you get lonely for the adventure?" Tomka pressed. "I mean, you were once an ace fighter pilot. Isn't there a small part of you that misses the action, speed, and companionship of your fellow pilots?"

"Maybe he just got old and soft like Dusty," Ragtar commented, before belching up a puff of black smoke.

"I don't think that's the case Ragtar," Dusty said, giving him a questioning look. "I may be old, but not as soft as you might think.

And, I still enjoy going out with my team and exploring the different chambers of the underworld, even if they are a little trying at times."

"Yes, I miss all the excitement of being a fighter pilot, but it's been so long now since I've flown I'm not sure…I…Well to tell you the truth, the last time I flew a fighter I blacked out and almost crashed. Ever since then I've had a confidence problem. Each time I think about climbing back in a cockpit, I get the shakes. Hell, I even have terrible nightmares about it to this day."

"That's the advantage of flying with a dragon," Naumy spoke up. "Unless they're hurt real bad, you don't have to worry about crashing. That's another reason you should consider Colonel Longhire's offer to be an instructor at the academy."

"I haven't completely dismissed the idea, but don't you think I should first learn how to ride a dragon?" Joe asked, pulling at his chin.

"I think that's an excellent idea," Dusty spoke up. "I am sure Hagnar won't mind if you swapped places with Naumy tomorrow for an hour or so until you get the hang of it. I'll even let you wear my old survival suit that Nathan's brother gave us last year."

Joe looked at the rest of them, like he'd been roped and hogtied into something he'd been trying to avoid. "Okay, okay," He said throwing up his hands. "I'll do it, if Hagnar doesn't mind this old man being on his back."

"It would be my pleasure, General. I look forward to it," Hagnar told him, letting loose a big dragon fireball, aimed at the ceiling, to seal the deal.

Later that night, Joe tossed and turned in his bunk, as he dreamt of a different time, in the long, distant past. He'd never told anyone, but for most of his life he had this sort of dream whenever he was stressed or under a lot of pressure. And most often, they would be about him and Nathan battling dark ships in space. He could see other pilots and personnel of a great ship in space and knew each one by name. It was strange, but in the last nine months he had again met many of those same people in the here and now.

"Joe, pull up, pull up," Nathan, yelled at him in his sleep. "You have one of those black bastards on your tail! He's firing, bank right! I'll take him out." Just then there was a loud blast as the black fighter exploded somewhere behind him.

"I'm hit! I'm hit!" Joe yelled, as he felt a reduction in engine power, and a sensor started flashing red on his forward instrument panel.

"It's not that bad, Joe, but let's get you back to the ship." Nathan said. Five minutes later he said, "Okay buddy, there's E-decks landing bay, I'll see you in a few."

"Nathan, bank left!" Arlie yelled over the radio. "A demon fighter is coming around on your six and I can't get a good shot!"

Joe heard Dad say, "I'm not leaving Joe until he's safely on board," and then another big explosion.

At that point, Joe woke up, covered in heavy sweat, and screaming, "No, No, Oh God No!"

Dusty handed him a cup of coffee as he made his way forward to the galley section of M-I-1. While the rest of his team was out on patrol, Dusty had started breakfast.

Joe felt weak as he sat down at the table and tried to bring the shake in his hands under control before taking a sip of the hot coffee.

"Have another bad dream, Joe?" Dusty asked, as he put the pancakes and sausage on the table, "The eggs will be coming up in a few."

"Yeah, they're becoming more and more frequent lately."

"Did you know that Nathan also suffers from bad dreams?" Dusty asked, as he put the syrup and butter on the table.

"No, I didn't know that," Joe said surprised, as he took his first sip of the hot black liquid. "Did he ever say what they were about?"

"Not exactly, but from the things he sometimes said in his sleep, I got the impression it had something to do with his war years. When I talked to Patricia about it, she said it may be better if we didn't bring it up. So we never asked him about them. However," Dusty paused at this point trying to find the right words, "You might think I'm crazy, but for some reason I got a feeling that not all his dreams had to do with this lifetime."

Just then Hagnar and Ragtar landed on the road just outside M-I-1. "Ah, here they are now," Dusty said as he started breaking eggs over a hot skillet and adding fresh wild onions, mushrooms, and green peppers along with a little salt and pepper. Dusty then opened a ten pound bag of fresh dragon chow, and poured it into two huge bowls for Hagnar and Ragtar. This food had been specially blended with all the nutritional values a dragon would need when it was away from home. It came in five different flavors, and even though it didn't smell that bad to humans, it looked like something someone had….well let's just say it wasn't pretty. However, the dragons found it quite delicious, and I guess that's all that matters.

"Good morning, gentlemen," Dusty said, as Tomka and Naumy came through the door. "By the time you get washed up, the eggs will be ready." Then Dusty headed outside to feed the dragons. "I hope you boys had a good flight this morning." He said as he put their bowls on the outside camp table. "Did you guys find anything we need to deal with or report to the Queen and High Council?"

"No, everything is the way we thought it would be in this chamber," Hagnar commented before taking a bite of his food.

"High mountains, dense forest, many rivers with waterfalls and just about every kind of animal on Earth," Ragtar spoke up before he too dug into his breakfast.

"Actually, you humans would probably think it a very beautiful chamber," Hagnar said between bites. "But for us dragons, there's just not enough sulfur-dioxide in the air for our tastes."

"Well after breakfast we'll get underway again and check it out," Dusty told them. "And ah, Hagnar, take it easy on the General, he's had a bad night."

An hour and a half later, after the dishes had all been cleared away and cleaned, Joe climbed onto Hagnar's saddle. "Don't worry about a thing, General," Naumy said, as he made sure Joe was all strapped in properly. "Hagnar will take good care of you."

When everything was in place, Hagnar leapt high into the air and spread his great wings with Joe hanging on for dear life. However, after the initial shock of takeoff, Joe adapted to this new ride very quickly, and he was soon encouraging Hagnar to go a little faster. And after a half hour of watching Tomka and Ragtar doing aero-acrobatics, Hagnar talked the General into trying some high dives from up near the five thousand foot ceiling.

"General, are you doing okay up there?" Dusty asked, after he and Hagnar buzzed M-I-1, just missing the roof by a couple of feet.

"This is the most fun I've had since Nathan and I used to do many of the same maneuvers with our F-4's in Vietnam," Joe said laughing, as the memories came flooding back to him.

"Well, who do you think taught us to fly like this?" Tomka asked, over the small helmet mounted headset.

An hour later M-I-1 approached the eastern tunnel to the Chamber of Exile, as it would come to be known. However, as he and Naumy drove down the steep winding road to the tunnel entrance, Dusty got the feeling there was something very wrong. "Tomka is there something amiss with the tunnel or the road ahead?"

"Not that Ragtar and I can see," Tomka replied. "What about you, General, do you or Hagnar see anything unusual?"

"Now that you mentioned it, we haven't seen anything out of place, but I do feel a little strange. At first I marked it up to flying on a dragon's back for the first time," Joe replied. "However, the closer we get to the tunnel entrance the worse it gets."

"I feel it now too," Hagnar suddenly spoke up. "It's a sense that danger is up ahead, even though I can't see any."

"Yeah, the way I would describe this weird feeling, is dread," Naumy said, as Dusty brought M-I-1 to a stop.

"Maybe we'd better stop here until we figure out what's going on."

Just then the ground began to shake violently, and the smell of sulfur filled the air.

As soon as the quake was over, Dusty sent off an email to Akakor telling the High Council what had happened.

Chapter Thirty Six

ANDEAN UNDERWORLD
26 September

Everyone had enjoyed their stay at the chamber of the Tree of Life. But now, that there was the possible penetration of the underworld by the Dark Demons, Pat felt she should get back to Akakor and make sure all that could be done, was being done to protect her realm. But then again, it may have been because of an email she received from Dad saying we would be visiting for maybe a week or two before training exercises began on our new Galactic Battle Cruiser. However, Dad had made it clear that we were first returning to Shambhala to finish our meditative training.

On the way home, Pat felt she needed to visit Dragon Isle, which was three chambers to the south, in the chamber of the Great Water. When they arrived at this chamber, everyone was awe-struck to find such a great body of salt water this far below the surface. Of course, it was impossible to see Dragon Isle from where they were, at the water's edge just inside the northern tunnel entrance. In fact, Dragon Isle was another twenty miles, over the water, to the south. The three great bridges that connected the Island to the tunnels and the other chambers were now permanently raised. However, last year when we passed this way, they had all been lowered beneath the water for well over a thousand years. This was because of the mistrust and loathing the dragons had for mankind. In fact, if it hadn't been for Dad's bold move in confronting Prince Draco right here at the northern entrance, the great wedge between man and dragon might still be in place.

"Is this the chamber where the big sharks live?" Lucy asked from where she sat with the other pups around the table. She was referring to one of the stories she remembered about last year's expedition through this chamber.

"Yes it is," Pat confirmed. "They are called megladons, and are very big, prehistoric sharks that some believe are akin to the modern-day great-white."

"How big are they?" Junior and Rufus asked simultaneously.

"Well, no one knows for sure exactly how big they get, but from what I've read, I'd say somewhere between forty and seventy feet." Pat replied.

"Will we be able to see one?" Molly asked.

"Why don't you guy's keep a sharp eye out as we go over the bridge, and let us know if you see a giant dorsal-fin in the water," Peggy told them, feeling a little uneasy about such a huge fish.

While here at Dragon Isle, Pat wanted to visit the parents of the new recruits at the academy, and thank them again for their participation in the unification of the underworld. As they drove into the central plaza of Dragon Town, the M-I units were welcomed with open wings and many fireballs. Even though they had to wear special mask, with re-breather-filters because of the sulfuric gases from an old volcano, everyone found this place fascinating.

A great celebration was held in Queen Patamaya's honor, where she healed and restored many old dragons to a healthy, younger condition, until late into the night. It was here last year, Pat used her special powers to restore King Drac, from a dragon on deaths door, with many battle scars, missing scales, and holes in his wings, to the more youthful vibrant ruler he is today.

"Dragons, living on a sulfuric island in the middle of a great sea, filled with mega-sharks, in an enormous subterranean cavern. Who would have thought it possible? Well one thing for sure, this beats the hell out of being sheriff of Flathead County Montana," Peggy mused to herself before finally falling asleep for the night.

The next morning everyone said goodbye to their new friends and were once again on their way. The next chamber to the south marked the start of a three chamber system that would continue down the continent to southern Chile and Argentina before going back to a two chambered system far below Patagonia. It was here, at the central intersection, they turned east. Pat wanted to go back to Akakor this way because she'd never seen any of the eastern chambers, and thought a true Queen should be acquainted with all her realm.

As the M-I units entered the massive eastern chamber system, they found a world resembling the jungles surrounding the Amazon River. In fact, at first, they thought they had driven out of the underworld altogether. However, their new GPS, which was specially made for the underworld, put their position at over four thousand feet below the surface, in chamber 15- 7465.

"These chambers never fail to amaze me," Matt said to Anthony from the copilot's seat in M-I-3.

"Yeah, I know what you mean. Each one is as different as night and day."

"Take that one where the dragons live. They say there are megalodon sharks living in the sea around the island," Matt said shaking his head. "However, that's hard to believe, because they've been extinct for thousands of years. But then, if you consider all the other ancient flora and fauna we've seen down here....?"

Lynn and Karen were listening in on their husband's conversation from where they sat at the table. Lynn spoke up, "I here there are chambers of all kinds down here, from hot deserts to a tropical rainforest and everything in between, with every kind of animal and bird that has lived on Earth since the Ice Age, and a few that existed long before that, such as those terror-birds and saber-toothed cats we saw at the beginning of this trip."

"When we were talking to Pat and Kim the other day, they said there were even pterodactyls, you know, flying dinosaurs, still living in a chamber just below Guatemala, if you can believe that," Karen informed.

Just then Anthony brought them to a stop behind M-I-2. "What's going on Pat?" he asked over the radio.

"I just thought this would be a good place to make camp for the night," Pat responded. "Bring your unit in behind ours, to the south, so they form an L shape."

Once Anthony pulled into place they could see why Pat had chosen this spot as a camp site. It was beautiful. Fifty yards from the M-I's was a pristine lake of about, 225 yards across, surrounded on three sides by 300 foot rock cliffs. With a beautiful waterfall poured from the cliff wall on the far southern side. There were also many varieties of tropical plant life including, banana, mango, and coconut trees, along with ferns, shrubs, and flowers of all kinds.

"This has to be the Garden of Eden," Peggy said, as she stepped from M-I-2 onto the sandy soil.

"Ms. Pat, can we go swimming?" Rufus asked as he and the other pups jumped from the unit.

"Maybe you guy's better wait until we've had a chance to check things out," Pat said, smiling at their eagerness. "You never know about these places. Last year we camped at a lake where there were forty foot crocodiles."

"Yeah, I remember Grandpa Nathan telling General Joe about them last Christmas," Junior woofed as he sat down atop a nearby boulder.

"What did you do?" Molly asked, as she looked in the direction of the lake.

"Well, after my dad, Dusty, shot one that was about to have him for lunch, they soon left us alone. But then, we didn't go swimming in the water either."

Peggy laughed, as she watched Pat carry on a conversation with the pups as if they were human. Then she realized, ever since she'd come to the underworld, she too could understand everything the pups were saying. It was about then, Anthony and Matt started toward the lake with pistol belts strapped on. "Hey guys, wait up. I'll go with you," she yelled as she went back in M-I-2 for a shotgun she'd seen mounted in the closet.

After a quick check of the lake and the surrounding area, the trio found nothing to be overly concerned about, or so they thought. Junior and Rufus had even tagged along, giving canine support to the small scouting party. They figured they could help flush any unwelcome critter out into the open, but was disappointed when they found absolutely nothing. After following a narrow, flower lined trail up to and across the waterfall, and then back down the other side and around to where they started. Nothing that is, except a strange looking depression in the ground that looked kind-of-like a small irrigation ditch.

However, when they returned to the M-I units where Dawn, and the other women had set up the camp tables and started dinner on one of the pullout barbeques, something occurred to Anthony just before they were going to report everything A-Okay. "Did you guys see any animal signs at all?" He asked a little perplexed, trying hard to remember if he'd missed some tracks.

"No, come to think of it," Peggy replied. "I saw no tracks or droppings anywhere."

Matt looked at Peggy, then at Anthony, "I'm sorry, but am I missing something here?" He asked before sitting down at a table.

"What Uncle Anthony is trying to figure out is, why," Arista said, helping her dog Skipper down from one of the seats at the table so he could go play with the other pups.

Matt flushed with embarrassment that an eleven year old girl knew what Anthony was talking about and he didn't. "Is that a problem?" He asked, still not understanding the concern.

Just then, Pat sensed it before she could see the ominous threat slithering through the thick surrounding plant life near the lake. "Listen up everyone, I want you in the M-I units NOW, don't ask questions, just move," she ordered, with authority.

Everyone looked around with surprise at Pat's command. Then the dogs sensed the coming danger and barked a warning as everyone quickly moved to their units.

"Anthony, where are the kids?" Karen yelled.

"They were just here a minute ago," Matt replied, a little panicked.

"There they are," Lynn said, as she spotted them running back, as fast as they could, with Junior and Rufus hot on their heels. Paige, Willard, Megan, and Arista had been picking flowers over by the trail when the pups went to get them.

Soon everyone was back aboard their unit still wondering what was going on.

"What is it, Pat?" Dawn asked, as she carried Skipper in for Arista and closed the door.

"That," Pat and Peggy said, simultaneously pointing out the front windshield.

Dawn, Duchess, and the pups all quickly gathered around the windows to see a giant camulatz, or basilisk like creature slithering toward the campsite.

"These were the creatures the Zipacna used to fly around the underworld on, and terrorize the different tribes," Pat explained. "Basically, a huge serpent with wings and a birds beak, but this one must be three times the size of any we saw last year."

When the creature came closer, Pat told Anthony to go to tactical over the radio, as she flipped the switch on M-I-2's computer system. "I thought we had destroyed all of these creature's months ago, but I guess we must have missed one. And it looks like it has been getting fat on the local animal population."

The camulatz came even closer to the M-I's, but at this point neither unit could use their guns to bring it down. They could have used a rocket, but because the venom of this creature was so toxic, Pat was afraid it would poison the water if any of the monsters head landed in the lake. It was already bad enough that the two large fangs were leaving small pools of acidic venom wherever it slithered.

"Come on big guy," Matt said, ready to fire the forward guns. "Just a few more feet and it'll all be over."

Just then the 30.cal machine gun on M-I-2's starboard side, fired a short burst, as Peggy squeezed the trigger on the joy stick.

"You got it, Ms. Peggy," Rufus barked, as he watched from the galley window just above the table.

"But it's not dead," Molly yapped.

"Shoot it again," Junior woofed.

"I can't. It's off my targeting scope for that gun. Maybe Anthony and Matt can hit it now," Peggy said, as she watched the creature twist in every direction.

As if on cue, Matt fired the forward 50.cal's, on M-I-3, tearing huge holes throughout the creature's sixty foot length. "That'll teach you to butt in where you're not wanted," Matt said, as the camulatz fell dead on the far side of the camp site.

"Everyone, stay here while Peggy and I go make sure it's dead," Pat said, as she asked Anthony and Matt to meet them there, with their weapons.

After the men left, Lynn and Karen sat down up front, to back them up with the unit's weapons systems. "Mama, where are dad and Uncle Anthony going?" Willard asked.

"They're going to help Ms. Pat make sure that thing is dead."

When she returned, about a half hour later, Pat immediately sent an email to Dragon Isle, asking for an extraction team to come and haul off the huge beast. They would probably end up making a feast out of it back on Dragon Isle. Pat remembered, all too well, how the dragons devoured the camulatz we encountered last year. But first, they would have to purify this area with dragon fire, and search for possible eggs, which would take at least three hours.

Needless to say, everyone would have to stay close to the M-I's tonight but, could probably go for a swim in the morning, before breakfast, if everything checked out okay.

Chapter Thirty Seven

MOON BASE ALPHA
27 September

The party had been going now for over three hours, as many old friends reunited in a victory celebration over the Dark Demons. Officers of both fleets recalled old memories of their school days at the Galactic Star Academy on Sirius, the battles fought during the Great War and conquest of their most recent fight. However, Dad and our group felt a little out of place. We'd been told about being part of all that had happened over the past thirteen thousand years and even as far back as the Great War in the Canis system, but there were many gaps in our memories. Perhaps that's what happens when you live, die and are reborn through reincarnation, instead of being rejuvenated every thousand years or so in a stasis-capsule. Don't get me wrong, there were bits and pieces of memories we had of that time, but most were vague and so brief it made one wonder if it was ever real. For example, have you ever had a dream where you knew everyone like a brother or sister, but when you woke up you could not put a name to a single face? Or, you were in a place that you were very familiar with because you'd been there many times during your lifetime, but when you woke, you could no longer remember where it was, or when you were ever there?

For each ship in both fleets, tables had been set aside for their officers in a massive hanger, which had been turned into a very large ballroom. Dinner had been served on seven large tables in a buffet style. And, the food had been prepared and brought out by the moon bases android kitchen staff, which was among the best chefs in the galaxy.

The fleet tables had been arranged in two semicircles on either side of a large half moon area, with an aisle down the middle so people could pass between the two groups. A podium had been set up on the straight or flat-side of the half-moon, where speeches and commendations were given after dinner. Between the tables and the stage was a dance-floor where a band played all the favorite dance music of days gone by, after all the dishes had all been cleared.

The Intrepid's officers all sat at five large oval tables on the east side near the stage. Everyone wore their finest dress uniform, with all the medals, campaign ribbons, and rank insignias. Let me tell you, I felt like a clown in that white monkey suit, trimmed in red with Colonels eagles on the collars, and I could tell Max felt much the same way, as he kept looking at me and rolling his eyes with boredom. That is, until a beautiful Black Lab from the Defiant started looking in his direction.

"Nathan, are you having the same trouble I am trying to figuring out just where we fit in this group?" Steve asked.

"Yeah, ah, don't tell anyone, Steve, but I'm having a hell of a time making heads or tails of all this déjà vu stuff," Dad told him. "Sometimes I feel like I belong here and have gone to this kind of function, with these same people many times before, but most of the time it all feels like a wired dream. It's almost like being in two different worlds at the same time."

"That's only normal under the circumstances," Dohna said, from where she sat to Dad's left. "However, your memory will slowly come back as time goes by. Take for example, when you climbed in to the cockpit of your fighter, did you feel like it was for the first time, or did you feel like you'd done it before?"

"Well, at that point, instinct took over and I suddenly knew what to do."

"Yes, but you have never flown anything like that ship before in this lifetime. The instruments and gauges are all completely different from any Earth made craft. Yet you knew how to fly it without hesitation or indecision."

"As I told you once before, Nathan," Chogyal spoke up. "Embrace your past, because that's who you are. And, if you can learn to accept your visions, you will be able to control your future. This was what we were trying to teach all of you at Shambhala. And yes, you all belong here and yes, you and your team have all been part of this fleet for many eons."

"He always was a little skeptical," Gabriel said, as he approached our table from the podium with Admiral Michael. Everyone stood, and shook the Admirals hand before they passed on to the other tables of the First Fleets ships. And, as he shook their hand or paw, Gabriel acknowledged each of our family and friends with a little bit of personal knowledge only he and that person would know. When it became Dads turn to shake hands, Gabriel told him. "General, if time permits I would like for you and your team to visit me at Avalon before starting training exercises on your new ship. I think we can clear things up as far as your memory is concerned."

"I look forward to it, sir," Dad said, as he pumped the Admirals hand.

With that, Gabriel and Michael moved on to Dohna and Chogyal where the Admiral once again congratulated them and their crew on a job well done, before moving on to the next table.

The party lasted for another two hours before breaking up. After saying our goodbyes to Chogyal and Dohna and a few other friends, we returned to our quarters on the Intrepid to change into more comfortable uniforms. It was about then there was a knock at the door. Robbie and Robo wanted to wish us luck with our new command, but when Dad told them they would be coming with us, they were overjoyed, and promised to make sure all our gear was transferred to our new quarters on the new ship.

"Well, Colonel, what do you say we round up our people and go have a look at our new ship," Dad said, smiling.

"Sounds good to me, General," I replied, as we walked out the door. "Did Chogyal say who will command the Intrepid?"

"No. But my guess would be, one of the original captains would take the helm, depending on their stasis rotation."

We met the others of our team, about twenty five minutes later in a conference room just inside Number 5 Hanger where our new ship was getting her final up grades. It was here Commander Clakrin met us to discuss any personal touches we might want. And after everyone had voiced their ideas it was time to see this new star bird.

"Ladies, and gentlemen, I give you the Galactic Battle Cruiser, Dragon Fire," Clakrin said, as he pushed the button that turned on the rooms viewing screen.

"Oh, Wow," David and Angela said, with wide eyed wonder, at the same time.

"Look at the size of that puppy," Jay commented.

"It looks to be at least ten percent bigger than the Intrepid," Larry guessed. "Or maybe it's just the difference in shape."

The Dragon Fire was made much differently than the oval-shape of the older three cruisers in the fleet. This one had a shape similar to a massive dragon in a steep dive, with delta-shaped wings, and short tail, or at least that's what we all thought at first.

After everyone had a chance to look over the outside of the new ship, Clakrin suggested we sit back down and view the inside, via-hologram, since it wouldn't be possible to go aboard for at least another two weeks. By using a hologram, we could see the whole ship at once, such as the med-bay, flight decks, and the bridge, as well as individual quarters.

"This ship is armed with 280 newly designed laser cannons with a range of five thousand miles, and has 20 newly designed ion cannons with a range of over twenty thousand miles. It also carries 1,000 inferno missiles that can be fired from cruiser and fighter alike, and 25 starburst missiles that now have a range of over 200,000 miles. I might add here, these weapons have more than twice the range of the ones on the older ships." Clakrin pointed out the different features with a small laser pointer as the program began. "This ship only has six decks plus the bridge, compared to the eight decks and bridge of the older cruisers. And you're right, Mr. Carver, this ship is slightly bigger than the others, but she'll make warp-eight when my crew is done tweaking the wormhole generator and the new hyperspace-engines. The most the old cruisers can reach is warp-six. And the fighter complement for this ship is 200, compared to the 150 for the old cruisers. Of course, we'll have to replace the F-47's with the new F-48-B star fighters." On our return after the battle, Dad had suggested a few changes to the F-48-A to Commander Clakrin and he promised to see to the upgrades.

"And finally, the crew complement for the Dragon Fire would be 2,000 humans, up to 300 dogs and 400 androids. And there are even accommodations for up to ten dragons. However, because of ceiling heights they have limited access to certain parts of the ship. Because of their size, they would only be able to use D-deck, where they would be quartered and the flight deck which is E-deck."

On the hologram, we could now see the ship was built in a giant triangular-shape with rounded edges. From its prominent, almost pointed-nose, it measured 3,000 feet to the center of the aft section, of which the far ends of what might be considered wings, were rounded somewhat in a curl-shape, and measured 2,100 feet apart. And what we thought was the tail, of a large dragon, turned out to be the rear thruster array-modules.

The dragon image had been so expertly painted on; it looked as if the ship would belch a giant fireball at any moment.

"Even the scales look real," Max commented.

"Why a dragon, I wonder?" Angela finally asked.

"Well, Admiral Gabriel thought it appropriate, considering Nathan formed the first dragon squadron in history," Clakrin explained.

"I'll bet King Drac will be glad to see the dragon-kind is duly represented by the fleet," Dad commented as the thought came to him. "That reminds me. I told Pat we'd pay the underworld a visit for a week or two before we put this ship through her maneuvers. However, before we visit her we have a little detour to make. Ladies and gentlemen, we leave at 0700, so maybe we should get some shuteye."

Chapter Thirty Eight

ANTARCTIC UNDERWORLD
30 September

The two sub crews were now enjoying life with their new found friends in the Antarctic underworld, and were beginning to adapt to this new Utopian way of life. So when they learned the underworld Chieftains had decided they should be returned to the sea, they had mixed feelings.

Some, from the Tennessee, wanted to go home, get their families and then return. There were others who didn't want to leave at all, but there were none who wanted to totally abandon their new homes.

The crew from the Dhul Fiqar just wanted to stay here. Not necessarily because they accepted or believed in what they'd been told about how these alien beings started the human race. It was because there was nowhere on Earth where they could go without being hunted down and killed. Besides, they had no family to go back to, and for the first time in a long time there was no war, death, or suffering wrapped around them. Here people worked together for the common good of all. They were safe and would do anything to remain that way.

"Come on, Husam," Malik said. "Let's go talk to Diaprepes and the local council and ask for at least a hearing before Poseidon, or even better yet, this Gabriel character. He seems to be the one with the final say in all this."

"I don't know, Malik. I'm not sure they will listen to the likes of us."
"We'll never know if we don't try."

Ten minutes later Malik and his bridge crew sat with Diaprepes and the other city leaders in a conference room at the cities administration building.

"Well yes, in the short time you've been here, you have become a welcome addition to our community and we would like nothing more than for you to stay," Diaprepes told them. "Not everyone can come down here and adjust to this way of life as fast as the crew of the Dhul Fiqar has. And I told father as much, but father and the others on the High Council, have……"

Before he could finish, the communication computer in the center of the table activated and rose slowly to reveal Poseidon, Cleito, Atlas, and Ampheres.

"Mr. Malik, I guess you and your crew are wondering why we would send you back out to the surface world to die?" Cleito asked.

"That's why we're here your highness," Malik answered. "It seemed a little strange to me, that you would take us in, treat us like your own, and then send us back out to die."

"How do you feel about what you and your crew did to humanity?" Atlas asked. "Do you think you should go without punishment?"

Sweat began to bead up on Malik's brow as he searched for the right words. "Sir, we have no excuse for our actions," He finally said. "All of our lives we have been taught to believe the western powers were devils. After the United States and Great Britain invaded Iraq and Afghanistan, where many of our family and friends were killed, we felt it our duty to avenge those deaths and to punish all those Arab nations that no longer resist the oppression these countries impose. Yes, what we did was very wrong, but dying for this wrong would not solve anything either. There will always be others to take up where we left off, which will fuel the fires of hate and vengeance." Malik leaned forward in his chair and looked Poseidon in the eyes, "Please, I beg of you, Sire, to let us prove our worth."

Poseidon stroked his chin as he considered Malik's words. "I agree that letting you die at the hands of others would not solve anything. However, if we let you stay here, you and your crew will obey our laws at all times or you will be put to death on the spot."

"We don't have much choice, Sire. Your wish is our command," Malik replied.

"Are we going to be able to come back here again," Paula asked Azaes, as they walked over to the South Point station with the other members of the local council.

"Yeah, we were just beginning to get accustom to this place," Chief Cloverdale spoke up before Paula's question could be answered.

"Well, there is no one here who is looking forward to your departure," Azaes told them. "You're all very good people in my book. But, we have to obey the High Council, even though we sometimes disagree with their decisions. You must know how that is, being in your countries military, given orders and having to carry them out whether or not you agree with them. However, I will talk to father again and try to convince him to appeal to the council one last time."

Josh had been very quiet until now, trying to think of a way those who wanted to, could stay in this new found paradise. "The way I understand it, you are sending us back to the surface world because of our warlike tendencies. Your High Council is afraid we will bring the death and destruction on the surface down here where your people live in peace and harmony."

"Yes, that's what I was told, Captain," Azaes replied. "We have too much to lose if someone reverted back to their old ways and started the lies, deceptions, and hate that has left your world in the shape it is now. As your kind might say, we are already taking a hell of a chance by trying to save what people we can from your world. For many of those people it will take years before they fully accept our ways and adapt to this environment. But, to bring a strict military minded group down here, such as you, could spell disaster for all mankind."

Josh and Paula took pause at the wisdom of Azaes words. "I understand what you are saying," Paula said nodding her head. "And I understand why it would be so hard to trust us to keep the peace in such a place as this. Sooner or later somebody would want to take control or start a fight. That's just the way it's always been in our world."

"It's ironic in a way," Josh Said. "We say we believe in the teachings of a just loving God and yet almost everything we do is contradictory to those teachings." Josh thought for a moment then continued. "It has only been since we came here that I can see, or should I say, truly understood for the first time in my life, the meaning of our religious teachings. I now believe this is truly what God had in mind for all mankind."

"I only hope the rest of your kind will be able to learn those lessons before it's too late," Azaes told him.

After everyone said their final goodbyes, the crew of the Tennessee boarded the train and was once again on their way back to their boat. Most were down in the dumps, with the feeling of being deported for no good reasons.

"Sir," Ensign Brooks said, as he leaned over the back of Josh and Paula's seat. "Maybe you could address the crew as to what's going to happen after we leave here. They're getting a little uneasy and may do something they will regret if not calmed down."

"I guess I could say a few words," Josh said, as he rose from his seat at the head of the aisle. "Ladies and Gentlemen of the USS Tennessee, can I have your attention? I know most of you would like to stay here for the rest of your days. I too would like nothing more. But we are members of the United States Navy and are duty bound to obey the oath we all took when we joined her ranks. I know the recent unusual circumstances have put us in this pristine underworld, but it is now time for us to return to our world and resume our responsibilities. Hopefully, we will be able to return here after our duty is done and reunite with our new found friends. Are there any questions?"

A hand of a seaman went up midway down the car. "Sir, are we still out to kill the Dhul Fiqar and her crew?"

"We will obey our orders to the letter even if we now know that may not be the best course of action," Josh answered, but as soon as he did he wished he hadn't.

"Sir," another young seaman spoke up. "With the recent battle in space, do you think our orders have changed?

"I don't know son, but we'll find out when we get back out to the Weddell Sea, where we can contact headquarters."

A half hour later, the super bullet train pulled into the city of Atlantia where it was met by Atlas and a contingent of guards. "Captain, if you and your crew will follow us to the Grand Palace, father would like to speak with you before you leave.

When they arrived at the palace the crew was shown to an anteroom, adjacent to the very ornate throne room. "Captain Worthington, Lieutenant Jones," Poseidon said, as they were led in. "It's been our pleasure to have had you stay here at Atlantia. We are sorry to have to say goodbye at this time, but we are looking forward to seeing you and your crew again soon."

"Are you saying we are welcome to return?" Paula asked.

"I'm not sure, but I think the recent attack by the Dark Demons will once again usher in a need for the interactions between my kind and yours. We will soon need trained human personnel to serve, not only in our Galactic Fleet, but on and under the Earth as well," Cleito Replied.

"What do you mean once again?" Josh asked.

"Once upon a long time ago, our two cultures interacted with one another. Your kind served in every service we had at the time, in space, on the Earth, and here in the underworld. We were so much a part of one another's lives; there were even a lot of intermarriages between the humans and the creator races. However, when you think about it, we are you and you are us. It was the attack by the Black Lords so many eons ago that left so much death and destruction around the Earth, many of your kind slowly turned away from the creator races and the Principles of Light. Then, over many thousands of years your kind forgot about us altogether. In fact until recently, the only hint we ever existed was only found in the different, distorted mythologies, some ancient religious text open too many interpretations, and of course the many megalithic stone structures around the world."

"What are the genetic differences between our two cultures?" Paula asked.

"Well, of course there are genetic differences between the twelve tribes of the Canis planetary system, but the main difference between us and humans is a rogue gene from an ancient humanoid creature found here on Earth. We thought over time we would be able to develop a being that would be more adaptable to the surface. And even though we did reach our goal, we failed to see at the time the gene that would make your kind as dangerous and unpredictable as any wild beast in the jungle. In fact, a wild beast only kills for food or self-defense, but humans will kill their own kind indiscriminately and without reason."

"Can you not do something about this rogue gene?" Josh asked. "I mean, you guy's created us, is there no way you could put that gene to sleep or cause it to be inert."

"We thought over time the natural evolution of the human race and the teachings of the ancient ones would take care of the problem, but it still has a strong influence on the human race, even after 300,000 of your years," Cleito informed. "However, we have now developed a special serum to help you cope with the problem."

"What does this special serum do?" Paula asked.

"All it does, is speed up the evolutionary process," Poseidon told them. "What it does, is enhances the genes you got from us and depress the more primitive genes of your ancient humanoid ancestor. It will make you smarter, stronger, and give you certain ESP powers. Basically, it brings our two species closer together."

"It won't hurt you," Cleito promised. "In fact, with the rapid cell growth that helps to heal your body and slow the aging process, you should live for many years to come."

"This is why we have called you here to the palace before your departure," Poseidon said. "Our son, Azaes, and the South Point Council, speak very highly of you and your crew. So, with your permission of course, we are going to offer you a chance to help advance the human race, by injecting your crew with the serum." However, Poseidon failed to mention the short-term amnesia drug, which would also be given the crew.

Two hours later the crew awoke at their stations on the Tennessee. They had no memory of being on Atlantia, except for strange dream-like images that flashed across their minds periodically.

"All stations report in," Josh said, after he awoke on the floor near the external monitor.

As each department responded, Bob Bixby interrupted. "Sir, we have sonar contact at two thousand yards. It sounds like the rogue and she's headed back for open water in the Weddle Sea."

"Chief, ready tubes one and two. Lt. Jones, plot a firing solution. I want to kill this bastard as soon as we come out from under the ice shelf. Mr. Brooks, contact the Chattanooga and let her know the rogue is coming her way."

Ten minutes after Brooks sent the message to the Chattanooga. "Sir, it's the Chattanooga," Brooks said, "Captain Northfield is sending you a personal message on the communication computer."

When Josh stepped over to the computer he was a little baffled by the message.

"WELCOME BACK TENNESSEE, WE THOUGHT YOU WERE GOING TO STAY IN ATLANTIA FROM NOW ON. FRANK FOSTER AND I WILL BE WAITING FOR THE ROGUE WHEN SHE COMES OUT FROM UNDER THE ICE, SEE YOU IN A FEW OLD BUDDY. Signed: Captain William Northfield, USS Chattanooga.

"What in the hell is going on here?" Josh asked, as Paula pointed to the day/date readout on an instrument panel. "We've been unconscious for over a week. And where's this place called Atlantia?" Josh quickly turned back to the computer and typed a return message. "WHAT'S GOING ON BILL? WHAT OR WHERE IS ATLANTIA? AND HOW LONG HAS FRANK FOSTER AND THE PORTLAND BEEN HERE?

A new message soon appeared on the computer. WE'LL TALK SOON.

Suddenly Josh knew they had to take the rogue without sinking it. So he gave the order to secure from general quarters. He needed some answers, and that was the only way he was going to get them. "Mr. Brooks, tell the Chattanooga not to kill the rogue, I repeat DO NOT KILL" Josh ordered. "At least not until we get to the bottom of this mystery."

When they reached the surface, just over an hour later, the Chattanooga and Portland already had lines attached to the Dhul Fiqar. "When she came out from under the ice shelf she just surfaced with her engines at all stop," Captain Foster explained, in the wardroom of the Portland.

Bill Northfield commented. "Our boarding party found absolutely no one below decks."

"Do you think it could have been operated remotely?" Paula asked. "And if so, what happen to the crew?"

"Well, if you had asked me that question a few days ago, I would have said there was no way this could happen," Bill finally said, shaking his head. "But, with what I've seen in the last few days I'd have to say anything is possible. And as far as the crew is concerned, it would be my guess they never left Atlantia. Which brings me to the question, why keep them and not you?"

"You say you talked to Paula and me the other night via computer and we were in this place called Atlantia," Josh said, with a note of skepticism.

"And just where were you two when you talked to us?" Paula asked. "I mean we don't have visual two/way computers on these boats."

Bill and Frank looked at each other with a question mark on their faces. They then tried to explain the events of the last few days, the battle in space, the shootout over the ice, and their visit to the big battle cruiser in space. The telling went on for over an hour, with plenty of coffee and sandwiches in between.

"We are to report to Atlantic Naval Command as soon as we can get there, for debriefing, and tell them exactly what we have just told you," Frank Foster informed.

"Wait a minute," Josh said. "Didn't you just say the whole world saw the battle in space on TV?"

"Yes, but my guess is, it's because we were the only ones who went aboard one of those big space ships," Bill said. "And you were the only ones who visited Atlantia."

Chapter Thirty Nine

WHITE HOUSE BUNKER
1 October

At the morning meeting, in the situation room of the subterranean White House, the President laid out his recovery plan. This new plan called for the military to work closely with the creator race in the cleanup of all the fallen ships. That is if it would be agreeable to Admiral Gabriel.

It was at this time, June Vanderbilt, reminded him there was still radioactive snow falling on the surface. And, it would probably continue to do so for some time to come.

"Mr. President, I don't think we'll have to worry about a recovery plan for the next twenty to forty years," June explained. "Even then there could very well be a mountain of ice a mile high, stretching across the northern half of the country. If you drew a line from northern Virginia across the country to northern California, and then north to the North Pole it might give you some idea how vast this situation could get before it stops. But at the same time, we could get lucky and be able to return to the surface in as little as ten years. It's just impossible to know at this point in time how long we'll be stuck down here."

"I guess what I'm trying to say, June, is that when we are once again able to return to the surface, I want a workable plan to be in place. A plan, that will help us determine what needs to be done as far as getting our major cities up and running as quickly as possible. A plan, that will provide aid and comfort to any possible survivors and at the same time destroy any mutants that may be a threat to our survival."

"Sir," Miles Standish spoke up. "I think we can count on the creator race for help with the cleanup. With their higher technology it will make things go a lot faster."

"That would be outstanding, Miles," the President agreed. "But how do we contact them when we need them. Do any of the Joint Chiefs have any suggestions as to how this could be done?"

After a long minute without any response from the others, except for shrugs and head shakes, Admiral Parks spoke up, "Sir, not to change the subject, but I have recalled our three subs from Antarctica. They should be here within a week. At that time, I'm hoping we'll know more about this alien technology after their crews have been debriefed."

"Three subs," Marcus said confused. "I thought you told me one of those boats had disappeared."

"Yes Sir. It seems the Tennessee suddenly reappeared on September 30th. Apparently out of nowhere. And the crew has no memory of being captured by aliens or disappearing for over a week." Parks paused for a moment before continuing. "The rogue also emerged from under the Ronne Ice Shelf at the same time. However, its crew has completely disappeared. We believe that crew is still being held by the aliens for reasons unknown."

"Sir," General Wells said, "This is exactly what we've been talking about when we say these aliens are a threat to our way of life. They are now harboring our enemies and by doing so, threatening all life on Earth."

"Or, could they just be making sure our enemies are in a place where they can't do any more harm to mankind?" The Vice President asked rhetorically. "I mean, they did send out the rogue sub for us to find. So in effect, they have completely disarmed the crew, and I would imagine they are holding them in a place where they can keep an eye on them." Katherine said and then paused. "That is, of course, if they have not already been executed."

"That's a good point, Katherine," Marcus commented. "I think one of the lessons the creator race is trying to teach us, is that killing something or someone is very seldom the answer to our problems. Take, for example, how many innocent people were executed before we started using DNA evidence. I think you'll find the number is just about fifty/fifty. And in many cases there are extenuating circumstances, such as long term abuse, or when a person is misidentified by a witness, and in cases where police have gotten a false confession through illegal interrogation methods." In this case, it was probably the illegal invasion of Iraq or Afghanistan, where thousands of innocent people have died. I know if a country attacked the United States and killed innocent civilians, every person in this room would want revenge, even if it meant using nuclear weapons."

"Well, now millions have died around the world," General Farmer spoke up. "Don't you think they should pay for the wrong they have done? Or should we just say all is forgiven and let those sons-a-bitches get off Scott free?"

"You know, Bill," the President said, "after the attack by the rogue I felt much the same as you, but those words Gabriel said to Dan the other day keep rolling over and over in my mind. "For the wrong you do, a greater wrong will be done unto you." And the wrongs have now been going back and forth for thousands of years. Where does it stop, Bill? When mankind has been completely wiped off the face of the Earth? Well, in case you haven't noticed, we can no longer live on the surface. So I'd say we're just about there."

"I'm sorry, Sir," Farmer said, as his face got red with anger. "But, I believe that sooner or later we are going to end up fighting a battle with these alien bastards, for the wrong they have done us."

"End up is right, General, if we ever dared to do battle with the creator race, I think the human experiment would be at an end very quickly" Mark Baker spoke up, nodding in sarcastic agreement.

"And what wrong would that be, General?" Miles Standish asked. "I mean, the military has known of the existence of these beings for many years now, even before Roswell. We have been trying to reverse engineer their space craft, weaponry, and other miscellaneous items with minimal success." Miles paused a second, waiting for a response. When none came, he continued. "The way I see it, these beings not only started the human race, they have helped us with every step of our development. It was not until we turned our backs on them after the last great battle with the Black Lords, did they let us walk on our own. And we've been making a mess of things ever since. And now, when we need all the help we can get to restart civilization, you want to go to war with them."

"If they were so helpful in man's development, why have they not shared their technology with humans?" Dan Wells asked. "It would seem to me, if they wanted us to become more like them, they would have given us the knowledge we need to get there a little faster."

The President looked around the table at the faces of those present to see if he was the only one who knew the answer to this question. "To put it very simply, Dan, it's the same reason you don't give a child matches to play with. A child has to learn to crawl before it can walk and walk before it can run. Besides, man's history is not exactly filled with peace, love, or forgiveness, but full of violence, death and destruction."

"Did we not just see a battle in space of two alien races killing each other?" Jeff Davis asked. "If we have a violent nature, it may be that we inherited it from our creators."

"I don't think that's the case here at all," Katherine West said, shaking her head. "It's one thing to go out and start a fight with someone in order to conquer or destroy that persons will to resist, making them a slave to the will of a would-be ruler. But, it is quite another to defend your family and friends from the would-be conqueror and the death and destruction he brings."

Jeff thought about her words a moment before responding. "Yes, I see your point, Madam Vice President, and I will concede that you are right. But, if not from the creator aliens, where does man get his urge to destroy or conquer all he comes in contact with."

"I wonder if it's not from our most ancient ancestors." Mavis Henley suddenly spoke up. "Maybe we have a rogue gene in our DNA that makes us fear everything we don't understand, and an overwhelming need to conquer it before we're conquered by it. If you think about it, at the time the aliens were supposed to have mixed the genes together, about 270,000 years ago creating the human race, it was a very violent, unpredictable world, fraught with danger."

"Or could it be the influence the Black Lords has had on mankind over the many millennia since the battle over Earth thirteen thousand years ago," Mark Baker interjected.

"Probably a combination of both," Marcus said just as another thought came to him. "But, now that you mentioned it, I do remember reading something in Masterson's report about mankind interacting with the alien race for many thousands of years before that battle. According to him, after an asteroid wiped out the continent of Lemuria, the two races became so close that man served side-by-side with the Lords of Light in every aspect of the rebuilding process. It seems there were even many cases of intermarriage between the two races. During that time mankind even served as part of the space fleet on the big battle cruisers. However, after the last battle with the Black Lords, the Earth sustained so much damage that the rebuilding process would take many eons. For most of those caught on the surface of the planet, it meant instant death or mutating into a different species altogether. This was due to massive flooding and high amounts of radiation in the air. For what few survivors there were, it meant a Stone Age like existence for many millennia. It was during this time the survivors of the dark demonic forces planted the seeds of hate, dissention, and greed into the minds of men, which turned many away from the Principals of Light."

The discussion went on for another forty five minutes before ending for the day, but not before the theme of working together to rebuild the nation was reiterated. However, the question became by which means that goal could be achieved.

Chapter Forty

HIMALAYAN UNDERWORLD
2 October

After leaving Moon Base Alpha, we returned to Shambhala with Chogyal, Dohna, and the rest of their personnel, in a borrowed shuttle craft from the moon bases shuttle-pool. Once there, we ended up staying for a week to complete what little enlightenment training we needed to finish our courses. It turned out that by doing so, we learned how to better manage our déjà vu episodes. For the most part we could now access those distant memories when we wanted, and not be surprised by suddenly reliving something out of the distant past. Chogyal told us that when we visited Gabriel at Avalon, everything would become even clearer.

Just before we left this wonderful paradise, the King asked us all to the palace where we found Chogyal, Dohna, and all the Masters dressed in their finest robes, in the great hall. They were all floating just above the floor in front of the throne dais. At this point, I wondered if we would ever learn to levitate like that. I mean, we could manage a few inches for a very few minutes, but nothing like that. Well, I guess that's why they were called the "enlightened masters". I don't know, but maybe they were doing this to show us what we could become if we continued to follow the meditation exercises we'd learned.

Ten feet in front of the Masters, we all lined up side-by-side for the short ceremony they had planned.

"We, the Masters of Shambhala just wanted to give you all something to remember us by, and welcome you to attend the annual alumni gala for Shambhala graduates," Master Jangbu said, before he approached us with Master Amrita, never touching the floor with their feet.

They stopped in front of Captain Yang, who was on the far left side of the line, and awarded him with a gold amulet and a small scroll tied with a blue ribbon. "May these words give you strength and wisdom throughout your long life," Jangbu said, as he handed Yang his Scroll of Light.

"And may this charm keep you safe from harm and evil," Amrita said, as she slipped the Talisman of Life around his neck and gave him a big hug.

After the same procedure was repeated for all eleven of us, the other Masters came down and said their personal goodbyes. At that point, we were almost sorry to be leaving this place of so many wonderful people and delightful wonders. However, at the same time, we were excited to know we would soon be with our family and friends again in the Andean underworld.

"You will have to come and fly with us on the Dragon Fire," Dad told Chogyal and Dohna.

"Just tell us when," Dohna said, as she gave Dad and I a hug.

Then Chogyal and Dohna returned to the throne with the Masters, and addressed all of us one last time. "For the past few weeks my daughter and I have flown to Mars and back with the finest crew we could ever hope to know. May the Great Creator bless all of you with a long and happy life, and always be your guide down the path of enlightenment," Chogyal said.

"And may you all find peace in your soul and happiness in your heart forever and always. You will always be welcome here, so be sure to come visit us often," Dohna said, as the Masters pyramided their hands and bowed slight

About an hour later we finally departed Shambhala and there were tears welling up in the eyes of our humans, as they were touched by the friendships they had made and would surely miss. As we flew fast and low toward the Pacific Ocean, no one spoke a word for the longest time.

We were in one of the new streamlined, chrome-colored, shuttleships that had the shape of a spear-point bullet fuselage, with delta-shaped wings and slanted stabilizer tail fins. Dad picked it because many of the instrument-functions were similar to the big battle cruisers and he wanted us to be ready for any situation when we took command of the Dragon Fire. This ship was about a hundred ten feet long, with three forward laser-canons on each wing, and two in the rear. It could carry up to twenty five people comfortably, and easily reach speeds of 16,000 mph in space, but only half that in Earth's atmosphere.

Before we'd left Moon Base Alpha, Dad said he wanted every officer to learn the operation of every position on the bridge, including command. This was because anything can happen in battle, and if any of our crew were unable to do their job, someone else could cover that position, instantly. Captain Perry was acting as our navigator since he and Captain Carver had done such a good job on the Intrepid. Captain Yang was filling in at weapons. First Lieutenants David and Angela Masterson were taking turns at the helm, while Captain Clayhorn taught Captain Carver the communications console, and Larry in turn, briefed Ron on the highly advanced version of alien long range radar. Of course, Colonels Steve and Jane Franklin, along with Captain Max, sat at the command center with Dad and I.

Dad also explained he was not real high on military protocol, so there was no need to address each other by rank unless we were in the formal company of Fleet Flag Officers. However, he did expect everyone to wear the proper uniform with rank insignia while on duty, because you never knew when an Admiral would hail us. And there were plenty of them to go around now that all the older Captains and Commanders had been promoted by Gabriel at the victory ceremony on Moon Base Alpha.

After a long time of quiet, Yang picked up another ship on his instruments and we started to sit up and take notice. The other ship was definitely shadowing us, staying just out of weapons range and refusing to answer our hails.

"What is our position, Jay?" Dad asked.

"We are three hundred miles southeast of Japan," Jay replied.

"The Dragons Triangle," Steve commented.

"Isn't that one of the two areas where Ixchel said the Black Lords still had small strongholds?" Jane asked, remembering our visit to the Mountain of the Gods last year in Guatemala. It was there, the android version of the Mayan jaguar Queen, Ixchel, who was in charge of the structure, showed us all the locations of the underworld cities around the world. She also informed us of our mission to the Andean underworld.

"Ron, can you bring that ship up on screen?" I barked.

Suddenly the craft appeared on the main monitor. It was disk-shaped, about a hundred yards in diameter and traveling at the same speed we were, 4,000 mph. It also seemed to be emitting a bright yellow light that pulsated like a strobe, which made the craft look ominous as it zigzagged across the night sky.

"Mr. Yang, show us all known designs of enemy ships," Dad ordered.

At that point the viewing screen split, showing the craft on one side and at least ten different types of ships on the other. From their large ancient battle cruisers they used to attack Earth in the past, to their newest medium-sized corsairs, but nothing matched the ship we saw on the other side of the screen.

"I think that's the type of UFO reported in many alien abduction cases," David spoke up. "It's also one of the types reported by many airline pilots, both military and commercial."

"Yeah, at the FBI we had a lot of those abduction cases reported, but until just recently we chalked it up to an over active imagination," Angela commented, thinking back to how crazy she had always thought those people were. "Now, I wish I had taken this phenomenon a little more seriously."

"Take us up to sixty thousand feet and increase our speed to 8,000 mph, David," Dad ordered. "Let's see if he stays with us now."

After we had reached the new altitude and speed, Ron reported the craft had mimicked the change and was still shadowing us.

"Mr. Carver, send a message to Avalon," Dad said. "Ask Gabriel whose ship this is and why it's following us. Include pictures."

"Nathan, were coming up on the radiation belt," Jay informed.

The radiation belt or Red-Zone as it was sometimes called was a thousand mile swath of extra-hot radioactive fallout that now circled the Earth.

"Raise shields and take us up and over it, David," I woofed.

Soon, we were in space looking down on the strange glow, which seemed to mimic the Northern Lights.

"Nathan, at this speed and altitude we will be over Lake Titicaca in less than an hour," Jay informed.

Dad sat strangely quiet at the command console studying the other craft, which had followed us over the radiation belt.

"Nathan, Admiral Gabriel is hailing us from Avalon," Larry informed.

"Put him on screen."

"General Masterson and officers of the Dragon Fire, congratulations to you all on completing your enlightenment courses at Shambhala," Gabriel said, as he appeared on screen. Chogyal told me the Masters were very impressed with how well each of you did on your final exams. Your scores were some of the highest ever recorded there."

"Thank you, sir, we learned many things while under the tutelage of the great masters." Dad told him. "And, we're looking forward to visiting with you at Avalon in a few weeks, where Chogyal said we will learn even more. However for now, we seemed to have an unidentified craft following us and we thought you might be able to help."

"Yes, well it looks like a Zeta-Reticuli ship of the race we, as well as humans, call Grays. No one seems to know for sure what their home planet is called, or even the true name of their race. We do know, however, they have been visiting the Earth for the last ten thousand years or so, and seem to always head off in the direction of Zeta-Reticuli when they are confronted."

"Are they, or have they ever been aggressive?" I asked. "I mean, do we treat them as a threat, or just ignore them and hope they go away?"

"Even though they follow Earth based aircraft once in a while, I've never known them to interfere with our ships before," Gabriel said, a little perplexed at their intentions. "The worst they have done is harvest the ova and sperm of humans and a few animal species, but except for scaring a lot of people half to death, they've never really hurt anyone as far as I know."

"Has anyone ever tried to communicate with them?" Jane asked.

"Yes, on many occasions we have confronted them, but as soon as we do, they just disappear. It's almost like they open a doorway to another dimension or parallel universe. By the time we respond and give chase, the doorway is already closed."

"Well, they've been following us ever since we crossed over the Dragons Triangle, off the coast of Japan," Steve commented. "And we thought that area was a demon stronghold, or that's what we've been told."

"Yes, we thought that for many years because it was one of the last two places on Earth the Black Lords had been found. And, since we only found a few of them we feared they'd been able to build a planetary transporter device, more commonly known as a Planet-Portal. The electromagnetic energy required to operate one of those units would certainly explain the boiling seas and electronic-fog, reported to have taken so many ships and planes." Gabriel thought for a minute. "I guess there is also a possibility they may have constructed a Space-Time-Transporter, which would also require massive amounts of energy. This last possibility worries us the most because it would mean they could travel back and forth through time and space, or even through other parallel dimensions."

"Could the Demon Lords, or even another alien race, have built this time machine and gotten trapped in a parallel universe controlled by these Grays?" Max barked.

"Yes, that's a very real possibility, Max," Gabriel agreed. "And if the other world is in chaos or their population is in decline, for whatever reason, it would explain why they are collecting so many reproductive samples."

Just then, Jay informed us we were coming up on our destination. The last thing we want to do was lead that ship to the entrance of the Andean underworld, Dad thought, as he bid Gabriel goodbye after thanking him for his help.

"Mr. Yang, go to tactical alert and arm all weapons," Dad ordered. Angela had moved over to the helm, for what she thought would be standard landing procedure, but now found herself in a possible combat situation. "Angela, you are going to learn a figure eight vector roll maneuver, ending up about ten miles behind our shadow."

"I'm going to WHAT?" Angela asked, unsure of what to do next.

"Just follow my instructions to the letter and you'll do fine," Dad told her. "First, speed us up to three-quarter power." The ship suddenly shot forward to 10,000 mph as Angela pushed the throttle forward. "Everyone, buckle up, this is going to get a little crazy," Dad warned. "Ron, put the other ship on a split screen that also shows our relationship to it in speed and distance."

"This is not a fighter, Dad," David reminded. "Do you think she'll be able to handle the G-forces of such a maneuver?"

"We'll be fine, son," Dad replied as we watched the other ship match our speed. At that point, he ordered Angela to turn us over on our starboard side and bring us around in a twisting roll in the shape of an 8.

As the scene unfolded on the screen, Angela now understood how the maneuver worked and reacted even before Dad could give her direction. First, she turned us on our right side, and then our left, as we came into the curves, and at one point we were completely inverted.

Then Dad ordered her to cut speed in half and turn us upright again. As the ship slowed, we found ourselves directly behind the other craft. We had caught them completely off guard, but not for long.

"Mr. Yang, target their port engine and fire," Dad ordered.

As our cannons fired, the ship made an evasive maneuver and disappeared at high speed. It was there one second, and then in a blink of an eye, nothing but a pinpoint of light heading off in the direction of Zeta-Reticuli.

"Well, I hope they didn't go away mad," Max woofed.

"Angela, you did an excellent job," Dad complemented. "Now maybe you can land this puppy, so we can visit our family and friends in the Andean underworld."

"It would be my pleasure, General," Angela said with a smile, as she looked over at David and winked.

Chapter Forty One

ANDEAN UNDERWORLD
6 October

After descending into the false volcano on the Island of the Sun, in the middle of Lake Titicaca, Angela brought us to rest on the landing-pad like she'd been doing it all her life.

There to meet us, was Pat, and the First Dragon Squadron. They looked very impressive as we exited the ship, all lined up as if to be reviewed, coming to attention as Dad and I appeared at the door.

After the rest had left the ship, Dad and I stood at the top of the ramp for a moment admiring, what was once a spur of the moment idea to defeat an evil demon. And now that idea had evolved into an elite fighting squadron. I raised my paw as Dad and I saluted before descending the ramp and walking down the line. As each human saluted and each dragon bowed low, Dad had words of praise for each one. Especially for Ragnon, because it was he that Dad had chosen last year to be his squadron mate. Then Dad stepped back and addressed the Squadron as a whole.

"I want you all to know how proud I am of you. You are the finest Dragon Squadron I've ever had the privilege to fly with. And I look forward to flying with you again before I have to leave."

"Well, I'm glad you feel that way," Pat spoke up as she handed Dad a new suit of armor and Arlie handed him his old gun-belt with its

M-I-45 and shotgun. "Dusty and his team, along with Joe Carter, are in trouble in a distant chamber to the south of here," she informed him.

"We were just on our way to find out what happen to them when we got your message about landing," Fred said, taking all the pomp and circumstance out of the moment. "So we decided to stop by and see if you wanted to go with."

Just then the two M-I units pulled up and parked just off the other side of the road, and everyone came running with open arms as soon as they hit the ground. For about fifteen minutes there was a lot of hugging, licking, barks and shouts of joy, while Dad got changed. Then, as the squadron took flight, the rest of us followed in the M-I-units.

"Can you tell me what kind of trouble they're in?" Dad asked over his helmet radio, as he and Ragnon came up beside Pat and Draco.

"We don't know for sure. My dad sent a message saying they were experiencing an earthquake on the 26th of September, but he said there was nothing to worry about, they had everything under control," Pat answered with concern in her voice. "Then yesterday, when we got back from vacation, there was a garbled message at council headquarters saying to send help. At least that's what the first two words were. We couldn't make out the rest."

The Squadron stopped briefly at Amaru Meru, after ten hours nonstop flight, and spoke with Captain Bitol, Paragon, and the city Elders. They informed them, there had indeed been severe earthquakes throughout the region, there was much damage reported in many chambers, and the death toll was mounting rapidly.

"We have sent repeated emergency messages to Akakor that have all gone unanswered," Nacon explained, a little frustrated at the lack of medical aid.

"The earthquakes must have knocked out a computer relay somewhere along the line," Pat said.

"If I can use one of your computers I'll send a message to our people coming in the M-I units and they will pass it on to Akakor. We have a medical team coming in M-I-2, Colonels Steve and Jane Franklin. They will stay here and help until another team can get here," Dad said .

"Thank you, General Masterson," Ajbit said.

"Have you heard from Dusty or his crew since they left?" Pat asked.

"Not since they were here checking into the problem we were having with the trouble- making newcomers. From what we understood they were headed to the Chamber of Exile at the High Councils request."

After they had the directions to the chamber in question, the squadron was once again airborne. Before they left they used the cities computers to send us the directions, because we were still many chambers behind of them. Steve and Jane and Max would stay at Amaru Meru while the rest of us continue on to Chamber 48-5390.

On the twenty seventh of September, Dusty and his team had just made it through the tunnel when a massive earthquake hit. The Chamber of Exile shook so violently a large fissure opened up around the edges of the entire cavern making it impossible to go back through the tunnels. Hot liquid magma could be seen flowing four hundred feet below at the bottom of the fissure, as sulfuric gases filled the air. Even though the ventilation system kicked on full blast, trying hard to filter out the bad air and replace it with good, it was still hard for the humans to breath. This type of environment was normal for Hagnar and Ragtar; dragons thrived on this type of air. Some believe it was what gave them the ability to breathe fire. However, the humans and animals of this chamber were now running in all directions trying to escape the carnage when Dusty pulled M-I-1 to a stop in front of the cliff dwellings on the south side. Just then the quake stopped as suddenly as it had started.

After the human part of the team donned the special helmets with built-in air-scrubbing filters, which allowed the wearer to re-breathe the same air for over an hour without changing the filter, they went to help the people of this chamber. Many had been hurt or killed from falling debris, such as rocks or trees, but there had been a few who had been boiled alive in the superheated water of the rivers. By the time all the aftershocks had come and gone, spanning a period of five days, twenty people out of the forty eight exiled here, had died. Many more would have perished if it hadn't been for Dusty's team, and the few people left from the original tribe, which were believed to have been killed off by the Zipacna raiders. There were only about forty of them left, and over the eons they had learned how to survive these periodical upheavals.

This tribe was known as the Hamawthan people, originally made up of many different tribes from the high Andes. They had joined together and followed Wiraqochha, or Holy Man, across the mountains several hundred years ago. They must have been like the multitudes that followed Jesus across the Holy Land, listening and learning from his teachings. Then, about five hundred years ago a small group of these people came here to the underworld to escape the Spanish Conquistadors.

Most, look like the brown skinned natives of the Aymara or Incan peoples of the high Andes, and wore very colorful clothing much like most Andean people wear today.

When they'd found this chamber with its abundant animal life, fresh water, fish from three large rivers, and long abandoned habitable dwellings in the cliffs, they quickly claimed it as their own. However, over the centuries the path they'd used in their decent had long since been destroyed by earthquakes. This made it impossible to return to the surface. What they didn't know until many years after their return route had been permanently blocked was that this chamber had been built a little too close to a fault-line by the ancients and suffered severe periodical volcanism episodes.

Of course, when the ancients realized their mistake a few thousand years earlier, they had installed many upgraded safety features, such as larger air purifiers to the ventilation system, and a diorite and granite lava-duct, coated with a special heat resistant metal to control magma flows. But even with the upgrades this chamber was eventually deemed unsafe and abandoned long before the Hamawthan people arrived.

At the center of the chamber was a strange looking black rock they called Yurak Rumi, which was over forty feet in length and between fifteen and twenty feet at its highest point. It had been carved into a ceremonial structure for the Hamawthan spiritual center. According to their leader, a man named Yupanqui; there was another one of these rocks on the surface at Rupa-Rupa, in the high jungle region of southern Peru.

Yupanqui literally stood out amongst his people. Being at least six foot five inches tall he stood a full head above the rest. And even though he had dark hair and much the same facial features as the rest of his people, he had bright blue eyes like those from Sirius or Atlantia of the creator races.

It was to this spiritual-ceremonial center the injured were taken, after Yupanqui explained everyone would be safe there. Of course, Dusty and his team had their reservations but decided to give him the benefit of the doubt. And, after all had been gathered together around the giant rock, Yupanqui climbed onto the surface of Yurak Rumi, knelt in front of what looked to be an altar, and began to pray. And sure enough, within just a few minutes a force-field engulfed everyone within a protective shield. The air became fresh and fit to breathe again, and the wounds of the injured begin to heal very rapidly.

After five days, when the tremors finally subsided, the shield was suddenly gone one morning as everyone was waking up.

"It is safe to return to our homes now," Yupanqui stated to the people. "There will be no more earth-shakes for a long time to come."

This should have been good news, but most were so overcome with grief of their lost loved ones, it mattered little to them. Now they would spend the next five days finding and burying their dead.

Every day Dusty had sent messages back to Akakor alerting them of the emergency, but had no idea none were getting through. Today he would send Tomka and Ragtar for help. Until now, they were needed here to help with the recovery effort. But now that the air had pretty much returned to normal, and most of the heavy lifting of debris had been done, it was the only way they were going to get badly needed food and medical supplies.

Chapter Forty Two

CHAMBER OF EXILE
8 October

"How long will it take for them to return with help?" Yupanqui asked, as they watched Tomka and Ragtar fly off toward the eastern tunnel.

"At least a couple of days, maybe as long as a week" Dusty replied. "They are going to Amaru Meru first to see if they can get a message out from there. If they can't, they'll have to make the trip all the way back to Akakor."

"Let's just hope they don't run into any problems along the way," Joe spoke up.

"If they do, it will only be from what has already happened," Yupanqui assured. "The earth-shakes only come once every forty to fifty years or so, and most are not near as bad as this one. They should be over for now."

Naumy and Hagnar returned about then to report everything was returning to some sort of normality, even though there was still a lot of debris scattered throughout the chamber. Even the exiled rebels now seemed to accept their losses and were helping the others bring order to this chamber without complaint. For a rebellious group, they seemed to get along great with the Hamawthan's, who had welcomed the newcomers with open arms. In fact, Yupanqui and the other

Hamawthan's seemed to have a certain calming effect on just about everyone.

Dusty had noticed this, and wondered if Yupanqui had some kind of advanced ESP powers like Patricia did.

Suddenly the radio earpiece in Dusty's right ear crackled. "Hey, Dusty, guess who I ran into on the way for help?" Tomka asked.

"Surprise me," Dusty replied, not wanting to play games.

"I'm on my way back with First Squadron."

"Well, that didn't take long," Dusty said, "You and Ragtar must have broken some kind of speed record."

Just then, they flew out of the east tunnel. "Look" Naumy said, "All the dragons have riders," He said as he watched them circle near the ceiling of the chamber, trying to assess the damage.

"You know who that is riding Ragnon, don't you?" Hagnar asked.

Dusty and Joe just stood there with their mouth agape as they realized Dad was back. "Well you two had better get airborne and welcome the General back to the underworld." Dusty said with a wide smile.

"Yes, sir," Naumy replied, as he and Hagnar leapt into the air.

When the squadron finally did land, about fifteen minutes later, Joe and Dusty came to attention and gave Dad a salute. After he returned it, they just laughed for a minute before shaking hands.

"Congratulations on your promotion, Nathan," Joe said as he pumped Dad's hand.

"I didn't ask for it, Joe. In fact, I would have been just as happy to have stayed at home with the family and lived out the rest of my years in peace, but now they want to give me a battle cruiser of all things."

"And with your background, Nathan, you'll be the best damn cruiser commander the creator race has ever seen," Pat said, as she gave Dusty a peck on the cheek. "My father here didn't exactly want to be our goodwill ambassador at first, let alone hold a military rank of colonel, but now he wouldn't trade it for the world."

"I must admit this job can be very rewarding at times," Dusty agreed as he turned to introduce the squadron to Yupanqui. However, as Dusty turned to where Yupanqui had been just a minute ago, there was no sign of him. "He was just here. Did you see him leave, Joe?" Dusty asked a little puzzled at Yupanqui's disappearance.

"No. We were just talking to him as you guys were landing," Joe said, looking around.

"What is that strange glow coming from the treeless area near the center of the chamber?" Prince Draco questioned. "Does it have anything to do with the human you mentioned?"

"Well, that's their spiritual center," Dusty replied. "There's a huge rock there they call Yurak Rumi. It's shaped much like the altar stone at Maccu Picchu, except much bigger." He then turned around and saw the pulsating white glow, about a mile away from where they stood on a hill near the cliff dwellings.

"Now that's odd," Arlie said as he and Fred walked over with Sean to shake hands with Joe and Dusty.

"Where are the people of this chamber you said needed medical help, Dusty?" Sean asked. "We've been up to the dwellings and found no one home."

"I don't know," Dusty said, completely baffled at this new revelation. "They were just here. We've been trying to put this place back in order all week, burying the dead, tending the injured and moving debris. Tell them, Joe, before they think I'm crazy."

"We got here just as the earthquake struck," Naumy spoke up when he saw how much trouble Dusty was having. "The chamber was a mess with falling rocks, trees, and plenty of sulfuric gas. As we got to the dwellings, there," Naumy pointed to the cliff dwellings about 100 yards to the east, "the quake stopped and we immediately went to work helping out in any way we could. I think it was about that time Yupanqui and his people appeared and told us to take everyone to the spiritual center where they would be safe."

"Yeah, that's reminds me. I thought it odd at the time," Dusty said. "Because no one seemed to have seen from what direction they came from."

"That's right," Joe said, after thinking about it for a moment. "But we were all so busy it didn't occur to us at the time. We were just thankful for the extra help."

Just then Tomka walked up with Ragtar. "Sir, now that I think about it. It seems to me those people came from the direction of the altar stone. But with the air so foul with dust and gas, I just marked it up to hallucinations. However, Ragtar just told me he also saw them come from that direction."

"Maybe it's time we go down there and investigate these people and their strange stone," Fred suggested. "I mean, that's the only way we're going to find answers to this mystery."

As the squadron mounted up Dusty and Joe headed for the cliff dwellings to see for themselves, but they were indeed empty as Sean had said. There was absolutely no sign of either Hamawthan or the exiled people from Amaru Meru. Even their belongings had mysteriously disappeared.

"I guess we should get down to that rock," Joe suggested, as he looked inside another doorway and slowly shook his head.

Dusty pulled M-I-1 up as close as he could to where they had helped tend to the inhabitants of this chamber just a few days ago. As they walked up, First Squadron was trying to figure out where the Yurak Rumi had now disappeared to.

"I'm telling you, it was right there," Naumy said shaking his head in disbelief.

"I saw it," Hagnar confirmed, puffing out a cloud of black smoke.

"Ragtar and I also saw it," Tomka agreed. "This is where we brought the people to be treated for their wounds. This is where Yupanqui climbed up on the altar-stone. It was about forty feet long and fifteen to twenty high."

"And this is where that same altar-stone covered us for five days with a protective shield," Dusty said as he and Joe walked up.

"Well, there's nothing here now," Fred commented, as he walked over to the exact spot where the rock was supposed to have been. "Even the grass around this area seems undisturbed."

"Maybe they were ghosts," Arlie commented with a smile.

"Well, the exiles sure as hell were not ghosts," Dusty said getting a little frustrated with the situation.

"We believe you, dad," Pat told Dusty, trying to calm him down.

"Besides, I found the Hamawthan people a little strange," Joe said. "For one thing, except for that Yupanqui fellow, they never said a word to any of us. And, the music they played seemed to keep everyone calm, even during the worst of the aftershocks."

"Music," Dad and Pat said at the same time.

"Yeah, you know, like a Pan-flute," Dusty explained, remembering the constant tune.

It was at this point, a strong cold wind started blowing across the clearing where the altar-rock had been. The temperature must have dropped twenty degrees in five minutes and cooling things down to a chilly 45 degrees.

"Let's get out of here before this gets any worse," Pat suggested. "We can regroup in the chamber to the east and figure this out."

"Hagnar you and Ragtar will have to pick up M-I-1 and place it on the tunnel side of the fissure when we get to it" Dusty said, as he and Joe climbed on board the motor home.

As they started off, the wind seemed to grow stronger in intensity, much like a twister in tornado alley. It was now picking up the debris, which had been cleared over the past few days, and tossing it in every direction.

When Dusty and Joe got to the fissure across from the eastern tunnel, straps were wrapped around M-I-1 so Hagnar and Ragtar would have something to grab on to. The problem was they couldn't fly the unit directly into the tunnel without hitting the chamber wall above the opening, which was only four feet above the roof of the motor home. The extreme heat coming from the bottom of the rift, also posed a serious problem if any complications with the maneuver arose. Everything would have to be timed just right. After the straps were in place, Dusty backed the unit a hundred yards from the fissure.

"We'd better go now," Naumy suggested over his helmet radio, as another twister formed two hundred yards behind them.

At this point Dusty floored the accelerator, the wheels squealed as M-I-1 started forward at full speed. Within fifteen seconds the unit was ten feet from the fissure. "Get ready boys," Dusty yelled over his headset.

"We're ready," Tomka said, as Ragtar clamped onto the rear strap and leaped upward at the same time Naumy and Hagnar did on the forward one.

It took everything both dragons could do to lift the forty eight foot motor-home into the air. At first M-I-1 rose very slowly off the ground, but picked up speed as the strong wind from the twister got closer. The wind not only helped lift the unit, but propelled it forward as well. However, as they neared the other side, it looked at first like the unit was not high enough to put the front wheels on the tunnel road, but with a little extra effort Hagnar and Ragtar put her in place without a hitch. As soon as the front wheels touched down, Dusty engaged the all wheel drive which started the unit forward with ease. At that point Hagnar let go before hitting the chamber wall. He and Naumy went vertical, pushing off the chamber wall like a diver on the high board doing a back-flip. This maneuver brought them around to the tunnel entrance where they followed M-I-1 down the road. Tomka and Ragtar followed after the rear wheels hit the road, just in time to avoid getting sucked into the whirlwind.

The rest of first squadron had landed and were setting up camp in chamber 48-5390 where everyone would wait for the other two M-I units. Then they would decide what should be done about the Chamber of Exile.

"I think this Yurak Rumi, or alter stone as you call it, may be some sort of transporter device," Pat suggested, after everyone had gathered outside M-I-1.

"But where did they transport to, another chamber, a parallel universe, or possibly even another planet?" Dad questioned, and then proceeded to tell the others the story of the strange ship that had followed us across the Pacific.

Chapter Forty Three

ATLANTIC NAVAL COMMAND

Norfolk, Virginia
9 October

The three commanding officers, along with Lieutenant Jones of the subs involved in what would become known as Operation Iceberg, were now sitting in an underground conference room at Naval Headquarters in Norfolk, Virginia. It reminded one of a small interrogation room used at the local jail. The room, made of concrete and stone, was all white with two long tables in the center, side-by-side, and a two way mirror along one wall.

Paula Jones was the only XO invited to this meeting because, she'd been the only one to visit Atlantia. Each of the four submarine officers had already submitted a detailed report on the events from 16 September when the Tennessee and Chattanooga first entered the Weddell Sea, to 30 September when all three subs, including the USS Portland, were ordered home with the rogue boat in tow.

Reviewing these reports, were three of the navy's highest ranking officers, Admiral Randolph Parks, (the chief of Naval Operations and member of the Joint Chief's), Admiral Mathew Clyburn (head of Atlantic Naval Command), and Admiral Philip Barns (the head of Atlantic Submarine Operations). They had already debriefed the junior officers and men of all three boats over the past three days, but now it was the senior officers turn to answer questions. Of course, these proceedings were being recorded and a copy would be sent over to the underground White House bunker for the President's review.

"And you two say you have no memory of this place called Atlantia?" Admiral Parks asked Josh and Paula.

"Sir, as I stated in my report, the last memory I had before waking up on the Bridge of the Tennessee, a week after we pursued the rogue boat under the Ronne Ice Shelf, was that of an unidentified submerged object heading straight for our position," Josh reiterated. "At that point the boat suddenly lost all power and became dead in the water."

"What about you, Lieutenant Jones? Just what do you remember about this incident? Admiral Clyburn asked with a skeptical look on his face.

"Sir, I'm afraid my memory is no better than Captain Worthington's. Just as I stepped over to view the outside-camera-monitor, we lost power. When we wakened, all power had been restored. Thinking we'd only been out for a few minutes, my first thought was, what on earth could have rendered us so helpless, so fast? It was only when we noticed the time/date readout on the computer and realized a week had gone by since our initial power loss. Even then we thought there had to be something wrong with the instruments. However, when we were able to contact the Chattanooga, Captain Northfield confirmed the lapse in time, and told us about a place called Atlantia."

"Captain Northfield," Admiral Barns spoke up. "You say you and Captain Foster were taken aboard a space ship where you met a Major Masterson?"

"Sir, I know how it sounds, but yes we were there for about four hours. We met some pretty interesting people during that time, including a couple of talking dogs," Bill replied.

"Do you confirm this nonsense, Captain Foster?" Admiral Parks asked, shaking his head in disbelief.

"Well, sir, I wasn't going to mention them because I didn't want you to think I was "NUTS", but yes, there were two talking dogs named Duke and Max, as well as many androids that could pass for human, on that ship. It reminded me of something from an old "Star Wars" movie.

And it was during our visit to that ship, we were able to talk to Captain Worthington and Lieutenant Jones via a highly advanced com-link."

"Just where were they at this time?" Admiral Barns asked.

"Capt. Worthington claimed they were in a subterranean kingdom called Atlantia. And Lt. Jones said it was like the Bible's description of the Garden of Eden," Bill Northfield explained.

"Can you tell us how you got on board that spaceship, Captain?" Clyburn Asked.

"Well, it was after we watched Major Masterson down three of those so-called "demon fighters" over the ice shelf. He then stopped long enough to ask if we needed help," Frank Foster told them.

"We thought it better not to challenge him with any hostile action after seeing what he could do with that advanced fighter," Bill Northfield added. "You can only imagine our surprise when we found out he was an American and just as human as you or me. So when he invited us to come aboard the bigger ship in orbit, I thought we'd better check it out."

"It was about then that Bill and I were struck with that strange light," Frank broke in. "The next thing we knew we were standing in the sickbay of that enormous space ship, talking to two doctors and a woman named Commander Dohna who claimed to be the ships second in command."

"How were you treated by these beings?" Parks asked.

"Sir, we were treated with the utmost respect that fellow officers around the world show to one another," Bill Northfield insisted. "They answered all our questions, thoroughly and without hesitation. Even though some of the things they told us were a little hard for us to accept at first. Such as how they had started the human race and how the battles with the Black Lords had brought mankind to where is today."

"What about you, Captain Foster, did you believe all they told you," Clyburn asked.

"Well, not at first, Sir. I must admit I had my doubts. However, once we put our heads together and thought about it for a couple of days, what they had to say made a lot of sense especially when you consider all the gaps in our history that science have no answers for, or at least no logical ones. And if you also consider the mega-structures around the world, built with huge precisely cut megalithic stones weighing in some cases hundreds of tons, like the ones used for the pyramids of Giza, Stonehenge in England, Tiahuanaco in the Bolivian Andes, and Teotihuacan in central Mexico. All these structures were supposed to have been built with ancient technology. A technology that is now lost to history and, in some cases, a technology that not even our best engineers can duplicate in this day and time. Scientists still debate why and by whom these structures were built."

"And if you look at all the ancient myths and legends from around the world, you will find many stories of beings from space, who in some cases fought fierce battles in the sky," Bill Northfield added. "Even the Bible is full of stories of what could be interpreted as extraterrestrial beings interacting with humans. For example: When Moses led the Israelites through the desert, they were guided by a long white cloud by day and a pillar of fire by night. When Abraham was visited by angels, there was no mention of winged beings, but beings that looked very much like humans. In II-Kings, Elijah was taken up into heaven in a chariot of fire, which some believe, may have been a shuttle craft from a bigger UFO."

"I think we get the picture, Captain. What else can you tell us about these aliens?" Parks asked. "Such as what kind of weaponry they have or just what it is that makes them so superior to humans."

At this point the sub officers realized what the admirals were searching for was a way to defeat the creator race in battle.

"Sir's," Josh spoke up. "It is my impression, from what I've heard here today, that these beings are so far ahead of the human race, in intelligence and technology, it would be like throwing rocks at a modern tank. As you have heard, they have the ability to shut down a modern attack submarine with ease, to erase memory, fly through space at light speed, and defeat an enemy that is just as advanced as they are." Josh paused a second before continuing. "I was told they were also able to tap into the international communications network and broadcast the recent battle in space to all nations on Earth. In my opinion, if these beings wanted to harm us, the human race would not exist."

"Don't you want to bring the men of the rogue boat to justice, Captain?" Admiral Barns asked a little irritated at Josh's statement.

"That was our intention, Sir, but to go to war with these beings over the rogue crew would be totally insane."

Something came over Paula at this point. It was as if someone else was talking through her. "Sir, that's exactly what we wanted at first. After the attack, we filled our hearts with hate and revenge. I would imagine much like so many Iraqi's did after our illegal invasion of their country." She paused for a second before continuing. "Justice, that's the key word, here isn't it? In one stupid act of revenge, or what they would call justice, that rogue boat killed one third of the world's population. But tell me, Sir, how many people responsible for the Iraqi war were ever held accountable for their actions? You know the war that cost the U.S. over four thousand troops and a trillion dollars. Not to mention all the innocent Iraqi people who were tortured and killed. But to answer your question, Sir, yes we want justice for the wrong that has been done to all mankind."

Admiral Parks looked at Josh and Paula with utter contempt. "You're out of order, Lieutenant. Another outburst like that and you'll find yourself in the brig. You may not remember your stay with those aliens, but I can see the influence they have had on you."

"Sir, there is something I don't understand," Frank Foster spoke up. "According to all that I've talked to about these beings, even though they came from another galaxy, they were here on Earth long before the human race. In fact, it is said by some that they started the human race. So why do we call them aliens when they could very well be our ancestral parents?"

With the sub commanders sounding more like they had taken the same position President Overton had now adopted, the admirals felt they had no choice but to relieve them of their commands until further notice.

Chapter Forty Four

WHITE HOUSE BUNKER
10 October

At the morning meeting, the President and Vice-President reviewed the debriefing of the sub commanders, with the Joint Chiefs, Miles Standish from the CIA and Stan Miller from the FBI.

"Sir," General Wells said, after they'd finished viewing the debriefing of the sub commanders. "I think this goes to show just how these aliens can influence our military forces. We should go in there and demand the crew of that rogue boat be turned over to us for trial. Otherwise, I feel there will be chaos around what's left of the world, with each country going its separate way without any kind of unification or stabilization like we have under the UN or NATO."

"First of all, General," Marcus said. "I think we have already reached that point. And I think if we ask anything from these beings, it should be forgiveness for the stupidity we have shown our fellow man and all that live upon the Earth. For years now, we've polluted our air, land, and water with so many toxins I'm surprised there is any life left on the planet. It's not enough that new viral diseases are killing thousands every year and global warming is threatening many polar species with extinction. But, every so often, we have to start wars so we can slaughter people even faster. We raped the land of all its minerals and natural resources, killing much of the human, as well as wildlife, populations in the process. And for what, General, I ask you, for what? For the almighty dollar, that's what!" Marcus just shook his head in disgust and shame. "Hell, General, the people that set off those bombs may have inadvertently saved mankind from himself. Because now we have lost everything and will have to work together with our fellow man, and these…other beings, if we have any hope of restoring life on Earth."

"Sir," Miles Standish spoke after a short pause. "Maybe we should contact General Masterson and his team. They may be willing to meet with us and help find an answer to this dilemma. They may even be willing to go to Atlantia on our behalf. Or even take a few world leaders to Atlantia to see for themselves what became of the rogues crew."

Marcus stroked the five day old stubble on his chin as he pondered Miles suggestion. "Do you know how to get in touch with him?" He asked after a moment's thought.

"Well, let's just say I know somebody that does, or at least I think I do."

"Sir, I would advise against going to this Atlantia," General Wells stated. "They may hold you and or the other leaders until the whole world submits to their demands."

"Since when did these beings make any demands?" Katherine West asked with a puzzled look on her face.

"That's just it, Katherine, they haven't made any demands and the General knows it," Marcus replied, giving Wells a suspicious look.

"Sir," Admiral Parks spoke up. "I think General Wells has a valid point. If the aliens have the world leaders, who knows what kind of mind control they could perform on them."

"Well, why don't we first visit with this Masterson fellow and see what he has to say about going down there. Then, maybe we can send a representative or representatives down to Atlantia to negotiate with the aliens," Stan Miller suggested.

"Miles, what do you think about Stan's proposal?" Overton asked.

"Sir, when I said Masterson might meet with us, I meant he may be willing to have an electronic two way communication with us, like he did shortly after the bombs went off.

I don't think he will come here under these circumstances."

"Why do you think that is?" Katherine West asked, trying hard to understand. "Have we done something to Mr. Masterson to cause him to distrust us?"

"Well, Ma'am, I think he became distrustful of the American government when he was a fighter pilot during the Vietnam War. And when his father died of a mysterious rare cancer a little over twenty years ago, he felt the government had something to do with it.

According to the agent I assigned to the Velasco case last year, Masterson is highly intuitive. He said, the man, including his family and exploration team were gifted with extraordinary ESP ability, including being able to telepathically converse with dogs like they were human, and to also read minds."

"I would say that makes him a possible threat to America, especially if he feels our government is responsible for his father's death," General Wells quickly accused. "And, if he thinks he can talk to dogs, it makes him crazy as a loon in my book."

"It's not that way, General," Miles countered. "I think the best way to explain what I'm saying is that he is a very patriotic man, as well as his whole team. They would do just about anything for their country. However, it's shall we say, those within the government that mislead, deceive, and downright lie to promote their evil agenda, or pad their own pockets at the expense of the American people, are the ones he doesn't trust. For example, like former CIA director Herbert Hedge and those we brought down last year."

"Wait a minute," Katherine spoke up, after a thought came to her from something Standish said a few moments before. "How could Masterson have served in the Vietnam War? When we talked to him a few weeks ago he didn't look a day over thirty five."

"Well that is a mystery within itself, Ma'am, but if I may venture a guess. I would say it has something to do with the company he keeps," Miles explained.

"Miles, contact Masterson if you can and tell him I would like to talk to him as soon as possible," The President said. "Maybe we can explore other possibilities to answer this question at that time."

Marcus then turned to Admiral Parks. "Randy, I want those sub officers returned to their commands immediately and sent back to Antarctica."

"May I ask why, Sir?"

"Well, because they have already been in contact with those beings from this so-called Atlantia and may be able to help in the negotiations for the rogue crew. However, tell them to go no further than the Weddell Sea until we've had a chance to talk with Masterson." Marcus looked around the table to see if anyone had anything else. When no one spoke up, he adjourned the meeting.

Chapter Forty Five

ANDEAN UNDERWORLD

City of Akakor
12 October

After much discussion it was decided, the Chamber of Exile would be shut down until a full investigation could be conducted. Answers would have to be found as to, who this Yupanqui character and the Hamawthan people were for sure, and exactly where they had taken the exiles? However, because of the limited time of our visit, the investigation would have to wait until sometime in the distant future.

"The ancient archives in Akakor should tell us who and or what we're dealing with here," Dusty commented. "So let's get back there and celebrate the return of our people to the underworld, before they have to leave again."

"I second that motion," Joe agreed.

Soon everyone was mounted up and headed north to Akakor, but before they left, the Queen inserted her royal medallion, with the Viracocha relief on it, into a hidden panel just outside the tunnel entrance and punched in the proper code on a concealed keypad. This procedure closed the massive tunnel doors to all three entrances, until a full investigation could be completed.

When Steve, Jane, and Max were picked up at Amaru Meru, Ajbit and the other city elders were on hand to express their deepest thanks.

The Franklins had helped save the lives of over a hundred residents in their short visit and were showered with gifts and well wishes before we departed. Of course, before we left, a huge feast was also held to honor us for defeating the dark demons in space. During the feast, I asked elder Ajbit about the possibility of another transport disk like the one they had at their government building, but he assured me there was only one in the Andean underworld. However, he'd heard rumors when he was a boy, of one on the surface.

"But," Ajbit said. "If there was another one, the formula for activating such a device has been lost for well over three millennia. So I doubt if this Yupanqui took the exiles that way."

"What can you tell us about the Yurak Rumi?" Dusty asked.

"All I know is it's a large, black, altar rock, which was used by the Hamawthan people in their religious ceremonies. I believe I read in the ancient text, about a legend that says, when the people you call the Spanish killed Yupanqui over five hundred years ago, the Yurak Rumi brought him back to life. They then found a way to escape their pursuers through a hidden passage in the mountains which led them to the underground. But that was so long ago I doubt if it's the same people," Ajbit said skeptically. "However, they may be the descendents of Hamawthan people. But how did they just appear or disappear and where did they go? Unless they are ghosts or, like you said, the Yurak Rumi can be used to open a portal to another dimension." Ajbit just shook his head at the enigma, unsure of how these people disappeared.

"I don't know, but for some reason I got the impression Yupanqui didn't want to meet the Queen or anyone else from outside their chamber," Joe spoke up. "As soon as First Squadron came through the tunnel those people high-tailed it for who knows where."

"I'm not sure that's quite right, Joe," Naumy said. "I mean, we were not exactly residences of that chamber, but they were there while we were and they even protected us with that weird bubble of a force-field for five days. I've never seen a rock do that before."

"I wonder if it has something to do with the special healing powers Patricia has," Dusty speculated.

"Or maybe the combined perceptive powers we all possess," Max woofed. "They may have been afraid we would see just what, or who, they really were."

First Squadron could have been back to Akakor a full day before the M-I units, but they chose to wait and enter the capital city as one unit. After all, this was the same team that had saved the city, last year, from an evil demon and restored it to its original beauty.

Pat had sent the High Council an email of our ETA, the day we left Amaru Meru, so the streets and main plaza were jam-packed with people as we entered the city. We pulled up to the front entrance of the palace where a big sign had been erected over the stairway which read, "Welcome Home White Knights." After three passes over the city First Squadron landed atop the palace. That was the only space left without people, dragons, and canines. They stood there for awhile waving to the crowd as they cheered, barked, and sent fireballs toward the chamber ceiling, before coming down to be greeted by the High Council.

That night, another one of those stuffy formal-dress-uniform banquets was held in our honor on the palace grounds. All of our family and friends from the surface were there along with most of the regional leaders from throughout the underworld. However, we became suspicious when we found Gabriel, Michael, Poseidon, and Cleito were also in attendance. We knew then something had to be very wrong, but no one mentioned a word as to what it may be. The good thing was that I was able to spend some time with Duchess and the pups. I think I'm going to ask Dad if they can come with us as part of the crew of the Dragon Fire.

The next morning we met with Pat, the High Council, the two fleet admirals, Poseidon, and Cleito, in one of the many large conference rooms. First Squadron, along with the officers of the Dragon Fire, was also in attendance.

"I was wondering when you were going to get around to telling us what's wrong, Admiral," Dad said to Gabriel. "Does it have something to do with the email I received this morning from Washington, telling me the President wants to meet with us?"

"Yes, I'm afraid so," Gabriel replied, with a serious look on his face. "As you know, we have always monitored the governments of the world without their knowledge to prevent mankind from completely destroying himself along with this fragile planet. But, sometimes a rogue event will happen that we have little or no control over. Like the one we've been dealing with for the last month."

"I thought the President along with the other world leaders agreed to work out their differences and work with us to rebuild a free...."

"Yes, that's true," Poseidon butted in before Dad could finish. "But there are still arrogant factions within the U.S. government that believe in world domination. Take my word for it; these people have nothing to do with peace or freedom, and everything to do with death, destruction, and total anarchy. We think they are still under the influence of the Black Lords, which started this nonsense thousands of years ago. And, your President doesn't really know how much danger he's in."

"Were you not able to capture and imprison all the Black Lords?" Pat asked.

Poseidon looked over to Gabriel as if to ask, how to answer.

"When we put away the last of them over six thousand Earth years ago," Gabriel began, "We were sure we had captured all that survived the battle. However, when you fought the battle here at Akakor last year and destroyed a Namaru class demon, we realized there may be others."

"This led us to two possible scenarios," said Poseidon. "Either we failed to capture all the demons, all those years ago, or at least one or more found a way to escape."

"So, after you liberated the city, we did a complete inventory of the lower regions, or what you call HELL, and found everyone present and accounted for," Gabriel assured. "However, it was rumored before their capture, way back when, that there were those who had children with human women."

"How could you be sure you captured all the demons involved in the 11,000 BC invasion fleet?" Larry spoke up. "I mean, could there not of been a few that survived without you knowing it?"

"At the time, we realized there was a possibility that some lesser demons may have survived," Gabriel conceded. "But, we thought we knew the two places on Earth they were hiding and decided to just put a powerful force field around them. You know these places as the Bermuda Triangle and the Dragons Triangle. However, in recent years those force fields may have been breached due to an electromagnetic anomaly."

"There has been an evil influence on mankind ever since the ancient Egyptian Empire," Larry commented. "Some believe it started shortly after the Great Pyramid of Giza was finished, and has found its way into many different cultures, under different names down through the ages. Today we know it as the Illuminati."

"Yes, that's true," Poseidon agreed. "That was just after the 11,000 BC battle, when the world was in chaos for many centuries. It was before we had recaptured the Black Lords and imprisoned them in the lower regions of the underworld."

"We are now of the opinion that a demon by the name of Belial landed on Earth during this last battle and is in command of a strike force aimed at freeing the others," Gabriel informed.

"It says in the Dead Sea Scrolls, in a document called the war-scroll, a demon by that name would come at the time of the Antichrist," Jay commented.

Ron then asked, "Getting back to the President, Sir, how do you want us to handle this operation?"

"Very carefully, Mr. Clayhorn," Gabriel replied, "Very carefully. The U.S. President is being manipulated by his military council and is in great danger of being assassinated. Of course, they want to make it look like we did it in order to start a war."

"That's happened many times in our two hundred year history," Arlie confirmed. "Some even believe the attack on 9/11 may have been one of these operations. A type of black-ops, called a False-Flag Operation. It's designed to get public support, or sympathy, for a military operation. Usually to start a war, which no one wants, or to make an illegal military strike on some country that doesn't deserve it. You might remember the one in 1967, during the six day war in which

Israel was attacked by neighboring Arab countries. President Johnson supposedly arranged for an American naval cargo ship, the USS Liberty, to be attacked by unmarked Israeli fighters, and torpedoed by one of their gun-boats. Some think the idea was to sink the Liberty and her crew and blame it on Egypt. This would have brought the U.S. into the conflict, on the side of Israel. However, the Liberty survived the attack, even though thirty four of her crew was killed and no help came from the U.S. fleet only a few miles away. At the time the Israeli government claimed it was a case of mistaken identity. But the real story came out about fifteen years later when one of the Israeli pilots involved in the attack, came forward to tell his story. He said the American flag was clearly visible and was told to ignore it and attack the ship anyway." Arlie paused. "At least you can now see how this kind operation is designed to work."

Everyone considered the possibility of Arlie's words, which triggered a heated debate.

"Are you saying you believe the U.S. government was behind the attack on 9/11?" Jane asked a little unsettled at the likelihood.

"They may not have planned the attack, but it wouldn't surprise me if they knew of it before it happen, and did nothing to stop it. Look, I'm just saying it wouldn't be the first time our government has carried out such tactics," Arlie stated. "Hell, back when I worked for the Agency, we went on many of these types of operations. After a while of just following orders, you become numb as to what was right or wrong. Killing this one or that one for whatever reason and never knowing whether or not they were guilty of anything more than standing in the way of some big deal to make a high-powered politician rich. After I lost so many good friends to the lies my country told, I decided to get out. I learned the hard way that Old Glory doesn't stand for what I was taught in school, or at least not for the common man."

"It seems to me I saw something on TV about that False-Flag operation you were talking about a few years back," Dusty spoke up. "It sure was odd that after the attack, the Bush Administration was able to get congress to pass the Patriot Act, which took away many of our rights and freedoms. And then congress gives him the go ahead to attack Iraq, even though the UN inspectors had told him Saddam had no W.M.D.'s. Nor did Saddam have anything to do with the 9/11 attack and there were no Al Qaeda in Iraq until after we attacked them in 2003. Yeah, I hate to think that's what happened, but when you start adding things up, as to what happed afterwards, I'd say the attack of 9/11 being a False-Flag operation is a real possibility."

Poseidon then brought them back to the present. "President Overton has ordered the return of the three subs back to Antarctica. His purpose in doing so was to open negotiations for the crew of said rogue boat. However, we think the military will try to use this as an opportunity to launch an attack on Atlantia."

"Admiral, we'll need a few days to draw up a plan of action," Dad said.

"Don't wait too long, Nathan, this situation could go critical at any time."

"In that case, Sir, you'll have the plan this time tomorrow morning."

Chapter Forty Six

WHITE HOUSE BUNKER

16 October

The President paced the floor of the Oval Office with his hands folded behind his back. His mood had become unusually dark. From his dour demeanor and bloodshot eyes, Marcus looked like death warmed-over. But then, he'd not slept for over thirty hours, nor had he showered, shaved, or even changed his clothes. With him in the Oval Office were, Secret Service Chief, Tony Barker, Miles Standish, Mark Baker, and Marissa.

"Sir, I have reason to believe the Joint Chief's will act soon to take over the government," Mark Baker informed. "And if I may say so, Sir, I don't think sending those sub's back to Antarctica was a good idea."

"Believe me, General. I now understand that it may play into the hands of the Joint Chiefs, but the officers I saw on the debriefing video were trying to convince the Naval high command against any military action on the Atlantian's, or whatever you want to call them." Marcus still had a little trouble accepting the fact there actually was a creator race, or that places like Atlantia and a vast subterranean underworld existed. Even though he had seen the battle in space unfolded like everyone else had, it was like his mind would not accept it as fact. Suddenly he stopped his pacing and turned to Standish. "Did you send a message to Masterson yet?"

"Yes, Sir, I sent it two days ago. It was his idea for us to meet here in the Oval Office this morning."

Just then, as if on cue, the widescreen office TV came to life as if by magic. "Mr. President, it's good to see you again. I'm sorry it took so long to get back to you, but we needed to work up a plan to get you and the First Lady out of there." As Dad looked at Marcus and the condition he was in, he realized this man was in bad need of medical attention.

"I'm not leaving my post, Mr. Masterson. I'm staying here for the good of the nation. If I have to, I will fire the Joint Chiefs and replace them with reliable officers. Officers I can trust. Besides, this bunker is heavily guarded by the military. So I couldn't leave if I wanted to." Marcus stepped over to where Marissa sat on the sofa and took her hand in his.

"Believe me, Sir, to stay here is not a good idea," Tony Barker told him. "My staff and I will give you as much protection as we can, but we're no match for the military."

"Do you have a plan, Mr. Masterson, or are you just going to give me more advice on what needs to be done?"

"Sir, you and the First Lady need to come with us now. And we'll have to get the rest of the cabinet out after we arrange a time and date for pick up," Dad explained. It was about then Anglia reported that we had a transporter lock, so Dad ordered them to be brought aboard.

Suddenly, in the blink of an eye, the President and First Lady disappeared from sight in the Oval Office and reappeared on the ships transporter-pad, across the hall from the sick-bay.

For this operation we had borrowed Pat's larger supply ship, because it had a very powerful transporter that was used sometimes for heavy equipment. This was no easy task since the First Couple was 250 feet below the surface, and the last eight feet of that was concrete and steel. Beaming them up through all the dirt, concrete and rebar, definitely had its dangers, but in this case we had no other choice.

When they materialized on the transporter-pad, Marcus asked in a whispered voice, "Where the hell are we?"

Max growled a warning, sensing something sinister about the President. Red lights also came on as the klaxon sounded an intruder alert.

"Welcome to our humble ship, Mr. President," Steve greeted, after ordering the alarms to be turned off, and then introduced himself. He and Jane then started checking the first couple's vital signs. "You and the First Lady are now on board one of our supply ships. From here we will take you to a safe location where we can decide on the best course of action."

Marcus and Marissa just looked at each other as if in disbelief of what just happened. "Where's Masterson?"

"The General is on the bridge, Mr. President," Jane told him, as she stuck her stethoscope to his chest. "He'll meet with you in the ships conference room after we're finished here."

In our continued effort to learn every station on the ship, it was now my turn at command. "Colonel, we have two F-22 Raptors coming fast from the southeast," Yang informed.

"Raise shields, Mr. Yang and stand by laser cannons to intercept any missiles they may deploy," I barked. "Mr. Perry, lay in a course to Akakor."

It only took a moment for Jay to comply with the course change. "Course is laid in, Colonel"

"Get us out of here, Lieutenant before more fighters show up." Just then the F-22's fired four missiles, but by the time they reached the space where we had been, our ship was well out of sight.

"Well done, Duke," Dad complemented me in a whispered voice. "I couldn't have done better myself." Then his thoughts turned to Joe, and his team, who had been sent to intercept the subs in our shuttle craft before they reached Antarctica.

"Where'd the damn thing go?" One of the Raptor pilots asked, just before the missiles exploded over the White House, instantly melting twenty feet of snow and ice.

"I don't know," the other one said. "But if they can just appear and disappear at will, we don't stand a chance of shooting them down."

"Yeah well, I'm just glad they didn't shoot back. If they had I don't think we'd be here."

After they checked out okay, the Overton's were showed to the small conference room where they took a seat, in comfortable well-padded chairs, around a long, oval-shaped table. When Dad arrived they were discussing the greatly advanced technology of the ship with Steve, Jane, and Max.

"Mr. President," Dad greeted with a smile and extended his hand. "I would like to welcome you both aboard our humble ship."

"I don't think all this was necessary," Marcus protested. "I could have handled the Joint Chief's."

As Dad shook the president's hand, he sensed something very dark and foreboding had taken over Marcus's body. This man looked like the President, but.... "Sir, I'm not sure you understand just what you are up against here. Do you remember what happen to President Kennedy? Well, that was when our government took a dramatic downhill change, and whether or not you want to believe it, Sir, the people behind his murder are still in control of our nation."

"I thought we got rid of them last year," Marcus said. "I know we either fired or sent to prison, about a third of our elected and appointed governmental personnel."

"The people I'm talking about are not actually part of the government, but they do have enough money and power to pull the strings of those that are. In fact, they put people in office to do their bidding. They control the congress, world trade, the military, and world finance, not only in the U.S., but worldwide. So, all you did last year was to remove a few stooges, who have already been replaced by other stooges." Dad paused when I reported that we were approaching the red-zone. At that point he turned on the window monitor so the President and First Lady could get a birds-eye view of the Earth from space and see firsthand the devastating effects the nuclear bombs had caused.

After the Ooh's and Aah's of being in space and the horrible shock of what had actually happened were over, The President asked, "Just who are these people you think are in control of the world?"

Dad telepathically read his mind and realized Overton already knew the answer. Dad also knew at that point, Marcus Overton, was not who he seemed to be. Or at least not any more.....a dark demon had somehow gained possession of the President's body. Probably from all the stress he'd been under over the last month, but exactly when or how it happened is hard to tell. Dad had not detected a demon last spring when our exploration team was invited to the White House, so it had to of been a very recent event, probably within the last few days. Without the others seeing Dad pushed a button on a hidden panel at his end of the table. "I think you know the answer to that, Sir, but......"

Just then Ron's voice came over the room's speakers. "Nathan, you are needed on the bridge."

"On my way," Dad said, excusing himself to the others. When he got to the bridge he told us what was going on and asked Yang to be ready to place a force field around the President, locking the demon in place. "We'll have to come up with a plan to separate the two, short of a full scale exorcism, before we get back to Akakor." Dad thought for a moment, then asked Ron to contact Gabriel for advice. It seemed the only way to remove a reluctant demon, without an exorcist, was to kill the host. Marcus Overton must die. Dad then called Steve and Jane to the bridge and informed them as to what Gabriel had advised.

When he returned to the conference room, Dad waited until Marcus was separated from the next nearest person, by at least five feet, before he signaled Yang to initiate the force field. Almost instantly Marcus was engulfed in a containment field, it was much like that of a transporter-beam, except in this case his atoms were not being sent somewhere else. Being that tightly enclosed in the beam there was enough electromagnetic energy to stop the Presidents heart.

"What the hell do you think you're doing?" Marissa yelled, as Marcus fell to the floor.

"Let's get him into the sickbay," Steve advised. "We'll be able to manage him better there." Just then, Max and Jane brought over a couple of magnetic stabilizer paddles, which allowed Steve and Dad to move the body without coming in contact with the containment field. Basically they were two forty-eight inch plastic rods with a ten inch magnetic disc on both ends.

Jane stepped over to the First Lady and led her back to the sickbay. "We have no intention of doing the President harm, Mrs. Overton. However, our sensors have detected an Asharu class demon inside his body. After we have rid the demon from the ship, we will be able to revive him."

Marissa looked confused, "A what?"

"Look, I know how it sounds, but some demons have the ability to become invisible, much like a spirit or ghost and actually take control of a human's soul and body. This can occur if the host human is under an enormous amount of stress, which breaks down the body's natural defenses, much like a virus can break down the body's immune system. In some rare cases, the demon waits until a person dies and enters the body after the person's spirit has left." Jane explained. "These we call, walk-in's. I'm sure you've seen the movie, "The Exorcist." Well, I can assure you that such things are not only possible, they happen all too often around the world. Even human spirits that have not crossed into the light at the time of death can possibly inhabit another body if the conditions are just right."

Marissa nodded, not sure if she believed or even understood all she had just heard, but she then remembered reading in our report how Queen Patamaya defeated the Namaru class demon at the battle of Akakor last year. "What are you going to do? How are you going to remove the demon without hurting Marcus?"

"The demon should exit the body on its own, now that the host is clinically dead," Steve explained.

After another minute, maybe two, a dark cloud-like mass exited Marcus's body, now stretched out on the examination table. No matter how hard the mass tried, it could not escape the containment field. Now that the demon was separated from the President's body, Dad and Steve were able to move the mass to the transporter-pad. There, a small lead-based receptacle, about the size of a breadbox, had been placed to hold the demon for all eternity. And once it had been sealed inside the receptacle, Dad transported the demon into deep space.

As soon as the demon had exited the Presidents body, Steve and Jane worked feverishly to restart Marcus's heart, with no luck. The President was dead.

Then Max remembered seeing a restoration capsule with a white sheet over it in one corner of the small sickbay. After twenty minutes in the capsule, the President was not only up and talking, but felt better than he ever had, physically. However, he had no memory of ever coming aboard our ship, or for that matter, the last few days.

"If they left Norfolk on the morning of the 14th they should be getting close to the southern end of the Red-Zone, Sir," Naumy explained. Naumy was acting as navigator on this mission, while Tomka served at the weapons station. Hagnar and Ragtar took this time to visit family on Dragon Isle since there was no room for them on this small ship.

"I think you're right, Lieutenant," Joe agreed, as he, Dusty, and Peggy scanned the red water, four hundred feet below, from the small bridge of our shuttle-craft, while sending a continuous hail.

Joe had been placed in command of this operation because of his military flight experience. He'd ask Dusty to come along, then Peggy wanted to come, and before long he had his crew. While Peggy learned the communication functions of the ship, Dusty figured out the helm.

Chapter Forty Seven

SOUTHERN ATLANTIC OCEAN
17 October

At a depth of 550 feet and 1,500 yards apart, the three submarines slowly made their way south through the dead-zone off the northeastern coast of South America at 28 knots. The dead-zone is what the radiation belt became for those who had the misfortune of trying to cross it on the surface. On land or sea, everything within this thousand mile wide belt, was either dead or dying. Even the water had taken on a deep red hue, much like the color of blood. But then, that is exactly what the book of Revelation had foretold the sea would be in the end days. It was only at a depth of five hundred feet that the radiation seemed to dissipate enough to allow the subs to pass with minimal danger.

"Don't you think it odd Atlantic Command is sending us back to Antarctica?" Paula asked, as she stepped over to where Josh stood, next to the boats monitors for the exterior cameras.

"Yes, it does seem a little strange, unless they're planning to start a war."

"A war with the Creator Race, now that's about as dumb as it gets," Paula whispered, shaking her head in disbelief. "It would be like going to war with your great grandparents. Besides if these beings are as advanced as we've been told, it would probably mean the end of mankind."

"That just goes to show the stupid, arrogance of our military and those who pull their strings." Josh replied getting a little upset just thinking about it. "It's too damn bad we don't have one of those bastards with us so they could see firsthand what we're up against."

"If we're ordered to launch our nukes, what are you going to do?"

"Don't even consider the possibility unless we're under attack, and then only if there's absolutely no other options." Then after Josh thought about it for a moment, "Hell, the way I feel now, Paula, I don't know for sure what I'd do, or what I even believe in anymore. But my gut feeling is that when all this is over the world is going to be a very different place."

"Sir, I'm picking up a strange sonar contact, coming up fast from the bottom," Bixby reported. "I thought they were whales at first, but...."

"I don't see anything on the screen, but then visibility is about nil in this red soup," Josh replied.

"Oh, my God, look at that!" Paula suddenly said, as a huge creature swam across the front of the boat blocking out one of the screens. "What in the world was that?" She asked, just before something big hit the starboard side with tremendous force.

"Sound general quarters, Chief," Josh ordered, as water sprayed from a ruptured line just off the bridge. "Mr. Brooks, contact the Portland and Chattanooga and advice our situation."

As the klaxon sounded they were hit again, this time on the port side. "Don't you think we should surface?" asked Paula.

"Negative, Lieutenant," Josh replied. "Our only protection from the radiation is to stay submerged."

"Sir, the other two boats are reporting similar attacks by an enormous unknown creature or creatures" Brooks reported.

"Sir, here they come again," Bixby advised. "There are about ten of them approaching at twenty knots from behind us at a thousand yards."

"All ahead full," Josh ordered. "Chief, load all forward tubes, set torpedoes to detonate on a spread pattern at a thousand yards."

"Look at that thing," Paula said, as a mouth full of giant teeth passed in front of one of the monitors. She estimated the head alone to be over eight feet long.

"Yeah, it definitely looks like a sea monster out of the age of dinosaurs," Josh confirmed, as one big eye passed by the lens. "And we're going to try to send it back where it belongs."

Just as the boat picked up speed, there was another strike, this time on the port side again, which rocked the Tennessee with tremendous force, knocking people around like they were pick-up-sticks. After the crew regained their balance, they scrambled to repair the ruptured pressure lines as water sprayed throughout the boat. "All stop," Josh ordered when the forward torpedo room reported flooding. Two minutes later, the Chief reported they were able to finish loading all tubes before they were hit, and the pumps were now taking care of the flooding.

"Where are they, Bixby?" Josh asked.

"About twenty five hundred yards in front of us, Sir," Bixby replied. "They're turning to make another run at us."

"Chief Cloverdale, flood all forward tubes, open outer door, and fire torpedoes."

The other two boats fired their torpedoes at the same time and caught the huge beast in a fiery blast that not only destroyed the creatures, but caught the boats in a hell of a backwash. As huge body parts floated past the subs, the crews could only speculate as to how these animals came to be.

"Do you think the radiation caused a mutation, or do you think the recent earthquakes may have released some unknown creature from Earths distant past?" Paula pondered, still trying to rationalize things in her mind.

"I don't know, but I hope we've seen the last of them," Josh replied. Then after he thought for a minute he added. "If they are mutants, I wonder how many other monsters have been created on land, as well as sea."

An hour later, after returning to full speed and standard operating procedure, they entered clearer water on the southern side of the zone. Ensign Brooks spoke up from his station at the radio. "Sir, we're being hailed. It's somebody named General Joe Carter USMC retired."

"Put him on speaker, Mr. Brooks," Josh told him. A little curious as to why a retired Marine Corps General would be calling them on a secure frequency. "Yes, General, what can I do for you?"

"Captains of the Antarctic bound U.S. submarines," Joe stated, since he was now communicating with all three boats at once. "We saw the explosions a while back, but are just now able get through to you by radio. What happen down there? Do you need assistance?

"We're okay now that we've destroyed the cretaceous sea demons," Frank Foster explained. Then, he realized this guy was either in another submarine or in an aircraft above them, and since there were no sonar contacts with another boat, it had to be the latter. But how did he know where they were bound or what frequency to reach them on.

"Well, I'm glad to hear you survived the ordeal with no casualties, but getting back to the reason I'm here," said Joe. "We've been sent as a representative of Queen Patamaya and the people of the Andean Underworld, to invite you and your crews to come stay at the Royal Palace in Akakor for a few days. There, you will meet some of the Top Brass of the creator race. I mean, that's why you were going to Antarctica in the first place wasn't it?"

Bill Northfield spoke up, still a little irritated after the ordeal with the Mosasaurus type creatures. "Just who are you and how did you get this frequency?"

"And how in the hell do you know what our orders are," Josh added.

"Well, Gentlemen, I actually am a retired USMC General, and I can understand your concern. Nathan Masterson said you would be a little reluctant to accept the Queen's invitation, but to bring you along anyway."

"You know Nathan Masterson?" Frank Foster asked a little surprised.

"Yes, I've known him for many years now," Joe replied. "He and I were in Vietnam together, during the war."

"I don't think the Nathan Masterson we met is old enough to have served in Vietnam," Bill Northfield said. "He looked to me like he was only in his early thirties."

"Yeah, I was surprised when I found out he was a Major already, when we first met him aboard that space ship," Foster said. "But then,

I thought maybe these aliens advance their officers a little faster than we do here on Earth."

"Well, don't let his baby-face fool you. I can assure you he is much older than he looks gentlemen. He'll be sixty three on his next birthday, and he held the rank of Major for over thirty six years in one service or the other, before just recently being promoted to Major General."

"Okay, General, let's say we accept the invitation of this Queen, what's her name, where do we leave our boats?" Josh asked a little skeptical. "I'm sure they don't have a dock for submarines in the Andean Underworld. Or would you have us go up in one of those fancy space ships?"

"Well, you should know a little of what they have in the underworld Captain, since you were the guest of Poseidon at Atlantia for a little over a week. But, you're right; there are no sub docks, this far north on the Atlantic side. The closest one is below an island near the Argentinean province of Tierra del Fuego. But then you were on your way to Antarctica anyway."

"We won't be that far south for another two, maybe three days," Bill Northfield broke in.

"Well, the way I see it, you have two options" Joe suggested. "We can take the commanding officers with us now and let your XO's continue on to Tierra del Fuego with the boats. Or, we can wait till you get down there and pick you and your crews up at that time. However, considering what's going on in Washington, I would advise you to take the former rather than latter option."

"Can you give us a few minutes to consider your proposals, General?" Josh asked, a little reluctant to commit either way at this point.

"By all means, but don't take too long, this situation could go critical at any time." Joe told them. "Let's say, thirty minutes."

Chapter Forty Eight

CITY OF AKAKOR

17 October

As the ship came to rest atop the landing site, Anthony and Matt were there with two M-I units to take us to Akakor. This chamber was dry and barren, with five thousand foot high vertical cliffs and little vegetation, but it impressed the President.

"My God, it is true, Marissa," Marcus uttered in awe, as he walked down the exit ramp.

"You haven't seen anything yet, Sir," Jane said, as she, Steve, and Max came down behind them.

"The underworld is a wondrous place with many mysteries. It can be very beautiful and at the same time, very dangerous," Steve told them. "I hope you will be able to visit some of the other chambers and see these things for yourself during your stay here."

"Are there really fire breathing dragons down here?" Marissa asked.

"I'm surprised they're not here to greet the ship," Dad said, as he walked down with the bridge crew.

"I'll believe it when I see it," Marcus said skeptically.

"And I suppose you still think dogs can't talk," Max barked, "Even though you and I carried on a lengthy conversation just after you came out of the restoration capsule, remember?"

Marcus had nothing to say to that because he was afraid everyone would think he was crazy.

Unbeknown to him, before they had placed Marcus in the restoration capsule, Steve had given him and Marissa, a shot of Ben's advanced G.E.F. serum. This gave him a highly developed telepathic ability, along with many other ESP enhancements. The shot would also protect him from every known disease and any future attempts by demons to posses his body.

A half hour later we made our way into the chamber of Akakor. The main plaza was filled with people, dragons, and canines, all straining to get a look at the U.S. President and his wife. Queen Patamaya, the High Council, including King Drac, Gabriel, Michael, Poseidon, and Cleito met us at the top of the palace steps, with all the pomp and circumstance shown to any foreign dignitary.

"Mr. President, on behalf of the people of the Andean Underworld, we welcome you and the First Lady, to the city of Akakor," Pat greeted them, holding out her hand. Then after the proper introductions, everyone moved inside the palace where the First Couple were shown to their lavish rooms, and were told of the dinner to be held in their honor at 7 pm. It was now 1 pm.

"Did you see them, Marcus?" Marissa asked excitedly. "There are dragons! And that pyramid in the central plaza. It must be at least as big as the smallest one at Giza."

"We can't go to a formal dinner tonight, Marissa," Marcus said, as if ignoring her excitement. "We have no clothes except for what we have on."

Even though he'd checked out medically, Marcus had been acting a little odd ever since he came out of the restoration capsule. It was like he was totally detached from everything around him. Steve thought it had something to do with dying and being brought back to life, after being transported through so much concrete.

She looked at him, wondering if there was not something more seriously wrong, or if he was just overwhelmed with the whole situation. About then, a buzzer went off on the intercom in their suite. "Mr.

President, this is Nathan Masterson, if you and the First Lady don't mind, Pat, Duke, and I would like to invite you on a tour the city of Akakor with us after you've had a chance to settle in."

"We would love to join you, Mr. Masterson," Marissa answered, a little annoyed at Marcus for shaking his head at the idea.

"Okay then, we'll meet you at the main entrance in say an hour," Dad said.

After the Overton's had a chance to clean up and put on fresh clothes, which had been delivered shortly after talking with Dad, we found them refreshed, and ready to go at the main palace entrance an hour later.

The Overton's were literally awestruck after touring each of the city's main buildings, the Temple of Viracocha, the Library and Educational Center, and even the Government building had been an eye-opener, as well as an awe-inspiring experience. As they walked around it, the great pyramid in the central plaza became the topic of much discussion. It was there, captured victims from throughout the underworld waited in the dungeons to be sacrificed, before we liberated the city last year.

For two and a half hours they viewed the colossal statues, both inside and out of each building. And we tried our best to answer the endless questions they had after listening to each of the many holograms.

By the time we returned to the Palace, Marcus seemed to be doing much better. He now understood how mankind came to be and accepted it without reservation. We could tell the G.E.F., which Steve had given them back on the ship, was now taking affect.

"How long will it be before we can visit some of the other chambers"? Marissa asked, excited to see more wonders of the underworld. "Are they all as beautiful as this one?"

"They are each unique in their own way," Pat told her. "Just as the surface world offers many different sides to natural beauty, the underworld is just as diverse in its flora and fauna. In one chamber you might find a great sea, and an arid desert in another, or mountains and great forest in yet another."

"But, along with the beauty there can be great danger," Dad commented. "There are many animals down here that have long been extinct on the surface…."

"Yeah, like those dragons," Marcus said, lifting his chin to indicate the two waiting at the palace's main entrance. "Why don't we wait here until they move on?"

At that, Dad and Pat laughed at the Presidents uneasiness. "That's Prince Draco and Ragnon," Dad said as they started up the palace steps.

"My, Queen," the dragons said, as they bowed their heads low to show respect.

"Father sent us to let you know Joe and Dusty are on final approach with the shuttle and it seems the mission was a success," Draco informed.

"Has an M-I unit been dispatched to pick them up?" Dad asked.

"Yes, your sons took M-I-2 over an hour ago," Ragnon replied.

That night at dinner in the crowded main dining hall of the palace, the Overton's, now dressed to the nines in a tux, for him and beautiful royal-blue evening-gown for her, sat at the royal table with Gabriel, Michael, Poseidon, Cleito, Pat, Dad, Dusty, Joe, Peggy, and the three sub Captains. Their table, being almost as big as the one used by the High Council, was only used on very special occasions, as in visiting dignitaries. I chose to sit with Duchess and the pups at a table reserved for Dad's children and grandchildren. I'd seen very little of them over the last month and wanted to catch up on what was going on in their lives. And of course, the High Council sat at their usual table because it was made to accommodate the dragon kind. Even with all their spouses there, including King Drac and his son Draco, they had plenty of room. King Drac's mate had died years ago, so he invited Draco to join him.

We dined on a choice of roasted wild boar in orange sauce, or prime-rib of mastodon, for the red meat lovers, and for those who would rather have seafood, there was calamari, giant lobster, or blackened sea bass. Each dish was served with an assortment of vegetables, and rice, or baked potato.

"If I didn't know better, I would think we have fallen through the looking glass into Wonder Land," Josh said, as he looked around the room.

"Don't feel bad, Captain, that's exactly what we thought when we first came here," Pat told him. "But after we got to know the underworld a little better and how things work down here, this place now seems as natural to most of us, as the surface world use to."

"But it does take getting use to," Dad reiterated, shaking his head at the memories.

"How on earth did you ever make friends with the dragons?" Marissa asked. "I would have been scared to death."

"As was I," Pat quickly told her. "But Nathan here decided he was going to confront these fire breathing monsters on his own and either make friends or die trying. As it turns out, we found that even though they are so different from us on the outside. They are very similar to humans emotionally. And now that we've gotten to know them for who they are, we've become very close friends, and in some cases, squadron mates."

"Nathan's new battle cruiser is even named the Dragon Fire, in honor of the first Dragon Squadron," Gabriel pointed out.

"Maybe you could arrange for a review of this famous Dragon Squadron we've all heard so much about, Patamaya," Michael said with a smile.

"It would be my pleasure, Admiral," Pat replied with a smile. "We could even give you a tour of the new academy at Akahim, if you'd like, and arrange for a little demonstration of the precision-flying being taught to our new recruits."

"That's something I'd like to see," Frank Foster said, followed by most everyone at the table nodding in agreement.

"It's really too bad the people of the surface world could not learn the love and respect that the people of the underworld have for all God's creatures," Marcus commented. "If they could, they would eliminate war altogether."

"Well, it hasn't always been that way down here," Dusty commented. "But I must admit within the last year we have managed to unite the underworld tribes under one government, which was no easy task I might add. But they now, for the most part, live together in peace and harmony, since Patricia killed the demon of Akakor."

"Pat, you are truly a person with many talents, healing the injured, riding dragons, and killing demons," Marissa whispered, shaking her head in disbelief.

"I know it's hard to believe, but last year at this time, I was just an ordinary veterinarian minding my own business. Believe me I didn't ask for this and at times would give anything to be able to return to the life I knew before in Kalispell, Montana."

"Well, how did you become Queen of this subterranean kingdom?" Josh asked.

"Well, to make a long story short, Captain, my father Dusty here, adopted me after my mother, Mayaset, was killed by Guatemalan Indians, years ago during an archeological dig. And, until last year when Nathan and his team brought me down here in search of the tomb robbers that were trying to kill me, I didn't have a clue as to who I really was. It was only after we visited the Hall of Records at the Mountain of the Gods in the jungles Guatemala that all was revealed to me."

"Yes, I read all about your teams fascinating exploits in the report Nathan gave Marcus last spring," Marissa said. "Marcus found it unbelievable. Until now that he can see it for himself."

"General, what do you and Peggy, think of this amazing place?" Marcus asked Joe.

"Well, Sir, we're still getting used to all the strange phenomena we've encountered in the short time we've been here." Joe replied shaking his head.

"Last year, when Nathan and Pat returned home in a space ship and told us about this place, we thought they'd fallen off the deep end of reality. But now that we're here and seen it for ourselves……. Well, all I can say is that it takes a while to sink in."

After dinner, a few speeches were made while everyone enjoyed coffee, or water for us canines, and a very tasty sugarless carrot cake. Pat spoke first, introducing the President and the First Lady and again welcoming them to Akakor. Then Gabriel spoke about the pending crisis and how he hoped we could all work together to avoid any further repercussions or fallout from what had happen over the last six weeks.

The President then said a few words on how honored he was to be a guest in the Andean Underworld, and how excited he was about seeing more of this wondrous realm. He also promised to do all he could to bring about a peaceful solution to the situation that now threatened to destroy the Earth.

The next morning, a meeting was held in the main conference room of the palace between the President, Gabriel, Michael, Poseidon, and Cleito to determine the fate of the rogue sub's crew. Of course, Dad and I, along with Pat, were also invited to attend.

"All I'm saying is that we need to bring some kind of closure to this situation," Marcus stated. "And we can't do that without a trial."

"I agree," Gabriel spoke up. "But where on Earth could a fair trial be held? And would the, so called super power countries be satisfied with the verdict? You do realize, don't you, that we have been monitoring every government on Earth, ever since their conception, and know the dirty little secrets of said governments, which could come out in such a trial..... At this point, let's just say, they wouldn't be in your favor."

"The way I see it," Poseidon interjected, "There are no simple answers to this problem. I hope you realize this is just as much the fault of the United States, as the people behind the attack. Because, for many years now your country has tried to dictate to the rest of the world what they can and can't do within their own borders. Tell me, Sir, just who gave your leaders such authority."

Marcus sat there quietly for a long minute before responding in a calm voice. "Yes, I agree, my predecessors and many members of congress have made a mess out of our government. Instead of working for their constituents, it would seem to me, they have sold out to the highest paying lobbyist. And in my opinion, they have chosen to betray the very principles our country was founded on. Now, every branch of my government has been compromised and I'm afraid it may not be able to be repaired. However, to put this issue to rest, I feel a trial in an international court will have to be held, regardless of what dirty secrets may come out. It might even help bring about the changes we need for a better Nation."

After another two hours of debating the particulars of where it would be held, what judges would preside and how many, from what nations the jury would be selected, and who would prosecute and who would defend, it was finally decided, that Poseidon would provide the defense attorneys. Nine judges would be selected from the UN ambassadors who were now surviving the adverse conditions on the surface, in a large bunker complex under the UN building in New York City. The prosecutors would be made up from the Super Power Countries. A jury, of forty eight, would be made up of people from every walk of life from around the world. However, it was a little harder to come to an agreement as to where such a trial should be held. Then, after much debate Gabriel suggested that we hold the trial at Moon Base Alpha, which was readily accepted by all.

Chapter Forty Nine

WHITE HOUSE BUNKER
18 October

Suddenly, Tom Pitt's office computer clicked on just as he was getting ready to call it a day. "Mr. President, how are you? We've been worried sick ever since you and the First Lady disappeared the other day."

"Hi, Tom," Marcus said with a smile. "We're just fine, so you can put your fears to rest. In fact, I've never felt better."

"Where are you, Sir? The Joint Chief's were mad as hell at your disappearance. I think they're about to stage a coup and take over the government. They wouldn't listen, even after I told them you had just taken a few days to sort things out. Katherine told them she would only take over as President, on proof of your death." Tom paused a moment to catch his breath. "So General Wells said he would get her proof and stormed out of her office."

"Calm down, Tom, everything is going to be alright. I can't tell you where I am exactly, but I can tell you it is an incredible place, as close to heaven as I've ever been." Marcus paused. "Say listen, Tom, I need a favor. I need you to call the Cabinet together in the situation room at 8 am tomorrow morning. Tell them I will be there with news that will bring the fate of the rogue crew to rest."

"I understand, Mr. President. Everyone will meet in the situation room at 8 am."

The next morning at exactly 8:01 the main screen in the bunkers situation room, came to life.

"Good morning, Ladies and Gentlemen." Marcus greeted. "I'm sorry I can't be there with you, but I've been busy the last couple of days negotiating with the Creator Race as to the disposition of the crew of the rogue sub." Then he introduced each one around the table of the main conference room at the palace. There was Gabriel, Michael, Poseidon, and of course Pat, Dad, and me.

"This ought to be good," General Wells said, as he rolled his eyes back and looked at the ceiling shaking his head in disbelief.

"Since when do we invite dogs to negotiations," General Farmer spoke up.

"About the same time they started putting idiot jackasses in military uniforms," I told him, as both rooms erupted in laughter.

"My God," Admiral Parks said, with surprise. "They can talk."

"Getting back to business," Marcus continued. "We have come to an agreement as to putting the rogue crew on trial. It will be held on an international scale and will be......"

Marcus then proceeded to fill them in on all the details, answering questions afterwards for over an hour. When the meeting finally adjourned, even the Joint Chief's seemed to accept the proposals without challenge. General Wells praised the President for coming back to his senses. General Farmer agreed, and added that after the trial we could finally put the matter to rest and get on with the rebuilding of the country.

Of course it would take six to eight months, maybe longer for the preparation of such a trial, and for everyone to be appointed, judges, juries, attorneys, etc. So until then, Marcus and the First Lady were going to stay where they were, to help in the final preparations.

Later that day in General Wells plush office at the pentagon section of the underground bunkers, the Joint Chiefs held a meeting of their own.

"You know, at first the idea sounded real good to me. However, now that I've had time to think about this trial, I've become a little apprehensive about the outcome. Especially, if those damn aliens have anything to do with the defense," Wells said, as he poured drinks from the mini-bar. "If we allow it to happen, I feel a lot of shall we say sensitive material, might be brought out. Material, which would be better off left buried where prying eyes can't see."

"Yes, I agree," Farmer said, as he took a sip of his twelve year old scotch, and then sat back on the blood-red overstuffed leather sofa. "If the press ever got a hold of said material, I'm afraid we would be at war with every nation on Earth, including the aliens."

"Such material may even bring some to believe the rogue crew was somewhat justified in their actions," Admiral Parks concurred from the other end of the sofa, "Or would have been, if they had used anything but nukes in their attack."

"Well, if it does come out, we can always blame it on the former administration. Everyone knows the former VP and CIA Director were in league with the Devil," Wells said with a laugh, drawing huge smiles from the other two men.

"If I remember right, the former administration had all their records sealed for the next twenty five years, even before the attack on 9/11," Parks commented. "So that would make it very difficult for anyone to obtain and introduce the material in question as evidence in a trial."

"Let's hope you're right, Randy. For all our sakes," Wells said.

"You know, it might not be a bad idea to stage another False Flag attack in order to turn world sentiment back to our side," Parks commented, while stroking his chin as if in devious thought.

A few minutes of silence followed as each man thought about the possibilities of this concept.

"You know, it would be too bad if that rogue crew were to somehow escape their captors only to meet with a terrible end before the trial ever began," Farmer speculated.

"Yes, wouldn't it now," Wells agreed. "Just what do you have in mind, Bill?"

"I'm not sure yet. Give Randy and me a few days to work out the details on a few different scenarios before we get too excited about this. Remember, we have a lot to lose if something goes wrong." Parks paused a moment as a thought came to him. "The problem would be how to penetrate the alien base without being discovered. With their advanced technology it might not be impossible."

"The way I see it," Wells said, as he sat down in the matching high-backed easy chair and took a sip from his bourbon. "If this situation goes wrong, it would mean all we've worked for from the very beginning, will be lost. And, gentlemen, if in fact it does go wrong, our life expectancy will be measured in hours."

Chapter Fifty

THE SOUTHERN OCEAN

Early Morning
21 October

The Tennessee led the way, as the subs approached their destination. The three boats had made good time down the coast of South America and were now off the province of Tierra del Fuego on the southern tip of Argentina. They had been able to run most of the way on the surface, which added almost ten knots to their speed. But now they would have to dive the boats before entering the hidden subsurface facilities Dusty had told them about.

"All ahead, one third," Paula ordered, as the Tennessee neared Isla de los Estados, a small island 3.7 miles from the mainland. "Dive the boat to 1,000 feet, Chief, at a thirty degree down bubble."

"We're at one thousand feet, Lieutenant," Cloverdale said, almost five minutes later, as the boat came level.

"Turn on outside lights and monitors, and make our course and speed 1-8-6 degrees at seven knots." Paula watched the monitors carefully as they slowly edged their way closer to the island.

"Island dead ahead, at one thousand yards," Bixby reported a few minutes later.

"All ahead slow," Paula ordered. Until suddenly at one hundred yards, a rock wall stood before them. "All stop," She ordered, as she scanned the massive underwater rock wall for a place to enter.

"Message coming through from the Atlantic Naval Command, Ma'am," Ensign Brooks reported.

As Paula read it she was a little uneasy as to its meaning. The other two XO's were unnerved by such an order as well.

"My God, what on earth are they planning?" Bob Dixon of the Chattanooga thought out loud. While Paul Wilson of the Portland, just shook his head in disbelief.

TENNESSEE, CHATANOOGA, AND PORTLAND, YOU WILL PUT YOUR SEAL TEAMS ON READY ALERT FOR THE EXTRACTION OF ROGUE CREW, IF AND WHEN THE SITUATION PRESENTS ITSELF.

Each sub carried a twelve man SEAL team for those, shall we say, secretive missions no one ever wants to talk about. But this was just plane crazy, Paula thought. Besides, the rogue crew was supposedly at a place called Atlantia, and if they understood correctly they would be going in the opposite direction.

Just then, a large section of the wall looked like it was being pushed in by some invisible force and then separated revealing a huge opening. "Looks like they're going to let us in after all," Paula said, as she reached for the subs intercom mike at the command station. "This is the XO speaking, we're about to enter an underground chamber to the unknown. Hopefully, Captain Worthington will be waiting for us on the other side. I want every crewmember at their station and ready for any situation. That is all." Then she ordered all ahead slow when the doors were fully open. With the Tennessee leading the way, each boat headed for the huge doorway. Each crewman stared in awe and wonder as they passed through the two hundred foot circular opening. Once inside Paula gave the order to surface and the Tennessee began to rise.

They'd only risen a hundred feet before breaking the surface alongside an ancient looking dock, which seemed to be cut from solid rock. In this chamber, there was enough room to tie up six subs the size of these three, side-by-side. But other than that, there was nothing spectacular about this place at all, just a dock inside a giant tubular cave that was about a 1,000 feet long, 200 feet high, by 150 feet wide. On the other side of the 25 foot wide platform, a high-speed bullet train waited to take on passengers. All three XO's were relieved when they saw the welcoming committee there to greet them.

All three Captains' along with Dusty, Joe, and Peggy were waiting there on the dock to meet them. Tomka, Naumy, Hagnar, and Ragtar had stayed back at Akakor. Dusty feared the dragons would cause too much of a distraction or adverse reaction from the crews. It's not just anybody that can accept dragons right off the bat without being scared half to death. So instead, they would take their place with First Squadron acting as security detail for the Overton's and the leaders of the Creator Race, as they toured the Andean Underworld in the M-I units.

The XO's were told to ignore the orders of the ANC, to have the SEALs on ready alert. The orders of the President overrode all others. And, their new orders were to proceed to Atlantia via bullet train, and wait for further instructions.

As the sub crew's boarded the train, the officers said their farewells to Dusty, Joe, and Peggy.

"It's been a real pleasure, General," Frank Foster said, as he shook Joe's hand. "The last few days have been very interesting to say the least."

"Yes, and before this adventure is over, I feel things are going to get a damn sight more interesting," Joe replied, before Frank stepped over to Peggy and shook her hand.

"I hope you gentleman enjoy yourselves in Atlantia," Dusty said, pumping Josh's hand.

"From what I hear, it's even prettier down there than it was in the Andean Underworld, but I find that hard to believe," Josh commented.

"I was told you and your crew spent a week there as guest of Poseidon, so you should know better than I as to what it's like. As for me, I haven't gotten that far south yet."

It must have been something in the way Dusty responded or maybe it was when they boarded the bullet train, for it triggered a memory in Josh, Paula, and the crew of the Tennessee at that very moment. "Yes,"

Josh said, as he looked back with an odd expression on his face. "I think it's coming back to me."

Then after Bill Northfield said his goodbyes, thanking Dusty and the others for their hospitality, the three sub crews boarded the train and headed for Atlantia.

After the train had pulled out of sight Dusty, Joe, and Peggy walked the short distance to the north end of the cavern and climbed the stone staircase to the cable-car platform where they boarded their ride home. Of course the plush-gondola wasn't as fast as a bullet train, or as down to earth as the M-I units, but it did offer grand vistas of the underworld, as it passed along near the ceiling of each chamber.

"Do you think they will be able to adjust to life in Atlantia?" Peggy asked.

"I can't say for sure how the others will do," Dusty answered. "But from what I've heard, Poseidon and Cleito said the crew of the Tennessee fit right in, and became a welcomed part of a chamber known as South Point. In fact, most wanted to stay there from now on, asking for political asylum, when they were told they had to go back to the surface world."

"Do you think they'll be divided up into different chambers?" Joe asked.

"I would think so," Dusty responded after a moment's thought. "Like ours, their chambers have already received many refugees from the surface. However, each crew may be kept together for morale purposes, but would be assigned to three separate chambers."

By the time the train reached the city of Atlantia, Josh and his crew had fully recovered from the temporary affects of the amnesia drugs they'd been given before they'd been sent back to sea. They now remembered the amazing cities, with their giant pyramids, temples with great statutes, and monuments lined with silver and gold. Then, there were the giant Ice Age animals, beautiful mountains, green forests with picturesque lakes and giant waterfalls of this wondrous subterranean island continent. Yes it was all there, like they had never lost their memories to begin with.

"Welcome back, Captain Worthington, Lt. Jones," Atlas greeted, after the doors slid open and the crews got off the train. He and Gadeirus had met the train with the royal guard, of about a hundred men, who stood along the wall at attention with their staff weapons at their side.

"It's good to see you all again," Gadeirus told them, with a smile, as he and his brother stepped forward and extended their hands. "When you left, father said we'd be seeing you again soon, and here you are. I hope this time you'll be with us a while longer than you were before."

"It's good to see you guy's again as well. And, if you don't kick us out again we wish to stay here from now on." Josh said, as he and Paula pumped their hands, happy to be in paradise once again.

After Josh introduced the officers of the other two subs, Atlas and Gadeirus led the procession into the city where the crew's were awestruck by its magnificence.

"You will all stay at the palace until we can assign a chamber for each crew," Atlas informed.

"Of course, Captain Worthington, you will be returning to South Point tomorrow, where I hear Azaes and his council have prepared a special homecoming gala for you and your crew," Gadeirus told them.

"But where will the other two crews be housed?" Paula asked, afraid they wouldn't be able to visit.

"We don't know for sure. As of yet, the housing in the other chambers is very limited," Atlas replied. "But Father and Mother will be back in a few days, they will know where to put the other crews."

"Until then, they will stay here at the palace," Gadeirus said, trying to put her mind at ease. "Don't worry, Lieutenant Jones, we will take good care of them."

Chapter Fifty One

PENTAGON BUNKER
21 October

"Are you sure you want to do this, Sir?" General Wells asked the dark figure on his office computer monitor. The figure was seated at the head of a large oval-shaped conference table in the middle of an unknown location. Because of the dim lighting, Wells could not clearly see the shadowy face of the one he was speaking to, just his upper torso, arms and hands. He also knew there were others seated around the table as well, but was unable to distinguish their identity either.

Admiral Parks and General Farmer had come up with the plan, and it involved using the Dhul Fiqar to attack the continent of Antarctica with its remaining nuclear missiles.

The shadowed figure, clad in a black suit, looked around the table to see if the other six members of the brotherhood agreed with this plan of action. After each one gave their nod, the man spoke with a computer distorted voice. "Yes General, we are sure. This battle has been too long in coming as it is."

"But, Mr. Chairman, this may mean the end of mankind altogether," Bill Farmer spoke up from where he was seated on the sofa. "I mean, the magnetosphere around Antarctica already has a lot of holes in it and a nuclear explosion down there would weaken it even more. It may even create another rift in the ozone layer around the world, which would cook the Earth with microwave radiation if it were hit with a solar flair.

"Exactly, and while the others are putting all their efforts into repairing the rift, the militaries around the world will attack. Oh, I have no doubt, General, that many will die, but the end of mankind? Well maybe, if we lose the battle. So you'd better not screw this up like the former VP and CIA Director did last year."

"We understand, Sir, and I will start putting together a crew for the rogue boat as soon as possible," Admiral Parks stated from the sofa. "Finding the launch codes for the rogue's missiles could be a problem, Sir."

"Admiral, you'd better hope it isn't," the shadowy figure warned.

After the link was broken with the seven man committee, the three officers sat there in silence for a long time, thinking about what they had been ordered to do. Each had suddenly realized the hopelessness in such an action. However, each knew the consequences if they failed to see the plan through. There was no quitting this organization. The only way out, was to die.

Each man thought of their family, and the shame they would have to endure, if it came out that they had carried out the many atrocities against humanity.... atrocities ordered by former dark administrations, over many years. Oh, I guess they could claim they were just following orders, if what they had done ever came out. However, like the defendants at Nuremberg after World War II found out, that would not hold water in a world court.

The three just sat there quietly searching their memory, trying to figure out just when they had sworn allegiance to the Black Brotherhood. Up until now, they had always believed their actions were best for their country. What they did, they did to ensure their country would always be strong against all enemies, foreign and domestic. However, somewhere along the line they'd lost sight of what America really stood for. Life, Liberty, and the Pursuit of Happiness, had become meaningless words on a piece of paper, or were only reserved for the rich and powerful.

Now, all that meant anything to them and the people that pulled their strings was Power and Control.

They had been recruited into the brotherhood directly out of their respective military academies where they had graduated at the top of their class before being put on the promotional fast track. They had learned the ropes quickly, and were soon put in command of very high level secret operations over more senior officers. And now, being members of the Joint Chiefs, they were in the position they had been groomed for, a position to stage a military-coup and take over the government. Together, with the shadow-men of the Illuminati's Black Brotherhood, they could now take over the world and declare a New World Order. However, now that everything was exactly where it should be for them to take control, they were having second thoughts. It was just then they realized exactly what they'd become, and had been working so hard most of their careers to bring about. Why they had not seen it for what it was before now, no one knew for sure. But now, there was no mistaking the blackest evil to ever enter the minds of men.

Finally, Admiral Parks asked. "Do you really want to do this, Dan?"

"What are you suggesting, Randy?" Wells asked a little surprised at his question.

"Yes, just what are you suggesting, Randy?" Bill Farmer asked, with an eyebrow raised. "I don't think we have much of a choice. Do we?"

"Maybe," Parks said, stroking his chin, while his mind calculated an alternative idea. "However, I'll need some time to figure it out. But whatever we do, it will be risky and I'm pretty sure we're going to need the help of Mark Baker."

Chapter Fifty Two

ANDEAN UNDERWORLD
22 October

When we left Akakor, we'd taken the northern route through the eastern chambers. All three M-I units were used for this trip, so the President and First Lady could get a good view of the underworld. Of course the Overton's were awe struck at the number of Pleistocene animals. Besides the mammoths and mastodons herds in almost every chamber, there were dire wolfs, giant sloths, and saber-toothed cats, just to name a few. In some chambers there were even older species, such as the terror birds like the ones they encounter on the earlier trip, the carcharodon megalodons in the chamber of Dragon Isle, or the pterodactyls that live in a chamber far north of here. Gabriel explained that these animals were on the surface of the Earth at the time they decided to colonize it, and after the global subterranean systems were constructed, a mating pair of each animal species along with a wide diversity of plant life, were brought to the underworld for study.

It had been many a millennia since Gabriel had had a chance to tour the Andean Underworld. Not since Viracocha had finished putting in the many chambers, extensive road system, and the connecting tunnels, had he visited this system.

Besides our high level distinguished dignitaries, there was Ron, Jay, Yang, Steve, Jane, and Max. David, Angela, Arista, Skipper, Duchess, the pups and I were also on board. And of course, the First Dragon Squadron flew along for security. The rest of Dad's human children stayed in Akakor. They'd had enough traveling for a while with young children.

When we arrived at the chamber of the Tree Of Life, we were formally greeted by the High Council, as most of its people gathered round to witness the proceedings. This was followed by a great feast and much celebration throughout most of the night. It sure was good to see our old friends Ben Franklin and his family again, but, to see my mom, (Gertrude) and brother, Lobo, who had been staying close to home anticipating the arrival of Howl's pups, was a real treat. And of course there were my two sisters, Gracie and Missy, who I hadn't seen since the wedding ceremonies last summer on Dad's sister Caroline's Caribbean island. While the humans partied, we dogs had a lot of catching up to do out on one of the higher balconies outside the cliff dwellings.

The next morning, Pat, Dad and I, along with Ron and Jay took M-I's one and two down to the main river to show our distinguished guest the namesake of this chamber. Steve and Jane, along with the rest of our group, stayed behind to visit with family and friends.

"But is it truly the Tree of Life?" Marissa asked, as she stared across the river in awe of the giant tree giving off a golden glow.

"Yes, I believe it is," Pat confirmed. "When we came through here last year we were given some of the fruit from this tree. Days later, in a chamber on the south side of Dragon Isle, we battled a demonic raiding party and freed their potential sacrificial victims. We gave some of the fruit to a young lady with a broken arm. It was a compound fracture which Steve and Sean had set before we went to bed that night. The next morning you could not tell the arm had ever been broken. Even the skin where the bone had protruded showed no sign of the slightest scar."

"I can assure you, Marissa," Gabriel said, after over hearing the exchange, "On this planet it would be considered a Tree of Life. We brought the seeds of these special trees with us from Sirius and planted at least one tree in every major underground colony around the world. Another very special quality they have is that they can bear fruit even if there are no others of their kind to be found."

"Is there any way we can get one of these trees in Washington?" Marcus asked. "I think it would be the answer to the Heath Care program."

"As long as the governments of the world would guarantee to give the fruit, FREE, to all people and not just a select few, I believe we could arrange to have whole orchards planted around the world." Dad told him. "But I can tell you right now, that as long as there is the greed and deception that runs most governments, including the U.S., it will never happen."

"You're probably right." Marcus agreed. "Besides, if we had a lot of those trees it would put many doctors and pharmaceutical companies out of business."

"Not completely," Gabriel said, shaking his head. "Even with our advanced technology we still have healers on all our bigger ships and throughout the underworld. Just as the girl in Patamaya's story, broken bones still have to be reset. Doctors are also needed to deliver babies, treat battle wounds, and offer medical advice on a wide range of maladies."

Just then, Naumy and Hagnar flew in fast and landed on the road not far from where our two M-I units were parked. This was Naumy's home chamber and he had stayed behind to visit with brother Ekno and sister Kinna before rejoining the others. "Sir," he said to Dad after saluting, then handed him a note addressed to the President. "This just came in." It was an email marked urgent, sent from Washington and relayed to this chamber from Akakor.

Marcus's mood immediately turned serious after reading the message. "Damn," he said. "The Joint Chief's are at it again."

"What now?" Marissa asked.

"Their putting a new crew together for the rogue sub which they plan to send back to Antarctica and use her remaining nukes to destroy the continent."

"Why would they do that?" Cleito asked, with concern.

"I'm not sure," Marcus replied. "I thought everything had been settled. Or at least they seemed to be happy with the idea of a trial."

"If I may venture a guess, Sir," Dad spoke up. "After the Joint Chiefs had time to think about what would come out in an international trial, I have no doubt they reversed their position on the matter in a hurry. However, I would say someone else is pulling the strings on this one. Someone that's not going to be satisfied until there is all out war between the forces of Light and Darkness."

"When the first three subs failed to check in, after receiving orders to capture the original rogue crew, the Joint Chief's must have figured their crew's had either been captured, sunk, or changed sides," Arlie interjected. "That's when, whoever is pulling the strings, decided to start an all out war."

"Who sent the message, Sir? If you don't mind me asking," Fred inquired.

"Miles Standish," Marcus replied. "He said the NSA had tapped into the communications between General Wells's office and a site somewhere in Switzerland."

"We've been monitoring that site for years," Admiral Gabriel commented. "They are the human equivalent to the dark demons. Their representatives on Earth, you might say. There are seven men, who control the world's Economy, World Trade, Science, Military, and all that's going on in the world today. They manipulate people, governments, and events through different secret societies, such as the Bilderberger's. The Illuminati is but one of their many names. However, they're also known as the seven headed beast that is mentioned in the thirteenth chapter of Revelation in the Christian Bible, and their Chairman is better known as the Antichrist." The Admiral paused when he saw the look of disbelief on Marcus's face. "Oh make no mistake about it, the Antichrist is very real and that passage from your Bible is very true."

Ron and Jay, who had been manning the communications computer in M-I-2, received almost the same message addressed to Admiral Gabriel. It had come directly from Captain Adams at Avalon.

"What do you think of this?" The Admiral asked and then passed it around.

TO ANC: MAKE READY ROGUE BOAT TO ATTACK ANTARCTICA.

"Could it be the Joint Chiefs want to switch sides in the middle of the game?" Dad asked. "I mean, why else would they send a non-coded message, such as this, over an open channel? They must know we have the ability to monitor such communications."

"You're right," Marcus said. "If they didn't want anyone to know about it, Admiral Parks would have sent it by a special military courier."

"Maybe they finally saw through the lies and deceptions of the Black Lords," Michael offered, "and now understand for certain how evil their puppet-masters and their agenda really are."

"Yes, it seems to me we've seen this kind of thing before. Remember how the Great War in the home system started," Poseidon reminded. Gabriel and Michael just nodded in agreement. "Are we going to have to fight this war all over again, or are we going to put a stop to it before it gets out of hand this time?"

"I think this time we're going to intervene and at least try to stop this before it turns into all-out war," Gabriel said.

"Sir, is there any chance they will have help from the dark demons? When we retrieved the Overton's, we had to extract one from Marcus," Dad reminded.

"I guess it's possible some of them survived from the ships we shot down and have now found their way into human host, but I think it would be on a very minimal basis, since most all the living population is now underground."

"Most of those, whose body died in the battle, will seek out living hosts on the surface," Poseidon suggested, "and with the amount of radioactive fallout in the air, they will become nothing more than mindless mutations, hell bent on killing humans."

"You said most?" Arlie questioned.

"Well, the possibility exists that those demons, which are still in their bodies, will have a controlling head, such as Belial, who would most certainly send them to find and release the Black Lords. They will try to work their way into the underworld as soon as possible."

Michael speculated. "And believe me if that happens, we will definitely have a full blown war on our hands, a war that would end in the total destruction of the Earth."

"That could be the very reason why they want to start a war, they know they can't win," Dad speculated. "It would act as a diversion, allowing them time to search out the subterranean colonies undetected until they find and release the Black Lords." Dad paused for a moment then turned to Gabriel. "Sir, it seems to me we should be drawing up a battle plan," Dad suggested.

"Yes, I agree, General," Gabriel said. "But first we need to get back to Akakor, and from there you and your team need to report to Moon Base Alpha and take command of the Dragon Fire. I'm not sure, but I have a feeling the dark demons are planning another attack from space and we need every ship up and running, ready for battle. I just hope you have enough time to put the new ship through her basic trials, giving your crew time to get familiar with her technology. I'll tell Commander Clakrin to put on extra androids to help instruct your crew."

"But Sir, we'll still need more personnel to man a battle cruiser, than my present bridge crew and a few extra androids," Dad reminded.

"I'm not sure, but I think I know where you might be able to pick up a few volunteers," Poseidon offered.

"And I think you know that First Squadron is at your command," Prince Draco spoke up.

"Well, pack your bags big fellow, because I think we're going to need all the help we can get on this one," Dad said with a smile.

"Well, then I'm going too," Pat said, not wanting to be left out. "The High Council can run things until I get back, or until Viracocha comes out of stasis."

"Well, that settles it," Gabriel nodded in agreement, before turning to me. "Duke, do you think those pups of yours are old enough to be drafted into the Galactic Marines?"

"I do indeed, Sir, but their mother might object. Besides they've had no formal training."

"You didn't either until you went aboard the Intrepid. And tell Duchess she's also drafted as well, and as many of Nathan's human children that want to enlist."

"In that case, Sir, there will soon be five new members to the Dragon Fire's canine corps."

"Well, I guess you now have your crew, General," Gabriel said. "After you get back from space trials, maybe we'll have time to get together at Avalon for a few days. If not, we'll do it when this is all over."

"Yes sir, I'd like that." Then Dad turned to Ron. "Mr. Clayhorn, please inform the Colonel's Franklin to report with the rest of our crew ASAP. Tell them to give our regards to the residents and council members of this chamber for their gracious hospitality, but duty calls and we have to go." Then Dad thought of something. "And tell Captain's Sean, and Lobo Franklin, and Zargon they are excused temporarily for maternity leave."

Gabriel then turned to Ron and told him to send a coded message to all underworld leaders around the globe, warning them of the danger and putting them on tactical alert. There was also a request, in the message, for volunteers for space duty.

Chapter Fifty Three

CITY OF AKAKOR

27 October

By the time we got back to Akakor, Dusty, Joe, and Peggy had already returned from Isla de los Estados. Agab and King Drac informed them of the situation as soon as they arrived, and the High Council had sent a general alert to all inhabited chambers warning the city leaders of the present danger.

It was well after dark when we rolled up in front of the Palace, but because time was short, a meeting was called in the government building's great assembly hall where the battle plan would be gone over with the High Council. Dad, his senior officers, the President, and the four members of the Creator Race had worked on a plan of action for two days, before we got back, and thought they finally had a workable solution. Now it was time to unveil it to the other underworld systems around the world.

The assembly hall was a large, elegant looking semi-circle greatroom, resembling a Greek amphitheater with a domed ceiling. It had many comfortable seats rising in thirteen rows in the circular portion of the room. Down front, there was a small podium for giving speeches to the general assembly of the Andean Underworld. This room was also adorned with all the finest sculpture and art the ancients had created. Many of which were dedicated to Viracocha and the creators of the

Andean Underworld. And, it was from this room that polices which affected this system were passed or rejected.

"May I have your attention please," Queen Patamaya announced from the podium, as the members of the council took their seats around the great hall, while everyone else took seats reserved for visitors in the front row.

"As you all know, we are now facing an all-out war with the dark demons and their human representatives here on Earth," Pat continued. "We have learned that many of the demons, who recently attacked our planet, survived the battle and are now trying to find and free the Black Lords. However, Admiral Gabriel assures me those chambers are well guarded and won't be breached." Pat paused. "The dark demons will most likely attack the manmade bunkers under Earths major cities first, and then try to find entryways into subterranean systems, like ours, around the planet. However, they'll need a much bigger force to accomplish that plan, which leads us to believe they are expecting reinforcements. However, we are unsure exactly where this other force will come from. This means we need to get our new battle cruisers operational as soon as possible. And since the Creator Race is mostly in stasis, we are asking all who can, to please volunteer to either serve on a battle cruiser in space, or to cover other important jobs here in the underworlds that are left behind by those that do. I will now turn you over to General Masterson, who has a few duty changes that you should be aware off."

"First of all, I think all of you have done a fantastic job over the last year, of restoring the Andean Underworld to its former glory. Admiral Gabriel has told me many times over the last few days how proud he is of all of you. It just goes to show what you can accomplish when we all work together to overcome any problem or adversity. However, getting back to business, as of tonight and until this new threat has been vanquished we are drafting the First Dragon Squadron into First Fleet's Galactic Marines or at least the ten senior officers."

"Where do Peg and I fit into all this, Nathan?" Joe asked from the first row of seats, thinking Dad might want him to go fly with him again.

Dad could sense Peggy's uneasiness about Joe's willingness to go into battle again after all these years. "Well, Joe, since Arlie and Fred are coming with me on the Dragon Fire, we would like for you and Peggy to take command of the academy at Akahim. With your background as a fighter pilot and Peggy's background in security, you should have no problems instructing the new cadets. I'm sure King Drac will assign you a few of his best dragons to replace Dagon and Fagon, as well as Prince Draco and Ragnon."

"What about me and my team?" Dusty inquired.

"There will be no changes at this time with your team Dusty. Since we can't take all the dragons with us, Hagnar and Naumy, as well as Ragtar and Tomka, will continue to aide you in your duties here in the underworld, at least until another new cruiser is ready for space trials."

"What about the Overton's?" Agab questioned. "Will they be staying here, going with you, or are they going back to Washington?"

"When we get back from putting the new ship through her paces, we'll decide whether or not to return the President and First Lady to Washington." Patamaya replied. "Until we can be sure of their safety, they will be our guest here in the underworld. And until I return, or until Viracocha comes out of stasis to take the helm of the Andean underworld, I'm going to ask that you allow Ben Franklin to act in my stead." Suddenly a lot of objections and debating broke out as to the credentials of this man, and his ability to be the head of the High Council. "Well the only other person for the job would be President Overton, but he has not been here long enough to understand how our system operates."

"Might I remind you, my Queen, that Mr. Franklin has only been in the underworld for about two months himself. Besides he's not a member of the Creator Race" Councilman Bolontiku objected. After which there was a lot of nodding in agreement by the others on the council.

Then Cleito asked, "How would you feel if I were to volunteer to fill in for your Queen until her return?" The room suddenly fell silent with the question. No one raised an objection, since Cleito was a member of the Creator Race and had thousands of years of experience running an underworld kingdom.

Finally, councilman Gukumatz spoke up after he had conferred with his fellow councilmen. "Madam Cleito, it would be our pleasure to have you fill-in for our Queen and lead the Andean Underworld until she returns." With that said, the room erupted with cheers.

Pat looked up at Dad and nodded then whispered in his ear, "How did you know that would work, and how did you know Poseidon wouldn't object to his wife remaining here for who knows how long?" When Dad had asked Pat on the way back to Akakor, who she wanted to temporarily take her place on the throne, she said, Cleito was the only one she could think of, which met the criteria, but she probably wouldn't accept the job because it meant being separated from Poseidon and her boys for who knows how long. So Dad told her to tell the Council her choice was Ben Franklin. Of course Pat knew the High Council would not accept him, but she decided to play along anyway.

We found out later, it was Poseidon who asked Cleito to take the job. But then, Dad thought he might.

After things quieted down a bit Dad announced that the White Knights of Avalon would be leaving Akakor within the hour. This should give everyone time to take care of any last minute necessities and say goodbye to their loved ones.

Two hours later Akakor's supply ship lifted off the landing pad and we were on our way back to Moon Base Alpha, via a short detour. We had to use the bigger supply ship because of the extra personnel. On board were our original crew, plus Pat, Anthony, Matt, my two boys Junior and Rufus, plus four dragons of First Squadron. Since Lynn and Karen had small children, they chose not to join us. So Dawn, Duchess, and my girls Molly and Lucy, also decided to stay behind to help with Arista and the other children.

An hour after takeoff we landed again, through a false volcano, on Antarctica's Mt. Kirkpatrick. It was the surface entrance to Atlantia. Here we picked up a few more volunteers, including the three American sub crews, who had finally decided a tour in space on a battle cruiser would be just a little bit better than their new found home in Atlantia.

Malik, Husam, and most of the crew of the Dhul Fiqar also wanted to volunteer, but under the circumstances, Dad thought it best they remain where they were, for their own safety. Besides, with all these extra volunteers, the supply ship was already going to be a bit crowded. However, since this ship was a little faster than our shuttle, we would only have to put up with the tight quarters for a little over four hours.

Chapter Fifty Four

MOON BASE ALPHA
28 October

"Ladies and gentlemen welcome to Moon Base Alpha," Commander Clakrin greeted us as we came down the ramp of the supply ship. "General, you will be happy to know the Dragon Fire is ready to go when you and your crew have acquainted yourselves with her new systems. I've assigned an extra two hundred androids to instruct your crew in their use."

"Thank you, Commander," Dad said, as we loaded onto a rail shuttle that would take us to our new ship. "Time is of the essence, so I would like to be able to take off early tomorrow morning. I know that means most of my crew will have to have on the job training, but sometimes that the best way."

"I understand, Sir," Clakrin replied. "Admiral Gabriel has already explained the situation, so the extra androids will be going with you. Commander's Robbie and Robo are already on board and will show you to your new quarters. You also have two hundred volunteers from here that were saved from the surface after the bombs went off. Some of them were ex-military and civilian pilots."

"Well, I'm glad to hear that," Dad replied, just before he boarded the train. "We also picked up about three hundred fifty human volunteers in Atlantia, but I'm not sure that will be enough."

"With the extra two hundred androids, it should be enough for the ships break-in exercises," Clakrin assured. "Have a safe trip, General, and may the Creator be with you."

When we pulled up in front of the Dragon Fire, tethered to her berth just outside the far northern hanger, all our new personnel were awestruck. She was huge. Everyone just stood there for a few minutes with their mouths open, taking in this magnificent ship. While the dragons all felt a deep sense of honor to be a part of this ships new crew, it was especially hard for the former sub crews to believe what they were looking at. Their officers must have asked three dozen questions as they looked the new ship over. Then Dad, Pat, and I led the new crew up the wide tubular gangway that extended from the hanger to the ship.

There, we were met by Robbie and Robo and shown directly to the flight deck where the other volunteers from the moon base had already been assembled. This was the only place, with the dragons on board, where the whole ships company could come together.

Actually, this deck was the size of two in height. It was enormous, much bigger than the one on the Intrepid. It had two separate massive bays with four runways, each wide enough for two fighters to launch or land at the same time, on either side of the ship. Down the middle of this deck, in-between the two main bays, was the section where the fighters and other craft were serviced, repaired, and stored out of the way when not in use. There were five large elevators with 12 foot wide doors that opened on both sides, capable of carrying up to twenty five people each, that were also located in this center section.

Dad and I stepped up on a movable platform, which was normally used by the maintenance crews to service all the different kinds of smaller spacecraft. "Ladies and Gentlemen," Dad began, after everyone quieted down. "I would like to welcome you to the Galactic Battle Cruiser, Dragon Fire. For those of you I have not met yet, I'm Major General Nathan Masterson, commanding officer on this ship, and this is Colonel Duke Masterson of the First Fleet Marines Canine Corps. Since this will be your home away from home for as long as you choose to stay in the service of the Galactic Marines, I think we'd better get you sworn in. If there are any among you who have had a change of heart and no longer want to become part of this most honorable team of heroic explorers and defenders of the Principles of Lights, you may back out now. I will ask Commander Clakrin to arrange transportation back to Earth." Dad waited a moment to see if anyone headed for the exit ramp. There were none. "Well then, I give you, my second in command, Brigadier General Patamaya, who will administer the sacred oath."

While Pat stepped up on the platform, a feeling of pride came over me as I spotted, Anthony and Matt standing with David and Angela. And there were my boys, sitting next to their Uncle Max and my sister's boy, Spike. The pups were only a year old, but were already grown and knew more than most humans. And now they were about to join an elite team of space explorers and probably spend most of their lives searching the stars.

"If you would all raise your right hand, paw, or talon, as the case may be, and repeat after me. "I, state your name, hereby swear my allegiance to King Adonai of the United Planets of Nirvana: To uphold the Principles of Light, to do my duty as a member of the Galactic Marines of the First Star Fleet of Sirius, and to the ship on which I serve: To keep my honor clean and to respect and protect my fellow Marines." Pat paused a minute as she looked out over the assembly. "Congratulations, Ladies and Gentlemen, you are now Galactic Marines of the First Fleet of Sirius." At that point a great cheer erupted from the crowd. Even a few fireballs flew toward the ceiling.

Then Dad spoke again, "Thank you Ladies and Gentlemen. It will be my honor to serve with each of you. For the first few weeks, things are going to be hectic until you all learn your new jobs and how to work together as a team. For those of you who have no military background or need to get into top physical and mental shape, you will start basic training immediately. For those of you who were already part of an Earth-bound military service or had previous military training, you will now start training for your new positions aboard this ship. At this time I will turn you over to Commanders Robbie and Robo. They head up our android corps on this ship. The android personnel will be your instructors until you not only know your job, but every job in your department. And, the androids will be the only ships personnel to go by a naval rank."

At that point, Robbie did a roll-call and assigned each person to their quarters, as well as an android instructor, who waited off to the side like a drill-instructor. Robo handed each one a communication badge as they walked by. Each badge had been programmed for that individual and should be worn at all times.

Except for the senior officers, bridge crew, and flight crews, each person's quarters would be on the same deck his or her work station was on. A device, which worked much like an iPad, was then handed out to each crewman by their instructor. A detailed diagram of the ship was programmed into the device showing each room, its use, and included all hatchways, elevators, and stairways. It also explained the function of each deck. For example: Bridge = (ships main control room). A-deck = (senior officer quarters, including eight conference rooms, and Captain's office). B-deck = (officer and crews mess, R&R areas for both officers and enlisted personnel alike, plus workout and exercise rooms for each). C-deck = (sickbay) and (7 Agra-bays), for growing food and a water reprocessing plant) unlike some TV shows, this ship didn't have replicators. D-deck = (supply deck, transporter bays, dragon and pilots quarters, as well as pilots ready-rooms, plus security headquarters and brig). E-deck = (flight deck). F-deck = (engineering).

While the rest of the crew got settled in their quarters, Dad and I, along with our bridge crew and Pat headed for the bridge. Four of the androids also came along to update us on the new systems.

The bridge was laid out differently than the one on the Intrepid. It reminded me of what the inside of a great raptors skull must look like. With the back of the room rounded, and then narrowing down to a rounded point in the front, about thirty feet across.

As you got off the elevators you entered the bridge on an elevated section which wrapped around the back of the room. To the right of the elevators, there were stations that displayed general ships function such as: engineering displays, deck conditions, location of personnel, flight-deck-logs (launches and landings), and sick bay data. The long and short sensor arrays, along with communications and science stations, were to the left of the elevators.

On the next level, which was about four feet lower and connected by a gently declining ramp on both sides of the room, was the command station with individual seating for five. In front of the middle seat there was a curved console that the captain could use to access information, or give nonverbal commands, to all departments in an instant.

On the lowest level were the final three stations. The helm was in the middle, navigation was on the left, and the weapons station was on the right. All the stations had very comfortable seats that conformed to the body of the occupant. The main monitor, about six feet wide, curved around the front of the bridge for about twelve feet. With its ten magnifications settings, something as far away as 5,000 miles would seem to be only 500 feet.

The small inset lighting, in a dark blue ceiling, could be raised or lowered to the wishes of the crew on voice command. That, combined with the earth tones of the carpeting gave one the feeling of standing on the ground, looking up at the stars.

Three hours later, after we thought we had some idea of how things were supposed to work, Dad met with the rest of his senior officers and department heads in the largest conference room on A-deck. Because of its size, this room could also be used for training purposes. Here the department heads and commanding staff officers sat with Dad on the wraparound podium down front. They waited to speak, as everyone took their seats.

"I hope everyone is happy with their new quarters," Dad said, after everyone that could be, was seated. "If not, contact Robbie or Robo as soon as possible and let them know." Dad paused. "I called this meeting to let you know how happy I am to have each of you as a member of this crew and look forward to working with you on a daily basis. You should all find new uniforms in your quarters, and now go by the Marine Corps equivalent of your former service rank. In the case of the former American Naval personnel, you will be responsible for similar positions on this ship as you were on the ship you left. As soon as possible, I would like a list of each subs personnel and their rank. I will try to keep your crews together whenever possible." Dad paused. "And now, I'll let my second in command Brigadier Pat Smith, introduce the department heads."

"Thank you, General," Pat said after she and Dad traded places. "Yes, Ladies and Gentlemen, there are some that call me Queen, but personally I believe the position is a little over rated." Pat paused until the laughter died down. "However, because of my bloodline, I have inherited not only that position, but the ones I now hold on this ship, such as XO, Science Officer, and Reserve Medical Officer. And, I promise you, I plan to perform each position in a professional manner." Pat paused. "Now that you know who I am, you're probably wondering who these other senior officers are? To my right is, Brigadier Arlie Longhire, he will be in charge of our Special Forces teams. Colonel Fred Holtz will be his second." Pat turned slightly as she introduced the dragons. "Brigadier Draco and his dragon contingent will be in charge of Ships Security. To my left are Colonels Steve and June Franklin and their canine, Captain Max, the will head up our Medical Staff. Our android officers include our Engineering Department Head, Lt. Commander Upsilon. Lt. Commander Epsilon will be in charge of our Flight-Deck Maintenance Department, and Lieutenant Omicron will head up the Basic, as well as AIT Training for the raw recruits." Pat paused before turning the proceedings back to Dad.

"With all the volunteers we picked up from the Andean Underworld, Atlantia, and Moon Base Alpha, we are still short by almost a thousand people. Admiral Gabriel promised to have the rest of our crew waiting when we returned from space trials but until then we'll just have to get by with what we have." Dad paused as a thought came to him. "If any of you are interested in becoming fighter pilots or know of anyone with such inclination, please meet me here at 0900 hours tomorrow morning. Colonel Duke and I will be pulling double-duty as head of fighter command. Now, if anyone has questions please stand, give your name and rank and we will try to give you an answer."

Paula raised her hand. "When we get into space, will we float around in mid air, like I've seen astronauts do on TV?"

Dad smiled. "No. This ship make's its own gravity so you don't have to worry about that."

"Can she really make light speed?" Bob Dixon, formally of the Chattanooga asked.

"Commander Clakrin assures me she'll do eight times that. But I'll let you know for sure when we get back," Dad replied with a smile as everyone's mouth dropped open in disbelief. "We also have the capability of creating worm holes. So we should have no trouble spanning the vastness of space in record time."

We answered questions for the next hour from almost every officer onboard.

Chapter Fifty Six

DEEP SPACE

29 October

The next morning we managed to get off the Moon okay and even into outer space. However, it took a bit longer for the ships crews to adjust to their new assignments, especially those assigned to the bridge. Even our regular bridge crew that had trained on the Intrepid had their share of snafus with the new systems. Don't get me wrong mind you, the whole purpose of this exercise was to familiarize all the volunteers with the new ship, and teach them how each of the many new and unfamiliar systems worked.

The morning we lifted off, everything went great, at first. Once the main screen was activated and we could see the breathtaking scenery with the huge craters of the Moon's surface and the stars in the background. For some reason, space looked a whole lot different here than it did on Earth. Dad said it was because there was no sunlight here on the backside of the Moon to interfere with the light of the stars.

As we lifted off, we saw the three older battle cruisers, tethered to their births, and the exterior damage they'd received in the recent fight with the dark demons. It would take Clakrin's androids awhile longer to restore and upgrade them to the newer technology. We also saw the three newer battle cruisers, each with a slightly different shape. It wouldn't be long before they would also be ready to go out on space trials. In fact, I think all they were waiting for was to be painted, christened, and a crew to fly them.

Once we were well clear of Moon Base Alpha, about a thousand miles out, Dad ordered Mr. Perry, who was learning the new navigation station, to lay in a course for Pluto at warp-speed. But, when he told Mr. Carver, who was at the helm, to engage, nothing happened. We still poked along at full impulse, or about three hundred thousand miles an hour. Commander Robo went over to the helm and showed Larry which button to push on his console. There was a moment's pause for the worm hole to form and the engines to switch to warp drive and then we shot forward at an incredible speed. At that point, I hoped Jay had plotted the course correctly around the asteroid belt between Mars and Jupiter, instead of through it. However, in the time it took for me to have that thought, we were already well past the belt and well on our way into deep-space, as we gradually increased our speed to warp eight. In fact, the whole trip of over three billion miles, took just a little under three hours. Of course, with light speed alone, it would have taken longer, but with the added advantage of a wormhole generator it almost doubled our speed. When we finally came out of warp, about five thousand miles from the little sphere, I could see why Pluto lost its status as a planet. It was only slightly bigger than Earth's moon.

The second crew to take over the bridge was Colonel Josh Worthington and the former bridge crew of the Tennessee. Each of the former sub crews would spend at least six weeks training throughout the ship. Dad figured that at least one or maybe even two of those crews might be reassigned after training, to one of the other new ships, because our bridge was over staffed.

However, at this point, training was going a little slow. Even with all the preflight instruction in one of the big conference rooms, the sub crews still had not gotten the basics down. Even though, the operational systems on this ship were much simpler than the archaic systems of their submarines. It took at least a couple hours of hands-on-training before each of the three former sub crews began to understand the many strange symbols and switches located around the bridge. All I can say is it was a good thing we had the extra androids onboard to help us out.

Dad and I had a bigger turn out for flight school than we first thought possible. Over a hundred men, women, and canines wanted to become fighter pilots. Many were ex military and civilian pilots used to flying earthbound aircraft. But, since each fighter needed both a pilot and a RIO, it would only be a quarter of the personnel we would need for our full complement of flight crews. However, it was a good start and Dad was sure we would have enough for all twenty squadrons, of seven fighters each, once we got back to Moon Base Alpha. And, we would get even more after the young cadets finished their basic training, in about six to eight weeks. I know that's what my boys, Duke Jr. and Rufus, as well as Anthony and Matt wanted to get into when they finished basic training.

After taking a day to explore Pluto and the surrounding area, and finding little we didn't already know, we decided to head for home, using impulse power for at least part of the trip, to give the new personnel time to learn the new systems and to document what we could about this corner of space. After all, this ship was as much a craft for science exploration as it was a ship of war.

On the second day, Dad and I did a walk through of the entire ship, inspecting each deck and the crew on duty, making sure that all systems were working as they should. We started with the bridge.

"General, on deck," Master Sergeant Tom Kelly, formally Master Chief of the Chattanooga, announced as Dad and I stepped out of the elevator.

"Well Bill, is this job more to your liking or do you want your submarine back?" Dad asked Colonel Northfield, as we sat down in the command section.

"Well Sir, I asked my men that same question not an hour ago and we all agreed, down to the last man, that this job is a whole lot better than being cramped up in a steel coffin at the bottom of some ocean."

"If I may say so, Sir, this is like being in heaven compared to that submarine," Captain Dixon observed.

"Are your men catching on to the new systems okay, Bill?" I asked.

"They are doing much better than I thought they would. We've only had a couple snafus, but we quickly recovered and have learned many valuable lessons in just a short time. I think they will be up to snuff sooner than expected."

"Well, that sounds good, Bill," Dad said. "Because in a few weeks, when we get closer to Mars, or maybe even before, things could get a little warm in this part of the solar system. To put it mildly, gentlemen, we could find ourselves in a combat situation sooner than we expected. So I'm going to ask Robbie and Robo to put this ship and its crew through every possible emergency, as well as battle scenario, they can think of. I want every man, woman, dragon, canine, and android to know every job in their assigned areas so well, that they don't have to think about how to respond to a situation."

"Sir, we will be up to the job," Bob Dixon assured us, before Northfield could respond.

"I hope so, Bob, because if you're not, this could be a one way trip for all of us," Dad told him with a dead-serious look.

After we had finished our tour of the ship, we decided to allow a few more days to pass before starting Commander's Robbie and Robo's exercise programs. This was for the crew to become a little more familiar with the ship. Most of these people had never been on a starship before, let alone a full size battle cruiser. And Dad figured that the next six weeks was going to be a grueling nightmare for everyone, especially those who had never served in the military.

So it was on the morning of the seventh day, around 5 am, the klaxons sounded and everyone scrambled to general quarters. Robbie and Robo had programmed an imaginary attack by the dark demons into the computers. At first, most everyone was confused and not exactly sure as to where they were supposed be, or what they were supposed to do. The first exercise took over ten minutes before everyone was at their assigned battle station. After two more of the same type exercises everyone was at their station within three minutes. And with a little more practice, Dad was sure we would be able to cut that time in half.

Usually, Dad gave a short address over the PA system after each exercise to let everyone know how he judged their overall performance and what needed to be done to improve. Then, an android officer would go over the material with department personnel in detail.

Dad and I would also address the pilot trainees and explained what would have happened if it had been a real attack. These would-be fighter crews had already started training in simulators, but as of yet, they had not climbed into a real fighter. So during the training exercise they gathered in the pilot's ready room on D-deck, to watch a video of an actual battle that best represented the particular exercise. During the video the trainees actually participated in the exercise by taking a test with a personal handheld keypad. It was much like playing a videogame. Afterwards, Dad and I would tally each individuals score and let them know if they would have lived or died, had the exercise been real.

This would continue on, day after day for several weeks. And sometimes there were as many as three exercises a day. Hopefully, the whole crew will not only know their jobs, but be able to work together as one by the time we get to Saturn. By then, Dad hoped to have the first seven fighter squadrons up and running, with a few exploratory missions under their belts as we passed by the Neptune, and Uranus systems, but their biggest test would come when we got closer to the demon outpost on Mars, or so we thought.

Yes, it would be a few weeks yet before we would have to tell the ships company, exactly what our mission was. But first we needed to teach them how to be ready for any situation, which could occur for real at anytime. In short, we needed to mold them into the finest Galactic Marines the fleet had ever seen.

Chapter Fifty Seven

WASHINGTON'S SUBTERRANEAN BUNKERS
31 October

Katherine West had been in her office for all of ten minutes, she had just sat down with her first cup of coffee and was looking over the list of judges suggested to sit on the trial of the rogue sub crew. Just then her intercom beeped, as the lights flickered off and on.

"Madam Vice President, there is something odd happening on the surface," her secretary advised. "The Joint Chiefs have called an emergency meeting, for 10 am, in the situation room."

Katherine looked at her watch, which showed 9:10. "Did they say exactly what the problem was? Oh, and what's up with the lights, Paul?"

"No, Ma'am, they didn't elaborate. However, I got the impression it may have something to do with a possible blackout throughout the bunker system."

At 9:30 one of the many battery powered golf carts used to transport people throughout the underground bunkers, picked up the Vice President. By 9:50 the cabinet was assembled in the situation room with the President on the main screen.

"General Wells, what seems to be the problem?" The President asked.

"Have you seen the surface, Sir? There is a total blackout. At noon yesterday it looked like midnight, which in itself is nothing new, it's pretty much been that way for the last month. But, now we're starting to lose the electric generators supplying the bunkers with power as well. These same generators also control the locks for the blast-doors to the bunkers. On one of our routine satellite passes of this area yesterday we got these pictures." An aide showed a recording of the surface of Washington DC dated 30 October. It showed thousands of human-like figures trudging through radioactive snow covered streets toward the five different entrances to the bunkers.

"These things are no longer human," General Farmer spoke up, as he motioned for the aide to zoom in for a close-up, which also showed dark, shadowy figures amongst the mutated human creatures.

"No General, they're no longer human, or at least not living humans. They are demon-possessed corpses and if they get access to the bunkers, everyone down there will die or have their soul stolen by the dark-legions." Marcus stated, remembering his own encounter with a demon. "Seal the doors any way you can, even if you have to weld them tight. And keep those generators going, no matter what. Those dark shadows can also come in through the ventilation or plumbing systems if they decide to abandon their host bodies, so I suggest you seal off all outside access, including doorways, air-ducts, and any plumbing that is not already protected."

"Sir, is there no way we can stop these fiends?" Katherine asked.

"If and when you have no other way of defending the Capital, I hereby authorize a napalm strike on Washington." Marcus said regretfully. "However, I'm told that will only destroy what's left of the bodies. It won't destroy the spirit-like demon inside the bodies. For that, you'll need an extremely strong Electromagnetic-Particle-Disrupter or E.P.D for short."

"A WHAT?" Stan Miller asked surprised. "I've never heard of such a weapon."

"I hadn't either, but here at our present location, we've seen a lot of things that we only thought existed in Sci-fi movies." Marcus explained. "Katherine, put all science, and engineering personnel on this problem immediately. We will send you the schematics for such weapons, via e-mail, before this transmission is done."

Just then, an aide to General Wells handed him a message. After reading it, he reported the same kind of chaos was going on around the world.

"It looks, to me, like the final battle for planet Earth has started, General," Marcus observed, after the satellite feed of world capitals, was put up on screen. "But what I don't understand, is why you Joint Chiefs, aligned yourselves with such evil."

Everyone in the room looked at the Chiefs with shock and disbelief. After a moment Admiral Parks offered a lame explanation. "Sir, we were led to believe that what we were doing was for the betterment of the country. We had no idea this was a fight between two alien factions, or that we were being used as pawns in their war."

"Damn-it, Randy, don't say another word!" Wells said, as his face turned red with anger.

"I think Randy's right, Dan. It's high time we try to undo the wrongs we've done over the years, but I fear it's going to be too little, too late," Bill Farmer commented, as he watched the screen, shaking his head.

"If you really feel that way, Gentlemen, then you'd better recall that rogue sub you sent to blow up Antarctica, before even more lives are lost." Marcus advised.

"How in the hell did you know about that?" Generals Wells asked, and by doing so admitted to the conspiracy. But his anger quickly turned to fear when he realized that if Marcus knew about what they'd planned, then the forces of darkness most likely knew they'd had a change of heart. He also realized just how little they actually knew about alien technology and how far that technology was beyond that of humans. Then with a sudden sense of overwhelming shame for being so stupid, he asked what they could do to straighten out this mess.

"I think you've already done enough, Dan. Most of it is detrimental to the principals this country stands for." Marcus said sadly. "I hate to have to do this, but I'm hereby temporarily relieving all three of you of command until this matter can be investigated more thoroughly.

General Baker will be in overall command of the military until I hear back from a review board. Until then, you'll be placed under house arrest at the service of General Baker. If you are truly serious about making amends and cooperate with the review-board, I'll think about giving you your jobs back."

With that, the Chiefs were escorted from the room by six MP's, who took them to their quarters. There, a sensor implanted ankle harness was strapped and locked to their lower leg and a two man guard was placed outside their door.

Andean Underworld

"So this is how the final battle between good and evil begins," Marissa said, after Marcus related the events of the cabinet meeting at dinner in the palace dining room. They sat at the same table as Poseidon, Cleito, Gabriel, Michael, Joe, Peggy, and Dusty. "Admiral, do you know how it ends, because I don't ever remember reading about this scenario in any Bible?" Marissa asked.

Gabriel sat for a long moment before answering the question. He looked around at the others of the Creator Race, like there was something that had not ever been told to humans. Then, with sad eyes, he told her the truth. "I'm sorry but contrary to all your religious text, no one really knows for sure the outcome of this encounter, or any encounter, with the Black Lords for that matter. I guess if they did, the war would already be over and no more lives would have to be lost."

"If you think about it, dear," Cleito spoke up. "Just because someone's interpretation of something is written down, doesn't mean that's exactly what's going to happen. It would make no logical sense to tell how an enemy would be defeated thousands of years before the war began, because he would simply change the battle plan."

Then Poseidon said. "As we tried to explain to the submarine crews a while back, so many of mankind's religious text has been written and rewritten and told and retold for thousands of years. They now contain only bits and pieces of mans true history. And the only thing they all seem to agree on at this point, is the morality lessons in each. The Ten Commandments, love thy neighbor as thyself, turn the other cheek and do unto others as you would have them do unto you. However, even those who profess to be the strongest believers, think its okay to go to war and kill his follow man because he interprets the text differently. Jew, Christian, and Islamic factions have fought a never ending war, almost from the time they first came into existence. And if that's not bad enough, factions of each religion, fight bloody wars between themselves, Catholic and Protestant, Shia and Sunni. It never ends, because every time someone disagrees with an interpretation, they write a new one and call it gospel. But then, the Black Lords have a lot to do with this. They have lied, deceived, and twisted the truth, throughout mans religious history, and it's no wonder so many people no longer believe in God or the Great Creator of all, as we call him."

"How fitting, that all this would start on Halloween," Marcus uttered, almost to himself, from the other side of the table, where he looked to be wrapped up in his own thoughts. "I hated to relieve the Joint Chiefs, but I had no choice."

"Don't worry, Mr. President, my nephew Mark is a good officer," Joe said, before he took a sip of his wine. "If nothing else, he's very thorough and will take every precaution to protect all those in the bunkers."

Marissa put a hand on top of Marcus's. She could see the worry building in his dark brown eyes. "It will be alright, dear, there's nothing else you could've done. I mean, if you left them in control of the military, there was no guarantee they would not continue to follow the dark forces of the Illuminati, Bilderberg Group, Antichrist, or whoever it is that's trying to take over the world."

Chapter Fifty Eight

ABOARD THE DRAGON FIRE
29 November

We'd been in space for a month now and we're just leaving the Uranus system. Because it was taking longer than first thought, Dad had decided to travel between planets at warp speed instead of impulse to save time. In this planetary system, all seven fighter squadrons were sent on exploration missions to the Planet and six of its twenty seven moons. Where, I might add, each performed admirably.

The previous Neptune system, however, had been explored mainly with probes. I say mainly because, most of our people were just not ready to go on an actual mission. However, Dad and I picked the seven best crews, the ones we figured would be future flight leaders, and led a short mission to one of the smaller moons just to give them a sense of how it's really done.

By the time we got to the Uranus system, the rest of the class was getting their turns on missions. Each squadron now flew as a single unit, with each fighter not only protecting their wingman, but every ship in the squadron. Dad and I were very proud of the individuals that made up these squadrons. They were shaping into very good pilots and would become valuable members of the Dragon Fire's crew. In fact, Commanders Robbie and Robo reported that all the ships personnel were far beyond expectations in their training.

Even the rookie cadets were excelling in their basic training and would soon be able to start AIT (Advanced Individual Training). This is where the cadet learns the job that he or she will be doing during his tour of duty aboard ship. I sure hope my boys score high enough on their final test to get into fighter school.

Now that we were on our way to the Saturn system, Dad felt it was time we let the senior officers and department heads, in on our mission. So this morning while our original crew manned the bridge, we met with the senior staff officers in conference-room-C.

"Ladies and Gentlemen, I've called you here this morning to inform you as to what we're actually doing out here," Dad began. "That is, besides being on a training mission that so far is going exceptionally well. My thanks to you all for the extra effort you've shown in helping to make this ship the best in the fleet." Dad paused as he put some figures up on the screen. "Before just recently, the last time the forces of darkness attacked Earth was over 13,000 years ago. At that time, they attacked with a force six times the one they used a couple months ago. And until last year Admiral Gabriel and the senior officers of the Creator Race thought they had all the Black Lords contained. However, when my team and I stumbled on one in the battle for the city of Akakor, they knew something was wrong, very wrong. After a head count of the Black Lords, that found them all present and accounted for, they thought at first he might have been one they had failed to capture from the 11,000 BC battle, but that didn't prove out either. Then, just recently, after receiving an updated list from the home world, they have determined the forces of darkness still have a sizeable armada somewhere in this star system."

"I thought you just destroyed that fleet two months ago," Frank Foster spoke up.

"So did we." I answered. "But, taking into consideration what is now happening on Earth's surface," and with that, I put the pictures Gabriel sent us from the Presidents last talk with his Cabinet. "And given the estimated reserve fleet of the forces of darkness, which should number close to the one of 11,000 BC, and would include at least four battle cruisers, we feel there is a strong possibility they are planning another attack on Earth, and soon. We think the attack of a couple months ago was just a ruse to find out how strong our defenses were, to infiltrate our underground bases, and if possible, to release the Black Lords from captivity."

"The staff officers of the Creator Race are under the impression that because the Second Fleet was there to help us win the day, the dark demons have put their plans on hold for the time being," Dad continued. "Now to the second and possibly the most important part of our mission...."

"Let me guess," Josh Worthington spoke up, "it is our mission to find this so-called black-fleet. But it seems to me, if the math is right, we would be a little outnumbered, even for this magnificent ship."

"Very good, Colonel," Dad said. "However, at present we are not to engage the enemy. We are just to find them and keep Earth informed as to their fleet strength. In other words, after we locate their bases, we will become their shadow."

"It is our hope that Commander Clakrin and his androids will have time to get our older battle cruisers ready and Gabriel will have time to find enough trained personnel to man the new ones. And that probably means pulling Creator Race personnel out of stasis early." Pat stated.

"If they don't find the needed personnel, we'll have to try and buy some time by using hit and run tactics," I barked.

"Now, does anyone have any questions?" Dad asked.

"Does this mean we will possibly have to go into battle, against an enemy of overwhelming odds, with only half a crew and can expect little or no help from Earth?" Paul Wilson, former XO of the Portland, asked.

"That pretty much sums it up, Captain." Dad nodded. "Now you know why I've been pushing the crew so hard these past few weeks."

At that point everyone started talking at once.

"Sir, what about Admiral Michael's Second Fleet, will they not be here to help us?" Paula Jones asked.

"Admiral Michael was called back to the home planet ten days ago," Pat replied. "It seems Admiral Uriel's Third Fleet will be coming our way soon, with someone very special and the King of Kings needs the

Second Fleet to return to Sirius to guard the home system. However, Uriel won't leave until the Second Fleet arrives home and they won't arrive home for another year, even at maximum warp."

"Sir, where do you think the enemy is hiding?" Bob Dixon asked.

"Captain, we found them the last time on a fluke," Dad informed. "If they had not exposed themselves by attacking the Intrepid and Scorpion as we did a routine check of Mars, the recent battle for Earth might have been lost. We would never have thought they would have built bases in the tiny moons of that planet, but that's exactly what they did. However, we got real lucky that Admiral Michael and the Second Fleet just happened to show up in time to give us a hand. So, to answer your question, Bob, I guess we could find the enemy just about anywhere between here and Earth."

"That means we must question everything, no matter how small it may seem," I reiterated. "Tell your crews to report every unusual tweak on the sensor arrays. And, from now on, we will run cloaked and silent at all times. This will cut down on our speed a little, but it may allow us to find them without being seen."

"If we have to search every planet and moon between here and Earth, we could be out here in space for a very long time," Bill Northfield spoke up.

"Yes, that may be true, Bill, but I can't see that we have much of a choice," Dad said. "I think it would be better to find them out here in deep space and do what we can to stop them, than to let them attack Earth with little or no warning."

"When we get to the Saturn system we will attempt a landing on one of its outer moons," Pat said, after putting the system up on the screen. Using a laser pointer she indicated the tiny moon of Phoebe. "This moon is believed to be not much more than a large asteroid that at some point in time got caught in the planets gravity field. If this is the case, because of its location it will enable us to see the whole system without being seen, and to monitor the strange sounds that have been reported coming from the planet itself."

"According to the information stored in the fleet's database, we think the largest moon, Titan, is a good possibility for an enemy base.

It has an atmosphere made up mostly of nitrogen with about one percent methane," Dad continued, taking the pointer. "This creates a smog layer not unlike very populated cities on Earth. And, although the temperature is extremely cold at 180 degrees Celsius, it's not that much different from the Planet Canis-2 in the Creator Race's home system, which just happens to be where some of the demon forces are originally from."

The next day, our long-range sensors picked up suspicious readings as we came out of warp near the Saturn system. It looked at first as if small asteroids were being knocked around from moon to moon. But, when we discovered they were leaving a plasma trail, we figured we'd found our enemy. And after we landed on Phoebe, in a nice, dark impact crater, all our speculations were confirmed. However, we had no idea the dark demons had amassed such a force. In fact, our estimate of a force close to the one of 11,000 BC was way off. The enemy had put together at least two full battle fleets, with at least seven or more battle cruisers in each and what looked to be hundreds of the new medium sized corsairs that they had used in the last attack. At first Dad figured with this many ships, the enemy had to have a base on just about every medium to large moon in this system. However, we were able to eliminate all but five of the larger moons because of geologically activity or radiation exposure from Saturn.

"Sir, there is a squadron of seven enemy fighters headed our way," First Lieutenant Trevor Horton, former sonar officer of the Chattanooga, advised Col. Northfield.

"Raise shields, Sergeant Major Kelly and sound general quarters," Bill ordered.

"Belay that order, Sergeant Major," Dad said as we got off the Bridge elevator. "What's the emergency, Mr. Northfield?

"Sir, I think we might have been spotted by a squadron of enemy fighters that are headed our way."

"If they had spotted us, Bill, I guarantee you they'd have sent more than a single squadron. Just make sure we stay cloaked and quiet. Most likely they're on a routine patrol and haven't got a clue we're here."

Five minutes later the enemy fighters flew over the tiny moon of Phoebe and paid no attention to us in any way.

"Sir, I apologize for such a rookie mistake," Bill told Dad after the threat had passed.

"Don't worry about it, Mr. Northfield. You did what you were trained to do. You know as well as I do, when it comes to this kind of situation, it's a judgment call and could have gone either way. So keep up the good work, Colonel," Dad told him.

Chapter Fifty Nine

WASHINGTON DC UNDERWORLD

30 November

Since the onset of the dark demon invasion, about a month ago, the underground facilities of countries around the world had fought a never ending battle. Not all the demon ships that were thought to have been shot down were out of commission. Some landed in the world's oceans, remote deserts, mountain tops, and forests, which were miles from any kind of population. There, they waited for the battle in space to end before attacking the underground bunkers of the major cities. Needless to say, Earth bound modern fighters, from around the world, didn't stand a chances against the demon craft. By the time Gabriel finally sent the outdated F-47 fighters, which had been replaced from the three older battle cruisers, to finish off most demon ships, many a good human pilot had been lost.

With the temporary demon air superiority, it seemed that most world governments were just hanging on by the skin of their teeth. Some in Eastern Europe, Southeast Asia, and Central Africa, had lost their battle with the forces of evil, and their people killed or forced into slavery.

In Washington, as in every other capital city around the world, the fighting went on twenty four-seven. Thanksgiving had come and gone with not much more than a prayer. For most, dinner had to be served and eaten on the run.

The schematics for the EPD plus a few hundred working models had been sent to the military scientist and engineers as promised. At the same time, Gabriel also sent the design for demon detectors, like the ones that had sounded a warning when the President was picked up in Pat's supply ship. These units were installed fairly quickly throughout the bunkers, but it took them over two weeks before they could come up with a working model for EPD's. The engineers then had the problem of mass producing them before they would even begin to have a fighting chance against such an advanced enemy. However, after another week, most countries had finally worked the bugs out and were now, not only making hand-held units but had even come up with a larger version of the weapon that could be mounted on helicopters.

The weapon worked similar to our ion cannons, on a much smaller basis, but instead of just blowing a hole in a target, as an ion cannon would, it completely vaporized it. One of the safety features for this weapon was a dampening field that made it ineffective on non-biological targets. For example, you couldn't shoot through a concrete wall or even a glass window, but if a person or animal gets hit with the beam from this weapon, they would be annihilated unless they are wearing special armor.

The ion cannons used on our space craft of both alien races had no such dampening fields. They used the combined force of both a charged particle beam disrupter many times stronger than that of anything found on earth, as well as an extremely strong electromagnetically charged beam. However, the protective shields on all space craft were designed to deflect these powerful beams from causing any real damage. That is, until the shields took more hits than the generator could handle.

When that happens......game over.

"What is our status General Baker?" Katherine West asked, after everyone was seated around the situation room's large oval conference table.

"I think we are finally beginning to gain the upper hand, Ms. Vice President. As soon as we started using the EPD weapons, the demons seemed to back off. And we have not detected any more activity outside the bunkers for the last twenty four hours."

"Do you think they will abandon the human bodies and attack our ventilation systems?" FBI chief, Stan Miller asked. "The way I understand it, they can pass through just about anything while they're in that black vapor form."

"If they do, the demon detectors should pick them up. And our scientists are now working on a way to enhance the detectors with what they're calling, demon scrubbers. These scrubbers are supposed to destroy the entity in just a few seconds after being detected. However, at this point the prototype will vaporize anyone that gets too close to the beam. Demon or otherwise."

"Are the EPD's effective when they take the form of the black vapor, before they reach a scrubber?" Miles Standish asked.

"Admiral Gabriel assures me they are. In fact, it was the EPD technology that gave our scientists the idea for the scrubbers. The Admiral also said, since the entity originally came from a biological being, the electromagnetic beam the weapon creates, will also destroy the spirit of that being, no matter what form it has taken. The bad thing about this is the dark demons have similar weapons. The good thing is they can't use these weapons while in the black vapor state. At least we are on an equal basis with the enemy as far as weapons are concerned. So now it will depend on our tactics and our ability to withstand their attacks, until help arrives."

"Why do you think they have pulled back? Jeff Davis asked. "I mean even if we are now equally matched, it seems to me that would not detour them from reaching their goal of taking over this facility."

"It's possible they've pulled back to regroup and are rethinking their battle plan. They may even be waiting for reinforcements." Mark Baker offered. "But, I think you're right, Mr. Davis. I don't believe they have just given up. Quite the contrary, I think they are planning to hit us again with overwhelming odds, and soon."

"Why do you think that, General?" The VP asked.

"The President told me that Admiral Gabriel will be sending us some help as soon as he can and I think the enemy will try to take us down before that happens. The problem is that all of the battle cruisers are currently being repaired or readied for their maiden voyage, except for one and it's already in deep space. So, the only thing he has to fight with, are the old F-47' fighters that are located on the moon base, and a few shuttle and supply ships located in each continent's subterranean colony system. Since these latter space craft no longer have to contend with enemy fighters, they've had much success in battles in some of the unindustrialized nations of the world that have fewer EPD's." Mark paused a second as he looked at the faces around the table. "The President assured me those ships should be here within a few days. At that time, I think, we should be ready to mount a counterattack, or possibly even evacuate the women and children in those ships."

"What about our planes and helicopters?" Mavis Henley asked. "Are they totally ineffective against this enemy?"

"No ma'am. We have used our aircraft to bring down many of their number since we equipped them with a more powerful EPD weapons, which have no dampening field and capable of blowing buildings apart. However, in doing so, we have turned much of the city into rubble. We have even, as the President suggested, used napalm, which started a fire that is still burning out of control. And now that we have this new weapon system mounted on helicopters, the enemy seems to disappear every time they get anywhere near the city. Hell, General North over at Andrews, tells me the demons have even attacked the air base many times.

"General, have you learned anything from the former Joint Chiefs, as to where the humans that are in league with these dark forces are located?" Stan Miller asked.

"Sir, it seems the only images they've ever had of these people were dark shadows seated around a large table, somewhere in Switzerland, they believe. I've been in contact with the NSA agent we met a while back and he assures me they are doing everything possible to pinpoint their location. He thinks they may be situated in a mountain bunker, far below the surface and have communication scramblers on their satellite transmissions. Even the Swiss Government, who are also involved in the search, are having extreme difficulty. The NSA think they have the location narrowed down to a region near the Austrian border, so we should know more within few days."

"Okay, General, keep us informed of any new situations," Katherine stated just before the meeting adjourned.

Chapter Sixty

ANDEAN UNDERWORLD
1 December

In Akahim, Joe Carter sat at his office desk, in the section of the grand palace that had been set aside for the academy's administrative offices. Except for large oval windows in the center of the south and east walls, the whole room was encompassed by very ornate bookcases, which held all the knowledge of the ages. Joe's large oak desk sat in front of the east window. On it, sat the most advanced computer system the Creator Race had. Even the ancient Library of Alexandria would have paled in comparison to the information stored it its database.

Joe leaned back in the overstuffed swivel desk chair and let his mind wonder a bit as he looked over the morning's schedule. He'd been a very disappointed when Dad had not asked him to join him on the battle cruiser. Even though he knew why his old war buddy had not included him as part of his crew, it still would have been nice to have been asked. But, NO, Nathan figured that a retired Brigadier and his new wife would be more comfortable with the safe position of Academy Commandant. "I was good enough to be his wingman in Vietnam, but not good enough to serve with him on a battle cruiser," Joe thought to himself.

Oh, this wasn't a bad job, he thought, if you like training humans and dragons to become one with each other while learning aerial combat tactics. One stayed very busy overseeing, not only classroom lessons, but actual flying exercises as well. And this was the type of job Joe would have enjoyed under normal circumstances. I mean flying, at high speed, on the back of a creature ten times your size while it breathed fire, was better than any thrill-ride at Disneyland. But even that paled compared to the thought of commanding a battle cruiser in deep space. Not that Joe had ever been on an actual battle cruiser, or even into outer space. However, he figured if Nathan could do it, he could.

"Joe," Peggy's voice came over his office intercom. Even though she never said anything about it, Peg knew what Joe had been thinking. She had plenty of experience reading him, since she had worked with Joe for many years as head of security at the Pensacola Naval Air Station in Florida. However, after a one night stand with the base commander, a Colonel Joe Carter, she resigned her commission in the Marine Corps and moved to Montana where she was elected twice as Sheriff of Flathead County. This is where she met Dad and the rest of the Masterson family, who lived on a remote manmade island deep in the mountains miles from town. It was during last year's investigation of the attempt on Pat's life that Joe showed up after a messy divorce from his wife.

"Yes, dear?" he answered as his thoughts returned to the present.

"Dusty is here to see us. He says we're needed in Akakor as soon as possible."

"What's going on, Dusty?" Joe asked extending his hand, as Peggy ushered him into the office.

"Well, to come straight to the point, Joe, Admiral Gabriel needs all the qualified pilots he can get. With your experience, there may be a battle cruiser command in it for you, after training, of course. Now, I know Nathan wanted to more or less protect you and Peggy from the coming war by assigning you to this job here at the academy, but I guess the fleet is coming up way short of qualified personnel. And, from the reports Nathan has sent back, the enemy is a lot stronger than Gabriel, or anyone of the Creator Race ever imagined."

Joe looked at Peggy with the most neutral expression he could, not wanting to show his excitement. "What do you think, Peg, shall we find out what a battle cruiser looks like?"

Peggy thought for a moment, letting out a heavy sigh. "I'll go along with whatever you decide, Joe." She said with a smile, knowing full well this was what he'd been dreaming of ever since Nathan was assigned command of the Dragon Fire. However, deep inside, Peggy was scared to death of going into battle with the dark demons. Ever since she'd learned the story of the true creation, she'd had visions of the evil demons in J.R.R. Tolkien's "Lord of the Rings" trilogy. But she didn't want to put a damper on Joe's moment.

"How soon do you need us?" Joe asked.

"Well, my orders were to ask you if you would like to voluntarily join First Fleets Galactic Marines at the rank of Brigadier General and for you, Peg, the rank of a full bird Colonel. If you accept these commissions, you, along with Sean, Lobo, and Zargon will be at Moon Base Alpha by midnight our time. Naumy and Hagnar, as well as Tomka and Ragtar, have also volunteered and will be going along with you."

"Without your helpers, how will you be able to do your job, Dusty? "Peggy asked.

"Well, I have now been reassigned to take over as academy commandant until a replacement can be found." Dusty rolled his eyes and shook his head at the thought of it, "As if I know anything about aerial-combat, especially where dragons are concerned."

"I think you will be surprised as to how much you do know, Dusty. However, if you run into trouble, refer to the schools manuals." Joe then turned and retrieved one from a nearby shelf and placed it on the desk before continuing. "In them, you'll find everything you need to know about dragons, their riders, and even tactics, complete with diagrams. There are even some pretty good films in the Palace library down the hall that Arlie and Fred put together during the training of the first class. Your four assistants were in some of them. I'm sure they will give you some insight as to how things are supposed to work."

Dusty looked at his watch, "Well I guess you guy's had better get packed if you're going to get to Akakor by noon. I'm sure you'll get new uniforms when you get to your ship so you shouldn't have to take a lot with you." He said, as he shook hands with Joe and gave Peg a big bear hug. "I want to wish you both all the luck in the world. From what Nathan reports, everyone on planet Earth will need a lot of luck when the next battle begins."

"How are we to get back to Akakor?" Peggy asked, not wanting to dwell on negative thoughts.

"My ex-assistant's are waiting outside to fly you there," Dusty said, as he walked them to the door.

An hour later, after they had a chance to update the student body, give Dusty some pointers to get him started as the new commandant, and to throw a few personal items into two large duffel bags, Dusty met Joe and Peg on the palace grounds where Naumy and Hagnar, along with Tomka and Ragtar, patiently waited.

"You guys hurry back and bring my daughter, Nathan, and all the White Nights back with you," Dusty said, as the two crawled up into the saddle behind Naumy and Tomka. "Oh, and teach these guy's something about respect while you have them out there in space," He added, with a smile as he pointed to the two dragons and their riders.

"Don't worry, Dusty. Peg and I will straighten things out and be back as soon as we can. Besides, we still have to figure out the mystery of the Chamber of Exile." Joe said as they waved goodbye. The two big dragons then jumped into the air and headed for Akakor.

When they landed on the Palace grounds in Akakor, they were greeted by Cleito and the High Council.

"The Admiral has sent a supply ship to take your party to the moon base, General. But before you go, the High Council and I would like to thank you and Peggy for volunteering for this duty." Cleito told them. "You might be interested to know the crew of the Dhul Fiqar have also volunteered and will be going with you."

"Do you think it prudent to allow the very crew that started this mess, to now become part of Earth's defensive force, Your Highness?' Joe asked with a look of confusion on his face.

"Joe, I know how this may look to you, but believe me, I would have never considered it if I was not absolutely positive of their loyalty. Poseidon put Malik and his entire crew through some pretty intense mind probes in the last weeks. We now know each man no longer believes in the Jihad or the Islamic leaders who promoted it. All they want is a chance to prove to everyone they are no longer the monsters who set the world on fire. So, I told them it would be up to you, General. Oh, and by the way, the crew of the Dhul Fiqar didn't start this mess. It was started long, long ago in a different galaxy many light years from Earth."

Joe wasn't happy with this explanation and suspected the motives of the rogue crew. But at the same time he knew the importance of giving everyone a second chance. "Okay they can go," Joe finally said, shaking his head. "But I want you to know I feel uneasy about this. And it's only because we are so short handed that I'm agreeing to this."

"Yes, General, I already know what you're thinking and why," Cleito told him. But before this battle is done, I think you will be glad you took these people with you."

"There are many here who have sons and daughters that have volunteered for space duty, General, some are going with you and some have already gone with Nathan," Agab spoke up suddenly. "So we ask that you to please bring them back to us in one piece."

Peg felt a little uncomfortable as she and Joe listen to the worry in their voices and after other councilmen spoke up. "Ladies and Gentlemen, we understand your concerns and rest assured we'll do everything we can to bring your children home alive. But, I must be honest with you, anything can happen in war. Each battle is unpredictable and can be very bloody, with great loss of life. That's why war should never be fought unless you are willing to die for what you're fighting for."

Peggy's words must have made them face the reality of the situation, because they just stood there in numbed silence for a moment or two.

It was only when Sean, Lobo, and Zargon came in for a landing, did the group show signs of life again.

"We were beginning to wonder if you guys were ever going to show up," Cleito said.

"Sorry were late, Lady Cleito, but my wife and new baby boy.... Well to tell you the honest truth, it was hard to pull myself away." Sean informed with a smile.

"I understand, Major Franklin. I have a few boys of my own," Cleito replied.

"Now that you are all here, we have put together a little going away party for the volunteers in the palace ballroom," King Drac informed.

They were greeted on Moon Base Alpha by Admiral Gabriel, and Commander Clakrin, along with newly promoted Rear Admiral Amun Re, Captain Montu, and their whole bridge crew who had come out of stasis six months early to help train the new recruits.

"General, it's so good to see you and Peggy again," Gabriel greeted as the new batch of volunteers came off the supply ship.

"Well, Admiral, I'm not sure we're glad to be here, but I'll let you know after we've had a chance to see what we've gotten ourselves into," Peggy said, still a little apprehensive of the situation.

After a thousand men, women, dogs, and three dragons from ten different supply ships from around the world, had gathered together on the hangers east end, Admiral Gabriel stepped up on a podium with Joe and Peggy, along with the other staff officers. After he introduced himself and the others, he proceeded to give a short, but affective speech, much like the one Dad had given after we boarded the Dragon Fire. Then, after everyone had been sworn in, they stepped over to the rail dock and boarded the train that would take them to their new ship.

Once there, Commander Clakrin introduced everyone to the Galactic Battle Cruiser Orion. The ships design was only slightly different from the Dragon Fire. I guess the only major differences between the two were the Orion was slightly smaller and painted to look like the constellation for which it was named. However, from the bottom side looking up, all one could see was a black body. Only on the topside was the outline of the Star Hunter visible.

Like on the Dragon Fire, Commander Clakrin had assigned 500 androids to help train the new crew and to fill in the gaps in the duty-assignments until the crew was ready to take over those positions.

Because this was the first time any of these people had ever seen a battle cruiser up close, let alone been inside one, takeoff for space trials would be delayed for two days while everyone became acclimated to the new ship.

Gabriel had accompanied the staff officers to the bridge after visiting each deck and learning their function. "Well, Joe, what do you think? Do you think you'll be able to handle this bird?"

"Wow," Joe said as he shook his head in disbelief. "Now I see why Nathan was so excited about these magnificent ships. Are they all like this one?"

"Not exactly," Clakrin spoke up. "The Orion along with the Dragon Fire and the two other new cruisers yet to be christened, are a little bigger, faster, and much more advanced than the three older cruisers."

"Don't you remember the Intrepid, Captain? I mean General Carter….," Amun asked.

For a moment Joe looked confused, not understanding the question. "You must have mistaken me with someone else, Admiral," Joe replied. I served on the U.S. aircraft carrier Intrepid with Nathan Masterson during the Vietnam War, but this is the first time I've ever been on a galactic battle cruiser."

"You're probably right, Joe, and I'm sorry if that's the case. I guess it's possible that the man I'm thinking of was a distant relative of yours, but you sure do look like an older version of a brash young Marine Corp fighter pilot I had on the Intrepid about the time of the last big battle with the Black Lords. I guess that's what happens when you come out of stasis early, your memory takes time to readjust to the transition."

"Well, if you will excuse me, I need to try to find some more recruits, and a couple cruiser commanders to train them." Gabriel said.

"However, before I go, may I have a word with you in the Captains anteroom, Amun?" It was here Gabriel explained to Amun that Joe and Peggy had no memory of their past lives. "But possibly by just being on this ship, distant memories may manifest in their dreams and if they do, it would probably be a good idea to help them understand who they really are."

Amun nodded in understanding. "I understand, Sir, and won't bring it up again unless they do."

Chapter Sixty One

ABOARD THE DRAGON FIRE

10 December

We had pretty much settled into a regular routine which meant sending out cloaked fighter patrols as well as long range probes of the demon bases in the Saturn system. The data they were bringing back would be essential in planning a defensive strategy against the enemy.

"Nathan, we are receiving a transmission from Moon Base Alpha on the encrypted channel," Ron informed.

"Read it to me, Mr. Clayhorn." Dad said from his seat at the bridges command center.

"It says the second of the new battle cruisers, the GBC Orion, has now left Alpha dock for space trials. She will be under the command of Rear Admiral Amun until the training exercises are completed, and then Brigadier General Joe Carter will assume command as the ships chief officer."

Dad smiled as he said to himself, "Well, I guess Joe got his wish after all. May God go with him, his crew, and his ship."

"Delta squadron is returning from routine patrol, Nathan. It seems their squadron leader, Lt. Colonel Mitchell Beebe, is reporting some unusual enemy activity on the moon Titan," Ron reported.

Dad was not only the commander of the Dragon Fire, but he had also appointed himself head of fighter operations, because no one on board had anywhere near the experience in aerial combat. "Tell Mr. Beebe I'll meet his unit in the squadron briefing room in ten."

Ten minutes later Dad listened to Beebe's unsettling report. Beebe had been an F-15 Eagle jockey in the Air Force for twelve years, until in 1991 when he retired after fighting in Desert Storm. During that time he had the call-sign of "Mad-Dog-Mutt," because when he locked on to something he didn't let go until he brought it down. Now in his early sixties, the five foot eight inch man was balding and had gained a few more pounds than he needed, but other than that, he was a very good pilot. And since we were short on capable pilots, especially of Beebe's caliber, if Steve gave them an OK medically, they flew fighters on the Dragon Fire.

"Sir, leaving the rest of the squadron in orbit around the moon, I followed an enemy shuttle craft below the heavy cloud cover until the smog cleared at around 2,500 feet above the surface. After the demon craft landed atop a strange looking hourglass-shaped tower, which stood about two hundred feet above the ground and must have been over a hundred feet in diameter at the top, it was instantly lowered deep below the surface." Beebe paused, "Now the strange thing about this is that there were hundreds, maybe even thousands of these landing towers within a twenty five mile radius. There also were thousands of cone-shaped structures spewing the smoke or smog that filled the atmosphere. It was hard to tell whether these mounds were artificially made or a natural formation. Then, after doing a flyover for pictures, my RIO, Lt. Dagg Peterson and I, spotted many enormous ships, about twice the size of a battle cruiser, on the outer fringes of the base. They sat atop even bigger versions of those landing towers."

"Do we have the pictures yet?" Dad asked.

"They're coming through now, Sir," Major Spud Sparks, the squadrons second in command, spoke up as he watched Peterson put them up on the screen. Sparks, a tall thin, blond haired man, was born on an Idaho potato farm, which is probably why his parents named him Spud.

The pictures revealed a barren, foreboding, rocky landscape, in a mountainous region of the giant moon. The smog hung like thick black clouds blocking out almost all light, which gave the surface the constant look of dusk. Beebe's cameras had captured everything he had reported in great detail. Dad speculated the bigger ships were most likely troop carriers, capable of transporting thousands of enemy troops across vast distances of space. Then as Beebe returned to where the rest of his squadron waited in orbit, his cameras caught what looked like a lake, many times the size of Lake Superior.

"What was the location of this base, Colonel?" Dad asked, as a large picture of Titan was put up on the screen.

"Here, Sir," Beebe pointed to an area near the southern pole of the moon.

"Well, it seems they must have a lot of those bases all over that moon. Alpha, Beta, and Gamma squadrons found similar bases, here, here, and here," Dad said, as he pointed out three other areas many hundreds of miles apart. "What we don't know is exactly how many of these bases there are and if Titan is the only moon they're on."

"Well, Sir, the enemy ship the Colonel and I followed down to the surface, seemed to be coming from the heavily cratered moon Dione, but we could not determine a definite point of origin," Lt. Peterson informed.

"Sir, I think we should back off a couple hundred thousand miles and hit Titan with one of those Starburst missiles," a young pilot, Lt. Rob Parsons, offered.

A small smile formed on Dad's lips at the thought of the typical response to most military situations. "It may come to that, Mr. Parsons, but for now we are going to bide our time until we know for sure just what we're dealing with here. Remember, there are the Jupiter and Martian planetary systems between us and Earth where the enemy could also have bases."

"Sir, is there any way we could attach a small probe to one of those demon ships without them knowing it?" Beebe asked. "If we could, it might just give us some insight as to how big the enemy base is below the surface."

Dad thought for a moment. "I'm not sure if that's possible, Mitch, but you're right, it would give us a heads up as to what's down there. I'll have to talk with Robbie and Robo and see if they can come up with something." Suddenly the PA sounded. It was Ron telling Dad a message was coming through from the Orion. "Okay then, if anyone else has any more suggestions, you can write them down and turn them over to myself or Colonel Duke." With that Dad concluded the meeting, after letting the squadron know how good a job they'd done.

"What was the message from the Orion, Ron?" Dad asked as he came out of the bridge elevator.

"Admiral Amun wants you to contact him, on the secure channel," Ron replied.

"Patch the link through to my office, Ron, after you ask Pat to join me there. Duke, you have the con." Dad said before stepping into a small, but plush office just off the bridge. The secure channel Amun had referred to meant the message was for Dad and or the top command officers only.

"Admiral Amun, it's been a long time," Dad greeted, as Amun's image came up on the large two-way computer screen that rose up from the middle of the desk. "I'm here with my first officer Queen Patamaya of the Andean Underworld."

Amun was a tall, slender thirtyish-looking man with black hair, coffee-colored skin, and dark blue eyes. In today's world he would probably be considered very handsome.

"Oh yes, Patamaya, I knew your mother, Queen Mayaset, quite well. Don't worry, child, she'll be with you again soon," Amun assured nodding his head. "Nathan, it certainly is good to see you again. I wasn't sure you'd remember me, because Joe had no clue as to who I am."

"I'm sorry, Admiral, Joe has not been to Shambhala and thus doesn't remember his past lives. It was only with the help of King Chogyal and the Grandmasters, that I was able to find reason for the strange dreams that had haunted me all my life. With their guidance and a whole lot of déjà vu that I finally realized who I really am. However, even now I find it hard to believe at times."

"Well, I'm glad to see you have finally been given a rank more suited to your abilities. You were the best fighter pilot I'd ever seen and should have been promoted long before we fought the last battle with the Black Lords." Then Amun paused before telling Dad and Pat the real reason he'd contacted the Dragon Fire on a secure channel. "In another week the three older cruisers will be fully refitted and again ready for duty. They will all be manned with the personnel from what most humans are calling the Creator Race these days. In fact, after this training mission I am to take command of the Intrepid again. But Gabriel is having a hard time finding enough personnel to man the newer battle cruisers as there are just not enough of the Creator Race out of stasis at any one time to man more than the three older cruisers. And commander Clakrin cannot spare anymore androids. He barely has enough to complete the work needed at Alpha Base as it is. So, Gabriel said to ask you, since you have four bridge crews, for volunteers to go to another ship."

At that point, Pat spoke up. "Well, Admiral, we'll see if anyone wants to volunteer. But, Sir, we are currently deep within enemy space and to leave our position or to send people through deep space in no more than a shuttle craft, would put our mission and the lives of the volunteers in great jeopardy."

"Sir, I'm afraid I must agree with Patamaya," Dad said. "We are in no position to send volunteers at this time."

"What if we came to you, Nathan? We might even be able to supply you with a little backup."

Dad thought for a moment. "Admiral, I wish we had a little help out here, but until your crew has the proper training it would be better not to attempt a meeting anywhere near the Saturn system. The situation here is so volatile the smallest mistake could end all our lives."

"I understand, General. I will contact you again when this crew is battle ready." With that, Amun ended the transmission with the traditional well wishes.

Chapter Sixty Two

SUBTERRANEAN BUNKERS NEAR ST MORITZ, SWITZERLAND

12 December

While those in the protected bunkers of every nation on Earth prepared for Christmas with hopes and prayers that this year would not be their last. In another, more secret bunker, far below the Swiss Alps near the Italian-Austrian border, a seven man panel went over the plans to bring about Armageddon. Each man was responsible for one continent, with the Chairman in overall control of the black-brotherhood known as the Illuminati. And it was this brotherhood, which dictated the hundred twenty member Bilderberg Group, who in-turn controlled the heads-of-state of most every major nation on Earth, as well as just about every aspect of human existence on Earth. In short, they controlled the New World Order.

With the Bilderberg members and other high level operatives on a highly sophisticated video link, the Chairman, dressed totally in black, began the meeting. He spoke in a low, heavily accented voice that made you think evil dripped from every word. "Ladies and Gentlemen, our quest to find and release the founders of our brotherhood, those who were wrongfully imprisoned by the Lords of Light so many millennium ago, is about to become a reality. Although we have recently lost many of our most trusted people in the United States, we are still in control in the rest of North America, as well as Europe and Asia." With that said the shadowy figure at one end of the large oval-shaped conference table seemed to sit back a few inches in his black desk chair and almost disappear from view. "Number seven can you give us an update on the battle for Australia and New Zealand?"

"Sir, the radiation levels from the rogue bombs are very low in Australia. In fact, they are only slightly above normal." The tall, bald man in a black suit, with the gray eyes, responded from the far end of the table. "There, the battles rage mainly on the surface and in my opinion, it is just about even. Our dark brothers from Mars were able to reanimate the bodies of fallen humans for awhile, until the Children of Light got a large supply of EPD weapons. Now it looks like the battles have started to swing the other way. However, our people within that government assure me they have everything under control." Number Seven paused before going on. "As far as New Zealand is concerned, we have all but lost any chance of taking control there. Unlike other nations of the world, their unity is very strong and it's almost impossible to drive the wedge of deception into their society on any level."

The Chairman drummed his fingers on the table in disgust as he digested the news of defeat and the lack of control of the two nations. "You will take control of Australia at any cost or face the consequences, Number Seven. Now, Number Six, would you give us your report on Africa?"

"Sir, most all of the Saharan countries have been subjected to so much radioactive fallout they no longer have any measurable life force of any kind," a black man in his early forties sitting just to the left of Number Seven, stated. "All the countries south of the Atlas Mountains, except for South Africa, are now under our control. We are presently engaged in a series of surface battles, with that country that are swinging back and forth, and at this point it's too early to predict the outcome."

"Number Five, have we taken full control of South America yet?" The Chairman asked, still unhappy with Numbers Six and Seven's reports.

Sweat began to bead up on the brow of the short portly man in the dark-gray suit. He sat to the left of Number Six and wished he had the news the Chairman wanted to hear.

"Well, Sir, the truth of the matter is, we pretty much have control over Brazil, Bolivia, Ecuador, and Colombia, but as far as the rest of the continent is concerned I'm afraid it's an ongoing struggle, despite our best efforts. While all the northern countries have been virtually wiped out from high levels of radiation, most of the countries of the Andes are getting a lot of support from a hidden cell of Light Children, and their creator Lords."

The Chairman leaned forward into the light so all could see his face. He looked to be in his early forties with strong handsome features. His long, black, shoulder length hair was combed straight back, but when his eyes went from coal black to blood red, everyone in the room and on the video link knew this was no ordinary human, and when he spoke, his words were almost hypnotic. "Let me make this clear to all of you. It's imperative we find the chamber where the Lords of Darkness are imprisoned before our brothers in space start their final assault. To do that we must have complete control of every continent on Earth."

In the Washington DC bunkers, the military was impressed with the suddenness in which the last battle had ended. On the surface, thousands of charred bodies lay rotting in the streets after the Vice President ordered the fighters in with another napalm drop, and followed it up with an attack from the helicopter mounted EPD's. Mark Baker suggested this tactic even though it may reduce all the national monuments and landmarks to rubble, it would most likely save the government for which they stood.

Another breakthrough came while the review board was questioning the former Joint Chief's. They had finally decided to tell everything they knew about the black brotherhood and the people and organizations they control. Now, dressed in casual civilian attire and under no pressure to say anything for fear of prosecution, the former Chief's told how they'd been recruited while still at their respected military academies, how they'd come up through the ranks believing they were doing what was best for the country, and how it was not until recently they figured out how evil the "New World Order's" agenda truly was. But the bottom line was that all they really knew about the shadowy figures in control of the world's most vital agencies was, they were somewhere in Switzerland, and were protected by every industrial nation on Earth.

It was General Wells who finally told the review panel how to contact the Chairman through a series of encrypted codes. But even then, it was uncertain if there would be any response, especially if he thought the Joint Chief's had been compromised.

Then General Farmer explained how this group had informants around every corner and how no one really knew who was working for whom. "Even though the Bilderberg Group is the best known, this brotherhood has many secret societies under its control."

"What about the Freemasons?" A member of the board asked.

"The truth is no one really knows for sure just where the Masons stand on anything. That's because only a very few from their inner core knows their real agendas. However, if you weigh all the circumstantial evidence you can deduce their involvement with the NWO and the black brotherhood. And, you may think Interpol and the governments of Europe are trying to help you in this investigation, but I can assure you, Gentlemen, all they'll do is mislead you with fancy lip-service down a series of dead ends and blind alleys," Admiral Parks informed. "The Illuminati control all the major banking systems in the world, so no government is going to help you find them."

"Do you think there's a connection between the recent bombings in the Mid-East and the Illuminati?" General Baker asked.

"I don't think so," Wells spoke up. "Even though they do control the world's purse strings and a whole lot more, it was Bin Laden and his Islamic terrorist groups that were standing in the way of complete world domination. Or at least that's the way it was before those nukes went off."

"And now that the knowledge of the Creator Race is out in the open and the dark demons have actually attacked the Earth, the black-brotherhood and the Bilderberg Group are pushing even harder to find and free the Black Lords," Farmer offered.

"Once freed, the battle of Armageddon would soon follow," Mark Baker finished as he realized the end game, while the former Joint Chief's just nodded in agreement.

Chapter Sixty Three

DEEP SPACE ABOARD THE ORION

25 December

Christmas Day aboard the Orion was just like all the others since they'd left the moon base. Now in orbit around Mars, training was now in its twentieth day. They had found the abandoned bases on the two moons where the demons had demolished them. And deep within the planets subterranean tunnels, an exploration team from the Orion found miles upon miles of still working power grids. The dark demons had utilized the massive rivers and lakes that were once on the surface before being hit with a massive meteor strike thousands of years ago. These power grids used great steam generators to produce enough clean electricity to power the planets subterranean cities for a million or more years.

However, only a few of these once demon colonies remained, totaling a few thousand individuals in each. And the beings that now lived here, wanted nothing more to do with war, hate, or the dark demons and Black Lords they had once swore their allegiance to. In fact, some of them had already started to change back to their original races, the races they belonged to before the Great rebellion against King Adonai in the Canis Star System. Of course, these beings would have to be monitored on a regular basis, but Admiral Amun thought that someday soon, if everything continued the way it should, this planet would be recognized as a colony of the United Planets of Nirvana the way Earth is today.

In much the same way, Dad had run a relentless training program of exhausting, unending drills and exercises, so was the daily routines aboard the Orion. Even though the crew had hoped today would be different, with possibly a few hours to celebrate the Holiday, it was not to be. When a young lieutenant asked why, she was told, by one of the android instructors that the Dark Demons and Black Lords wouldn't hesitate to use this weakness against them. "When you finish your training and have become as sharp as the keenest blade, then you can celebrate."

Before leaving Moon Base Alpha, Admiral Amun realized he had his work cut out for him. He would have to be the ships Commanding Officer as well as conduct a highly affective training program in two months, maybe ten weeks, for a program that would normally take two years to complete at the United Star Academy on Sirius. This meant around the clock exercises and drills that he knew would break the spirit of most humans by the second week. However, if the threat of war was as bad as he'd been told and personnel were truly limited, then there were no other options to consider.

Even before they'd lifted off the moon, Joe and Peggy, along with many other officers, had spent a couple days learning the basics of each department. When it came time to leave moon dock, Amun asked Joe to take command of the ship for departure. Now it was Joe's turn to show how much he'd learned in such a short time. Needless to say the Admiral was very impressed at just how fast Joe had caught on. "I've never seen anyone take to this job so quickly," Amun commented. "It's as if you were born for it."

"Well, Sir, it's not all that different from flying a fighter, except a battle cruiser is a lot bigger and you have other people working the controls for you," Joe said with a smile.

"Well, now that you understand the operations of the Orion, General, I would like for you to take over the training of its fighter pilots, because, Commander Clakrin didn't have time to program the android instructors with any real aerial-combat knowledge. So other than knowing how to start the craft, and the different functions of its instruments, which the pilots can read from the operations manual," Amun, just shook his head, in a not knowing who else to ask gesture. "Our android instructors know nothing of actual combat."

"Sir, I understand, and I'll be happy to take the job, it's the same one I've been doing for the past forty years. Besides when we go into a fight, I want to know I have only the best trained fighter pilots under my command."

"I knew you would understand."

"What station do you want me at, Admiral?" Peggy asked, after Joe headed for the pilots briefing room on E-deck.

"Well, Colonel, I think you should start out at the helm." Amun replied as he pointed to the middle seat directly in front of the command station. Then, he proceeded in assigning the other stations around the bridge to the remaining volunteer officers. An android stood by to help each person learn the function of that position.

At this time, Malik and his crew were learning other stations throughout the ship. Joe and Peggy thought it best to split them up until they were sure they could be trusted. If they worked well with others and followed orders to the letter, as well as learn the jobs they were assigned, the bridge crew of the Dhul Fiqar would then be allowed to take positions on Orion's bridge. Amun, on the other hand, had no doubt Malik and his crew would perform admirably once they understood the workings of the ship. But then, Joe and Peggy had only recently been exposed to the enhancement serums, which allowed a person to look deep into the soul of another and really know that person for who and what they truly are. Of course, in time this would come as natural to them as it did to the Creator Race and, to them, it was almost like breathing.

The Orion had now been in space for about twenty two days and Amun could not believe how well the training had gone so far. Except for just a few minor mishaps due to the over zealousness of those who fell short of impressing on others what they thought they could do, or to fatigue that seemed to hold the whole ship's crew in its grip, both crew and ship were exceeding all expectations.

Joe had even made great progress with the two hundred or so volunteer pilots, many without any prior training whatsoever. Some of these volunteers were given to Tomka and Naumy, who had been temporarily assigned to fighter duty and promoted to the rank of Captain. Zargon, Ragtar, and Hagnar, were now in charge of the ships security personnel, as well as the hundred or so assault troops that may be used to take and secure an enemy base without blowing it all to hell.

Even though they had never been inside a fighter before now, Tomka and Naumy's training at the Dragon Squadron Academy helped them to understand the dynamics of aerial-combat tactics. And, after learning to fly the F-48 fighter with precision in simulators, they along with a few other volunteers who were ex-fighter pilots, could now help Joe train the other recruits.

In one of the bigger conference rooms where Joe usually held his training briefings, he addressed all his fighter personnel. "Now that we've finished our research here in the Martian system, I want to congratulate each of you on a job well done. It's not often that a group such as yourselves has caught on as fast as you have. However, there is a lot more to learn if we are going to be battle ready by the time we get to the Saturn system and hook up with our sister ship the Dragon Fire. In the meantime, we'll be moving on to the much larger Jupiter system. Because this system has a wide variety of moon types, I'm going to assign each of you to a seven ship squadron, for a total of fourteen squadrons. Each squadron will go by a letter from the Greek alphabet, starting with Alpha and going through Xi. Each ship will have the name of its pilot and RIO just below the cockpit. And, as we get more personnel, we will be able to add more squadrons." A hand went up in the back of the room. "Yes, Mr. Lee?"

"Sir, the Greek alphabet only has twenty four letters. If we had a full complement of fighter squadrons, they would number twenty eight. What would we call the other four?"

"Well, Major, the remaining 32 ships will be held in reserve in case one breaks down or....." Everyone knew the "or" meant a ship and crew had been lost. Joe then pushed a button on the daises control panel displaying the Jupiter System on the main screen. "We will only be using our fighter squadrons to explore the four largest moons: Io, Europa, Callisto, and Ganymede." Joe used a laser pointer to indicate each moon. "For the other 57 smaller moons, we will send probes."

When Joe asked if there were any questions, hands went up all over the room.

On these new ships the officer's quarters were as plush as a five diamond resort. There was an outer room with sofas and chairs, a desk with an advanced computer system, as well as a table and chairs for dining in. There was also a huge bedroom with all the latest in sleep comfort, and a nice large bathroom with all the amenities.

That night, Joe tossed and turned in his large king-sized bed, as visions of a long distant past once again invaded his dreams. It was the same nightmare he'd had for years now, the one where Nathan's fighter is on fire as they landed on the Intrepid.

"Joe, wake up," Peggy said gently as she shook his shoulder. "You're dreaming again." Suddenly, Joe sat straight up yelling Dad's name. Sweat had soaked his pajamas as well as the sheets on his side of the bed. "That same dream again, I'll bet," Peg guessed.

"Yeah, it seems like I'm having it almost every night, now that we've come aboard this ship."

"Have you ever talked to someone about it, Joe?" Peggy asked as she gently rubbed his back.

"I talked to Dusty about it a few weeks back, but no, I haven't seen a professional shrink if that's what you're asking." Then he remembered something Dusty had told him. "However, the morning Dusty and I discussed it he said he thought Nathan had similar nightmares as they explored the Andean Underworld last year. Dusty said Nathan would wake up yelling and covered with sweat, much the same way I do. When he asked Pat if there was anything they could do, she said it may be better to ignore it and hoped it went away. But it never did. And, from what she could decipher from what Nathan was yelling, the events that caused these dreams were very real. However, she got the feeling they hadn't happened in this lifetime."

Peggy looked confused as her brow wrinkled. "Why did she say that?"

"Well, because the nightmare was about a big battle in space. I guess Nathan's ship was hit pretty bad and on fire, but he manages to get it into the landing bay. He and Duke are immediately taken to the sickbay but…..they don't make it." Tears started to well-up in Joe's eyes as if he'd been there and the memory was just too horrible to bear.

"Why do I get the feeling the dreams you are having are the same ones Nathan has?"

"Look, I can't explain it," Joe said shaking his head. "But these dreams are so real."

At that point something came to Joe he'd not thought of before. "Wait a minute Admiral Amun was there, except in the dream, Amun wore the insignia of a Captain."

"Well you know when we met Amun at Moon Base he thought he recognized you," Peg reminded.

"My God, it did happen, but how can that be?" Joe said shaking his head.

A half hour later Joe and Peg met with Amun in his anteroom adjacent to the bridge.

"Well, Joe, Gabriel told me not to bring the subject up unless you mentioned it and I assured him I wouldn't. However, now that you have, I can see why you are so confused. After all these years, having the same dream, lifetime after lifetime," the Admiral said sympathetically shaking his head. "Yes, it is true, Joe. You were Nathan's wingman in the battle we fought with the Black Lords about 13,000 Earth years ago. And, yes, it's true that Nathan and Duke died that dark day, as did you, Peggy and your canine RIO, Lieutenant Spike, about two months later." Amun paused as he noted the shock in their faces. "You were on your honeymoon, if memory serves me right. It seems after the battle, many demon ships came down and hid in the dense forest, mountains, and deserts all over the planet. I guess they figured from there, they would slowly infiltrate the human race and spread their poison to all mankind. Well, when we found your bodies in a shuttle craft that had been shot to pieces and a crashed demon ship nearby; it wasn't too hard to figure out what happened."

"But how can that be?" Peggy asked, confused at hearing her name mentioned.

"Well let me start at the beginning. At the time of the battle, Nathan's squadron, which consisted of many of the people you have been recently reacquainted with, were assigned to the Intrepid. After the battle, Gabriel was literally heartbroken. He looked upon Nathan as if he were his own son. In fact, he had a real close relationship with his entire squadron which was known as the White Knights of Avalon. So, he appealed to King Adonai and the Great Creator, El Shaddai, to come up with a way to return the many souls we'd lost."

"Reincarnation," Joe said skeptically, shaking his head in disbelief.

"Well, when we first started the program it was called soul-rebirth and the only problem was that, in most cases, it takes many lifetimes for the soul to remember who they truly are. Usually their only clue is through strange reoccurring dreams that make little or no sense, such as the ones you've been having, or equally puzzling déjà vu visions." Amun paused. "In each lifetime, we try to keep family and friends together. That's why you feel closer to certain people than others, even though you may have only just met them."

"Does everyone go through this reincarnation process after their body dies?" Peggy asked. "Even those individuals filled with evil such as, Hitler or Stalin?"

"Most everyone is given the chance to redeem themselves over many lifetimes, even the most vile, but sometimes, in rare cases, the evil goes so deep the soul has to be, shall we say, sent into oblivion," Amun answered, with sadness in his voice. "Then there those that can be saved from that fate. Take for example, those beings we found on Mars a few days ago who were once filled with the blackest hate imaginable, but now they have begun to return to the light. And, I guess that's what King Adonai hopes will happen to Lucifer, because he won't allow us to knowingly kill him. Personally, I think he's a lost cause, but it's not my call."

Chapter Sixty Four

THE JUPITER SYSTEM
2 January

As the Orion approached the Jupiter system at full impulse, all seemed to be as it should. However, everyone was at general-quarters, with shields raised to maximum and the cloaking system engaged. Amun didn't want to be caught off guard, so he told Joe to launch a fighter squadron as soon as they established high orbit around Callisto, the outer most of the four larger Galilean moons.

Joe had picked Alpha squadron for this mission and placed Beta squadron on ready-standby to back them up in case Alpha ran into trouble. In the preflight briefing he told his pilots to stay off the radio, and to use coded messaging when communicating. "Make your altitude no less than 30,000 feet, and stay cloaked at all times. If you pick up anything you're unsure of, send the data to the Orion immediately. We will analyze it and let you know whether or not it requires further investigation. Are there any questions?"

"Sir," a young lieutenant from Beta raised his hand.

"Yes, Mister Parks?"

"Exactly what are we looking for down there?"

"Well, I would think if the enemy had a base here in the Jupiter system, it would look much like the ones we found in the Martian system. They will probably be hidden in impact craters, or maybe disguised to look like rock-outcroppings, or even in subterranean facilities hidden below the moon's surface. These bases might be huge, hiding many ships, or small like an early warning substation. If your instruments pick up a metal return or anything that might remotely indicate something artificial, you might want to give that area another flyby."

"Sir," The flight leader of Alpha squadron raised his hand.

"Yes, Mister Pike?" Joe said pointing to the Colonel.

"Do we have permission to attack a target if we deem it to be hostile?" Before joining the Galactic Marines, Ed Pike, a slender man, forty-eight, with salt and pepper hair, had flown F-14 Tomcats for the U.S. Navy until he retired last year after twenty years of service. He wanted to spend more time with his wife and family, but after the recent attack on Earth by the dark demons, he knew he had to help defend the planet.

"Only if you are fired upon, Colonel, otherwise get all the Intel you can on the site, pictures, co-ordinance, size, you know the drill." Joe looked around the room before continuing. "If we actually find an enemy base and are able to keep our presence hidden from him, we may be able to send in a strike team and capture valuable data such as: other bases, ship strength, or find out if they're planning an another invasion of Earth. However, if you're fired upon, it means your cover is blown and you should attack and eliminate the target as quickly as possible before they can call for help." Joe looked around the room for more questions, and then left them with a final warning. "Remember; don't ever let your guard down. If the enemy is down there, he could blow your ship to pieces in a blink of an eye. At the end of the day, you're not going to step out of a simulator and say I passed. This is the real deal people, be smart, stay loose, and good hunting. Prepare to launch in fifteen." With that, Joe turned and walked out of the room with Tomka and Naumy following close behind.

Joe, Amun, and Peggy watched the fighters launch from the bridge. Their emotions were mixed, but it all boiled down to one question. Are they ready?

"Well, we'll soon know the answer," Amun stated as the last of Alpha Squadron left E-deck and headed for Callisto.

When they reached their altitude they turned on their cameras and high-resolution sensors that could record even the slightest irregularity or unnatural anomaly on the surface. Almost immediately they picked up the low-frequency radio waves radiating from Jupiter, which was normal considering its size and the massive amounts of radiation it gives off. However, the fighters picked up nothing artificial or unusual, except for the fact that almost every square mile of Callisto was covered in impact-craters. I guess one could say this moon, about the size of Mercury, had truly taken one hell of an asteroid beating over the years.

After Callisto, there was Ganymede. This moon, larger than Mercury by 234 miles in diameter, also has many dark craters. Naumy was flight leader for Beta squadron which had been chosen for this moon. Gamma squadron was on ready-standby, with Tomka as flight leader.

Soon after reaching their assigned altitude, Naumy's RIO Lieutenant Lora Clark, a raven haired, twenty six year old, beauty, with blue eyes, picked up a movement in one of the darker impact craters.

"What was that?" Naumy asked.

"It was like a huge door opening and then closing again."

"Advise the Orion, Lora. Let them know were turning around for another pass."

But just as Naumy started his turn he spotted twenty enemy fighters at 28,000 feet, heading in their direction. At first Naumy thought they had been detected and this was their welcoming committee coming to meet them. But, when the demon craft went by without a challenge, he ordered his squadron to follow. "Well, I guess that explains your readings, Lieutenant," Naumy said while rechecking his instruments to making sure they had not been seen. "You'd better let the Orion know we are in pursuit."

After five minutes the demon fighters headed out into space at high-warp. "Orion, please advise, do we continue to follow?"

"Negative Beta, get a positive location on enemy launch bay and return to base."

"Return to base?" Naumy said confused, after Lora passed on the message. He wasn't happy about it, but an order, was an order.

It took about fifteen minutes to find the enemy's underground base and get some pictures before heading for the Orion. Once there, they found Orion's entire fighter command in the main briefing room.

"How many enemy fighters did you see?" Tomka asked in a whispered tone, as Naumy sat down in the seat beside him.

"Twenty."

"Do you know where they were headed?"

"I'm not sure. They hit hyperspace five minutes after we picked them up. Then we were ordered back to the Orion."

It was at that point Joe walked in.

"General on deck," A young lieutenant called out.

"As you were," Joe said as he made his way to the screen at the front of the room, where an image of Ganymede seemed to magically appear. "First of all, I want to congratulate Beta squadron on a job well done. They found a subterranean demon base located here in an impact-crater." Joe used a laser-pointer to show the exact location of the enemy base, which now filled the screen. "As you can see, it is well defended with many ion and laser cannon installations, as well as what we believe are missile silos. This facility looks to be impenetrable, but the situation computer is working on the possibility of a commando strike as we speak. And, if the computer gives us a likeable scenario, we plan to send down a team and extract what information we can about demon bases throughout the solar system."

Flight Leader Major Bob Lee of Delta-Squadron raised his hand at the back of the room. "Sir, are we to understand that we're going to land troops down there?" Major Lee, 45, was of average height, slender build, with green eyes. He had reached the rank of Lt. Commander in the U.S. Navy where he had jockeyed F-18's until retiring two years ago to become a test pilot for a big aerospace company. Now he was the Delta-squadron flight leader and loved the adventure of space.

"Yes, Major, that's exactly what I'm proposing."

"But won't that destroy our element of surprise?"

"Not unless someone gets careless, but they're probably going to know we're here shortly after we blow the place up." Joe paused as he once again weighed the possibilities in his mind. "However, it will be worth the risk if we can retrieve the information we're after."

At that point Naumy raised his hand. "Sir, do we know yet where those enemy fighters were headed."

"Given their co-ordinance when they hit hyperspace, and the direction they were heading, it looks like they might be headed for the Saturn system. We have sent the Dragon Fire a coded heads-up and informed them as to how we're planning to take the enemy base on Ganymede."

Four hours later a shuttle craft launched from E-deck with a commando strike team on board. The ten member unit consisted of five men, three women, and two dragons. The mission commanders, Hagnar and Ragtar, had been fitted with special suits which served the same purpose as the space suits the human team members wore, except these suits had special vent's that allowed dragons to expel fireballs whenever needed, and a fifteen percent mixture of sulfur-dioxide added to their air supply.

Each of the human members carried an advanced version of a laser weapon. It was a hand held weapon, and came in both pistol and rifle versions, and could be set to different firing settings, from stun to meltdown.

And since they had found this base, Beta-squadron was dispatched to provide support in case their fighters made an unexpected appearance. Gamma-squadron would be on ready-standby.

Chapter Sixty Five

THE SATURN SYSTEM

3 January

Dad, Pat, and I sat with the senior officers and department heads in one of the smaller conference rooms on A-deck. In this morning's meeting we discussed duty-roster changes and crew concerns in a more relaxed environment.

"Commander Robbie, are the cadets still on track for graduation next week?" Dad asked.

"Yes, Sir, and I might say they have all passed with excellent scores." Robbie answered.

"And General, you and Colonel Duke will be glad to hear that Second Lieutenants Anthony Masterson, Mathew Dodson, Duke Masterson Jr, Rufus Masterson, and Spike Franklin will be part of our fighter personnel," Robo added.

We didn't have much of a chance to visit with the boys since they'd entered training, but with that said, Dad and I swelled with pride at the thought of our children becoming pilots and RIO's in a fighter squadron.

"Does anyone have any major concerns or problems that need immediate attention?" Pat asked.

"What about bridge personnel are there any concerns we need to address here?" I asked looking in the direction of the former sub commanders who were sitting together at the far end of the table.

"Sir, I hate to say this but my men are being overcome with boredom, just sitting here waiting for something to happen day after day," Josh Worthington spoke up.

"Yeah, so are mine," Bill Northfield agreed. "Sir, I know our being here is of the utmost importance to the future of planet Earth, but...."

Frank Foster just nodded, and then added, "Yeah, my people are so bored they seem to constantly argue over the smallest things. I constantly have to put people on report for letting these squabbles get out of hand."

"I understand your frustration, Gentlemen, but until the enemy makes a move there's not much we can do," Pat said. "I'm sure if you ask a cop he'll tell you that stakeout duty is the most boring of all police work."

"Besides, I think they will be making their move before long" Dad spoke up. "We have uncovered over a hundred enemy bases now on twelve moons. And, I believe those fighters that came in from the Jupiter system yesterday are a sign of something big about to happen."

Just then a beep sounded on the room's intercom. "Nathan, we have just intercepted an emergency message from a base on Ganymede in the Jupiter system. It's addressed to the High Lord on Titan and says they are being attacked by humans and dragons," Ron informed.

"Thanks, Ron, please keep me informed as to any transmitted response from Titan or if any ships suddenly leave this system."

Thirty minutes later, Mr. Yang beeps in over the intercom. "Sir, there is a full battle fleet taking off from Impetus. There are at least four battle cruisers and twenty of those smaller corsairs accompanying each cruiser. And Sir, I'm picking up plasma trails of even more clocked ships."

"Sir," Larry Carver cut in. "It would seem by their last heading before going to warp that they could very well be going to the Jupiter system."

It was at this point Dad started rapidly giving orders. "Ron, recall all our patrols squadrons and get a message to the Orion. Let them know what's possibly coming their way. Then send a priority-one message to Adm. Gabriel informing him of the situation. Mr. Perry, as soon as all our patrols are back aboard the Dragon Fire, lay in a course for the

Jupiter system at maximum warp." Dad then pressed a button on the ships intercom and asked Lt. Commander Upsilon in engineering, for warp-eight in twenty minutes.

Then Dad turned back to his senior officers and said, "Well, Gentlemen, it would seem the boredom you spoke of, is now over."

When we came out of warp, about two hours later, there was no battle of any kind going on. We had expected the Orion to be fighting for her very life. However, we found her still cloaked and in orbit around Ganymede. There was not even the slightest plasma trail, which would indicate cloaked ships, so where had the enemy fleet gone?

Ron established on screen contact with the Orion. "Well, Joe, it looks like you and Peg made it into space after all," Dad said smiling. "Congratulations on your new command."

"Thank you and it's good to see you too, Nathan. Where are all these demon ships you told us about?"

"Well, according to my intel, they were headed in this direction, and they may still be on their way. We were able to kick our engines up a few notches over what we believe theirs are capable of. So we should be about eight to ten hours ahead of them depending on whether or not the larger troop transports can do more than warp-two."

"Nathan, the ships you detected leaving the Saturn system may not even be coming here. Since this year marks a rare alignment of the planets in this star system they may be heading straight for Earth as the spearhead of their invasion fleet," Amun advised.

"I agree, Admiral," Dad said nodding his head. "They wouldn't send that many ships just to defend a listening station that was most likely lost anyway."

"Were you able to get any useful information from the demon base, Admiral?" Pat asked.

"Yes, we found out the demons have bases throughout the Saturn system, with many small moon listening stations, like the one here on Ganymede, and throughout the whole star system," Amun replied solemnly. "In my opinion, we have gravely underestimated the enemy's strength and should return home at maximum warp."

"Captain Clayhorn, get Adm. Gabriel on a secure deep-space com-link."

"Aye, Aye, Sir." Ron responded.

Five minutes later, Admiral Gabriel, suddenly appeared on a split screen and after being advised of the situation, ordered both ships to return to Moon Base Alpha at maximum warp. We were told to except some changes in crew assignments at that time, and to ask for volunteers to transfer to other ships.

On the trip home, both ships deployed deep space sensor buoys in an extremely wide pattern, to alert the home fleet of the enemy advance. These buoys could pick up any movement, no matter how small, for a million miles in any direction. They could identify the object, calculate its speed, and relay the information to the moon base or Earth in a matter of seconds. And it didn't matter if the object was cloaked or not. So we should have plenty of notice as to when and where the demon ships were going to strike.

Once we arrived at the moon base things started to happen very quickly. We discovered all our battle cruisers were now operational and ready to be deployed. Gabriel had been busy these last few weeks finding personnel to man them. Of course, he had to finally draft over six thousand people from the different militaries around the world, and brought over two thousand of the Creator Race out of stasis early. And, Commander Clakrin and his androids had been training the new recruits day and night for weeks now.

Once we established a link with the docking tethers, the shift in personnel went smoothly. Of course, the Defiant, and Scorpion already had their new crews on board and had taken up defensive positions around Earth. The Intrepid would be leaving as soon as Adm. Amun and his crew transferred over from the Orion.

King Chogyal and Dohna were now in command of the Defiant, with a crew mostly from Shambhala. They had been assigned over a thousand new recruits to fill in the gaps in their personnel roster. The King would also be in overall operational command of the coming battle in space.

Commanding the Scorpion would fall to the newly promoted Admiral Tyr and Captain Freyr. Since they already had a full crew complement from Asgard, they only needed a few fighter crews to replace the ones lost in the recent battle with the dark demons.

Joe and Peggy assumed total command of the Orion, with Major Malik and the former crew of the Dhul Fiqar as their primary bridge crew. They had also been assigned a thousand new recruits from whom a secondary bridge crew would be formed. A few of our newly graduated cadets also volunteered to go over to Joe's ship. My nephew Skip was among them.

Admiral Amun took command of the Intrepid with Captain Montu and his original bridge crew. He was assigned 1,600 new recruits; over half were from the Creator Race. Androids filled in the rest of ships personnel.

Josh Worthington, Paula Jones, and the former crew of the USS Tennessee, took command of the newly commissioned GBC Polaris, named after the North Star. They were assigned 1,600 new recruits and around 400 androids.

Frank Foster, Paul Wilson, and the former crew of the USS Portland took over command of the GBC Leo. Their whole ships company was made up of new recruits.

Bill Northfield and his crew decided to stay with us on the Dragon Fire, which was fine with Dad because most everyone on board liked the Colonel and got along well with his crew. We were only assigned a thousand new recruits, which brought us up to a full crew complement. We even had enough to round out our fighter crews to a full twenty eight squadrons.

Chapter Sixty Six

HIGH EARTH ORBIT

4 January

Since the direction from which the dark demons would launch their attack was unknown at this time, King Chogyal decided to send the four newer ships to points about a half million miles out from Earth, with one ship in each of the four quadrants. The three older cruisers would take up a triangular position in high orbit around Earth at equal distances apart. Admiral Gabriel would be in overall command of Earths defenses. He and the other underworld leaders had worked frantically since receiving Dad's message about a pending attack, to bring Earths ancient ion and laser cannons on-line and ready for action.

The Dragon Fire was assigned to the Alpha Quadrant, which was straight out toward the sun and the most likely the point the main attack would come from. Joe and Peg had the Delta Quadrant, on the exact opposite side as ours, which was the second most likely attack possibility. This put the two ex-sub commanders between us, with Josh and Paula, a half million miles straight out from the North Pole in the Beta Quadrant and Frank Foster in the Gamma Quadrant, a half million miles out from the South Pole.

Once all our ships were in position, Admiral Gabriel appeared on every viewing screen throughout the fleet and throughout the underworld on Earth. He told us how proud he was of everyone who had volunteered to defend Earth from the evil that was coming to destroy it. "I think you all know what we're faced with here today. The enemy has an overwhelming force that is determined to accomplish three things; to free the Black Lords, to destroy the human race, and to enslave the Lords of Light. As soon as I got General Masterson's message about the size of the demon armada, I sent a message to Sirius and advised them of the situation. I got a return message from King Adonai this morning, which read: Gabriel you must hold out until help arrives. I am returning Michael and the Second Fleet to Earth at maximum warp. They should be there in about a week maybe two, Earth time. May the Creator be with you and your fleet." Gabriel paused a moment as he refolded the communiqué. "To the men, women, dragons, canines, and androids of the First Fleet of Sirius, and to all those of the underworld colonies who will help fight off the coming threat, I salute you and all that you stand for." With that Gabriel broke the transmission.

Ten seconds later King Chogyal replaced him on each ships bridge screen to make sure we all knew the battle plan. "Sensor-buoys and space-mines have been placed in all quadrants which should help equal the playing-field, but whatever comes through after that, I'm afraid we we'll have to take them on, ship to ship. As soon as a deep space buoy goes active, the closest cruiser will fire five Starburst Missiles in a wide spread pattern, to detonate two hundred thousand miles out from your present positions. If possible, I will send one of the older cruisers to help defend a quadrant if I feel it's going to be overrun." Chogyal paused. "I don't have to tell you how important it is to stop these demons before they get to Earth and establish a foothold. If they do, this whole star system could be in danger of collapse. Are there any questions? Just then Ron turned to Dad. "Nathan, one of those sensor-buoys is signaling a massive force of over a thousand ships, a little over a million miles out, traveling at warp- two."

"Sound general quarters, battle stations" I barked. "Raise shields and make us invisible, David."

"Mr. Yang, fire starburst missiles," Dad ordered as he looked over at Pat and saw the fear in her eyes. "Ron, get a message off to Chogyal letting him know the battle for Earth has just begun."

About twenty minutes later a blinding light lit up the sky when the Starburst Missiles went off. With the bridge screen on maximum magnification, we could make out ship after ship exploding in space. Then, a series of periodic fireballs as the enemy ships hit the minefield. At warp speed they were unable to detect the mines until it was too late.

"Stand by to launch fighters, all squadrons," Dad ordered.

"Fighters are ready to launch, Sir," Angela said after a couple minutes.

"Launch fighters," Pat ordered after she finally found her voice. "Bring ion cannons to bear and open fire as soon as targets are in range."

As the remainder of the demon ships, about three hundred, came out of warp just under a thousand miles away, they were instantly hit with cannon fire. Most were the smaller Corsairs which meant the big cruisers had been either destroyed or put out of commission. At this point our fighter squadrons attacked with all the fury of a hive of mad hornets.

"Sir," Ron said. "The Orion is also under heavy attack. One of the enemy cruisers came out of warp in the Delta quadrant, but it had suffered heavy damage and was blown to bits, with the Orion's ion cannons, before they could launch their fighters."

"Good shooting, Ole Buddy, Dad thought to himself.

"What about Beta and Gamma quadrants?" Bill Northfield asked a little worried about the former sub crews.

"As of yet there has been no activity in those sectors, Sir," Ron replied.

On the fighter to ship intercom, Alpha and Beta squadrons were inflicting heavy damage to one of those huge troop transports, which had somehow made it through the gauntlet of missiles and mines. It was probably because it was a lot slower than the rest of the enemy ships and came through after they had cleared the way. Since there were no enemy fighters to contend with in this quadrant, the rest of our squadrons were taking on the corsairs with much success. Dad was impressed with how well our fighters were doing, but his main concern was that Anthony, Matt, and my two boys were out there somewhere with Lt. Colonel Beebe and Delta Squadron. Duke Jr. ended up as Anthony's RIO, while

Rufus became Matt's. They had been assigned to Delta Squadron on our way home, before we got the new recruits at Moon Base Alpha.

"Sir, all sectors are now repelling incoming enemy ships," Ron informed.

The Orion was now engulfed in a sea of enemy corsairs and troop ships, but like us, she was holding her own. It was the Polaris and the Leo that Chogyal was most concerned about. At least two enemy battle cruisers had come through in each quadrant and had launched fighters as soon as they came out of warp. As soon as he realized what had happened, Chogyal sent the Intrepid to help the Polaris and the Scorpion to help the Leo.

"Damn! We've thrown everything we have at these demon bastards and they still keep coming!" Paula said.

"Sir, a message coming in from the Intrepid," Ensign Brooks informed.

"Put Adm. Amun on screen, Ben," Josh said.

"Colonel, what is your status?" Amun asked, as soon as he appeared on screen.

"Sir, we've sustained heavy damage to shields and our port impulse engine and we're down to only twelve fighter squadrons. However, we were able to take out a battle cruiser, as well as a troop ship, about fifty of those corsairs, and around a hundred enemy fighters. Their second enemy cruiser is heavily damaged, and won't last long, but at this rate, Sir, I'm not sure we will either."

"Hold on, Mr. Worthington, we're about a hundred thousand miles out and should be there in fifteen. I want you to move the Polaris 122 degrees to starboard and hold that position until we arrive. We will de-cloak at the same time and unleash everything we have."

"Understood, Sir," Josh replied just before the Admiral ended the transmission.

"Mr. Brooks, inform our fighter squadrons of our new heading," Paula ordered.

By the time the Polaris was in position, the Intrepid pulled up about two hundred miles away. The enemy squadrons had completely missed the movement of the cloaked ships and were still concentrating their fire where the Polaris had been. But when both ships suddenly de-cloaked at a different location, the demon ships were under the impression two new ships of Light had entered the battle. When the combined fire from both ships ion cannons hit what was left of the enemy force, only a few demon fighters remained and they were headed out into deep space as fast as they could go.

"Thank you, Sir, for your help. I don't think we would have lasted much longer if you hadn't shown up." Josh said as Amun appeared on screen.

"It was my pleasure, Mr. Worthington. I'm sure you would have done the same for me."

"Do you need a tow into the moon base?" Captain Montu asked.

"Well, my android engineer said the port engine will be back on line in about an hour, which will be just enough time to get all our fighters back on board. So, we'll see you later, Intrepid, and thanks again for all the help." With that, Josh ended the transmission as the Intrepid turned toward home at full impulse.

In the Gamma Quadrant, the Leo was not in as bad of shape as the Polaris had been. Even though she was greatly outnumbered, she was still holding her own when the Scorpion materialized less than a hundred miles off her starboard side.

"Sir, we have an incoming transmission from Admiral Tyr aboard the Scorpion," Lieutenant Phelps, the communications officer, informed.

"Put him on screen," Frank Foster said as the Scorpion de-cloaked.

"Colonel Foster, the Scorpion is here to help. What's your status?"

"Sir, our ship is still in overall good condition, except for some minor battle damage and some weakening of our shields. We've taken out at least one enemy battle cruiser, two of those big troop ships, and a whole slew of corsairs. Our fighters are now going head to head with the enemy fighters which outnumber ours almost three to one." Frank Foster paused a moment after the Leo's shields absorbed multiple laser blast from another enemy cruiser. "And, oh yes, there's that big bastard off to port, that won't go down no matter what we throw at it."

"Our instruments are showing one enemy cruiser a thousand miles out and 110 degrees to port," Captain Freyr stated.

"That's him," Paul Wilson confirmed.

"Well, let's try this together, shall we," Tyr said. "Bring all guns to bear and open fire."

At that point, the demon battle cruiser was vaporized by the combined firepower of both ships. However, just as the battle looked to be over, ten demon corsairs de-cloaked and attacked both ships with a vengeance.

"Where did they come from and why didn't our instruments pick them up?" Frank Foster asked.

"Sir, they came in cloaked until the last possible second," Lieutenant Emma Grace, the Leo's weapons officer informed him.

"Well, two can play that game," Foster said. "Make us disappear, Ms. Grace." "Helmsman, take us 25 degrees to port and hold position."

While they were moving to the new location, Mr. Phelps informed the Scorpion of their move. The Scorpion then made a similar move. When both ships de-cloaked they were able to make short work of the enemy's corsairs, and after the fighters were once again on board, each ship headed for Earth.

"Sir, I can't raise the Defiant," Ron Clayhorn spoke up, as the Dragon Fire sped through space toward Earth.

"Inform our other ships of the situation and that we should approach Earth, cloaked with shields up."

Ten minutes later. "Sir, we are now a hundred thousand miles out," Larry Carver said.

"Slow to half impulse, Mr. Perry," Pat said.

"Put Earth on screen, Angela, full magnification," I barked.

As it appeared on screen, we could see the Defiant taking on an enemy battle cruiser and about ten corsairs. She was firing her guns as fast as she could and Earths defense were giving as much support as they could, but the odds were that she would not last much longer.

Just then Joe appeared on a split screen. "What's our battle plan, Nathan?"

"Well, what's bothering me at this point, Joe, is what we don't see. If there are cloaked demon ships in the area, we need to make them reveal themselves. So I'll take the Dragon Fire in uncloaked and try to draw some of the enemy fire away from the Defiant. I want you and our other ships to follow me in, but don't de-cloak unless the enemy does."

We were now at full impulse and very quickly closing the gap between us and the demon ships. On our arrival, many of the corsairs that had been attacking the Defiant broke away from that battle and headed in our direction. However, when our cannons fired there were not as many as there were before, and when we launched fighters the demon ships turned and fled back toward their battle cruiser. Once there, the whole horizon was suddenly filled with enemy ships, with at least six battle cruisers.

At that point, Dad ordered the fleet to spread out and launch fighters. They would take on enemy fighters with their laser cannons and use their inferno missiles on the corsairs and troop ships. Our cruisers would have to take on theirs, head to head.

Chapter Sixty Seven

EARTH'S SURFACE

4 January

Even though we were doing everything we could to stop the dark demon invasion, many enemy ships had managed to slip through our defenses. At least a hundred of these were troop ships had offloaded 50,000 of the most evil military troops in the universe, onto almost every continent on Earth. The rest of the enemy ships were made up primarily of fighters and a few corsairs, which would supply air support for their troops. They were met by the shadowy, half human forces here on Earth and together set out to find and free the Black Lords.

Gabriel and the other underworld leaders were already mounting their forces for a counter attack. Everyone that could be had now been brought out of stasis early and had been informed of the dire situation. Gabriel had also convinced the human leaders of every nation on Earth, that the battle of Armageddon had just begun, and if the forces of Light lost this battle, mankind would no longer exist. At this point, the world leaders immediately transferred total command of their militaries to Gabriel and the Lords of Light. And, for an instant, everyone on Earth held their breath, as they prepared to repel the dark invaders.

Fighting side by side, against the invading demons, the Creator Race and the human race won many early battles. But, no matter how much effort they put forth, the enemy soon covered the globe, including the Red Zone, in their determination to find their Black Lord leaders. I guess the bottom line was, until they received help from our ships in space, the best the people of earth could hope for was, to break even against the awesome weapons of the dark demons.

Even the powerful Earth based weapons of the Creator Race were of little help. They'd been dormant for so long, that Gabriel just didn't have enough time to bring them all on-line before the enemy broke through. Those weapons in the Red Zone had been affected by the high amounts of radioactive fallout and only fired sporadically.

When all seemed lost it was General Wells and the former Joint Chiefs, who came up with the idea of using the laser mounted military satellites against the enemy. Even though they were less than two percent as powerful as the ones on our ships, they helped to slow the enemy's advance, especially in the Red Zone.

High Earth Orbit

"Sir, the Defiant is still not answering our hails," Ron said.

"Put the Defiant on screen, Angela, magnification factor three," Pat ordered.

We could see the ship had taken many hits from enemy cannons. Her guns were silent now and she listed twenty degrees to port. We all feared the worst when Mr. Yang reported an imminent engine core breach.

"Sir," Mr. Yang said. "My instruments are now showing the Defiant's engines have just shut down like something or someone turned them off."

"Mr. Perry, bring us within transporter range," Dad ordered.

"What do you have in mind, Nathan?" Pat asked, with a worried look on her face.

"I need to get on board that ship. Ron, have Steve and a medical team meet me and Duke in the transporter room. We will also need

Commander Robo and an engineering team, along with Arlie and a security squad."

Twenty minutes later Dad and I materialized on the bridge of the Defiant. People were lying everywhere. Steve and his team went to work immediately helping the injured. King Chogyal and Dohna lay in front of the command station barely breathing.

"If we can get them to sickbay they should be okay, Nathan, but they are in bad need of a Med-Bay Rejuvenation Capsule" Steve said.

Dad hit his com-badge and asked the transport officer to transport both of them directly to the Dragon Fire's sickbay.

Just then Robo called from main engineering. "General Masterson, both impulse engines were hit by direct laser blast. Most of the plasma coils have been fried. We should have the problem fixed in about ten minutes."

"Is she still battle worthy?" Dad Asked.

"As far as I can tell at this point, but when we get the plasma coils replaced and the engines going again, I'll be able to let you know whether or not she'll be able to re-enter the fight."

"Thanks, Robo, keep me posted."

Just as I looked up at the screen, there were two of those corsairs coming in to finish off the Defiant. But, unbeknown to us, Pat had sent Delta Squadron to cover us. When they materialized in front of the ship and fired their inferno missiles, the corsairs were blown to bits.

"Thank you, Mr. Beebe," Dad said as his heart started to beat again.

"No problem, Sir. It's a good thing Colonel Northfield reminded Miss Pat you guys were defenseless over here until you got this old gal going again."

"Well, thanks again, Colonel. Commander Robo assured me his team will have her back on-line any minute now."

And, as if on cue, the power was suddenly restored. However, before the weapons systems, or shield and cloaking generators could be brought back on-line, the Defiant would need a lot more work at the moon base.

"How much speed can we get out of her?" I asked.

"Oh, I'm sure she'll do quarter-impulse, but not much more than that," Robo replied.

"Will she make it back to Moon Base Alpha?" Dad asked.

"As long she's not attacked again, Sir, I think she'll hold together, but it wouldn't take much to finish her off at this point."

Since none of the bridge crew was in any condition to go back to work, Dad had Bill Northfield and his crew transported over to the Defiant. As soon as Steve and his med-team had revived most of the ships medical staff, Northfield would take the Defiant back to the moon base for repairs and extended medical care for its crew.

After we recalled the Defiant's five remaining fighter squadrons to escort the ship to Moon Base, we all transported back to the Dragon Fire where Dad informed the fleet that he was assuming full command of combat operations in space until King Chogyal and Dohna were back on their feet.

In the final count, 158 were dead, 596 were unconscious and near death, 722 had severe life-threatening injuries, and only 524 had minor non-threatening injuries and could go back to duty after being treated. The only thing that had kept the Defiant from being completely destroyed was its android staff. They had shut the engines down seconds before an ion-plasma breach would have blown the ship apart. We would find out much later that just after Chogyal had sent the Intrepid and Scorpion to help the Polaris and Leo and their rookie crews, almost five hundred enemy ships materialized in high Earth orbit. Chogyal knew they had no chance against such odds, but if he didn't try to take out as many as he could, they would swarm down and overpower Earth's defenses. The Defiant had taken out at least three of the closest enemy battle cruisers and her fighters had blown up at least eighty corsairs, two troop ships, and an unknown number of enemy fighters.

But, now it was up to us to finish off what was left of the demon fleet. They still had a very formidable force of at least six battle cruisers, two hundred corsairs, one troop ship and around 700 fighters.

Dad met briefly with our cruiser commanders on screen. "Ladies and Gentlemen, we will spread out at fifty thousand mile intervals and take the enemy fleet head on, slowly encircling them until they have no place to go. The Dragon Fire will take the lead. Make sure your fighters have a full complement of inferno missiles. Use them on enemy cruisers, troop ships, and corsairs only. Our battle cruisers can also fire these missiles, but we are too close to Earth to use Starburst. Good luck and good hunting, everyone."

"Sir," Josh Worthington spoke up. "Are we going in cloaked?"

"I think every other ship should go in cloaked. Maybe we can confuse the enemy as to just how many ships they're up against. And all our fighters should remain cloaked until they have their targets dead-to-rights." Dad paused to see if there were any more questions, then he added. "May, the Creator be with you all." With that Dad broke the connection and ordered Mr. Perry to bring the ship 100 degrees to port.

We waited for ten minutes while the other ships got into position and then we started forward at one quarter impulse. To our port, at 50,000 miles, was the Intrepid. The Orion was to their port at the same distance. To our starboard were the Polaris, the Leo, and the Scorpion on the outer edge.

"Sir, we are now within cannon range of the nearest enemy cruiser, she is powering weapons," Mr. Yang informed. Yang, David, and Angela were in charge of the weapons computers.

"Angela, bring all our guns to bear and open fire on the nearest enemy cruiser," Pat ordered.

"Launch our remaining fighter squadrons," I barked

Just then the Dragon Fire rocked hard from an ion-cannon blast to our shields.

"Sir, shields are down by ten percent," David informed.

"Mr. Yang, what's our range?" Dad asked.

"A thousand miles, Sir," Yang replied.

"Fire five inferno missiles at five hundred miles."

Another cannon blast rocked the bridge, this time to our port side. A corsair had suddenly materialized and fired before Beta Squadron could take him out. Our first four fighter squadrons were assigned to guard the ship, with Alpha Squadron two hundred miles in front and fifty miles lower than our position, so as not to be in line with our guns. Beta Squadron was to port at the same distance and lower position. Gamma Squadron was to our starboard and Delta Squadron protected our rear. All the other squadrons were cloaked and spread out between our other cruisers, to make sure the enemy didn't slip through the cracks.

Like two great chess masters, Dad and the demon leader, Belial, had just made the opening moves in the final battle in space, for Earth.

"Sir, we are now within five hundred miles of the first enemy cruiser," Mr. Yang informed.

"Fire missiles, Mr. Yang," Dad ordered.

When the missiles hit the lead demon ship it diminished their shield capacity to almost zero. When it was hit with our cannons a half minute later, the ship exploded. At that point many of their ships started going down as our cruisers and fighters let loose with everything they had.

"Admiral on deck!" a young Lieutenant called out as Chogyal and Dohna got off the elevator.

"Carry on," Chogyal said as he went to the command center and sat down in the seat I had just vacated for him. Dohna sat down next to him.

"Sir, it sure is good to see you and Dohna up and about," Pat said as the ship rocked with another cannon blast to our shields.

"What's our status, Colonel?"

"We have the enemy surrounded, Sir, at 10,000 miles, and are picking them off one by one," Pat replied

"How many ships have we lost?" Dohna asked.

"At this point, Admiral, we still have all our cruisers," Dad answered. "Admiral Tyr, however, has reported the most battle damage, with one impulse engine out and three of his cannons no longer in use. He's also reporting a loss of 20% of his fighters. But he ensures me the Scorpion will hold together. The rest of the fleet has minimal damage to all ships. And, you'll be happy to know the Defiant made it back to Moon Base Alpha and will live to fight another day." Dad paused as a smile came to Chogyal lip

"Sir, General Carter is hailing us from the Orion," Ron interrupted.

"Put him on screen, Ron."

"Nathan, I have what I think is their flag ship in my sights, because it's one hell of a big cruiser". Just then the Orion shakes from multiple cannon blast. Joe and Peggy are almost thrown from their seats.

"From the looks of it, Joe, I would have to say he's got you in his sights as well."

"No, that came from a couple of those sneaky little corsairs, of which our fighters just took out. But that big cruiser is heavily damaged and listing to starboard. Don't you think we should board her and capture what data we can?"

"Take it out, Joe. They could be playing opossum, don't get near enough to fall for that old trap," Dad told him.

With that, Joe just ordered his weapons officer to fire. Ten seconds later a great explosion rocked the center of the enemy fleet. The blast was equivalent to a hundred 20 megaton nuclear weapons and sent a shock wave through the heart of the demon fleet.

"To all ships, reverse course at full impulse!" Dad ordered, as soon as he saw the blast.

The shock wave took out most all of the remaining enemy fleet. And, it almost took us out when it hit our ships at 10,000 miles out. It's a good thing Dad had ordered us to reverse course when he did or we wouldn't be here.

"Good Lord!" Pat said. "Did somebody on the Orion accidently use a Starburst Missile instead of an inferno?"

"I don't think so," Dohna said. "It's an old trick used by the demon fleet ever since the Great War in the Canis system. When they know their beat, and have no chance of escape, they often program one of their bigger ships for a warp-core–breach, and then abandon ship. When their enemy comes in for the kill, the ship explodes and takes out every ship in a radius of many thousands of miles."

As the broken enemy ships started to get caught in Earth's gravity and pulled into its upper atmosphere, we went back in to vaporize what was left of them before they came crashing down on the planet. At that time, we found out there were still some of those corsairs still alive and giving our fighters a hard time, but for the most part it was just a mop up operation here in space. However, we could now send our fighters and strike teams down to help Gabriel with the surface battle.

Chapter Sixty Eight

THE BATTLE FOR EARTH

6 January

On the surface, great battles raged on every continent, except Antarctica, and in every nation on Earth. The dark demons and their human counterparts were systematically slaughtering everyone and everything in their path to find the Black Lords. Even though they had not found a way into the much deeper subterranean colonies of the Creator Race, they had blown up many of the underground bunkers that most humans now called home.

Gabriel had used every weapon he had to fight with except for nuclear weapons, and had even modified weapons in the human arsenals to more powerful levels. But even with this added support, humans, as well as their creators, were barely hanging on and wouldn't last much longer unless help arrived soon.

So when Chogyal, after resuming command of the fleet, told Gabriel that half the fleet's fighter squadrons were on their way down to engage the enemy on the ground, a big smile came across his face. He knew then we had won the battle in space and the demons on the planet would soon be defeated as well. Gabriel immediately sent the message to all the forces of Light on the surface that help was on the way.

Each battle cruiser would hover in low Earth orbit over its assigned continent, giving tactical support to their fighter squadrons. From this vantage point in space, the cruisers could track the enemy's position as far as six hundred feet below the surface. The Dragon Fire would take North America, the Orion would take South America, and the Polaris had Europe. The Leo was assigned Asia, the Intrepid got Africa, and the Scorpion had Australia and New Zealand.

The battle plan was a relatively simple one, with the fourteen squadrons chosen from each ship; seven would start on opposite ends of a continent and push the enemy toward the middle where they could be disposed of in one final battle.

However, when we got the news an American outpost was about to be overran, Dad decided to personally lead a flight of four fighters to the surface. Against Pat's strong objections, we picked three android crews from the remaining fourteen squadrons to serve as wing support, and headed to where the fighting was the worse. We could see the battle on the surface was going badly for the Americans at one of those expensive new bunkers in the Colorado Rockies. On the ground, the demons used strange looking laser firing machines that looked like something out of "Star Wars" to blast their way through the American defenses. The American's fought back with heavy tanks, 40 mm mortars, a few 105 howitzers, and of course the rifle battalions, but none of these could penetrate the enemy's shields.

In the air, even the F-22 Raptors, with the modified EPD weapons, were no match for the demon fighters, let alone their corsairs. And here again, the missiles the Raptors carried had little or no effect on the enemy's shields.

Our four fighters were in a diamond formation as we caught up with a friendly flight. "This is General Nathan Masterson of the First Fleet of the United Planets of Nirvana," Dad said as we slowed down to match the speed of what was left of a Raptor squadron. "We're here to give you boys a hand."

"Boys! I beg your pardon, General. I'm Colonel Sue Carson USAF, flight leader of this squadron, and there are no boys in it! All of our male pilots were drafted into the space squadrons by that Admiral Gabriel of yours!"

"Sorry about that, Colonel. I hope you can forgive my mistake. We're here to help, by upgrading your aircraft and then teach you how to kick some demon butt!"

"You have our undivided attention, Sir."

"We have four enemy fighters coming in at ten o'clock at a hundred miles to port," I informed, "and one of those corsairs at three hundred miles to starboard."

"I see them, Duke," Dad confirmed. "Colonel Carson, we have multiple bogeys coming in fast from two different directions. Just stay put and let me and my people handle them." With that, Dad and I, along with our starboard wingman, peeled off at incredible speed to attack the oncoming corsair. Our other two fighters did the same to port, to take on the enemy fighters.

The corsair open fired almost immediately with their laser cannons, but our shields held fast. Then we rolled over and returned fire with our five forward cannons, which brought their shields down to almost zero. Then we each launched two of our inferno missiles at ten miles, blowing the corsair into a thousand pieces. Then, after we'd cleared the skies of any immediate demon threat, all four of our flight attacked and made short work of the enemy ground forces.

At that point we followed the colonel back to her base, which was built into the side of a mountain at 2,500 feet off the valley floor. When the huge hanger doors opened we could see the runway extended clear through the mountain with huge blast doors on each end. This was so the planes could takeoff or land at the same time from either direction.

Once we had landed, one of our supply ships, loaded with inferno missiles and some laser cannons which Commander Clakrin had removed from the old F-47, landed shortly thereafter.

Of course, when Prince Draco and Ragnon exited the ship in their armored uniforms, it caused quite the panic. They, along with three former Navy SEALs from the Chattanooga, had come along for security. Then there were the ten androids from engineering that Commander Robo had sent along to refit the new ordinance to the American planes.

It was a good thing Dad and I were there to quell the situation before it got out of hand; otherwise someone might have gotten shot or roasted with dragon fire as the case may be.

"Damn, General, are you sure you're on our side?" Carson said after introductions. "I mean a talking dog as a RIO and now armored dragons." She just stood there shaking her head in disbelief. The green eyed, thirty something, red head, with an athletic figure, was actually easy on the eyes, even though she had a quick temper, Dad thought as he shook her hand.

"Colonel Carson, meet Prince Draco and Colonel Ragnon," Dad introduced, as they took up positions on either side of the exit ramp, then bowing their horned heads down to the Colonel's level to say hello. "They are in charge of our security forces on the Dragon Fire."

"What's going on here?" An officer yelled, coming across the two mile long, three thousand foot wide runway, in a jeep with a squad of armed marines.

"General Masterson, meet Lt. General David Brooks, Base Commander," Carson introduced. He was a man in his late fifties and a little over weight, stood about six foot, with balding salt and pepper hair and brown eyes.

"You're not the General Masterson we've all heard so much about lately, are you?" Brooks asked, as his men kept their rifles trained on the two dragons.

"I'm afraid so, Sir," Dad replied while pumping Brook's hand. "But, could you have your men lower their weapons? I can assure you the dragons are on our side. Besides, if by chance you manage to shoot at one, he might take offence and level this whole facility after turning everyone in it into crispy-critters."

"They could do that?" Brooks asked taking a step back, as he eyed the huge creatures with fear and suspicion.

"Oh, believe me, Sir, you have no idea what a pissed off dragon can do," Dad told him.

Then, after telling his men to stand down, Brooks went over to have a closer look at the androids just coming down the exit ramp with the new equipment "And, exactly what do we have here?" The General asked, staring face-to-face at the nearest android.

"Sir, I'm Lieutenant Commander Chi, in charge of the flight-maintenance and engineering staff on this mission. We are what you would call an artificial life form. We have a posatronic main frame that can compute 80 times faster than the most intelligent human brain, a synthetic outer covering that looks and feels like real human skin, and we are at least ten times stronger than the average human. We are also programmed with a complete knowledge of history, mathematics, science, and engineering, as well as philosophy, human emotion, and logic." With that Chi paused for a moment while Brooks took it all in. "Now, Sir, if you don't mind we should get started adding the new weapons-ordinance to your aircraft."

General Brooks was completely taken aback. He just stood there in disbelief for a long minute with his mouth agape before finally stepping aside with a backhand wave. "By all means Lt. Commander, please give us something to fight with."

Colonel Carson just smiled as she looked over at Dad and whispered. "I think that's the first time I've seen General Brooks searching for something to say."

While the androids went to work installing the new hardware onto the bases fighters, we stepped over to our F48 Star-fighters.

"Now that's what I'm talking about," the Colonel said as she and the General looked the craft over.

"What kind speed can you get out of this bird?" Brooks asked.

Dad just smiled and replied. "She'll do 45,000 mph in Earth's atmosphere and twice that in space."

"And, if you kick her into warp drive, she'll go twice the speed of light," I added.

"Did the dog just talk?" Brooks asked as a strange look came over his face.

"Oh, how rude of me," Dad said, "Let me introduce you to my RIO, Colonel Duke Masterson, of our canine corps. And, to answer your question, yes, the Colonel can not only talk but has an IQ of 270, which means he is smarter than most humans."

With that, Brooks got all red in the face, then turned around and headed back to his jeep, without saying another word, unable to accept the possibility Dad was telling the truth.

"I think he believes you were joking at his expense," Carson said. "His IQ is only 180."

"Yeah, well, believe it or not, he's not the first person to react negatively to my abilities or accept the possibility talking canines could ever exist. But, regardless of what he thinks about me, I'm pretty sure it's a good thing we didn't tell him the dragons can also talk."

With that Dad and Carson busted out laughing, at the absurdity of it all.

Just then we got a call from the Dragon Fire on our head sets. It was Ron patching through a call from Gabriel. Dad climbed up into the cockpit of our star-fighter and activated his view-screen. "Sir, how can I help you?"

"Nathan we have the main enemy forces bottled up in the Sinai Desert and in Northern Israel in the Jezreel Valley at Megiddo, as well."

"Are those locations what I think they are?" Dad asked referring to the gateway to the devils domain.

Gabriel just nodded slowly.

"How strong are the demon forces in that area and how close are they to finding the entrance?" Dad asked.

"With their combined force, the demons along with their human counterparts have around two million on the ground with a whole lot of air support, both alien and domestic. They have set up at least a dozen super shield generators, which will make our efforts to stop them most difficult. They create a multi shield barrier that is immediately replaced if one is knocked out. So far the black-chamber safeguards are holding at all the doorways. But, I have no idea for how long."

"I understand, Sir. Duke and I will leave immediately."

"Oh, and Nathan, I know a good commanding officer should go out in the field once in a while to maintain his tactical edge on reality, but ..." Gabriel paused before he expressed his true feelings about thinking of Dad as a son. "Well, I guess what I'm trying to say is, a commander with your experience would be very hard to replace."

"I understand how you feel, Sir, but as you also know, a good commander does not ask his men to do something he would not do himself." Dad had picked up on Gabriel's feelings but chose not to mention it.

Before we left, we advised Draco of the situation and told him we would leave our other three fighters here to escort the supply ship back to the Dragon Fire after the new hardware had been installed and the human pilots instructed in their use.

Chapter Sixty Nine

JEZREEL VALLEY, NORTHERN ISRAEL

7 January

We found the Dragon Fire and four of our seven ships in low orbit over the Middle East. The Intrepid and Scorpion were in high Earth orbit on opposite sides of the planet watching for any enemy ships that might try to sneak past our defenses. The Defiant was still in space dock at Alpha Base where Clakrin's androids were tending to her battle damage.

As we landed on E-deck, the maintenance personnel were franticly getting all our remaining fighters ready for launch. It was at this time that most of our first fourteen squadrons were returning to the ship for reassignment and to re-arm with missiles.

"Hey, Dad," Anthony called from across the flight bay near the elevators. Afterward he realized it was not a good idea to call the commanding officer of the ship, Dad, for obvious reasons. Delta Squadron had just landed before we did and was headed for the ready-room on D-deck for debriefing.

"General, we heard you led a flight to the surface, but until now I would not have believed it," Lt. Colonel Beebe said as we got on the elevator still in our flight suits.

"Well, Mr. Beebe, you know how it is with commanders keeping their tactical edge," Dad told him, quoting Gabriel. Dad and I then stepped over to where Anthony and Matt stood with Duke Jr. and Rufus. We looked them over very carefully as they came to attention.

"Colonel, we've heard a lot about these four," Dad said, trying hard to sound like a stern commander, while doing his best at suppressing a smile. "How are these new Second Lieutenants working out for you?"

"Sir, in my opinion, they are two of the best flight crews on the Dragon Fire and it has been my privilege to have them in Delta Squadron."

"Well, keep an eye on these characters, Lt. Colonel, they look pretty shady to me," I said as they exited the elevator on E-deck.

In our quarters, we changed into our regular uniforms, and then returned to the ready-room on D-deck where all of the ships fighter squadrons waited for their new assignments. Dad had asked Draco and Ragnon, who had now returned from the surface, as well as Arlie and Fred to be at the meeting as well. A com-link would also be opened with our other ships, as well as Gabriel and the underworld leaders.

"Attention, General on deck!" a lieutenant called out as we entered the ready-room.

"As you were," Dad told them. "Ladies and Gentlemen, I'm not going to stand up and lie to you about this next mission. You are literally about to fly into the gates of HELL and are going up against an enemy that is determined to free the devil himself. The demon forces number approximately two million on the ground with about five thousand fighters in the air. These forces are made up of both demon and human hybrids alike. Their weapons range from the more advanced laser cannons used by the demons from space, to the most modern human guns, missiles, and fighter aircraft. We believe the manmade aircraft have been modified with demon shield and laser generators, which would allow them to operate within the Red-Zone. They are also using multiple super shield generations on the ground, which will make it very difficult for our weapons to penetrate. If one is taken out, another one immediately kicks in to cover their positions."

Just then, flight leader Major Michael Mulkey, of Omega squadron, asked as he raised his hand from the back row. Mike was from the UK where he had been flying fighters for the R.A.F. for almost fifteen years before being drafted by Gabriel into the Galactic Marines. He was a tall man, in his late forties. "Well, Sir, if we can't knock out their shields, how are we supposed to attack the enemy forces with any hope of success?"

"Good question, Mr. Mulkey," Dad answered. "Our tactical situation computer is working on that very question as we speak. However, I suspect it will come up with us launching a ground attack to knock out the enemies shield generators before we attack from the air. The only problem with that is putting a strike team with enough protection from the radioactive fallout on the surface, while figuring out how to get them under the enemy shields."

Just then the intercom beeped. Chogyal had the solution and put it on the ready-rooms situation screen. "This is Mt. Serbal," Chogyal began as the picture of a desert mountain appeared on the screen. "Or should I say, it is the real Mt. Sinai, the one where Moses received what is known as Ten Commandments. I know because I was there when he got them. It is 6,791 ft. in height and is located at Wadi Feiran in the southern Sinai desert. And, it is here that there exists a third entrance into HELL. A back door if you will. The main entrance, presently under the enemy shields, is in a secret tunnel at Megiddo that runs under the ruins for five miles before opening up into a massive pit-chamber." Chogyal paused. "The strike team would have to enter here at Mt. Serbal, near the ruins of this fourth century monastery, and travel 150 miles down an irregular tunnel, full of dead-ends, false-leads, and booby-trapped chambers."

"Are the demon forces also at this site?" I questioned.

"They are in the area, but are concentrating their efforts on the wrong mountain," Dohna replied. "As far as we can tell they are at the other Mt. Sinai, the one that bears that name in modern times."

"I hate to say it, Sir, but I think this is a job for the White Knights and the First Dragon Squadron," Dad offered.

"I came to that same conclusion about a half hour ago, Nathan," Gabriel agreed. Until now he'd been listening quietly trying to think of a better plan, but no one had a better understanding of the dangers of the tunnels like the White Knights. And, after their exploits last year that ended in the freeing of Akakor, Gabriel knew they were the only ones that might be able to survive this mission. "Even though it is not what I considered to be the best option, it's the only one at this point that stands a chance of succeeding."

"Sir, we will need…"

"I have already taken the liberty of ordering a supply ship, from Alpha Base, with all that you and your team will need, including, Commander Clakrin's version of your M-I units, a new body armor that should protect against lesser laser fire, and a few very powerful hand-held weapons, that under no circumstances should you let fall into the hands of the enemy. Chogyal will program your route into your transports navigational computers, as well as the helmets of First Squadron. This route won't take you directly into HELL itself unless you are unable to exit at the Megiddo Gate, so don't get off the designated path. When you come out near the ruins of Megiddo, you'll be under the enemy's shields so we may not be able to receive any communications. And, if for some reason, you are unable to come out at Megiddo, you will have to go on to Mount Hermon on the Syrian border. This exit is just barely inside the enemies shield coverage, but will be enough to let you and your team get into a good tactical position. The Mt. Hermon location will also be loaded into the TTT's computers, as well as the helmet displays. Oh, and by the way, if it does become necessary to exit at the Mt. Hermon Gate, you will have to pass through the very heart of HELL itself." Then with sad eyes, Gabriel wished us luck and added before signing off. "May the Creator be with each of you."

Three hours later we were on the surface with not only our original White Knight team, but the dragons of First Squadron as well as thirty six former Navy SEAL's. Dusty, was the only member from our original team that would be missing from this trip.

Dad had also tried to talk Pat out of coming, but she wouldn't listen to a word he said.

"If you're going, I'm going!" She told him without hesitation, and that was the end of it. Dad had long ago quit trying to tell a woman with her mind made up, what she should or shouldn't do.

The supply ship from Alpha base had landed on E-Deck thirty minutes after the last of our team had ferried over from the other ships. And, while we donned the new body-armor, an android Lieutenant explained the use of the new equipment.

The three new TTT"s, short for Tactical Troop Transport, were, as Gabriel said, Commander Clakrin's answer to our M-I units. They were 50 feet long and tubular in shape, with a maximum capacity of twenty one adults each. They were capable of limited flight of up to 300 hundred feet above the surface with an average speed of 310 knots. When in flight, fifteen foot delta-shaped wings extended from either side near the top of the craft, as well as a six foot tail fin in back, and the smaller tail wings extend from hidden compartments.

The wheels folded up inside a sealed compartment when in flight, and when extended, the unit could be driven like any big semi truck. For water landings, four twenty foot extendable stabilizer pontoons extended seven feet from the sides, and with a flip of a switch, you have yourself a boat, complete with a prop that dropped down from a rear compartment. Unlike our M-I units, which had a chameleon option, the TTT's had a complete cloaking device.

The armaments, as well as the tactical computers on these puppies, were the best the fleet had. On the rounded-shaped nose there were no less than five laser cannons at the same strength as the ones on our fighters. There were three more cannons in the rear, as well as four retractable ones along each side and four more along the belly. They also had two rotating-retractable rocket launchers set on either end of the roof, capable of firing eight inferno missiles each. And there was a shield generator, equal to the ones on our Star-Fighters.

On the inside, the TTT's were not at all plush like our M-I units, they had seven padded seats on either side of the vehicle directly behind the pilot and co-pilot seats, with five seats facing forward across back of the cabin and a command seat set two feet behind and between the pilot and co-pilots seats. To the rear of the main cabin was a small area for preparing food, with a counter, sink, and a large, very advanced microwave oven, across the aisle from the four foot diameter table. Two fair-sized restrooms on either side of the hallway came next, each with a shower, sink, and toilet. And in the very back, there were six sets of bunk-beds built into the walls. This area could also be used as an infirmary for the wounded.

Our personal gear consisted of the new body armor, which not only, protected the wearer from lesser laser blasts, but also protected against the high amounts of radiation, as Gabriel had said, but it also kept the body temp at an even 98.6 degrees even if the outside temperature was 300 degrees Fahrenheit or 210 degrees below absolute zero. This suit also came with a detachable helmet and a small re-breather unit, giving the wearer up to three and a half hours of oxygen when the outside air became foul or when the wearer was underwater.

We were also given a small communication device that was about the size of a small hearing aid. It had a range of fifteen miles, and was similar to the ones we had last year. As well as the goggles, with telescopic lens that made objects a thousand yards away look like they were only 100 feet away. And, with a touch of a little button, these goggles also allowed one to see, perfectly, in zero light or in light as bright as the sun.

The SEAL teams used their laser-blasters, issued at the time they became Star Marines in First Fleet. Clakrin had especially designed a new lightweight hand held laser-pistol and rifle for the First Dragon Squadron and the White Knights, with a six option settings for each. The handgun looked just like an old western Colt 45. revolver and the rifle resembled a Winchester lever action 30-30. I guess it was Clakrin's idea of humor, or he was trying to tell us he thought we were modern-day cowboys, because, the pistol came complete with a quick-draw holster and gun-belt, and the rifle had a case that attached to the dragon saddles, just like the ones of old had attached to a horses saddle. However, these were far from the weapons they were modeled after. When Arlie decided to test the pistol at max power on a section of rock-wall, a hole opened up about 6 x 6 x 6 feet. We knew then that these were very powerful weapons and would serve us well on this mission.

Dad finally shortened the TTT's to Tactical Transport or TT-1, -2, and -3 to save time in communicating. In TT-1 were, Mr. Yang, Larry, twelve former SEALs from the Tennessee and me. TT-2 would have Steve, Jane, Max, and twelve former SEALs from the Chattanooga. And in TT-3 were Ron, Jay, Lobo, and twelve former SEALs from the Portland. And of course, First Squadron was made up of Dad and Ragnon, Pat and Draco, Arlie and Dagon, Fred and Fagon, Sean and Zargon, Naumy and Hagnar, and Tomka and Ragtar.

Chapter Seventy

HELL

8 January

After landing on the surface a hundred yards from the back door to HELL, we stared at a solid rock wall towering over six thousand feet from the surface that went on for miles around the mountain. After checking to make sure these were the right co-ordinance, we then searched until finding the control panel for the door concealed behind a giant boulder. Like many of the doors to the underworld we encountered last year, this one needed a special key to open it. However, the medallion Pat wore around her neck, would be of little use here. For this door, which no one could see at this point, Gabriel had teleported a special key along with an encrypted code in a small box, to Dad just before we left the Dragon Fire.

With First Squadron, as well as the TT's standing by, all mounted up and ready to go, Dad punched in the code and turned the key. Nothing happened at first and Dad was going to repeat the process when what look to be a blast of steam came from the wall. At that point we could see the outline of a giant doorway 100 x100 feet, which slowly begin to separate in the middle.

We entered into a blacker than black chamber with zero light of any kind once the doors closed behind us. Almost immediately, a feeling of extreme dread closed in around us. Even after we donned our goggles and could see the massive cavern for what it was, the feeling didn't go away. Maybe it was the dense darkness that caused this feeling, because even when the main monitor on our TT unit, located where the windshield would normally be, was activated, we could only see about a hundred feet or so. At full magnification, it brought in maybe twice that. With just our goggles at normal range, we could see about fifty feet and at full magnification, we may have been able to see up to seventy five feet.

The massive cavern was void of life of any kind. Everyone stared in awe at the oddly twisted stone walls and huge weird-shaped boulders that seemed to dominate this entrance. Even the usual stalagmites and stalactites found in caves around the world, were missing.

"Let's get this show on the road, people," Dad finally said, as he and Ragnon took the lead down a tunnel to the left.

Because of the kaleidoscope affect these tunnels had on our eyes, all we could manage was a 100 mph and even that was pushing the realm of sanity to its limits, as we descended deeper and deeper into the bowels of this horrid-realm. At least in the TT units we could look away and let the auto-pilot keep us on course, but, it's a wonder the dragons of First Squadron didn't go mad from all these weird twisted shapes. I would imagine it had much the same affect as LSD or some other hallucinogenic drug. One of our SEALs commented about how this reminded him of something going down the toilet.

After about twenty minutes we entered a massive chamber that reeked not only of sulfur, but the rotting stench of decaying flesh. Personally I think this was much worse than any sewer ever smelled, but the SEAL's analogy was pretty much on the money.

We suddenly found ourselves flying over a large expanse of black liquid, where fire seemed to float on small islands. No one uttered a word as we took in this horrible place. But the question on everyone's mind was, "Was this really the heart of HELL? Where lost souls go to spend eternity, or, like in "Dante's Inferno" was this just one of the many levels of this terrible environment?"

Just then we entered another tunnel on the far side of the black sea, where bleached white bones of all kinds of prehistoric animals dotted the stone floor. It was a good thing this passageway was over 250 feet high and over 125 feet wide, or we might have been brought down by a long, dead dinosaur.

When we emerged from this tunnel about fifteen minutes later, we entered a chamber many times larger than any we'd encountered so far. In this chamber the intense darkness seemed even worse. Our visibility dropped in half as our auto-pilot lowered us another 1,000 feet. When we finally leveled out, our instruments said we were only a hundred feet above the bottom of this pit and this is where we got our first glimpse of its inhabitants. They numbered in the millions and seemed to have a black, smoky outline of a head and upper human torso, but quickly trailed off to not much more than black shadows moving in every direction at once. Then there were the awful, never ending screams of agony that even earplugs could not keep out of one's mind. And here, too, was that overpowering stench that made one want to puke. The smell seemed to permeate every inch of the TT's, even through the filtered ventilation system was on full blast. We finally had to put on our helmets to get any relief.

"Raise shields," I ordered, just in case these entities could pass through the TT's fuselage.

"These things remind me of those spirits that came out of the Ark of the Covenant in that first "Indiana Jones" movie, except these are black instead of white," Larry commented, from the pilot's seat.

Just then Dad's voice came over our headsets. "TT-1, come-in."

"This is Duke, General, go ahead."

"This next tunnel should take us to the Megiddo ruins where the main demon force is trying to break into the entrance. So as to be on the safe side, First Squadron is going to seal this entrance from the inside. I want you and the Tactical Team to proceed on to our alternative exit at Mt. Hermon, and set up firing positions on the enemy's super shield generators. We will join you as soon as possible."

"Understood, Sir, and proceeding to Mt. Hermon exit point. Good luck to you and First Squadron. Duke, over and out."

"I have already plotted our course into the computer, Duke, and advised TT-2 and 3 to do the same," Mr. Yang informed me before I had a chance to say anything.

Just then, instead of following First Squadron into the next tunnel, our TT unit made a sharp turn to port, missing a solid rock wall by just a few feet. It was a good thing these units had seatbelts or we would have been thrown all over the place.

First Squadron reached their destination eight minutes after entering the tunnel, landing near the huge, stone doorway. They could hear explosions on the other side, which indicated the demons were trying to blast their way through the massive stone wall. So far they hadn't found the spot, but it was just a matter of time before they would line up a shot on the ten foot thick doorway and thus gain entry into this realm.

"Let's find the control panel for this side," Dad said.

"What do we do with it after we find it?" Arlie asked.

"On the control panel for the door where we gained entry, I noticed the monitor flashed the message "security systems deactivated" when I turned the key."

"That should mean the security systems for this door are still activated," Pat said, from a distant wall.

"Well, let's hope so," Fred spoke up.

"That's what we're here to find out," Dad stated.

"Just what kind of security features are we talking about?" Sean asked, just as he got too close to the entrance and was thrown off his feet by an invisible force-field.

"Well, it would seem that at least one of the security features are still activated," Fred said with a little laugh, as he helped Sean to his feet.

Five minutes later Tomka called out from twenty yards down the tunnel, "Sir, it's over here." He and Ragtar had uncovered the control panel accidentally when Ragtar belched a fireball at the wall and blew off the rock-looking cover that hid it. It was an oval touch screen display, about one foot by one foot, built into the wall of the tunnel about five feet above the floor. A small flashing-green light next to the security display, at the top of the panel, indicated all systems were on and operating normal. In the center of the unit was a keyboard with the letters of the Greek alphabet, below that a row of numbers from zero through nine. And, just like Gabriel and Chogyal had explained, on the very bottom of the unit, was a red button which immediately activated a powerful force-field on the outside of the door and eight minutes later would double the strength of the systems already in normal mode. However, at that time it would also turn the whole tunnel into a death trap for any living thing still in it.

"Alright people, get mounted and get out of this tunnel, Ragnon and I will be right behind you," Dad told them.

As everyone mounted up and took off, Pat looked over at Dad and said. "Nathan, let's go."

Dad pressed the red button just before the whole tunnel shook from a demon blaster. They had finally zeroed in on HELL's gate, at Megiddo. The doors held tight, but huge rocks began to fall from the ceiling almost taking out the tunnels last four remaining occupants. As Dad climbed up into Ragnon's saddle, a boulder fell where he'd been standing seconds before. And once in the saddle, both Prince Draco and Ragnon took off like a bullet going down the barrel of a gun.

"Nathan, I think the whole tunnel is collapsing!" Pat yelled into her headset, just as Draco turned up on his left side to avoid a falling boulder.

"The exit should be around this next bend," Dad yelled back. But when they made the turn, the exit was sealed with huge rocks. At that point, Dad and Pat quickly drew their pistols and fired twice, at the same time Draco and Ragnon let loose fireballs. The blocked exit instantly exploded into the chamber beyond without the dragons having to skip even one wing-beat.

For most of the trip north to Mt. Hermon we continued to fly through the black-spirit chamber with the wailing, moaning, and stench of forgotten souls in the domain of the damned.

Suddenly we crossed over a massive river of magma that must have been over mile wide. Aided by the light given off by the fiery glow, we could barely make out what look like thousands of hideous creatures on the higher ground of the far side.

As we passed over these hideous beasts, heading straight for the next tunnel about fifty miles away at Mt. Hermon, Mr. Yang uttered from the co-pilots seat, "I sure hope our cloaking device is working properly."

"Did you see those monstrous devils?" Larry asked. "Hell, no wonder Gabriel doesn't want them to get loose in the world. It would be the end of mankind for sure."

"And to think, at one time, those creatures looked like the rest of the Creator Race. Some even went to the "Star-Academy on Sirius" with Admiral's Gabriel and Michael," I mused.

"Now you know what hate, greed, and arrogance can do to even those far more advanced than humans," Yang commented.

Aboard the Dragon Fire, King Chogyal turned to Bill Northfield, who had just got back to the ship from Alpha Base with his bridge crew. "Mr. Northfield, we should be ready to attack as soon as the strike team brings down those super shield generators."

Dohna had already briefed him and Mr. Dixon on our mission before their crew reported for bridge duty.

"Sir, wouldn't it have been easier just to use our laser cannons to eliminate those generators?" Bob Dixon asked a little confused.

Chogyal thought for a second then asked, "Mr. Dixon, have you ever seen the Grand Canyon?"

"Yes, Sir, I have."

"Well, Mr. Dixon, if we use our laser cannons the Jezreel Valley will look like the Grand Canyon. Now normally, that wouldn't matter, but when you consider the fact that the bowels of what mankind refers to as HELL, are about five thousand feet below this valley......well, what it boils down to is, we would actually be releasing the Black Lords, and that is what we're trying to prevent."

"I understand, Sir. Thank you for taking the time to explain it to me," Dixon said, a little embarrassed at the thought of Chogyal thinking he was a little slow on the uptake.

"When all this is over, and the world is once again on the mend, I suggest all the new cruiser commanders take time to complete the courses at Shambhala," Dohna told Bob.

"Gabriel has already told me that the courses at Shambhala will be required learning for all officers in the First Fleet," Chogyal informed them. "It's been a long time since humans have assumed such duties, so they have a lot of catching-up to do."

"I look forward to it, Sir." Bill Northfield interrupted. "But, we must first win this battle."

Just then a sensor flashed on David's screen. He and Angela were still at the weapons station. "Sir, a signal has been set off at the ruins of Megiddo."

"That would mean the interior security measures at the Megiddo gate, have been activated," Dohna informed with a smile. "Looks like Nathan and his team are right on schedule."

"And, if everything continues the way it should, the shields should come down in about an hour and a half at the most," Chogyal finished. Then he turned to the communications officer, "Lieutenant Parker, send a message to the other three ships in this battle group. Tell them to have their fighters ready to attack as soon as the enemy's shield generators come down."

"Duke, we have a problem," Ron called from TT-3. "Our instruments are picking up bogeys in hot pursuit of our TT units."

"Can you bring them up on your rear screen?"

"We've tried that but all we're getting is an invisible echo. In other words, we can't see whatever it is, but our sensors are telling us something is there and gaining fast."

"Duke, we're now picking up the anomaly as well," Mr. Yang said.

"Steve, are you guys getting these readings as well, in TT-2?"

"We're seeing it, Duke, but Maj. Ming, our SEAL team commander, thinks it may be the magnetic iron ore on this side of the magma river. He said this sort of thing is quite common and can play hell with the instruments."

It was about then we began to slow as the next tunnel system presented itself. Once inside, we discovered an upward spiral similar to the one we came down.

Chapter Seventy One

LOW EARTH ORBIT

9 January

"Sir, we are receiving a message from Adm. Amun aboard the Intrepid," Second Lieutenant Sam Parker informed from the communication station.

"Put him on screen, Mr. Parker, as well as the other commanders in the battle group." Bill Northfield ordered.

"Chogyal, our long range sensors just picked up a massive fleet heading for Earth at high warp. They just passed Jupiter, so they should be here within two hours."

"Sir, Adm. Gabriel is also hailing us," Lt. Parker interrupted before putting him on a split screen with the other commanders.

"Amun, ask them for the standard identification and pass codes," Gabriel ordered.

"We have, Sir, but so far there's been no response."

Then suddenly Amun's communication officer spoke up. "Sir, a message is coming through now, S, S, F, F, A, M, C, was all it read." The code stood for Sirius Second Fleet, Fleet Admiral Michael in command.

"Hold your fire, Amun, that's Michael and the Second Fleet," Gabriel said with a smile.

"Sir, I was just told that now there are two fleets. One is coming in from Beta Quadrant and another from Delta Quadrant." Amun informed. "They both can't be Second Fleet."

"How close is this other fleet?" Chogyal asked.

"About a hundred million miles out, Sir," Amun replied.

Both Gabriel and Chogyal quickly calculated the direction from which Second Fleet should arrive and answered at the same time. "Second Fleet should be coming in from Beta Quadrant."

"However," Gabriel paused a second. "Amun, ask both fleets again for their I.D. codes."

This time a two coded message were received. The new one read S, T, F, F, A, U, C.

"That's Third Fleets I.D. code," Chogyal declared.

Gabriel looked perplexed. "Could the King have also sent Uriel and the Third Fleet?"

"Well, Sir, if the Black Lords are somehow set free, we may need all three fleets to contain them." Chogyal suggested.

"Do we know the status of our strike team?" Gabriel asked.

"We got a signal from the Megiddo Gate about a half hour ago, indicating it had been sealed from the inside." Chogyal replied. "But we have not heard anything since."

"Sir, Duke should be exiting the Mt. Hermon Gate with the TT units, any moment now," Joe Carter spoke up from the Orion. He and Peggy were monitoring the current situation from their ready-room computer, as were the other cruiser commanders.

"As soon as the strike team knocks out those shield generators we must attack with all our fighters," Gabriel reiterated.

"Sir, our fighters have already launched and are standing by for the attack order," Josh Worthington informed from the Polaris.

"Our fighters are also standing by," Frank Foster added from the Leo.

"Sir," Malik's voice came over the Orion's ready-room intercom. During the time the former crew of the Dhul Fiqar had been with the Orion, they had proven themselves time and time again as a loyal and reliable addition to the ships company. During the initial demon attack in Alpha Quadrant, Mr. Malik and his men had exceeded Joe and Peggy's expectations and were now, in their opinion, some of the finest officers they'd ever served with.

"Go ahead, Major." Joe acknowledged.

"Sir, our instruments are picking up large explosions on the surface in the vicinity of the enemy's super shield generators."

"That must mean Duke and the White Knights have started their attack." Peggy said.

Joe sat back in his chair with a worried expression, and reflected on Peg's comment. "Yes, it would seem so. I just hope Nathan and First Squadron were able to get through the gate before it closed."

Just then, Chogyal ordered the Polaris, Leo, and Orion, to attack the Valley of Jezreel and the ruins of Megiddo with their fighter squadrons as soon as the enemy shields came down. The Dragon Fire's fighters would attack the demon forces in the Sinai and surrounding areas.

"Mr. Malik," Peggy said after pushing the intercom button. "Launch all fighter squadrons and attack the surface at the Valley of Jezreel.

We'd exited the Mt. Hermon Gate on a high ridge, about 8,200 feet above the valley. A small dirt path, just barely wide enough for our TT units, wound its way up another thousand feet to the mountains central summit, where we pulled in behind some large boulders and locked our inferno missiles on the enemy's shield generators, heavy weapons arrays, and airfields that dotted the northern Israeli valleys below. Of course, the demon version of the F-47 Star Fighter didn't need an airfield with a runway to get off the ground, but we were able to ground much of the enemy's man-made fighter-aircraft that did.

At the time we thought this was going to be a walk in the park, however, that was not to be. Dad and First Squadron should not have been less than thirty minutes behind us. So when they failed to show up or check in forty minutes after we reached the summit, we began to get a little worried. And, with all the enemy fire we were taking, it was impossible to put together a rescue until our fighters came.

"First Squadron, come-in," I called repeatedly, but got no reply.

"Nathan, there's something following us." Pat said over her headset, shortly after they crossed over the river of magma.

Dad looked back but couldn't see anything but shadows. However, like Pat, he had a bad feeling something horrid had indeed picked up their crossing and was giving chase.

Prince Draco and Ragnon also felt the presents of an evil more-vile than anything they'd ever known.

"Arlie, come-in," Dad called.

"Go ahead, Nathan," Arlie replied.

"Are you guy's at the next tunnel yet?"

"We have it in sight."

"I want you to hold up in the chamber at the exit gate. I think we have attracted some unwanted company and may need your help before we can safely open the door.

"Understood, we'll wait for you."

What we had dismissed as a magnetic anomaly turned out to be a lot more sinister than we had ever imagined, and it was gaining on Dad and Pat. Suddenly, Pat heard her dead mother's voice in her head.

"Patamaya," Mayaset said, as her image appeared on the inside of Pat's helmet.

"Yes, Mama," She replied.

"You are in great danger. The High Lord of the great black-pit has picked up your scent and is in pursuit with his legions. The weapons your team carries cannot defeat this beast. Only you have the ability within you to slow it down, but not even you can destroy him."

"Mama, what do we do?"

"Get through the gate as quickly as you can. Remember, I'm here with you and will help you all I can."

"Arlie," Pat called over her headset. "We are being chased by the devil himself. We need you to open the gate and hold it open until we get through. Wait for us on the other side."

"Will do," Arlie replied.

"What was all that about?" Dad asked. "Why did you countermand my orders?"

All Pat did was look in his direction, with tears welling up in her eyes, and said, "Mama told me what to do." Then Dad understood just what they were up against, because Mayaset only appeared to Patamaya when the lives of her or the team, were in extreme peril.

By the time Arlie and the others reached the massive doors of the exit gate, Dad and Pat were just entering the tunnel. Draco and Ragnon, flew like there was no tomorrow, as they could sense the powerful evil forces that was slowly gaining on them.

When the heavy stone-doors opened, Arlie and the others could see the chaos on the other side. Laser and missile blasts were going off in all directions. The red-sky was filled with fighter aircraft of all kinds, both alien and man-made. And in the valley below, every kind of cannon, tank, and even small arms, was being fired.

"Duke, come-in," Arlie called.

"Go ahead, Arlie."

"We're at the gate, but can't exit with all this laser fire. Can you bring the TT units down and give us cover? We'll also need the supply ship for team extraction, ASAP.

"Will do," I replied "Give us about five to get there."

We brought the TT units in and hovered on the open sides of the cliffs using our shields to cover First Squadrons exit from HELL. As the heavy doors began to close, Dad and Pat shot through the gate just after everyone else had gotten out. As they joined together and headed for the top of the mountain as fast as the tired dragons could fly, we followed behind continuing to cover their rear.

Just after we landed on the top of the mountain and offloaded our SEAL teams, who took cover behind the large boulders, a giant black shape similar to that of a dragon, but over twice as big as any of ours, rose out of the mountain with an earsplitting scream. The creature opened its huge wings and hovered, just out from, and slightly above, the boulders we'd taken cover behind. This thing was enormous, with a wing span of at least forty eight feet and a body, from horned head to the spear like point of its tail, close to sixty feet.

"OH, NO!" Pat exclaimed, as she hit her headset button, running for the protection of the boulders. "Ron, inform Chogyal the black-beast is loose. But I think the gate must have closed before his Legion could escape."

"Understood," Ron replied.

Except for one or two people still left in the TT units, everyone had now found cover behind the huge boulders that were laid out like the ruins of an ancient temple complex.

Just then, an over excited corporal from one of the SEAL teams, started firing at the thing with his laser weapon. Everyone else followed suit a moment later. Even our dragons belched large fireballs at the creature, but the beast just seemed to absorb the blast with no lasting effect. Pat knew our weapons were useless. She also knew this was not the true form of the monster.

"Can you do anything?" Dad asked, just as the creature loosed a deadly fireball of his own, which resulted in five of our SEALs being instantly charbroiled.

"I'll try," Pat replied as the beast grabbed up one of the TT units in a large, clawed talon.

At that moment, the Orion's Alpha Squadron, led by Colonel Ed Pike, attacked with pinpoint precision, causing the creature to release the Tactical Transport. However, when the beast released another fireball, two of Alpha Squadrons fighters were sent spiraling toward the valley floor.

Pat's heart sank as she watched the fighters go down, but there was nothing she could do about their crews. Hopefully they were able to eject the escape pods before the craft crashed. She then reached up and touched the medallion around her neck and mentally asked Mayaset for help. With that her mother's voice was once again heard in her head. "Patamaya, you can't kill this creature like the one at Akakor. Instead of using your kinetic energy, you must use your gift of healing."

Confused at her mother's advice, Pat then turned to Dad and asked him to cease fire. Dad cocked his head to one side and gave her a strange look, as if to ask "what in the hell are you thinking," but ordered everyone to cease fire anyway. Everyone thought the order was crazy, but immediately complied. At that point Pat climbed atop one of the large boulders and held her arms out with her hands turned up, as if trying to stop something. The beast zeroed in on her with a fireball that seemed to be blocked by an invisible bubble-shield.

"Ah, yes, the great, great, granddaughter of Viracocha," the creature roared and came close, as it sniffed the air. "You will not defeat me with your puny powers."

Pat closed her eyes and calmly let two balls of blue-light fly straight for the heart of the beast, which caused an unexpected reaction. It twisted and turned in all different directions and almost fell out of the sky, as it instantly took on the form of many different beings, before returning to the black dragon shape.

While the creature reacted to Pat's healing light, a supply ship landed about fifty yards away. Chogyal and Dohna floated up to where Pat stood atop the boulder. "Mama said to use my powers of healing on this beast and it seemed to weaken him." Pat told them as all three stared at the beast. Then all three loosed more of the healing balls of Light. This caused the Black Dragon to scream like a banshee as it clawed its way higher in the sky to get away from the three Lord's of Light.

"Patamaya, you now know what Lucifer has become," Dohna informed.

"There are only three beings in the whole universe that can truly destroy him," Chogyal added. "The Great Creator, El Shaddai, Lucifer's father; Adonai, Great High King of Sirius and the Canis star system; and......" Chogyal stopped mid-sentence, as fast moving black storm clouds suddenly darkened the red sky. For the first time since the nukes fell here in September, it looked like a very serious storm system was going to dump a whole lot of rain here in a very short time.

As the wind began to pick up, the great beast looked skyward and let out a deafening roar. He then let go with a huge fireball, as if he sensed something or someone that no one could see. As heavy rain began to fall, he turned and flew off in the direction of the ruins of Megiddo, where the great demon Belial and what was left of the dark forces were making a last ditch stand.

Epilogue

MOON BASE ALPHA

16 January

The battle of Armageddon ended that day, with the sound of trumpets announcing the arrival of the second son of Great King Adonai.

The huge storm clouds parted and the combined fighter squadrons of the other two fleets flew through, led by a single gold-colored shuttle craft. As the fighters peeled off to help take out what was left of the enemy aircraft and gun batteries, the shuttle came down and hovered over the ruins of Megiddo.

It was there the demon ground forces finally laid down their arms. Even the Great Black Dragon reverted back to his true form, a handsome looking thirty year-old with golden hair and heavenly blue eyes. Suddenly another figure appeared next to Lucifer. This being could have almost passed for Lucifer's carbon copy, except he wore white and blue robes, with a golden crown of thorns atop his head of long dark brown hair.

As if by magic, the doors of HELL opened and the person who wore the crown just pointed. And without saying a word, the demons obeyed, filing into the pit without delay or recourse. However, when it came time for Lucifer to follow the rest, his eyes turned a fiery red as he looked back and said, "This is not over, little brother. We'll meet again on another day."

When the doors to HELL were once again sealed and we started looking for our fallen comrades is when the true reality of this terrible battle began to sink in. The blood of the dead ran like a river in the Jezreel Valley. There were so many, it was impossible to walk through it without stepping on someone's skeletal remains, which deteriorated quickly in the rich, radioactive atmosphere.

With a sad, solemn voice the Great Prince Immanuel said to leave the demon dead where they lie, to serve as a warning for the price of hate, arrogance, and greed. That seemed a little strange to us because by the time this area was once again inhabitable, at least a thousand years would have passed, or so we thought. However, when Immanuel lifted his arms toward the heavens a fresh rain began to fall. The air freshened and a strong wind began to blow, as the blood red sky faded away. We all looked at each other with wonder when our instruments on the TT units indicated the radiation levels had fallen off to almost normal. Even the 1,000 mile wide radioactive Red Zone, which had encircled the globe, was now returning to normal levels.

Okay, now that was impressive and way above my head. But now I understand why the ancient humans thought this being was a God when he was here the first time.

As for the demon dead here acting as a deterrent to war, well that remains to be seen, even if the story of this epic battle is written down and taught to future generations, as I'm sure it will be. In time there will be those who believe it to be no more than a myth or legend, like so much of Earth's history has already become.

Personally, I believe there will always be that rogue faction throughout the universe, which thrives on the destruction of those planets that are unprotected or underdeveloped.

Even here on Earth, there were still those small pockets of demons around who, for now, will fade into the shadows. But in years to come, they will once again tempt and deceive the Children of Light with visions of glory and grandeur. And yes, the dark demons and those humans who followed them will once again, in time, become a force to be reckoned with.

A week after the battle, at Moon Base Alpha, instead of the usual victory gala, there was a very solemn memorial ceremony for all our lost friends who had given their lives defending Earth, both in space and on the surface. With most of the underworld colony leaders awakened now from stasis and the higher ranking officers of all three fleets, the huge hanger was filled to capacity. The ceremony would also be broadcast to all underworld colonies, as well as the underground bunkers of every major city on Earth.

Gabriel stood on the curved platform, waiting for everyone to take their seats before starting the ceremony. Seated on the stage behind him was Prince Immanuel, as well as the other two fleet admirals, Michael and Uriel. Once the proceedings got underway, it took over an hour and a half just to read the list of those that had lost their lives in the great battle. As their names were called their picture was shown on five large screens around the huge hanger. Then, after all the names had been called, Gabriel unveiled a wall, on which each name had been written down and gold plated, so their sacrifice would never be forgotten.

After that, Prince Immanuel spoke in such a voice that made you believe everything was once again right with the world. After giving his father's blessings, he praised First Fleet for their courageous stand against the dark demons and promised that the souls of the fallen would soon be returned to us again as Children of Light. He also explained how fortunate we were that the rest of the Black Lords had not escaped the pit. If they had, he emphasized, their combined power would have taken many more lives before they could've been brought under control. If in fact, we could have stopped them at all, even with all three fleets.

"I would now ask that the White Knights of Avalon and the First Dragon Squadron of the Andean Underworld, as well as the three SEAL teams, to please rise and step up to the dais for special commendations," Gabriel said after the Prince had finished.

Dad looked over at Pat with a suspicious eye. "What's this about?" He asked.

Pat just shook her head and shrugged her shoulders. "I have no idea."

On the way down to the podium, Steve whispered to Jane. "Maybe they're going to shoot us for setting Lucifer loose."

Because there was not enough room on stage to allow the dragons to stand with us, so we all lined up in three rows just below the platform. We now stood facing the audience with dragon and rider of First Squadron standing together in the back row, the rest of the White Knights in the second row, and the SEALS in the first row. Admirals Michael and Uriel then came down from the platform to stand in front of us. Uriel held a very ornate box which he held out to Michael, who reached inside and pulled out a golden medallion on a chain. Then, as Gabriel read our names from atop the dais, Michael placed a medallion around our necks.

It was then that Prince Immanuel spoke again. "I want to congratulate these brave souls for being the only beings to pass through Satan's realm, besides myself, and live to tell about it. But then, I even had to die for a short while before going there." At that, most all the Lords of Light and even some humans, broke out laughing.

At this point Dad had to say something, and he turned and faced the Prince. "But, Sir, it was our presence there that allowed Lucifer to escape in the first place. So, I wouldn't think our mission was very successful, or at least not enough to get a medal for."

The Prince peered at Gabriel and the other two fleet admirals with a questionable look on his face before continuing. "Well, General, all three fleet Admirals and I looked into this matter very carefully before we decided to award you and your team with this honor. For you see, if it wasn't for your combined courageous efforts, the demon forces would have blasted through the Megiddo Gate and released all the Black Lords, which would have ended in disaster. So yes, General, I would say the beings of this planet owe you and the brave men, women, dragons, and canines who stand with you, a huge debt of gratitude." The Prince paused as everyone in the hanger rose for a standing ovation, and then continued when they'd taken their seats again. "As it turned out General Masterson, Lucifer was not free long enough for him to regain much of his real power. That's why he returned to the pit without a fight. However, from what I understand, his son, the one you call the Antichrist, and the false prophet were not captured, so this world is still in great danger. They too, have great persuasive powers and deceptive abilities. So, beware of their lies and stand together strong in the Principles of Light." With that the Prince came down to congratulate each of us personally before mixing in with the rest of those present in the large hanger.

Six weeks later, Third Fleet left Earth's orbit, with the Great Prince aboard. They had one more stop to make before returning home to Sirius and that was the planet Mars, where the once demonic population was in the process of changing back into beings of Light. If they really wanted to return to the Light, the Prince wanted to help them in any way he could.

During his visit here on Earth, he visited each of the seven underworld colonies and the capitals of every nation on the planet, where once again these cities were being rebuilt on the surface.

The week after the Prince left, Gabriel called together a high court, of both human and Creator Race, on Moon Base Alpha, to decide the fate of the former crew of the Dhul Fiqar. And after a month of testimony and cross examination from everyone who had gotten to know the crew since they had attacked the Mid-East with nukes, they were found guilty of terrorism and war crimes against humanity. However, due to Joe and Peggy's testimony as to their heroic service aboard the Orion, Malik and his crew were sentenced to serve a period of not less than twenty five years each, in the service of the Galactic Marines, and would also be required to pass the course of studies at Shambhala.

Of course, there were the usual objections from the prosecution, General Wells and the former Joint Chiefs, that the terrorist should be executed for their crimes. However, when certain documents were produced that indicated <u>the Joint Chiefs</u> in many military actions against innocent civilians around the world, they were happy to let the matter drop.

When we finally made it back to the Andean Underworld, a great gala was given in our honor that lasted for a week. We, of course, traveled to every city or chamber of any size and were greeted as heroes everywhere we went. It sure was good to see Duchess and my girls again, as well as the rest of our family and friends throughout the underworld. But I guess what I wanted most, was to return home to northwestern Montana, and once again touch base with all the happy memories of when Duchess and I were pups.

This must have been on all our minds because one night at dinner, Arista asked her dad if we could all go home now. Everyone at our large table, which consisted of family and close friends, nodded in agreement.

But this was not the case with all the newcomers to this subterranean realm. Many of the displaced people had no homes or family to go back to. So they opted to stay here in the underworld where they were now accepted as part of the local population.

It was about then Dad pulled a diamond engagement ring from his pocket and asked Pat to marry him. Dad had asked Dusty if he could have his daughters hand shortly after we got back. Pat smiled as she leaned over and kissed him. "Are you sure?" She asked, as everyone in the main palace dining hall stood, clapped, and cheered. Marcus and Marissa Overton came over to congratulate Dad and Pat personally. This started a whole procession of everyone in the great room. Even King Drac, Draco and Ragnon made their way over to our table.

"But who will oversee the underworld?" Pat asked.

"Well, Gabriel told me after the Ceremony for the Fallen, that Viracocha will be coming out of stasis early, in about six months. I'm sure the distinguished representatives of the government can run the underworld until then. And, if you want, we can wait till then and let your acclaimed ancestor do the honors."

"That would be wonderful."

"Besides, our duties aboard the Dragon Fire will leave little time for you to spend here at Akakor."

And that's the way it was, Dad and Pat were married six months later with all the Pomp-and-Circumstance of a military wedding. Because of the large number of guests, the ceremony was held in one of the larger hangers on Moon Base Alpha just inside the Dragon Fires mooring tethers. Commander Clakrin and his robotic staff had turned the hanger into a thing of real beauty. There were flowers, fountains, and blue and white ribbons and bows throughout the hanger. Chairs had been set up on either side of a golden path that led down to a beautiful altar. Here the White Knights waited on one side of the aisle, while the dragons of First Squadron stood on the other, with everyone wearing their dress gray-blue uniforms of the Galactic Marines.

As Pat started down the aisle holding Dusty's arm, everyone rose to their feet. She wore a beautiful white gown with a long train that Megan and Paige kept off the floor. Arista went before her throwing rose petals from side to side. Dad waited at the altar with Joe Carter as his best man. Viracocha stood at the altar in blue and white robes with arms extended, as an aura of golden light seemed to envelope Dad and Pat when they exchanged their vows.

Also attending the wedding besides every officer above the rank of Captain in First Fleet, was all the Creator Race hierarchy that was out of stasis: Gabriel, Leah, and Captain Adam represented the North America Underworld colony of Avalon. King Chogyal, Dohna, and all the Grand Masters represented Shambhala and the Himalayan Underworld of Asia. Amun, Osiris, and Isis represented the North African Underworld. Zeus, Hera, and Apollo represented Mt. Olympus and the Southern European Underworld. Poseidon, Cleito, and all ten sons represented the Atlantain Underworld of Antarctica. Odin,

Thor, Freya, Admiral. Tyr and Captain Freyr represented Asgard and the Northern European Underworld. And, then there was Viracocha, the whole governmental body and many family and friends from the Andean Underworld.

"Where are you going for your honeymoon?" Steve asked, after the ceremony was over and everyone was standing around drinking champagne, waiting for the wedding feast to begin.

"Do you remember the mountain we came out on when we left Gabriel's Avalon last year?"

"Yeah, I remember. There was a house on top that was supposedly built by you in another lifetime. I remember the scenery from there was spectacular, with the surrounding mountains and the crystal blue lake far below."

"Well, in the last six months it seems that Gabriel had it fixed up for us. Besides, I've been promising him another visit for a while now."

"But if I remember the story right, you built that house, so long ago, for you and Maggie," Jane interjected, and instantly wished she hadn't.

Dad thought for a moment before replying. "I don't know why things turned out the way they did in this life, but Maggie made her choice, and now I have made mine."

With Dad and Pat on their honeymoon, the crew of the Dragon Fire enjoyed an extended shore-leave. Duchess and I went home to Montana with our pups, as well as Dad's human children and grandchildren. It sure was good to see our home again, which had suffered very little damage from the radioactive snow storms because of the protective shields that covered the island.

Every day now, while on morning rounds, Duchess and I sit for a while at her favorite spot on the north wall which overlooks the lake. There we reflect on all that had happened since we were last here, and how happy we were that our family and friends had survived the great battle. However, at the same time, we feel a heavy sense of sadness for all the Children of Light who had lost their lives defending the planet. "May the Great Creator be with them and guide them home again soon."

www.ingramcontent.com/pod-product-compliance
Lightning Source LLC
LaVergne TN
LVHW041738060526
838201LV00046B/847